^{BY} FORCE ALONE

LAVIE TIDHAR

HEAD
of ZEUS

First published in the UK in 2020 by Head of Zeus Ltd

Copyright © Lavie Tidhar, 2020

The moral right of Lavie Tidhar to be identified as the author
of this work has been asserted in accordance with the
Copyright, Designs and Patents Act of 1988.

This is a work of fiction. All characters, organisations,
and events portrayed in this novel are either products of
the author's imagination or are used fictitiously.

9 7 5 3 1 2 4 6 8

A catalogue record for this book is available from
the British Library.

Typeset by Divaddict Publishing Solutions Ltd

ISBN (HB): 9781838931278
ISBN (XTPB): 9781838931285
ISBN (E): 9781838931308

Printed and bound in Great Britain by
CPI Group (UK) Ltd, Croydon, CR0 4YY

Head of Zeus Ltd
5–8 Hardwick Street
London ECIR 4RG

WWW.HEADOFZEUS.COM

'From this amphibious ill-born mob began
That vain ill-natured thing, an Englishman.'

—Daniel Defoe, *The True-Born Englishman* (1701)

'Britain has kings but they are tyrants. They plunder and
terrorise the innocent, they defend and protect the guilty
and thieving. They sit with murderous men.'

—Gildas, *On the Ruin of Britain* (c. 510-530 AD)

'Fuck 'em if they can't take a joke.'

—Aristophanes of Athens (431 BC)

PART ONE

THE RISE AND FALL OF UTHER PENDRAGON

1

King Vortigern the usurper sits upon his throne and waits for the end of the world. Outside the castle walls the invaders slaughter his men and are slaughtered in turn, and the air fills with the stench of blood and the cries of the dying. King Vortigern, the usurper, is no longer a young man, and the joints of his fingers are inflamed with arthritis, but by damn he can still hold a sword.

He sits upon his throne. It is his by right. He had schemed for it and he had killed for it and it is his by force alone. The throne is carved of old cedar brought long ago from across the sea. It had been decorated in the past with intricate inlays of Welsh gold and set with amethyst, but the usurper had ripped those and many other valuables when he took the castle and now his throne is bare.

He prefers it that way.

In the old days, travelling through the deep, dark forests of the land, preying on travellers or hiring out, they had slept in burrows in the earth, by burning fires, and sat on fallen trunks and logs. Sometimes he misses them, those who were there, those who had gone. Many had taken the fairy roads and were vanished, erased, but he remained, and he was hungry, and strong, and now the throne is his by right, by force alone.

The last vestiges of battle can be heard. Sunlight drapes across the room. The king hears the gates fall and the invaders storm into his sanctum. He hears the clash of steel on steel. The throne smells pleasantly of cedar.

After a time, there is silence. King Vortigern, the usurper, hears the tread of heavy footsteps outside his door. They come closer, unhurried, and the doors of the throne room are thrown open. First through the doors comes the tossed corpse of his son, hurled like a rag doll onto the floor. Half of his son's face is gone and his left leg below the knee, and his sword arm hangs crooked and bent backwards, broken in several places like kindling for the fire. Vortigern looks on his son, whom he had held in his arms when he first came out wailing into the world from his mother's quim, when he had placed a kiss upon his forehead, his first boy. He remembers how small he was, how strange it was to hold this tiny, defenceless animal with something like love.

Behind the boy's broken corpse comes a man. He is a tall man, and broad-shouldered, and his hair is yet strong and black, and his sword is bloodied. The man looks at Vortigern and smiles, and Vortigern is angered by how many teeth, healthy and whole, the man still has left in his mouth.

'Uther,' he says.

'Vortigern.'

They watch each other. And Vortigern remembers one night, it must have been December, and the woods filled with snow, and the moon aglow over the trees, casting down molten silver. They had chased three Jutes across the forest, their breath foggy in the cold, and no sound but the breathing of the chasers and the chased, until they came upon their quarry like two foxes on a brace of hares, and made easy work of them until the snow was dark with the Jutes' blood. Who the Jutes were and what they were doing this far from home and on a night like that he never knew, but they had emptied their purses all the same and stripped them of their coats and boots until the three lay naked on the snow. More snow fell, then. They raised their heads and watched the moon glow through the flurry of snow. He remembers that night, the silence, and the three naked bodies on the ground. How still it was.

'My wife,' he says now. 'Did you—'

'You mean, your daughter?'

'What's mine is mine,' Vortigern says; and that's all there is to say. 'But is she—'

'Dead?'

Vortigern nods. 'I sent her away,' he says unwillingly. 'But I did not know if she made it out in time.'

'Who gives a fuck?'

Vortigern rises from the throne. The great sword, how easy it once was to lift it. Uther smiles. He waits, at ease.

'As it comes to me it will come to you,' Vortigern says.

Their swords clash. Uther kicks the other man in the ribs and as he falls he lunges with the hidden knife and buries it in Vortigern's neck. The blood spurts out, so much blood. It sprays the throne, the floor, Uther's face. Vortigern raises his head one last time. For a moment he thinks he sees Merlin, standing quietly by the drapes, near the window.

Uther waits. The usurper falls.

Uther wipes the blade clean and takes his place on the throne.

2

The torches burn over Dinas Emrys. Uther's soldiers are drunk on beer and mead. In the storerooms of the castle they had unearthed old Greek amphorae, imports from the vanished empire. Uther drinks the foreign wine, which tastes of the lead it is flavoured with. He stares out over the valley. Vortigern's corpse burns on the pyre outside the gates. The moon rises in the night sky. Uther traces features on its face, light and dark areas that could be valleys or seas. The Greek, Democritus, believed it was a ragged world, hanging in the sky, with lofty mountains and hollow valleys. And once, escorting an Irish chieftain in that barbarous northern land, they had come across an ancient mound, built there who knew when, and there, upon a stone, were carved a set of maps of the lunar face. He remembers tracing the dark features with his finger, and as the new moon rose its light traversed the passage until it hit upon that same carved stone. Uther wonders if it is possible to reach the moon, somehow, perhaps by hitching a skein of geese to a carriage, and if so, what manner of warriors would be found there. The Greek, Democritus, believed that the world and everything in it was made of tiny things called atoms, beyond which there was no division, with only a void between them. And he believed, further, that there were many worlds, some young and growing, some old and in decay. And some had moons and some had none, and some had suns and some lived in eternal darkness. And though the Greek was dead centuries before, who was to say he was wrong. For Uther too had been offered a glimpse of other worlds than this, and he had seen his fallen comrades rise, and cast in silver moonlight walk the fairy paths to the place where the fair folk dwell. He has no love for that realm or for those who dwell there. Now he drinks of the old Greek wine, and stares out into the darkness, and the charred smell of the burning corpses on the pyre fills the air. It makes his stomach rumble.

'My liege.'

'Pellinore. What word?'

The boy bobs his head. He has a long pale face and mournful eyes that remind Uther of a frog's. He sways slightly on his feet, the effect of too much beer on someone ill-accustomed to it. His shirt is specked with dried blood.

'The tally is complete. To wit, three working silver mines, a gold mine in Dolaucothi, fifteen garrisons collecting road toll, seven wineries of which only four are operational, five foundries, thirteen leather workers' shops, fifteen hundred heads of cattle—'

The list goes on. Uther nods in time to the words. His now, all his.

'Three sail ships, twenty skin boats, five flat-bottoms, one Roman warship, a quinquereme, unseaworthy and with no crew who have the knowledge to pilot her. Finally with regards to Dinas Emrys, a full inventory has been carried out. Three chests of coinage, five of jewellery, some of good quality, one hundred amphorae, seventeen serving girls in working order, thirteen hundred and twelve sacks of grain, a well-stocked library of seventeen books, my lord—'

Pellinore sounds wistful, here. Then he pauses, hesitant.

'Well, boy?'

'And one prisoner, sir.'

'A prisoner?'

'Perhaps it would be best if you saw him for yourself.'

Uther rises. The campfires burn to the horizon. Overhead the stars are thick as dust. This castle rises high above the hill, overlooking the river valley. Uther follows the pageboy down and down and down, along a Roman spiral staircase, until it feels to him that he is burrowing into the ground, descending into the chute of a mine.

At last they reach a shaded glade. Though there are soldiers everywhere in the castle grounds there are none here, and Uther's skin itches. The glade is lit by molten moonlight and sitting at its heart is a calm pool of water. Uther can taste it on his tongue, the witchery of this place. He draws not his sword but a short, nasty blade he carries with him always. Meteorite iron, and crudely fashioned, by a race of people who had lived and died long centuries before any Roman engineer ever set foot in this savage land of Britain.

The pool, he sees on his approach, is not abandoned. A youth lies on the bank, pale and pretty with straw-blond hair, naked from the waist up. He is chained in iron to a metal rod driven into the ground. The moon shines down on the youth, the pool, the short tended grass. Uther's boots sink into the soft ground. Though Uther moves softly the boy is aware of his approach. He turns his head and smiles.

It's in the eyes, Uther thinks. The eyes that remind one of a cat or a lizard or a snake. Something not quite human, anyway. Disconcerting eyes. And the boy's flesh is unmarred by life's little indignities; no scars or blemishes of any sort, no pox, no acne. A lazy smile, for all that Uther is certain the iron shackles give the creature pain.

'The king is dead,' the boy says. 'Long live the king.'

'Why did Vortigern have you imprisoned here?' Uther inquires.

'He had asked for a prediction, and got one he didn't like.'

'What did you predict him, boy?'

'His death. Your coming.'

'I can see how he would not take to it kindly,' says Uther.

The boy shrugs. 'Many would make out that they want to know their fate,' he says. 'But no one ever does, not really. Besides, what's there to say? Every prediction ends in death.'

'An easy trade, then.'

'If you say so, liege.'

'You have a mouth on you, don't you, boy.'

'Yet here I am,' the boy says, and laughs, and lifts his arms to rattle at the iron chains.

'You have a name?'

'Who doesn't?'

'May I inquire what it is?'

'What's in a name,' the boy says. 'By giving names to things we lose perception, a way to see more clearly. We give a name to things and think, by doing so, we know them.'

'His name is Merlin, sire.'

The boy, this Merlin, sticks out his tongue.

'Profession listed as astrologer and wizard. Parentage, of no mortal man.'

'Such things as you I've seen, in villages and hamlets all across this land,' says Uther. 'And usually with their skulls bashed in as infants. How is it that you live?'

'Looks can be deceiving.'

Uther sighs. 'I can see why Vortigern chained you up,' he says. 'You'd try the patience of an Eastern saint.'

'Look, sire, bash my head or set me free, but I grow tired of this conversation. I mean you no harm.'

'What future do you see for me?'

'I told you, there is but one answer, lord.'

'Before my death, you impetuous cur.' But he says it without malice.

'You'll live,' Merlin says, simply.

'Live well?'

'You are a king.'

Uther laughs. 'Why should I let you go?'

'I bear you no ill will, King Uther. And perhaps I can be useful. Sire, you have power.'

'So?'

The boy licks his lips; perhaps nervously. Though Uther doesn't think the boy does anything without a conscious purpose.

'As bees are drawn to flowers so it is with me, lord.'

'Bees feed on flowers,' Uther says. He frowns, for he does not like the implication.

'Yet they also help them.'

'Let him go,' Uther says.

The pageboy, Pellinore, just stares.

'I said, let him go!'

'Lord, he's a—' Pellinore says, and then stops, confused. 'I know not the word for such as he.'

'Never question me again, Pellinore.'

Uther strides to the chained boy. He kneels beside him and pulls roughly on the iron shackles. The boy grimaces with sudden pain, the iron chafes against his naked wrists and ankles. He hisses, like a snake.

'It burns,' he says.

Uther leans in close, speaks softly. 'You will serve me?'

'I will serve.'

Perhaps it is that the ambiguity of the boy's answer registers with Uther, but does not concern him overmuch. For he *is* king. He pulls on the chains one last time, until the boy lies sprawled belly down on the grass, his head nearly touching water. Uther holds the back of Merlin's head and pushes, until the boy's face is submerged. He watches the bubbles rise and the boy's slim, pale body buck and thrash. At last, as the boy's struggle grows weak, he lets go. Merlin's head rises above the water and he sucks in air, coughing and spluttering.

'Remember this moment, boy,' Uther says. 'Remember I cupped your breath in my hand, so it would not extinguish.'

'And I am ever grateful, liege. Now will you let me go?'

'I will.'

He unties him. The chains, still tethered to the iron pole, flop to the ground, useless now. No longer earthed, the prisoner regains his smile. He rubs his wrists, but makes no mention of the pain.

'It's funny,' he says. 'I waited here for you all this time, yet when you came your eyes were green, not brown.'

'Get up, Merlin.'

'My King.'

Uther strides away. The banquet waits, his men, the flames, and seventeen serving girls in good working order. 'Get him something to wear and some scraps from the kitchens,' he says.

'Yes, my lord,' Pellinore says.

And this is how they meet, more or less. It can't have meant that much to Uther. The moon shines down on that quiet glade, the placid pool. They're creatures with an affinity to water. As Pellinore goes to help the boy, Merlin lunges at him and Pellinore jumps back, frightened. Merlin laughs and shakes his arms at him. 'Woooo…' he says.

'Freak!'

'I see a great big beast riding on your back,' says Merlin; but he says it without meaning harm, and perhaps Pellinore sees that, for again he offers Merlin his arm, and after a moment the wizard accepts and, leaning on the pageboy, he accompanies him out of that place and back into the world.

3

It's a beautiful day when they set out riding. Dew glistens on the grass, and snow dusts the Eryri mountains. As they ride along the hills the sea comes into view far in the distance, a flock of seagulls dark like ash over the swell. The air smells fresh and clear. Wild daffodils and creeping buttercups and honeysuckle. A village to the east, nestled at the foot of a hill, with cooking smoke rising.

They ride at an easy canter, Uther leading, his sword on his hip. And he remembers a day much like it is today, with the sun shining and few clouds in the clear blue sky, but the air was filled with the smell of blood and smoke and the fields strewn with the corpses of men. It had been on the wrong side of the Picts' Wall, and he no longer a sword-for-hire but a commander, if in someone else's army and in someone else's war. What king or lord it was it no longer mattered, for the man lay dead at Uther's feet with an arrow through his cheek and another in his chest, and he had gurgled out his last words not long before, and then the Picts were upon them.

Awful they were, in their tribal tattoos, like carrion birds they came upon the dead. And he, Uther, with his sword arm bleeding, hid. He crawled under the corpses of his fallen men and there he lay, for all that it was such a beautiful day, he saw nothing more of it but the flesh of his comrades, their stench, their blood, and there he lay as the Picts walked amidst the dying and the dead, assisting the former to hasten their final journey, assisting the latter by stripping and robbing them bare. He bore them no ill-will, in their place he would have done the same, it was just common sense. But it was the taste he could never quite rid himself of, the taste of that day, how he bit into cloth to stifle his own screams from the pain, a dirty shirt soaked in blood and piss, but he kept quiet as the dead, and when the Picts departed night had fallen.

He had crawled out from under the corpses, amazed to be alive. He had lost a lot of blood. There was no moon that night, and nothing stirring. He bound his wound, then retched against the Romans' wall. That night he searched by touch as much as vision until he found at last a broken section and crawled through. He wound his way away from the boundary of the Caledones, delirious, sick and half convinced that he was dying. But by morning he was still alive.

He swore that day that he'd return to that savage land, return with his sword and subject it to his will. That he would piss from on high on the Picts and make them his. It was on that day, perhaps, that he finally understood his destiny, emerging into daybreak after that infernal day and night. A clear morning, and heathers bloomed, and nary a cloud in the sky. And he thought, I would be king.

And so it was. So it is. They make good time but still the taste is in his mouth, but by noon they stop at a garrison that is now his by rights, and the soldiers welcome him with joy, and he washes away the stench of that long-forgotten battle with watered ale. He supervises the storerooms and examines the soldiers' weapons and observes them in practice, and he checks the records, so many carts, so many horses, the tariffs levied and the totals earned.

In truth he finds it dull. They lunch but sparsely, and resume their way. Uther thinks of wide-hipped women, tall, strong women, black-haired, doe-eyed, full-lipped women. Uther's hard. Of the seventeen serving girls in Dinas Emrys only eight are left who can work and he'd had three of those the other night. They don't fulfil him. A camp meal, nothing more, hastily eaten and shat. He needs a queen.

'A king is not a king without an heir.' The soothsayer, Merlin, appears by his side. He steals a glance at the king's crotch and leers, the expression unbecoming on his youthful face.

'Do not trespass into my head again, astrologer.'

'Sire, I speak only the plain truth. It is there for all to see.'

Uther shifts uncomfortably in the saddle. He needs a vessel for his seed. The wizard boy is right.

'You ever fuck a woman, boy?'

The wizard shrugs. 'I don't discriminate,' he says.

'I bet you don't.'

'You must have sired children, lord.'

Uther shrugs. 'Born on the road, perhaps,' he says, indifferent. A fighter on the road is but a dandelion, his seed spreads everywhere.

The wizard nods. 'You have time, yet,' he says.

That night they camp under the stars. Uther sits by the fire whittling wood with his knife. The wizard, Merlin, sings softly by the stream. His pale white hands submerged in water, he catches fish, quick as an osprey. The song speaks of the land under the stars, of ash and silver birch and fern, of moors and fenlands. The horses whinny, softly, paw the ground.

Uther sleeps. Uther dreams of islands.

4

White sails and dark clouds, a storm on the horizon. Sea spray and crying birds, and a single boat, sailing on the sea towards a distant shore.

5

They ride for days across the land. Across his land. His kingdom. This land is riven, tribal. Silures, Demetae, the Ordovices.

Wales, the Saxons call this land. Filled with petty chieftains, men dressed in the rags of Roman generals and ruling villages of farmers and their farmer wives. But not to be underestimated. And as the riders pass they must sit with the chiefs and share a meal and give gifts and receive them, a kingdom's like a spider's web, it's a delicate weave of fragile alliances. Uther promises peace. He promises stability. He is a soldier, they respect the sword. It is not that long ago that Rome had fallen, and this island still remembers the tread of the booted auxilia. The ships still dock at Fort Constantine, carrying pottery and wine, glass, silverware. Traders still come, though they are more wary now. There's profit still to be made with this land of his and by damn he intends to make his profit.

Five days' ride, to Dolaucothi, and the gold mines there. His mines. His gold. A wide estate along the valley of the River Cothi. Here it is as though the Romans never left. Aqueducts and water tanks, trip hammers worked by water wheel. The miners and engineers live in an adjacent village, children run naked and shrieking, splattered in gold dust.

'My lord,' Chief Engineer Magnus says. 'We are honoured by your visit.'

He is a youngish man, who speaks quietly but with authority to his men. Not slaves, these. Mining's a specialised job. This one is of this land, they all are, but he has the air of the old world about him. 'We try to maintain the gold field operations, but we are sorely lacking in equipment.'

'What do you need?'

'The furnace needs repairing. We need dewatering machines. The aqueducts are never properly maintained. And we need timber for the beam supports. You wish to see the tunnels?'

It's a familiar litany. Everywhere he goes there are needs and requests and demands. He grows weary of it all. But gold! He follows Magnus, born and raised here like his father before him, but with some Gaul or Palestinian in him. He sees the molten gold in the furnace, how bright it is! The water as it floods and strips the land, the miners searching for the tell-tale signs. Then down the shaft into the tunnels, following a seam, the specks of shiny matter in the walls. The miners move like ghosts below the surface. They have their own language, one he does not understand. Merlin follows behind, seemingly fascinated, he asks questions of a technical nature and Magnus answers in that same incomprehensible tongue.

It's eerie down there. He'd rather face a man in open battle than skulk in tunnels underground. His chest feels tight. But Merlin moves at ease, he's like a lizard. He says, 'What gold we have fell from the heavens, it isn't native to this Earth.'

'Is that correct,' Uther says drily.

'I think so, yes. It's why it's rare.'

But Uther doesn't care, beyond that gold is pretty and it shines, and people covet gold. He'd make a crown fit for a queen, and earrings too, perhaps a pendant.

'The next shipment will be ready in a fortnight,' Magnus says.

Uther is relieved to be back above ground. There is a soldier encampment to watch over the mines and what they hold – his soldiers. His mine. That night they sit around a fire when

Magnus brings out a small bag from which he extracts a handful of dry leaves.

'A little present from the traders,' he says. He places stones in the fire and when they are hot he places the weed on the stones. It releases a pleasant aroma, Uther thinks. He feels his muscles relax and his mind grow heavy. Merlin hums a wordless tune. The stars swirl overhead, so many stars, how had he never seen the shapes they make? He laughs. Merlin smiles a goofy smile.

Uther sees a falling star. He thinks of gold.

6

ight miles from Dolaucothi, they climb atop Pen-cerrig-
mwyn where a lead mine is in operation. So much metal
carried out of the earth, and his, all his. Tunnels follow
the veins underground but he politely abstains from going
down below again. The dirt removed is carefully packed and
stacked against the slope. And Uther thinks, they are building
a mountain here, in a hundred years' time a visitor may come
and find a taller, broader mountain where this one once stood.
But he has little interest in lead, and the Chief Engineer of this
place bores him with more demands, salaries for the miners,
which number two hundred and fifty or so, and the need for
new chits for the toll roads, and the problems with brigands in
the hills who covet the shipments.

'Brigands?' Uther says. This he understands. And there is
indeed a tribe, or at the very least, a family, well-known to
all the local lads, it seems, who make a trade of hijacking
the loads. So Uther mounts up and his soldiers follow. Less
than a day's ride and they come upon a nestled valley and a
lovely stream, and huts of mud and straw and women at their
washing, children in their play and men who sit and play dice
by the cooking fires.

There's no discussion. No man will take what's his by right
and force alone. That day they swoop down on the robbers,
the horses thundering down the slopes, the women screaming,

children run, the men draw weapons, but they're no match for Uther's force.

It's a distasteful business.

When it is done there's no one left alive but one, an elder. They set to make a cross and nail him to it, like the Christ in Palestine. The water in the brook is spoiled, but it will wash the detritus of that place and, downstream, the water will make people sick. Let it be a warning to them, he thinks. And after all the water will be clear again before too long.

In the heat of the slaughter, as his sword caught a woman with her babe in arms, he thought he saw Merlin, just for a moment. The boy's rapt face. Those eyes. Uther kills for killing is his business. But Merlin doesn't kill so much as watch. He finds the wizard, at times, distasteful.

They leave that place. They ride into the night. More falling stars. The via lactea, the Milky Circle in the sky. The riders' shadows are as long as blades or elves, they flit like ghosts under the moonlight. They sleep, they rise. The sun is hot. The road slopes down by degrees, the air becomes enriched with salt, and Uther sees the sea. They ride into Dinas Maelor.

The giant steps out from his fort, and Uther marvels at the sight of such a thing. A great coarse being with wild hair and a beard in which birds make their nests, and on his head a crown of thorns and thistles. They say it takes the weaver women seven days to spin one of his shirts. He wears gold on his fingers, and his teeth could chew through rocks. He stands with hands on hips and glares at them. He dwarfs the men. They say he eats a sheep each day for supper.

'So you're King Uther.'

'Aye.'

They stare. The giant's eyes are flecked with gold and cobalt.

'You came to… what?'

'I am the King.' He says it simply. It is merely fact.

The giant nods. 'I heard you did for the lead thieves of Bawddwr.'

'It is so.'

They stare again. The giant nods. 'My liege?'

'Yes, Maelor Gawr?'

'Be welcome in my castle. Lord—'

'Yes?'

'I have a problem with sheep thieves.'

And thus it's ever so.

'Of course you do,' sighs Uther.

They enter. Into the giant's giant hall, the fireplace is like a furnace, and three skinned lambs turn slowly on a spit. 'Rubbed with olive oil, sea salt and garlic,' the giant says, with pride. The smell of fat makes Uther's mouth water. They're served a dry hard cheese, fresh bread, a brace of dormice cooked the Roman style. The giant plucks the lamb meat off the bone, but delicately. He's dainty in his habits, and wipes his fingers on a cloth as large as a military tent. The soldiers eat with less restraint. All but Merlin, who picks at a honey cake.

The giant puts the carcass down. The gold glints in his eyes.

'And what is this?' he says, 'You have yourself a plaything, liege?'

'My wizard, Merlin.'

'Is that so.'

Merlin nods politely.

'Is the food not to your liking, wizard?'

'I find the company so much more nourishing,' the wizard says.

'Indeed, you look well fed.'

'I thank you, kindly.'

Uther frowns. 'Perhaps you could do something about these sheep thieves our host finds so inconvenient, Merlin.'

'Me, lord?' The boy looks startled.

The giant laughs, like boulders falling from a hilltop. 'You haven't earned your keep yet, imp?'

Merlin bites on the last of the honey cake and scatters crumbs onto the floor. 'If this is my king's desire.'

'It is,' says Uther.

'Then be it so.'

The boy stalks out. 'Sheep? Sheep!' he says.

'A knife's no toy to play with,' says Maelor Gawr.

'But it is useful,' Uther says.

That evening with the fall of dusk, a shout brings them to the battlements. They see the dust at first, and then the herd of sheep that storms towards the castle. The giant's herdsmen catch the sheep and lead them to the kitchens. Behind the sheep comes Merlin, sauntering, chewing on a blade of grass. 'Sheep? Sheep!' he says.

'Are those...?'

Merlin just shrugs.

That night they feast on flanks and chops and loins and legs, yet Uther sticks to watered ale and Merlin to another honey cake. But Maelor Gawr eats hungrily, and grease runs down his cheeks and in his beard, where mice gnaw on the scraps that fall into their paws. The torches burn in Dinas Maelor. The fire roars. And all is well.

7

In this manner they circumnavigate this green and pleasant land of his. Along the coastal road and in the shadow of the snowy mountains, ever present, to see his people. Fisherfolk and sheep herders and barley farmers, weavers and potters and brewers. They welcome him gladly, the safety he brings, they come out to see him pass and ask him in for cakes and ale, and often he accepts, he and his men, and so the journey's slow. He basks in the warm glow of his people's affection. In one village they erect a bonfire and host a fair for him, they spit a pig over the coals and serve him beer. He entertains the children with a song, young mothers come to touch his hand for luck.

A king is not a king without an heir. And on that journey he spends much of his time examining the maidens of that land, dark haired and brown eyed and fair to see, and there is nary a night that he spends alone.

Farther along the coast they come across a group of semi-feral boys collecting crabs along the shore. They run after the knights and try to mimic them with sticks instead of swords. Uther takes out his sword and shows it to the boys. He calls them soldiers. He shares their food, boiled crab and periwinkles, and gives them coin, and tells them to come seek him when they're ready. In truth, he knows his battle's far from over, for all that Vortigern is dead. His enemies are ever present, scheming in their castles, hiring men. He cannot be complacent.

This coastal part becomes more densely populated. He sees the remnants of Roman fisheries long since abandoned, and makes a note to try and bring them back. Along this coast fishermen go out in boats and come back with a daily catch, and the fish markets do good trade, but this is small scale work, and he doubts there is much tax revenue generated. A king is not a king without his tax. He sees a great blue shark for sale and orders half to be prepared. He bites into white flesh and fat runs down his chin. He tastes the sea. He notices Merlin has more of an appetite for the creatures. The boy's eyes flash and his hair turns white as sea spray. His skin is almost scaly, Uther thinks. That night they stop in yet another village to take their hospitality. The night is cold, a wet cold wind blows from the sea. The skies amass with clouds. Uther wraps up in a heavy blanket and sits by the fire, staring out to sea. Sometimes he dreams of a shining white island, far in the distance, and it seems to call out to him. But tonight sees nothing but the coming storm, a solitary cormorant diving against the gathering clouds. The tide rises against the beach, the waves are high. And down there, as though it were his bath, is Merlin, frolicking, at ease. An eel is what he reminds Uther of. He strains his eyes to try and make out details – it seems to him that Merlin's not alone, that there are others with him in the water, graceful figures moving in a dance of foam and spray. But he can never make them out clearly.

Uther warms his hands against the fire. The nights are growing longer. It is well known that the world is a sphere. The Greek astronomer, Eratosthenes, had performed complex measures and concluded that the circumference of the world is some two hundred and fifty thousand stades. And Philolaus believed that the Earth spun on an axis. And in the battle between light and dark that spins and spins across the world, Uther, recently crowned king of all this land, nevertheless has an affinity to night, when sun turns its face from the world.

For in the darkness one can bring a stealthy death upon one's enemies.

It is those enemies that occupy his mind now, and chief among them Gorlois, Duke of Cornwall, or anyway that's how he styles himself, the fat buffoon, a merchant, not worthy of a castle or a crown, how much he'd like to wrap his fingers around the bastard's throat and squeeze and squeeze. That fat and wealthy land, Belerion, Land's End, that joshes at the Celtic Sea and leans to Gaul. They mine for tin and trade it with the continent, and have the means to raise an army that made even Roman generals of old think twice.

He has a deal with Gorlois. Isn't this the way these things work? You have your patch and I have mine, and no one wants a war, it's bad for business.

Only Uther doesn't like to deal. Uther wants what Gorlois has. It's always been that simple. And the fat bastard's the same. Still. The deal holds.

Then there's Leir, the clever old man of the ridings, with claims to royal Roman blood, whose power spreads over York and the entirety of the Brigantes. They make fearsome warriors, again, even the Romans feared them. Leir makes his home in no one fixed abode but moves around, and they say he has eyes everywhere.

For now there's an understanding.

Uther warms his hands by the fire and frets, and drinks ale. The Earth spins, the nights lengthen, and soon it will be winter, but not yet. And he is king.

Fort Constantine, at last, feels like the jewel in the crown. The bustling city makes one think of empire. The roads are clean, the markets bustling, the harbour is alive with ships both foreign and domestic. Across the strait is Druid's Island, with its sacred groves and menhirs. He has no fear of druids, who Tiberius and Claudius both hated, hunting them until they vanished. Uther relaxes in the public baths, his arms on marble: this is the life, he thinks.

'My lord?'

It's Merlin, sliding into the water.

'Yes, wizard?'

'What are your plans?'

'I thought I'd have a drink, followed by women,' Uther says. The wizard sighs. 'I don't mean now.'

'I know just what you meant.'

'And so?'

'I want this land united under one authority, Merlin,' Uther says.

'Your own.'

'Of course.'

'You need money. Men. You need arms.'

'Can you magic them for me, boy?'

'Lord, for what you want, you don't need wizardry, you just need swords.'

'I know, you fool.'

'But I'll be by your side.'

'I know that, too.'

He'd grown accustomed to the little wizard. A knife's a dangerous toy, but it is useful. And he knows Merlin, has known things like Merlin. They're drawn to power, feed on it. There is a trust in knowing that you cannot trust them. But you can use them, even as they think they're using you.

'This daughter-wife of Vortigern's,' says Uther. 'She's hidden well. My men can find no sign or trace of her.'

'My liege?'

'I cannot have' – he waves a hand – 'usurper brats running around. Perhaps you'll see if you can find her?'

'Of course, my lord.'

'Then go.'

The little wizard vanishes. Uther relaxes in the public baths. A rare luxury, these days. Civilisation. He'd only heard the stories of how Britain used to be under the Romans. Now Londinium's a shithole, the roads lie unmaintained, the courier network's a distant memory, and good luck sending any mail. If it were up to him he'd clean the aqueducts and build new sewers, maybe start a library to rival those of Alexandria and Antioch. Well. He would do those things, perhaps, but where are the engineers to fashion sewers or the archivists to catalogue dusty old scrolls? Gone, gone with the empire, and he, the king, has better things to do. How can he build when he must rule first, how can he rule when there are men still who oppose his will?

It's much to think of.

Uther relaxes into the warm piped water.

8

Merlin steps out into the streets of Fort Constantine. The sun in the sky shines most pleasantly. A heavyset flower seller stands at a street corner and smiles at him, most pleasantly. He buys a primrose and inhales its scent – it is most pleasant, he thinks.

Merlin struts down to the sea. Along the harbour, stalls are set and fish are sold, but he is drawn to an upturned crate and a shifty-looking man and a game of dice. Merlin puts down coin and picks up dice. He throws, contemptuously.

'Two sixes. Pay.'

'Triple for a snake eyes.'

'Call.'

He throws. The man stares at the dice.

'Pay,' Merlin says.

'Double or nothing, all bets are final, player's call,' the dice man says.

'A crucifixion,' Merlin says. He throws.

A double three, two lines intersecting, form a cross. The dice man pulls a knife instead of paying, but Merlin laughs, snatches the money on the crate and runs. He loves to gamble and he loves to cheat, and as long as games of chance exist and men will play them, then he would never lack for coin.

It was in this manner, of a sort, that Vortigern's embittered wizards found him. For Vortigern, the usurper, had asked his astrologers and witchers to cast a spell of protection for him against the coming of Uther, his enemy. And so the astrologers worked their spells and incantations, and then declared that only blood would serve. Blood!

The useless fools, thinks Merlin.

Blood? the usurper says.

The blood of a youth born without mortal father, smeared on the foundations of the castle, the witchers say.

And where might such a youth be found? Away they go, these ruffians, to hunt for one with foreign blood in him.

That day, and he was running, he was being chased by other boys who jeered and cried and threw stones at him, calling him every name under the sun – 'Go! Go back to your eldritch father, Thing, go back to the realm of gnomes and sprites!'

How they spat at him, how they would have done him harm had not the witchers and their soldiers stopped them. Instead they shackled him and brought him back to Vortigern.

He smiles now, remembering, but his smile is bitter. He steals an apple from a cart and skips to shore and pays for passage. He has unfinished business over yonder on Druid Island.

It's a big island, a kingdom unto itself. The Romans, when they came, tore down the sacred groves and executed druids, built forts and mined for copper. Since their departure, Irish pirates had made it into their stronghold, but old Vortigern and local chieftains fought them off, at last. Now it's just an island. Merlin likes islands. He loves the sense of security of being surrounded by water. He loves the sea, its fathomless depths, where strange blind creatures swim in eternal darkness. He loves its moods, its unpredictability, its lethal reach, he loves the song the drowned men sing and the whisper of the water through their bones, he loves to dive and close his eyes and listen to the whales cry out across the thousands of oceanic miles. There's magic in the sea.

There's magic everywhere you look. Just pluck a leaf and hold it to the light. How magical it is. That it is there, how it had formed and how it grows. There's magic in a stone – oh, yes, he knows his stones. There's magic in the earth and in the sky and in the heavens. He drops the leaf. He walks unhurried. Off the Roman road, deeper into the interior of the island. He has no obvious destination in mind, no visible purpose. Yet minute things decide his journey. A scratch on the bark of a yew tree there. A patch of meadowsweet there, where a corpse might be buried. Ah, there, a menhir, twice taller than a man. Ah, there, an apple grove. He picks a wizened apple from the ground and bites into the flesh and finds a worm. He sucks it in and lets it wriggle in his mouth. A tiny vestige of the power such as Uther has. It's like a delicacy. He hesitates, to spit the worm out or to swallow.

'Don't fucking move, Merlin,' a voice says.

Figures come into the clearing in the orchard where he stands. They're robed and armed, and two have thick and bushy beards, one has a scar and lacks an eye, another is a woman.

Merlin swallows.

'You have some nerve.'

'Is that you, Caradoc?' Merlin says. 'Didn't recognise you there without your eye.'

The disfigured man scowls. The woman laughs – a sound like a knife against a whetstone.

'Darling Merlin,' she says. 'Always so droll.'

'Nimue. I have no fight with you.'

'Indeed?' she murmurs.

'Lady, this company does not befit you.'

She smiles. Her eyes remind him of a fish, her teeth are needle-like.

'Why are you here?' she says.

'I come in service of my lord.'

'You're awfully confident, little wizard–' from one of the gruff and bearded men.

'Nennius. It's been a while.'

'Not long enough, you little shit.'

The woman, Nimue, looks at them. Her eyes meet Merlin's. She nods, an almost imperceptible gesture.

'Boys, I'll leave you to your games.'

With that she turns into a crow and flies away. The others turn, with staffs and blades. They grin.

'Three against one seems hardly fair.'

'We missed your blood.'

And Merlin remembers the long days of his captivity, chained there in the sacred pool under Dinas Emrys.

Blood for the foundations, they had told their lord. Shed the little freak's blood, and your castle will stand. And every day one of these men came down the spiral staircase, and every day there was the iron knife. He watched his blood drip slowly into sacred water. He watched the blood, he watched the life.

'Time to finish the job.'

Then they are upon him. He snarls, his skull shifts shape, his mouth fills with wolf's teeth. His fur bursts out. He moves with speed, he tears off Caradoc's ear and Nennius' quadriceps. He leaps on the third man's back, Claudius, whose wizardry is of the continent, and tears out his throat and tastes the blood, it tastes of grapes and warmer climes. Wolf-Merlin snarls, the one-eyed man lashes with the iron knife, the wolf howls rage and tears and bites, and blood runs down and soaks the hungry earth of that old sacred grove.

Nennius backs away, but his bleeding leg won't let him run. He falls back against an apple tree. The wolf snarls. Then Merlin re-emerges out of that suit of muscles, tendons, blood and guts, and dusts himself, and he looks older now. He stands above his vanquished enemy.

'Well, Nennius? I spoke no lies to your master. My blood helped him not, and his death still came.'

'The castle stands,' croaks Nennius.

'You fool. The castle stands, but not the head that wore

the crown. Your master's dead. It's time you joined him in the other world.'

'Then... fucking kill me, freak.'

'That I could do. But there is still the matter of your master's daughter-wife. Where may I find her, please?'

'Fuck y—' he screams as Merlin, kneeling, twists a knife into his shoulder.

'I did say please,' says Merlin.

Then it is done. It's quiet there, under the apple trees. The grove, he feels, is grateful for the offerings. He steps over a corpse and reaches down for an apple.

He takes a bite.

9

They ride deep into the mountains and the mountains are wreathed in fog and snow. The horses' breath forms into whitened shrouds, the tread of hooves is eerie in the silence that the mist creates. After a time the horses slow, then stop and won't go further.

'Are you sure you have it right, Merlin?' Uther says.

'It has a dying man's sincerity behind it.'

Uther gives him a thin smile. 'Then lead the way.'

They walk. The execution party's small, just Uther, Merlin, two retainers and the page boy, Pellinore. Merlin navigates by scent and recall: here, the smell of a woman's desperation, here an infant's cry, here they stopped to argue, here to eat, here – the remnants of a fire, however much disguised.

Snow falls. The climb is steep. They follow narrow mountain trails, one at a time; the king speaks not, but breathes heavily. He's armed and ready, and Merlin admires that about him, that ruthless determination that no one and nothing should ever stand in his way. This is no matter of guilt or innocence. To be a king the innocents must die, to be a king the guilty live, to be a king is to be judge and executioner both, and rule by force alone. Merlin can understand that. There are two types of men, those with swords and those without, and Merlin likes the men with swords. You know where you are with one of those.

He leads the way. The trail grows clearer, stronger, here a

crushed flower releasing its scent, here the dried excrement of a child, here, beyond this ravine, the corpse of a handmaiden who fell. And something else, too. Something foul.

He feels rather than sees the mountain move. The snow above falls in a great big clump of ice. He shouts, 'Pellinore, move!' and shoves the page boy in the back. The boy is thrown against the rocks and Uther turns, his sword raised high – 'Betrayal, Merlin?'

'No, you fool!'

Then Uther sees it too. The moon, for just a moment, peers behind the clouds. A figure rises from the mountainside, all stones and brambles, ice and rocks and trees. It forms a vaguely human shape the size of a grand dolmen. It roars and gnashes ice in teeth of rock.

'Ogre!'

They try to duck for cover, but it's no use. They run, blindly, into the swirling snow, into the rising fog, into the trap that Vortigern's daughter-wife had set for them. A guardian, and what nefarious trade must she have made to secure such a guardianship?

'Do something, Merlin!'

But ogres have no love for Merlins and their kind. The druids had it right, of old – 'How did you gain your crown, lord?'

'With blood—'

Realisation dawns.

'Not Pellinore.'

'No,' Merlin says. The ogre swipes at them with fingers made of stout oaks. They duck. 'But you have those.'

'My men have served me well!'

'Then let them serve you one last time.'

And Uther sees the logic in the wizard's words. He must. He draws his blade. Not sword. A knife, a dirty weapon for a dirty deed. Then comes upon his men.

The knife speaks. The knife makes a compelling argument.

The storm of rage above them slows. The ogre smells the

blood. It's fresh. It's good. The ogre likes. A sacrifice. The way it's right and proper. The ogre leans into the mountainside. Becomes once more a bed of rocks, a copse of trees, a path. The blood soaks into its hide. The ogre sighs. The howling winds make Uther's flesh run even colder than it is. He follows Merlin up the mountainside. His page boy comes behind him. Two eyes as large as wells blink sleepily at him. Then they are through.

When they find the place at last it is a temperate valley well hidden within the crevices of Eryri. The snow falls elsewhere. The air is humid. Flowers grow thickly on the slopes. On the valley floor, beside a running stream, there is a lean-to building made of stone, so low they almost miss it. They trudge down the slope, approach with caution. A cooking fire had burned only recently, Uther notes. The door's a stout oak. He gestures. Merlin shrugs. The wizard puts his hand against the wood and seems to listen. He pushes and the door just opens. They go inside, where it is dark, the ceiling low, it smells of stagnant water, mushrooms, moss.

'Step carefully, my lord,' whispers the wizard.

But Uther has no fear of orphan-widows. He finds the trapdoor just as he expected. He lifts it up though he must strain his muscles, pulling at the iron ring. A slab of stone and, down below, some cavernous space. But whether it's an old abandoned mine, or burial ground, or sewer, he doesn't know. Down they go, with Pellinore above to watch the hole. And down there he finds her, at long last, the daughter-wife of Vortigern. She stands with a staff and tries to ward him off but he is stronger, and he knocks it from her hands and socks her on the chin and drags her back above and to the brook.

She glares at him. 'As I die so shall you, you inbred sword-for-hire.'

'Why did you marry him?' he says.

'I loved him.'

'You wanted power.' He says it kindly. 'How will I die, lady?'

She laughs. 'For you, I forecast death by water.'

'Then you'll die by the sword, lady queen.'

She spits at him. He lifts his sword. He brings it down on her head, the blade cuts through, he splits her open, like a pomegranate.

'Oh, fuck!'

'Get them off, get them off! They're everywhere!'

She opens like a husk and from the pod come slithering out snakes, at least a hundred, usurper's brood, the poisonous little vipers. He stomps upon their tiny skulls and lashes with the sword, he has to catch them all, catch them before they slip away.

'I'm bit! I'm bit!' – it's Pellinore. He stares aghast. A snake has fastened on to Pellinore's arm, it holds on by its poison teeth. The sword moves through the air, the body drops but the snake's head's still attached to Pellinore. The boy's face turns purple. His eyes turn in their sockets. Merlin catches him as he falls. He pulls the head of the snake off. Two nasty marks, but little blood. Yet Pellinore's arm is swollen. He is infected.

Uther stomps and stomps with renewed fury on the baby snakes. He loses count of how many he's killed. Their bodies glisten on the ground, their guts and blood, crushed baby skulls. At last he's done. He thinks. He breathes heavily. An awful smell, he doesn't think he'd ever wash this smell off. Snake's shit, snake's piss. But nothing moves. Perhaps there's one who's playing dead, the way he, Uther, had at Picts' Wall. He goes methodically, one by one he brings the sword down, one by one until he's certain every single one of them is dead.

10

That night, as they ride back to Dinas Emrys, he sees something miraculous in the skies. A bird of light, or so it seems, a glowing red object trailing through the heavens, with a long scaly tail and wings of flame, and it's moving fast.

'A dragon,' Uther breathes. He watches the being of flame as it traverses the night. 'This is a sign, Merlin, and I shall take it for my name and for my emblem.' He raises high his sword. 'Uther Pendragon!' he shouts, and his men raise their arms in turn and echo his cry.

But Merlin has other thoughts regarding the nature of this celestial apparition. And he watches this comet, this star stone, as it travels to the horizon until it disappears somewhere over Britain, and still he waits. Then comes a sight the likes of which he'd never seen, far in the distance, a huge, mushroom-shaped cloud rising, with flames inside it. Then comes the sound, this terrible roar, until the horses lose their balance in fright and Uther barely holds on to his mount, then shouts, in ecstasy – 'Hear the dragon's roar! Pendragon! Pendragon!'

And his men join in, all but for those two who were trampled underfoot and now are left to feed the crows – 'Pendragon! Pendragon! Long live Uther! Long live the king!'

They ride on, in frenzy, to Dinas Emrys. There they light great fires, and roast pigeons and sheep, and get roaring drunk.

A banner is hastily made and raised to the top of the tower. The serving girls are passed from hand to hand.

The wizard climbs the spiral staircase to the tower. The Milky Circle's myriad of stars are obscured above by smoke and dust. The air is cold. They wouldn't notice, down below, not now, not with the fires and the drink. But later. The wizard thinks, it is going to be a cold winter. He looks out into the dark. He'd love to know where the thing had landed. There would be traces left, an impact crater. He summons birds: a wren, a tit, a warbler and a raven. He sends them forth to be his eyes and ears. He hopes they will come back.

Merlin stares into the dark. It's lonely at the top of the tower. Down below they chant, 'Pendragon!'

The wizard broods.

11

That winter turns out long and cold and dark and dust covers the sky. It's cold and dark the world over, messengers confirm. Few ships arrive that year in Britain and there is little to trade, and the people of the land starve as crops fail. 'The sun gave forth its light without brightness,' writes Procopius from Caesarea. In the capital and port cities of Byzantium a deadly plague kills millions. And the birds Merlin sent out never return. The location of the fallen star stone's lost to him.

It is a long and bitter year, with the sun permanently in eclipse. The people starve and Uther quells rebellions, for hungry people have nothing left to lose. The king is not dispirited, but he is frustrated. 'Is there no magic you can do?' he demands of his wizard.

But Merlin mutely shakes his head, then says, 'This thing will pass.'

'I want to believe you,' Uther says. 'I do.'

There is little to do throughout that long year but close in and wait. Even the king subsists on gruel, in Dinas Emrys the stores of grains are all but depleted. They say some people have resorted to cannibalism. If so, there's naught the king can do. He shrugs. 'The flesh is not so bad once you get used to it,' he says. Merlin forgets, sometimes, where Uther comes from. It is a world where only ruthlessness survives.

That summer it snows in mid-day. The corpses of birds litter the fields and fish rot on the seashore. 'This can't go on,' the king says in frustration. He summons augurs, druids, priests of Christ. None can help but cast aspersions or demand a sacrifice. In the north beyond the sea the Norsemen bury hoards of gold to try and buy the sunlight back from heathen gods. A wandering Jew far from his home in Persia makes his way to Uther's court. He says, 'Perhaps the fault is not with God but is a matter of natural philosophy.' He says, 'Did not Aristotle argue that the Prime Mover is not the efficient cause of action in the universe, and plays no part in its construction or arrangement? If so' – this merchant says, warming to his subject – 'perhaps this blight is but a grain of dust that clogs the orderly mechanism of Physis, of nature, which soon must revert back to its prior form? For though the vagaries of the material cause are subject to circumstance, and thus to change, nevertheless every object has a nature, attributes that is, which make it behave in its customary fashion. And so—'

But Uther, bored, dismisses the traveller, though the man and Merlin speak long into the night on all manners of santa natura.

That summer is a miserable one, and the winter that follows promises nothing but more hunger and death. Yet spring comes suddenly. The sunlight brightens and the dust eases in the sky and it is warm again. Flowers bloom over the slopes of the snowy mountains, and fish return to the shallows and what crops the farmers planted grow. That year brings promise with it, life is renewed, the earth is healed. A summit is planned between the kings of Britain, to be held in Tintagel. And so with spring returned they ride once more across the land, to Cornwall.

12

alfway they stop at Caer Odor, the Fort on the Chasm.
The Roman villas are abandoned, but near the gorge a
settlement of Christians persists, and a wooden cross is
erected high over the Avon. These new religionists bring food
and drink to Uther and his men. Their priest is learned, a man
of letters, who is comfortable in Latin.

'And have you considered the word of the Saviour from
Galilee?' he asks the king. The priest brings out a sacred book,
called the New Covenant, and attempts to engage the king in
discussion of the rise of Christ, and the rebellion of the Jews
against the Romans, and of tales of many miracles, such as
when the Saviour spoke to and calmed a storm, or when he
cast out demons into a herd of swine and drove them to the
sea, where they promptly drowned. But the king yawns, for he
has little interest in distant Palestine and far-fetched tales of
fancy, and besides there is the matter of Pellinore.

Pellinore lies sickened in a room inside the fort. His bloated
body is distained, his skin is stretched and taut over his
glistening belly. He groans and sweats, hot and cold in turns,
he cannot grow comfortable.

This condition had arisen since the boy was bit, and it had
grown in stages, all through that long and terrible year, until
now he can no longer ride a horse or hold a sword or fetch or
carry for his master. And a noise arises from inside his stomach,

an awful keening sound that drives even hardened men to fright, so that they stay well away from Pellinore.

'I can't go on,' whispers the boy, 'please, lord, put an ending to my suffering.'

Uther stares at him in annoyance. Pellinore has royal blood. He turns to his wizard.

'Will he live or die?' he says.

'This affliction has a cure, my liege.'

'Then cure it.'

Merlin sighs, for he has seen such things before, if only rarely. And so he summons towels, boiled water, soap. He lights a candle in the room. The night is dark, there is no moon. His shadow hovers right beside him. He burns herbs that send forth a pleasant aroma.

'Not long now, Pellinore,' he says.

'Help me, Merlin.'

'I'll do what I can.'

He takes the knife. The young man's eyes stare at the blade in horror.

'Bite on this,' the wizard says. He sticks a piece of wood between the young man's teeth. This job's unpleasant, Merlin thinks. And yet a job's a job.

He removes Pellinore's garments. Pellinore's belly glistens so awfully. The skin is so pale it is near translucent, and within it Merlin sees the thing moving inside. Big, now. That awful keening sound.

'Hush, Thing,' says Merlin. He speaks soothingly to the belly. He sings the creature songs to calm it down. He lifts the knife. Places the tip against the skin, and presses.

Pellinore screams. Merlin cuts, gently, carefully, tears open Pellinore's belly. He pulls at the flaps of fat and skin. A gush of mucous liquid, blood and slime pours out onto the floor, the awful keening sound returns in earnest as Merlin reaches deep within the recesses of Pellinore's makeshift womb and puts his fingers round the creature. He lifts it up – it's large – it's heavy

– it's made of Pellinore's own flesh and blood and bones. It comes away with a wet sucking sound. Pellinore screams. The beast kicks Merlin in the chest. He falls back and the beast squats on his chest and thrusts its face at him, hissing.

'Get it off me,' Merlin says, 'get it off me!'

Pellinore sits up upon his sickbed. The beast hisses in contempt at Merlin and leaps into Pellinore's arms. Pellinore holds it in his arms, weeping. He strokes its hide. The beast purrs. Merlin scrambles away from them both, disgusted.

'The beast will have to die,' he says.

'No! Never!' cries Pellinore. The beast turns and glares at Merlin. That awful screeching sound again. Merlin covers his ears to try to block it out. He staggers. The beast leaps to the window. It knocks the candle on the floor. It looks back at Pellinore.

'Go…' says Pellinore. 'I'll find you. Wherever you go, I will find you.'

The beast coos. It turns its head and looks at Merlin, and spits. He moves, just in time to avoid the poison, which hits the wall and hisses as it eats through stone. The beast screams in rage and loss. Then it jumps out of the high window, into the night, and vanishes from sight.

'No!' cries Pellinore. He settles on his sickbed, desolate. A shaken Merlin rises, goes to him. He tries to summon some professional pride. He picks a thread and needle.

'This will hurt,' he says. He begins to sew the stomach shut. The flesh, he sees, knits together neatly. This is not nature that has caused this.

'You'll heal,' he says.

'But I'll never be whole.'

Such despair in his eyes. Merlin turns away.

'There'll be a scar,' he says.

At the door, he hesitates. He turns to look. Pellinore is lying back. His breathing's better, his colour's back. Merlin says, 'You'll be alright?'

'I'll live.'
'Yes,' Merlin says.
He goes.

In the morning when he comes to check on Pellinore, the man's no longer there.

13

They cross the border into Cornwall on a sunny day in summer. A glorious day. Falcons and razorbills and puffins in the skies, and elms and oaks as far as the eye can see, and bees buzzing lazily amidst the flowers, and the smell of grass trodden on by hooves, and the horse's tails wagging and the fresh smell of their shit, and the men lolling in the saddles, drunk on the heat and the light, and in the distance the cries of seagulls and the smell of salt and tar.

Uther breathes it all in. This rich land, and all the fish in the sea and all the birds in the sky should be his. He covets every castle, every hamlet, every field and every foundry, every head of cattle, every working aqueduct, every road and every tree and every fucking soul that ever lived upon this land.

His hand grips the pommel of his sword. His thoughts are dark and filled with murder. He would see this land riven by plague and washed in blood if it is not to be his.

Yet his it will be.

They ride to the sea. Tintagel Castle sits atop an island, a dark, malevolent force of nature as impervious to attack as the moon. Surrounded by open sea, its only link to the mainland is by a tall and graceful footbridge, heavily guarded on both sides. The castle rises high into the air. Its stonework has enchantment woven into it. Guard towers watch the four winds, land and sea. The men of Tintagel are armed with catapults and scorpions.

When Uther and his entourage approach, already they can see the banners of King Leir, whose men and horses wait in their encampment, watched over by the forces of Gorlois.

'Gorlois, Gorlois!' Pendragon says. 'Would that I spit and roast the fat bastard on a fire!'

'Patience, lord,' his wizard mutters. Uther snorts contempt. They come to the place and stop. The men dismount. Pendragon's banner's raised.

'You are expected, lord. Please, follow me.'

Uther strides along the narrow bridge. The wind runs its fingers on his short-cropped hair. The sea spray leaps into the air far down below. He watches rocks. He watches mermaids singing in the depths. He watches seagulls crying as they hunt. His thoughts are bloodied, but he masks them with a smile. His wizard follows meekly, and a handful of his men. The rest stay on the mainland.

They reach the island. They enter. He feels as though he's entering the belly of a dragon. Inside it is cavernous, filled with light. Soft music plays, tuba, tibia and horn, a lute and lyre. A children's choir sings, so beautifully. 'The little angels,' murmurs Uther. Their singing fills the air.

That night there is a great big feast to rival ancient Rome's. There's wine from Gaul and Greece, and spitted ewes and suckling pig and dormice, there are oysters and cherries and carrots and crabs. There are musicians playing, and the Grand Hall is filled with the sweet singing voices of the children. Servers move like charmed and captive angels amidst the throng of British kings, fetching and carrying, and the smell of burning herbs pleasantly fills the air. Merlin eats like a starved gutter rat, for once. There's so much concentrated power in the hall that his stomach rumbles. He feeds on cheese and bread and a preserve of grapes, and drinks the wine, but watered. He watches Leir, a man with dangerous blood. That king catches his eye and nods in recognition, and Merlin looks away.

But Uther has no mind for peace talks, and no eye, this once, for his rivals. Uther Pendragon has no eye for the serving girls for once, he pays no heed to the enchanting music, and he barely notices the piece of bloodied cow flesh he is desultorily chewing on.

At the head of the table sits their host, Gorlois. And beside Gorlois sits his queen.

And what a woman! Not too tall and not too slender, but fine all the same, with a full head of hair, long and rich, a woman blossoming in womanhood, a mother only made more fetching in her changes, with a welcoming smile and a graceful way of gesturing, and a pleasing voice and a calm demeanour, and she wears a crown of slim gold and tourmaline that frames her face.

But it's her eyes that capture Uther, her eyes that make him unable to pull away. There's something deep and haunting and unknowable behind her eyes, he thinks, as though some of her blood, a ways back, is of the good folk. And how Gorlois parades her!

'This is my queen, Igraine, my wife, the mother of my little princesses—'

How Uther loathes this fat lord of Cornwall!

And how, oh how, does he desire the man's wife!

'A pleasure, lady.'

'Be welcome in our castle, lord.'

But welcome he is not. He knows it and she knows it just as well. The next few days are busy with discussions. The kings negotiate. They must discuss this climate change that's happened, the famine on the land that's now averted, at long last, the state of roads and ancient boundaries, the rising threat of Saxons coming from the north.

'There must be peace,' declares King Leir, 'there's plenty land for each of us to have.'

'There must be peace,' says lord Gorlois, 'there's more for any one of us to have.'

And Uther sits there, listening to them all: Gorlois and Leir and the others, Eldol of Gleawecastre, and Outham the Old, and Conan Meriadoc. And he says what they wish him to say. That there will be peace, there must be peace upon this land.

And how, he thinks, will there be peace when every scarecrow with a sword is lord of someplace or another? They're children, squabbling over rubbish heaps. A king there can be only one. He knows it, and they know it too. Still, they persist in this fiction.

Uther makes his excuses early. Once more he traverses the narrow bridge over the sea. And Gorlois' men watch him go. His men wait on the mainland. They have been growing restless, playing dice and catching mice and sparring with the other kings' men.

'We should leave, lord,' Merlin says.

'Yes,' Uther says. 'We should.'

But they do not go far. A small band, and seasoned soldiers all. They route around and backtrack, and shelter on a wooded hill to watch the road.

King Leir leaves first. Back to the ridings. His men surround him. They vanish quickly – 'In a hurry,' Uther says, in satisfaction.

'What is the meaning of it, lord?' says Merlin.

'Leir knows the wind's direction,' Uther says. 'He'll burrow deep when he gets home, and he'll be kept awake waiting for ambush all the way there.'

'War, my lord? Are we ready for more war?'

'Hush, Merlin. We are mere observers.'

The rest depart the keep, the last being Meriadoc. Uther watches, broods. They kip under the trees, always on watch. They watch the castle. Tintagel, impenetrable, bewitched.

'What is it, lord?'

But Merlin knows. The way a dog can scent its master.

'Igraine,' he says.

'Igraine,' says Uther.

'But lord...'

They wait and watch. It isn't long, then, that Gorlois emerges, two, three days after the confabulation. He's lord of Land's End, after all. His business takes him all about his land. Thus he departs, calm in the knowledge that his castle and his wife remain secure, for none can breach those stony walls, and none can reach the island save by his say so.

'Now, Merlin...' Uther says. 'I wonder if I may have a word.'

This is how it happens, you see. This is how the boy's conceived, a starry night, the moon swims in the blue-black sky, a seagull dives against the setting sun.

Uther stands still, like a man at his barber's.

'This will hurt,' Merlin says. His fingers move, dextrously. They pull a cheek here, an ear there, they stretch a fold of skin, push up an eye and then another, widen the forehead, pull back the hairline, they rearrange the nose. Merlin shifts bone and skin, working from memory. Uther stands stoically, though the pain must be not insignificant.

Then it is done. Merlin holds up a vanity and Uther stares at his reflection. The stars are overhead. They say a mirror can trap your soul. He stares at the man in the mirror and at last he nods.

'You've done well.'

'My lord.'

Uther leaves their hiding place. He walks alone. Lust makes men do awful things. This is how the boy's conceived, the one who would be king. Uther doesn't hurry. He walks at ease. His footsteps feel strange to him, his face is not his own. He approaches the bridge.

'Halt! Who goes there!'

'At ease.'

'My lord! But are you back? Where are your men? What—'

'Speak not, and step aside,' says Uther.

'Yes, lord. Of course.'

The soldiers part. He crosses, to the castle. They welcome him, their king. He says, 'Where is my wife?'

'In her chambers, lord.'

'Then take me to her.'

A steward escorts him. Up flights of stairs and down corridors. Oh, how he covets Tintagel. Oh, how he covets the oyster within its impregnable shell. At last, a set of doors. He waits. The steward hovers.

'You may leave me now.'

'My lord.'

The steward withdraws.

This is how the boy's conceived. The one who would be king. This is how they tell the story.

Uther enters. She stands by the window, looking at the moonlit sky. The moonlight's in her hair. She turns, surprised.

'My lord Gorlois! I hadn't thought—'

'Igraine,' he says. 'I couldn't bear to be without you one more night.'

She smiles. It lights her face. 'My lord...'

He comes to her. He reaches to disrobe her. He lifts her shift up, slowly. She stands before him, naked in the moonlight. Pale, full thighs. A dark triangle of hair. He says, 'I want you—' his voice thick with desire. That liquid sense that flames inside him. She comes to him, willingly. Her husband. He lifts her up and carries her to bed.

14

This is how it happens, this is how the boy's conceived, this is how a nation's born. At dawn he leaves the way he came, over the bridge, and there he fades from Tintagel like morning's dew. Uther Pendragon returns to his own castle and he lays his plans.

In Tintagel, the lady Igraine grows heavy with child. Imagine Gorlois' reaction when he at last returns to his impregnable castle, having been busy on his rounds, collecting taxes, checking on his fortifications, recruiting soldiers for his army (for a war is coming) and so on, only to find—

'Wife? What ails you?'

'My lord?' She places hands over her belly. So serene, the lady. Moonlight woven in her hair. She smiles, with so much hope. 'Perhaps a boy.'

He is no fool, Gorlois. But a cold fury builds inside him and he says not a word more to her. And he finds out, he does find out the truth. It's there to taunt him. This act of Uther is an act of war. It is what men have always done in time of war to women.

He is provoked. He says not a word to the lady Igraine, the mother of his daughters. But he marshals his men and his war machines, his horses and carts, his supplies. He sends spies ahead. And he begins to march upon his enemy.

Perhaps it is too soon. Perhaps he's not equipped enough.

One might say honour is at stake, but what is honour? It is a word as empty as a skin of garlic, blowing in the wind. It is the shit the chickens leave, that farmers use for fertiliser. It has no meaning. Perhaps, more accurately, it's pride. A king is not a king if he is made a fool. And so Gorlois marches to war against Pendragon. Sword versus sword. And blood alone will tell.

Of course, while he was gone King Uther laid his plans and amassed men. And so these opposing armies march, one from Cornwall, one from Wales.

These lands are separated by the Sabrina. A mighty river ruled over by one of the ladies of the water. The armies dare not raise her wrath and so they march on land and skirt the river, though Uther and his forces wait, and Gorlois crosses round and over river's source and to the southern bank.

They meet at Monnow-mouth. A Roman fortress, Blestium, still stands there, where once the Roman invasion into Wales began. A colony of ironworkers still remains where once a garrison held room for full two thousand soldiers.

So it begins. The armies clash. Steel catches steel. It cuts through bone, it severs arteries, it tears men's arms off, separates heads from necks. Horses cry and die. Men vanish into smoke. Gorlois and army take the fortress and withdraw within. King Uther's men surround the structure.

Night falls. The carrion crows hover, watching the fallen with hungry eyes. Fires burn. The Romans built well, Uther thinks. The fort can hold for days or months, depending on supplies. He marches to the gates.

'Gorlois!'

A flight of arrows, and he laughs. His wizard turns them into birds and, beating wings, they rise into the sky and disappear.

'My land, my wife? We had a deal!' says Gorlois.

'I want your land, I want your wife, and most of all I want your head,' says Uther.

'Then come and get it, hired man!'

That rankles. This is the thing about a king, he's either born or made. And Uther's just a hired sword, a thug, they'd say. And how else does one become a king? he'd counter.

But still. It rankles.

And so they wait each other out.

In Tintagel the lady Igraine is heavy with child. Her belly swells. Her skin is hot. She supervises servants, tends her garden, weaves with her maids, clothes for the baby. It doesn't have a name.

Time passes. The moon waxes, wanes. Her husband's absence grows ever long. The child's strong inside her. She feels it kick. She dreams of freedom. Of walking by the streams in spring, collecting pines, of fishing in the rivers of her distant home. Of running free, and laughing, how she used to run when she was small, before men noticed her. Perhaps in time, she thinks, all women will be free. Some fantasy: control over their bodies and their lives, not subject to transactions, nor incubators for an endless stream of children, nor to the needless deaths of so many small souls who never make it. How many had she lost for each one that was saved? She'd rather not recall, but each remains a scar that's etched inside her. A woman's like a soldier, not worse or better, and subject to the same relentless force. A woman lives and dies by force alone.

Time passes with the moon. At last it happens, as it must. The pain rents her asunder. When it is over there's a boy, alive and strong.

She cradles him.

'I think,' she says, 'I'll call you Arthur.'

The baby gurgles, happily enough, and fastens greedy lips around a nipple. What's in a name. She strokes his hair. He's got good hair, the baby. Arthur.

He's got so much to look ahead to.

*

'About the baby...' Uther says.

'My lord?'

'You will take care of it?'

'My lord.'

With that, the wizard's gone. Uther Pendragon stares across the river to the fortress. They cannot hold out much longer, Gorlois and his men. Another night, another day, but soon.

And then, he thinks, the others.

Igraine wakes in the night. A young man stands beside the crib. He's cradling the baby. So tenderly. He doesn't look at her. The window's open. He says, 'It is the king's command.'

'Please,' she says. 'Please.'

She doesn't ask, which king.

'He will be safe.'

Her breasts ache, to feed. She won't beg. A woman's but a soldier in an ancient war. She thinks, I've lost another.

'He will be safe.'

And I? she wants to ask, but doesn't.

The wizard nods. She knows his kind. He holds the baby like a precious cargo. She nods.

'Then by your leave,' he says. So softly.

She turns away.

When she turns back, they're gone.

15

'Look at me!' says Gorlois. 'Look at me, I'm the king of the world!'

Uther laughs uncontrollably as he makes the head speak, as he makes the lips move. Gorlois' head is mounted on a spit. King Uther stands on the top battlements of the Blestium fortress. He makes the dead traitor speak from beyond the grave – not that he will ever have a grave.

'Look at me! Look at me! I'm the king of the world!'

He tires at last of this game. The head remains up there, to stare blindly across Uther's land. Gorlois and his men had held up in Blestium, for too long they had held against Uther.

Summer turned to autumn. A bitter winter came. By spring the fortress fell, at last. Now he can turn his attentions elsewhere. So much work yet to be done. But they will know his name, he thinks, now and echoing all down the centuries. They will remember Monnow-mouth and his victory. He will not rest until he's king of all this land and everything that's in it.

That summer he amasses his troops and consolidates his holdings. As a victor he comes to Tintagel, for it is his now, by force alone. He marches into the grand hall and surveys his domain, and he summons the woman, Igraine. How still she stands! How lovely she is! He reaches for her and she comes. Their marriage is performed under the canopy of stars. The dragon's banner's raised over the castle. At night he takes her eagerly, a victor's spoils, he ploughs her like a field.

When it is done he lays back, sated.

'Wife,' he says. 'I thirst.'

'My lord.'

She rises. How beautiful she is, he thinks, Igraine, nude in the moonlight. She moves so softly. She vanishes beyond. He sits back as she returns. A goblet in her hand.

'My lord.'

He drinks. The water's cool, refreshing.

He marvels at his fortune. Soon, he thinks, all this island shall be his alone.

Anon it befell that the king was seized by a lingering distemper.

Something in the guts. It feels as though he is being eaten from the inside. The king grows wan. He suffers noxious gas. He finds it hard to keep down food. He has the shits.

A medicus comes. He examines his urine. He draws a star chart. He takes measure of the four humours. He prescribes blood-letting.

But the king grows ever weaker.

Another medicus comes. Of the Methodic school, he observes Uther keenly. He explains that the circulation of atoms through the body's pores causes disease. At last, he prescribes liquorice. This helps, for a little while, but the king sickens still.

The king's wizard comes. He examines the king. He tsks sympathetically. He offers no useful salve.

The king sickens.

At this time, too, Saxons once again make their excursions into the land. Octa, son of Hengist, had returned to the land with his pirates, landing first on the island of Thanet, then marching onwards through Kent. Vortigern's old allies, mercenaries from the continent, desiring settlement. How they had slaughtered the Picts and the Britons! Well he remembers those days, when friend and enemy made common cause. Now they challenge his rising authority, and sickened or not, he would have none of it.

'Bring me my sword,' the king whispers. A sword is brought, though he can barely hold it up. His wife is brought, though he can hardly embrace her. She kisses him softly. How like water she is, he thinks.

'Bring me a horse.'

But he cannot ride a horse. A litter is made, and the army marches to battle. Goodbye, Tintagel. Goodbye, the lady Igraine. The march is long and hard. At last they meet the forces of the Saxons at Verulam. A Christian town, the scene of a cult. A Roman soldier called Alban had lived and died there. Sheltered one of those Christian priests, and was converted, and then when the priest was wanted, this Alban allowed the man to escape and took his place. They took him up a hill and chopped his head off, though it's said the executioner's eyes popped out of his skull and rolled down the hill alongside Alban's head. He's worshipped there still, this Alban.

The Christians flee from the besieged city. He drafts them to his army. Thus engorged they clash with the Saxons, who jeer and call him the Half-Dead King. Well, fuck them, he thinks. He sends his men with fire. He would see no one left alive. He watches from a distance as the city burns. The Saxons burn. Those who try to flee are slaughtered. He feels a savage satisfaction rise. They bring him Octa's corpse, what's left of him. The king has gas. The king, he gets the shits.

'My lord, your lady wife sent water from a blessed spring to ease your pain.'

He takes the goblet gratefully. The water's cool and sweet.

'Merlin, regarding the matter of the child—'

'The child's taken care of, lord.'

'Good, good.'

His stomach cramps in pain. 'Oh, fuck this!' Uther cries.

'My lord?'

But Uther's dead.

PART TWO

LORDS OF LONDINIUM

16

The boy who would be king lies on the hard stone floor. He's curled up against the wall, under the window. His master, Hector, snores next door beside his whores. The floor is hard, the room is cold, the boy's long story is not yet told.

Kay sleeps besides him.

And in his sleep, Kay dreams.

The alley cats are squabbling in the alleyway beyond the wall. They hiss and fight. Londinium, in this new year of Our Lord, that saviour from distant Galilee. To bring in morning, the bellmen ring their bells, as sanctioned by the Roman, Paulinus. Beyond the wall the sun is yet to rise. The cockerels crow. The cats hiss at each other. The boy turns, restless, on the hard stone floor.

'This boy, he is the one?'

'He's mine, Morgan. Keep your paws off him.'

'A likely chance of that, Merlinus.'

'I told you not to call me that.'

'So touchy.'

Two cats, with moonlight-silver fur, watch the sleeping boy from the windowsill.

'He doesn't look like much,' the female says.

'They never do.'

She licks her lips. 'He smells of blood.'

'The boy is mine.'

'You mean, you're his.'

He doesn't disagree. The boy turns, restless, on the hard stone floor. Only fifteen. He's wiry, there's no fat on him, and he's surprisingly strong. An alley rat for these alley cats to fight over.

'They would kill him soon as look at him,' Morgan says.

'They are distracted,' Merlin says.

'You made sure of that.'

'And besides, don't underestimate the boy.'

'He looks like a chicken bone with all the meat stripped off it.'

'Then leave him be!'

'And let you have all the fun? I hardly think so, Merlin.'

The cats squabble. The boy, this Arthur, tosses and turns. The cockerels crow outside. Londinium awakes. Dawn breaks against the sky.

Next to Arthur, Kay awakes.

Londinium, in this new year of Our Lord. He wakes alertly, like a cat himself. He shakes Arthur. 'Get up!'

The other boy blinks up at him and smiles. He steals upright. They leave Sir Hector to his boozy sleep. They exit through the window. At dawn the city's theirs. Like cats or rats or pigeons they roam the city. Its Roman masters gone, Londinium is pale and cold in the light of the newborn sun. Its avenues are strewn with rubbish, a cold wind blows along the Strand road that the Romans built to reach Calleva Atrebatum. The boys move fleetingly through fog and damp, they steal like magpies, hunting treasure. A baker shop provides them with a loaf still hot, they run laughing as the baker follows with a poker, screaming obscenities in several languages.

Kay loves this city. This vast metropolis, its thousands of people, its narrow thoroughfares and muddy marshes, the cry of birds and the whistle of oars on the Tamesis, the smoke that rises from a thousand cooking fires and stoves, the whisper of steel and the clink of old coins from the continent, which they do not mint anymore in this land, since the Romans are gone. He doesn't know them. They're merely ghosts to him, these vanished strangers, who came one day with ships and arms and men and took this island and inhabited it, and kept it for a century and then another and another, and then, just as abruptly, left. As far as he's concerned the city's always been there, ancient, muddy, twisting, dark, a maze for him to wander in, explore, and profit from. Kay and Arthur follow Fleet, past the old ruined governor's palace and the great occult stone, and to Billingsgate under the White Hill, where already the boats have come in and the traders are setting their wares and the air smells of fish and of tallow and tar.

'Boys!'

They come at Arthur's whistle – Tor and Geraint, and Elyan the White and Owain, the Bastard. His boys. He doesn't need to tell them what to do. They aren't... subtle. They don't have swords, but knives and heavy sticks. Like him, they're lean. Like him, they're always hungry.

'Where is the fucking rent, Wilfrid? Where's the fucking rent what's due!'

They surround the fish stall, banging on the wood with their sticks, toss the fish to the ground, make a racket. The seller's an old Saxon, one of those who came to this land as mere babes. He's as much of Londinium as they are – which means he knows the score.

'We're your protection, Wilfrid, we look after you.'

'Without us the Wolves will take you, Wilfrid, or the Frankish mob—'

'Tear you up and drink your blood, they will—'

'Not like us, Wilfrid, we're your friends, see? We look after our own.'

The grizzled old fisherman knows the score. His countenance

is dire. But he's in thrall – he must be, the last time he tried fighting back his nephew, Aelfric, got a knife between his ribs and that was that. But still he hesitates.

'The fishing's been bad the past fortnight, and the cost of caulking's up and fish are down, and—'

Now Arthur slips silent as an eel behind the stall and puts his cold iron blade to Wilfrid's throat. The old man doesn't dare to swallow.

'Well?'

The old man pays. The coins are old and some are bent and on their sides they bear the faces of all kinds of kings and emperors, the only common thing they have is that they're all now safely in the earth and in the hands, so one presumes, of God.

It's meagre earnings. Yet the performance is repeated all along the edges of the market. Not at the heart. Those sellers who can well afford it have their own form of protection, to keep the riffraff such as Arthur and his boys away. But not the weak, the poor, the elderly – they need him. They need his help, his counsel, his force. He helps them, he is their protector.

From there to breakfast in the ruins of the Roman wall. It stands, still, but it crumbles. Sir Hector has a line of trade in bricks, when Kay and Arthur were yet striplings they worked on Hector's roaming gangs stripping the wall. There used to be more of it, then, and less of them. Now Arthur and his boys build a fire where the wall is black with soot already, and they cook fish for their breakfast, and share the stolen bread.

Elyan the White counts the money. But money on its own is not enough. Swords. Power. Kay watches Arthur at his meal. He knows that Arthur hungers – for something more, something nebulous. He's never been beyond the city. And yet this land – Kay knows that sometimes Arthur dreams of it. He dreams of northern snow and moorlands in the spring, and castles standing over green, green hills and seagulls crying over white-sailed ships approaching shore. He tells the boys his father is a king. They don't believe him. His father is a king who rules all of the land and one day he'll come back for him. An evil sorcerer has separated them. His father loves him. His real father loves him. Sir Hector is a boorish man, a fat old ogre with bad teeth that smell of rot. His pisser's riddled with the clap. He thinks he's lord, he speaks pig Latin and reads Greek pornography in the latrines. The whores he runs are little better. He takes a cut from everything he can: the whores, the brick trade, grain, protection, the cut-throat gangs, the rub-and-tug emporiums. Lord of Londinium, he styles himself, but he is nothing more than a jumped-up rent-boy who used to blow fat merchants for his supper.

This is what Arthur thinks, and what he says to Kay: for all that Kay is Hector's son.

Kay chews on fish. He watches Arthur think his darkened thoughts.

17

That dream, Kay thinks. Those talking cats. They keep recurring.

He finds the cats unsettling.

Londinium in daytime's bad enough. At night, under the moon, the witching hour starts. Things walk the streets that shouldn't. Swaithes and tod-lowries and Robin Goodfellows.

It's best not to draw attention to oneself.

Kay's not like Arthur. Kay's afraid. He's scared of blood, of violence, of goblins and his father whom he also loves.

Sometimes he thinks, uncharitably: Arthur's too dumb to be afraid of anything.

After breaking fast they scatter. The day is theirs. The city's theirs, or so they think. Kay follows Arthur. As fast as rats they scuttle down to the forum.

Here they come on sufferance. They steal inside. They have no power here, the forum's under Sir Carados' own protection. All in the city pay a tithe to Carados, he is the omnium ducibus dux, the boss of bosses.

The White Hill Gang, the Wolves, the Frankish Mob, the Knights of Bors, they're all subordinate to Sir Carados. He styles himself the Governor, for all that the city had not seen one since the Romans left. He makes his home in the old governor's palace. To him the boys are like the summer flies that plague the banks of the Tamesis. One careless slap from him and they'd be nothing but a bloody splatter on the Roman wall.

Kay loves the forum. He loves the cries of merchants from their stalls, the hustle and bustle of trade and negotiation, the shouted arguments and the whisper of exchange. He and Arthur steal among the throng, wary of the guardsmen, these burly ruffians of Sir Carados.

Here there is gold from vanished Greece, hand-wrought anklets, bracelets, earrings – 'For your girlfriend!' says the seller with a lewd laugh, and makes Kay blush – and local silver worked into pendants and rings. Kay is enchanted by the jewellers' section, the dazzle of precious metals and stones: of pearls from Persia and emeralds from Egypt, amber from Gedanum on the shores of the Mare Suebicum. Kay loves it, the artistry of it, the beauty that is not of anything but of itself.

He watches Arthur. His friend moves like a thief among the stalls. He cares not for the beauty of these things, not even for their value, but for what they represent. Wealth is power, and power is what Arthur craves. These trinkets mean nothing to him, these gaudy baubles, these decorations for the human frame. It makes no woman more desirable, no man more fetching. These are mere indications of their place in the world, and Arthur knows the place he wants to be.

Kay admires his friend for his ruthless determination, his absolute conviction of who he is, of where he wants to go. Kay follows him willingly, for to be with Arthur is to be dazzled, to have one's mind opened to infinite possibilities. It is but a dream that Arthur has, but what a dream! And Kay will follow him anywhere, even into the mouth of the underworld itself.

Past the jewellers into the arms market: old helmets and shields, short stabbing swords and javelins. Arthur lovingly fingers the hilt of a sword. Kay examines a legionnaire's old pair of sandals, the tough leather studded with metal spikes. Alongside the Roman junk are other weapons: Pictish axes and pikes, short nasty daggers, and next to these a range of bows and arrows all of different makes and ages – a cornucopia of arms, a profusion of weapons!

The arms trade's bustling in Londinium, that great cesspit of a town to which, even now, the dregs of the known world are sometimes drawn. This island is a wild country, a host of warring tribes who scrabble for scraps in the ruins of civilisation. It's each man for himself, and a man with the right attitude – and the right arms – can make or lose a fortune.

The boys scuttle past, wary of the guardsmen's attention. The best arms in the city go to the Guv'nor and his gang, Carados still believes himself the heir of Rome, its rightful representative on this dark and fertile soil. The Romans came, they killed, they built, they ruled – they left.

'Well fuck the Romans,' Arthur says, 'and fuck good Sir Carados in the ass.'

'Hush!' Kay says. 'Not so loud. His men are here.'

'I will piss into the empty sockets of his skull and watch him grin as I do it,' Arthur says. But he speaks softly, now.

Somehow that's scarier to Kay. Arthur seldom raises his voice, and when he speaks there's an authority beyond his years behind his words. Perhaps it's being orphaned, or perhaps he truly does believe himself a king. Though what's a king? They're all, each one a king, these lords of Londinium, each with their turf, each with their share of the spoils. There'll always be a need for swords and whores, there'll always be a need for men to take what's theirs. Or so they think, at any rate. They think themselves kings in their tiny domains.

Yet Kay's dreams take him elsewhere. In Sir Hector's house there were several buckets of scrolls tossed in a corner, the debt plus vig repayment of some ancient loan. Handed over along with some blood and teeth by some travelling priest with an unfortunate predilection for games of dice and little boys, and a thirst for knowledge. In Hector's manor no one read them, it was left to the boy Kay to learn his letters from a hired tutor, he and Arthur huddled on the floor beside the window. But to Kay the letters came more easily.

He loved those scrolls, from vanished Rome they came, just common scrolls on grade four amphitheatre papyrus, the sort the scribes copied by the bucketload back on the Aventine. Just common scrolls, just scraps from vanished Rome, these typo'ed badly copied fragments of cannibalised classics.

He had read them till they began to crumble, and any time he can he reads them still. There is, for instance, a fragment from Lucretius, in which the poet proposes that the universe is but an endless void, filled with an infinity of atoms. In all of Nature, the poet says, there is but bodies and the void.

Kay wishes he could read more of Lucretius. They say the Guv'nor has a library still inside the fort, a treasure trove of codices and scrolls, for all that he's illiterate. It's just more *things* to own and thus more power, like jewellery or whores. Kay thinks of life, how passionate it is to be alive. Death scares him, and to walk by Arthur is to skirt always close to death. The poet, Lucretius, says that death is finite, the body and the spirit both summarily end. Yet in another fragment in his father's house, an evangelion, written by some curious Jew from distant Palestine, Kay reads of a death and a resurrection in Jerusalem.

He thinks that city must be grand indeed, this Jerusalem of white towers high on its hill. As grand as Rome or Athens. So different to Londinium, this beggar town where beggar knights and kingpins dwell. Kay longs for something more, a knowledge of the world. Lastly in his father's store of scrolls there is a map based on Ptolemy the Greek's *Geography*. For hours Kay had sat and studied it, for days and through the years. It shows him continents and seas. It is the world made comprehensible, it is the world as it is *known*. There is Rome and there is distant Qin where they make the silk, there's India where spices come from, there's Germania, Hispania and Palestina. There's savage, ancient Egypt where the pharaohs ruled before Greeks or Romans ever dreamed of civilisation. The world is vast and interlinked in trade and roads, by ships and seas – it must be wonderful, Kay thinks, stuck on this dismal, rainy island.

He'd never even gone beyond the walls. Londinium is all he knows.

But he can dream.

'Run, fool!' Arthur hisses, and Kay startles. A merchant raises the cry and the guardsmen turn, but Arthur, laughing, is as fleet as wind or faun and Kay must hurry after. Together the boys run, upending a table laden with fruit, leap over a sheep, push an old woman out of the way and burst out of the forum. They run along the Via Publica and down a side street, not far from the main mithraeum. There in the alleyway they collapse against a stout stone wall, panting and laughing, and Arthur shows Kay his treasure: an exquisitely crafted flint dagger, of the sort men made in days gone by, before they learned the art of metallurgy. It must have been ancient, centuries old. Arthur turns it over and over in his hands. His long fingers stroke each careful notch the ancient stonemason had made. The blade's still sharp as ever before it was.

'But what good is it?' Kay says, practical. Such techne, as the Greeks had called it, is surely obsolete.

'It's beautiful,' Arthur says. It is a word he never uses lightly. For arms or women, only, and what does Arthur know of women yet?

Kay shakes his head, for his friend never ceases to surprise him. Arthur is not given to much sentiment.

'If they'd caught us they'd have beaten us to death,' he says.

'And yet they didn't,' Arthur says, and smiles. He's so happy at that moment, with his toy. So pure. There is a purity to Arthur that can be sometimes terrifying.

'What do we do now?'

'We need to hook up with our Trinovantes connection.'

Kay looks down at his own, nail-bitten fingers.

'If my father finds out we're dealing outside the family...' he says.

'What Sir Hector doesn't know should not concern him,' Arthur says.

'We swore an oath! He *is* my father.'

'And like a father to me, too,' Arthur says – not too convincingly, Kay thinks. 'But we are men, are we not, you and I? We have a right to make our own way in the world. Besides' – he punches Kay on the shoulder – 'it's only Goblin Fruit. What's the harm?'

'The *harm* is that—' Kay starts to say, but doesn't finish.

Something comes barrelling down the dark alleyway towards them. It makes the most awful and terrible sound.

A horrid, giant, shrieking beast shambles down the alleyway. Kay cannot bear to look at it directly. It has too many eyes, too many mouths, too many teeth. Its shriek is like a pickaxe in the mind. Its crazed babble invades the psychic sphere, it conjures images of nightmares in Kay's mind. It shambles down the alleyway and passes them. Eyes on a stalk look down on the boys. A slender, flexible appendage like a tentacle strokes their faces like a blind man seeing.

Then it is gone.

It vanishes so swiftly, like a dissipating dream. Leaving behind it the sense of vast incomprehension, and something else – a disappointment in the boys, a sense that they were not the things it seeks.

A questing beast.

'Well that was weird—'

Behind the questing beast there comes a knight – bedraggled and ill-kempt. A vagabond with sword and hammered breastplate, unshaved and with eyes wild.

'The beast!' he says. 'The beast, where did it go!'

'It went that way—'

He rushes past them, cooing.

Silence settles once again.

The boys exchange glances.

'What *was* that thing?'

Arthur just shrugs. 'An aberration.'

And Kay thinks of the Greek, Plutarch, and a story he'd read in one of the scrolls in his father's manor, of a maze and the creature that was forever trapped there. And he thinks, this world is beset by fantastical beasts on all sides, and man is but a tiny thing beside them. He'd longed to see the giant elephantus, or that creature it was said Julius Caesar brought to Europe, a tall and terrifying creature with a neck so long it reached the tallest trees, and which the Romans called a cameleopard. He'd seen their images once in a bestiary.

'Perhaps it was a unicorn?' he says now, dubiously. For was it not Julius Caesar who said he had seen their like deep in the forests of Germania?

'Where then was its horn?' Arthur says and, dismissing the subject with a wave of his hand, stands up. 'Come on, Kay. We have business to attend to.'

It's easy to dismiss the strangeness, for such things are not unknown. And anyway it harmed them not.

And so they go.

18

'Who's the runt? Your bum boy?' their Trinovantes contact says, and Arthur laughs. Kay blushes.

The Trinovantes man is burly, dark, with greasy hair and cold clear eyes. He wears a coat of dead bear's fur. His boots are studded. His sword is steel.

'My associate, Sir Kay.'

'A sir, is he?' the man says, and laughs. He has good teeth, Kay notices. 'Such lords and ladies in Londinium you are, boy.'

'Don't call me boy,' Arthur tells him. There's cold iron in his voice to match the alloyed metal in the other man's weapon. There is this thing about Arthur, for all his youth men do respect him. The other nods.

'You have the cash?'

'You have the merchandise?'

The man scowls. 'We are nothing if we are not professionals,' he says, with slight reproach. Opens his coat. Removes a bag and hands it over.

Arthur tosses the bag to Kay. Kay looks inside. The smell is unmistakable.

It's Goblin Fruit.

Nevertheless he sticks a finger in. Puts it to his mouth but doesn't swallow. A putrid thing. Some sort of rye infected with a fungus. It's nasty stuff.

He nods. 'It's pure,' he says.

'You ever try it?' the Trinovanti says.

'I never use the merchandise—' from Arthur.

'And you, Sir Kay?'

The man leers at him knowingly. The pit of Kay's stomach feels warm.

'Once or twice,' he says – as though there's nothing to it.

Where the Trinovantes get the merch he doesn't know. They rule directly to the east of Londinium and as far as the sea, and have dealings with Saxons. They say back in the day they'd sent emissaries to Rome itself, then rose against it in rebellion with Boudicca. They're tough bastards, Arthur always says, admiringly.

'It's nasty stuff,' the Trinovanti says. 'Well – my money?'

'Kay?'

Kay puts away the bag of Goblin Fruit, removes the payment in its stead – a smaller bag, of rubies and garnets, a lady's diamond ring set in gold, several gold denarii and silver Tyrian shekels from who knows where. The flotsam and jetsam of empire. He hands the bag to Arthur. Arthur hands it over to the Trinovanti.

'Pleasure doing business with you, boys – men, I mean,' the Trinovanti says. 'Begging your pardon.'

He gives a mock bow.

'Next time we need double,' Arthur says.

'This shit's hard to come by,' the Trinovanti complains. 'I'll see what I can do, but it's not like it just grows on trees. I'll see you, Arthur.'

'And you, Ywain.'

He vanishes towards the Cripplegate. As they walk back, Arthur is elated. This area's dark and dodgy, Kay just watches for attack. They pass the place where Lady Boudicca, the Iceni, is resting.

'Now there was a queen,' Arthur says, in admiration. Kay thinks of the city reduced to ruin, the bones of Boudicca's enemies strewn across the ground. This new Londinium of theirs is built on bones and graves. And how long shall it remain? Without its Roman masters the city's but a shade of what it was. There is no rule of law, nothing but the gangs, like king rats they scrabble in the ruins for domination.

Soon, he thinks, it will wither and die, its populace will vanish, and nothing will remain but a thick layer of black ash, gathering over the dark age of centuries.

'Cheer up,' Arthur says, not unkindly. 'What's got into you?'

'I was just thinking,' Kay says.

Arthur says, 'You think too much.'

The safe house is off King Lud's Gate and the adjacent cemetery. Kay's still uneasy. Night has fallen and the witching hour's sure to soon be struck. The others wait for them, Tor and Geraint, and Elyan the White and Owain, the Bastard. The only piece of furniture they have is an old driftwood-crafted rickety round table. They fall on the package. With crude utensils they cut the merchandise, divvying up the pure Goblin Fruit, mixing and cutting in bowls.

The Roman soldiers brought it over, originally. Some sort of hallucinatory substance they called kykeon and used in the mithraeums. A mithraeum was a temple to Mithras, some old Persian god who liked to slay bulls. Really it was just a sort of officers' club, where the men got together in dark subterranean rooms to feast and booze. It was all proper religious and stuff. Then the Romans left, but some of the old boys remained behind one way or another and, well, it turned out lots of people liked the taste from a bite of what they started calling Goblin Fruit.

In Londinium at present, *everybody* wants a little escape.

Problem is, it's hard to get and, subsequently, expensive. Which means the profit margin's huge. There are mithraeums everywhere, lots of demand – and never enough supply. Even those rich fucks who live up-river in Todyngton and Tuiccanham on their country estates beyond the tideway. Especially them.

So Arthur's boys cut the fungus up with flour and dried rosemary. They make several batches of different strengths, then package them into individual wrappers. Elyan the White's in charge of mixing, Owain and Geraint package and wrap, Kay does the counting and the numbers.

'Well?' Arthur says.

'It's good.'

Arthur nods.

'Then let's take it out.'

19

Once more the boys split. At night Londinium is dark and quiet. But not all dark, and not all quiet. Torches splutter, casting murky lights. A dog barks. A cat hisses. A woman screams. A pot smashes. The sound of dice, the laughter of men, the smell of cooking porridge and mutton fat seared in a fire.

Overhead the via lactea swirls in the sky, so many stars like diamonds. No moon, which makes the going hard. And Kay has a sense of two cats on a wall, watching. Something in their perfect stillness gives him pause.

A bellman rings his bell in the arch of a closed shop. 'Who goes there?' he cries.

'It is I, Arthur, king of Britannia!' comes the reply, and the boys laugh, running fast down the narrow alleyways.

The mithraeums line up on the road along the main one, that temple to the bull-slaying Persian god. Men stand outside. The darkness masks their faces.

'Well? Have you got it?'

'The best and freshest, guaranteed to give you dreams from out of this world!'

'How much?'

'Cheap at the price and twice as good!'

The punters part with cash, receive the Goblin Fruit, descend back to the underground lairs.

'What if we get robbed?' Kay says.

'What is it with you, Kay? Stop being so afraid.'

'I do not like the night.'

'We *own* the night!'

Kay only nods. They sell the Goblin Fruit and Arthur and the boys carry the profits back. A look of understanding passes between him and Arthur. Then he departs, Kay slips into the shadows and is gone.

It's true. He fears the night. But not because of spooky cats, or centaurs, Pans, Jack-in-the-Wads or mormos.

Not because of the Guv'nor's goons and what they might do if they catch him dealing Fruit, either.

Not because of brigands or back alley cut-throats. Not because of rabid dogs or wild wolves or an escaped bear from the amphitheatre.

None of that.

Kay fears the night's *potential*. He feels aflame with heat. His heart beats faster. He hugs the shadows and the shadows whisper back, caressing him.

He makes his way to the Via Amare, not far from the amphitheatre and the nearby gladiatorial schools. In Rome in the Empire's heyday they had been popular institutions. Here in Londinium they are not quite the same, for all that men and beasts still die in the arena, and there are always spectators to cheer on the sight of blood.

Kay makes his way to a small door in a stone building with a sign above it that says *The Gogmagog*. Two men with nasty cudgels by their sides part silently to let him enter.

Inside, Kay finally relaxes. The air's scented with sweat and oil and flowery perfume. The light is dim, the room's illuminated by oil lamps. It's hot inside, flames burst out of fresh logs in the large fireplace. He removes his apparel. Men move across the room, softly. Figures whisper in the shadows, recline on couches. Clay cups clink. Men nibble pastries.

Men move across the room. Musicians play the flute and

harp. Kay walks through rooms. Men brush past him. Small men and large men, fat men and thin. Gladiators from the nearby schools, naked but for a loincloth, muscled arms and torsos oiled and shining. Britons, Angles, Jutes, a panoply of free men. In one room a group of sailors from the continent, Gauls or Germanic, stand in a circle round a fierce little Iceni. A man who might be a druid watches them from the corner eagerly, stroking an immense erection. He notices Kay's stare and smirks. It's not an invitation.

Kay moves on. The smell of oil and sweat and semen, cries of excitement, grunts of effort, in one room a fat merchant strokes a Libyan gladiator's member with bejewelled fingers. They notice Kay and call out to him merrily to join them, but he declines, politely. A passing server offers him a goblet and he takes it, sips watered wine. In other rooms men sit already sated, making conversation. The Gogmagog's a maze of rooms, it's like a box of wonders. A buffet of delicacies sits on the tables. Kay finds the room at last, *Reserved*. He goes inside.

'You came.'

He grabs Kay roughly. Strong boorish hands, with gnarled fingers. The sort of hands used to the beating of a man half to death for not paying his debts or showing the proper respect. For expressing their master's displeasure. The hands pull Kay's face to the other's face, to his rough roguish beard, to his hot, full lips. Kay's breath is knocked out of him and the flame in his belly erupts as their lips meet, as he kisses the other man, as he wraps his own arms around him, as he lets his own fingers run over the man's short-cropped hair, over the uneven scalp, and then there is no need for words.

'...I am undone,' the other says.

They lie there on the fur, on their backs, sated, emptied, at peace.

Peace! How Kay craves peace. This is the closest he can come to it: here, now, he is fulfilled. He props himself up on an elbow and turns to look at the other.

Bors the Younger looks back at him, smiling. He is not handsome in any conventional sense, Kay thinks, yet he is so arresting. The Knights of Bors are the worst of all the bands of knights who terrorise Londinium. Even the Guv'nor merely tolerates them, for they cannot be ruled. Boorish and violent and unpredictable, more ogres than men, and Bors the Elder is their paterfamilias, a half-giant, they say, who tore out his mother's womb out of viciousness and committed his first murder in the very moment of his birth – they say.

They say a lot of things.

Kay strokes Bors the Younger's hair.

'I missed you.'

'My father has a shipment of Goblin Fruit coming, a big one.'

He's not much for pleasantries, is Bors.

Kay grows alert. 'When?'

'I don't know yet.'

'How big?'

Bors moves his hands, stretching them wide.

Kay says, 'Why are you telling me?'

Bors the Younger does not reply. The silence lies between them like a shameful confession.

At last Kay nods. An understanding between them.

Later, they rise. Too soon. Dress, and Kay marvels again at Bors' rough hands, how gently and deftly they handle his weapons. They draw to each other for one last, stolen kiss. Then they are gone from there.

At home, Sir Hector's sound asleep, his wenches by his side. The remains of a roasted pheasant on his table. Kay's heard it was the Romans who brought the birds to Britain. His father's fabulously fond of a pheasant. Kay helps himself to the remains, tears chunks of bread to soak up the oil, washes the lot down with more watered wine. His father snores, his wenches senseless by his side.

Kay goes to his sleep. Arthur's already there, curled by the dying fire, and Kay admires him, how small he seems in sleep, yet still so forceful, like a resting blade. He treads in softly, but Arthur stirs all the same.

'You smell like a whore,' he says, not unkindly.

'And you would know how?' Kay says, for Arthur is surprisingly prim.

He tells his friend of Bors' news. Arthur sits up, cross-legged on the stone. He mulls it over.

'Can we trust him?'

Kay shrugs. He stretches on his bedding. The day was long and he is tired. Sometimes he dreams of being elsewhere, a farm boy on a village somewhere, tilling and hoeing on the fertile farmlands of the beaver lea brook, perhaps. And was it not said by the Hebrew prophet, Isaiah, that men should turn their swords into ploughshares? He is sure he had heard it somewhere, though were he to mention it, no doubt Arthur would laugh and call him fool.

And so he doesn't.

He falls asleep as Arthur broods.

The alley cats are squabbling in the alleyway beyond the wall. They hiss and fight.

Goodnight, you knights of New Troy, you lords of Londinium.

Goodnight.

20

Time passes, as time is wont to do. A year it is. The seasons change as the gangs of Londinium scrabble for scraps in the ruins of a fallen metropolis. Children are born. Leaves fall. People die.

Outside the steps of the Temple of Apollo stands now the wizard, Merlin. He thinks of time. The Greek, Parmenides, said that time was an illusion, and what exists is now, all at once, one and continuous. Yet Aristotle argued that time is a function of movement, that it was a measurement of change, and continuous. The followers of Mithras, that bull-slaying god, saw time as a wheel of a fixed duration of some twelve thousand years in which a battle raged between the forces of two gods, one good, one evil. It was the sort of idea soldiers were fond of, Merlin reflects, the sort that drew them to the mithraeums. The sort his dear old master, Uther, would have liked.

Time, Merlin thinks. There's never enough time.

He finds he misses Uther. In the years since his master's death he's had scant feeding. The fae are drawn to power but human power is so fleeting. Oh, but to have lived in Imperial Rome! Oh, to have fed in the presence of Caesars! He thinks of pharaohs and the monuments they built, the power they commanded. He thinks of emperors in distant Qin, of the great kings and queens of India, of the Persian Shahs. If only he had time.

He wonders, is it possible to travel back through time? There are stories elsewhere, filtering from the wider world onto the shores of Britain. Merlin collects knowledge like a magpie lusts for coins. There had been a man in Judea, so they say, whose name was Honi, who could raise the rain or calm the sky, and it was said further that he had travelled through time. But in that story Honi only travelled sideways, had slept and when he woke after a night seventy years had gone. And besides it was said that he had raised the ire of some rebels, and they had stoned him to death.

Merlin fidgets. The temple's a bit of a mess, he thinks: cracks in the walls, and overgrown with vines. In time it might be torn down and some western abbey be built there. Perhaps. Were you to ask Merlin his thoughts of time he would not answer truthfully, for time to such as him is a sort of coalescence of strands, which undulate and pulse in and out of probability and existence. Was it not the Greek, Plato, who spoke of the nature of reality as being viewed as shadows, dancing on cave's wall? This is what people see, the shadows, while Merlins and their kind see the things that cast the shadows... Or so he likes to think, at any rate.

A young man stands on the steps and has been standing there for quite a while. Now Merlin goes and stands beside him, comradely, and looks up at the artwork.

'Wonderful architecture,' he observes.

The young man turns. He sees only a Merlin, which is to say, an equally young man, of pleasant countenance, surely no threat and, besides, the day is young and the sun pleasingly high in the sky.

'They built to last,' he says, and smiles in a friendly fashion.

'Yet nothing lasts forever,' Merlin says.

The boy, Sir Kay, frowns but accedes the point.

'What brings you here, then, stranger?' he says.

'An old story,' Merlin says. He runs his fingers over the cracks in the walls. Peers at them closely. 'Of a man who attempted to fly.'

'Ah,' Kay says. 'Bladud, the leper king.'

'Yes. You know the story?'

'I often think of it,' Kay says. 'They say he invented a set of marvellous wings and strapped them to his body. He climbed to the top of this temple and soared into the air. For a short while, at least. Then... well.' He raises his thumb, then points it down. A gesture adopted from the Romans in their gladiatorial blood sports.

'Splat,' he says.

'Quite,' Merlin says. He ponders. 'Was his contraption ever found?' he asks.

'I do not think so.'

'Such a device...' Merlin says. 'Would be most useful.'

'Surely, sir, it's but a myth.'

'They say the Qin have flying techne,' Merlin says. 'And centuries ago there was a Greek by name of Daedalus who made wings with bird feathers and wax.'

'Begging your pardon, sir, it sounds flimsy,' Kay says politely.

Merlin examines this young man. He looks at him closely. 'I see blood in your future, Kay,' he says.

'Excuse me? How do you know my – what did you say your name was?'

'I didn't.'

Merlin pats him on the shoulder.

'I'll be seeing you,' he says.

He waits. Kay stares at him, then shakes his head and leaves. Merlin watches him go, a slight figure, disappearing down the avenue back towards the city walls.

'Meow,' Merlin says softly.

Kay had not dawdled long at the temple. He had gone there hoping for a prophecy, for Apollo is the god of oracles and omens. But he had not expected this eel-silvery youth with the unsettling dead fish eyes, and he is uneasy, for all that today is a good day.

Today he is going to be made.

He reunites with his father outside the old governor's palace. Sir Hector is resplendent in furs and the sword that he wears is magnificent. He hugs Kay, and Kay feels a wave of affection, even love for his father.

'Are you ready, boy?'

'I am ready, father.'

Arthur is there. He too hugs Kay.

They enter the palace.

Really it is a ruined old place and a bit of a dump. Stone statues of imperial eagles lie broken on the ground, dirty puddles collect on the uneven ground, and the once grand mosaic floor is ruined. Yet the Guv'nor's men line up the reception, big burly men with the stillness of stone-cold killers, and Kay is reminded that true power resides here, still. This is the home of the paterfamilias.

There are some new additions since the last time he'd been to this courtyard. A wooden cross hammered into the ground and, strangely, a large rock with a sword stuck into it.

As a child Kay had accompanied his father here when his father delivered the one-tenth tax. The low always kick up to the top, and each month the family heads would come to the omnium ducibus dux, the boss of bosses, to deliver his share of the profits. How awed Kay had been, then, by the glamour of the place. The burning torches and the burly men and the comely wenches and the open display of wealth, the looted statues and the tapestries and the gold rings on the women's fingers.

Too many broken wine amphorae on the ground now and nobody to sweep them. The smell of piss from drunks who didn't stagger outside but went wherever. Years of neglect and plain indifference. Dead flowers in Greek vases.

It must have been so grand once, Kay now thinks. When

the true governor ruled Britannia from this palace, the traders came and went, centurions kept order, musicians played. How grand it must have been! No longer but an isolated, dreary island with a thousand trifling tribes squabbling with each other, but a part of some vast tapestry that was the Empire, that was the known, civilised world. He wishes he could have seen it as it must have been.

Yet there is only now. There is only this. And he is being made.

He's being knighted.

'Is this the boy?'

The Guv'nor sits on a throne of stone. He is a corpulent old man, bare-chested, extensively scarred, with a few good teeth remaining, the left ear missing, and he's chewing on a chicken leg. His personal cook squats by an open fire, turning coals.

'My son, Kay.'

'He's got less meat on him than this chicken!'

The Guv'nor's goons laugh.

'Good one,' Sir Hector says.

Kay steals a glance. He watches Arthur, watching the gathered dignitaries. He knows – he *thinks* he knows – what Arthur thinks. How he hates them all and how he longs to be like them. To be a made man. To be a knight.

It's the highest honour they can give you, it means you *belong*. Arthur could never be one of them, he could never be made. To be a knight is to have *family*. It's to be *known*. They're all here today, to see Kay knighted. The Frankish Mob and the Wolves and the Knights of Bors. He tries not to look at where Bors the Younger is standing. To Kay, all this just means his dues. He was always going to be knighted. But for Arthur it means something deeper, it means no one can fuck with you and you can fuck with anybody, long as they're not also a knight.

But this is Kay's day today.

'Well, come closer,' the Guv'nor says.

Kay does, obediently.

'Kneel.'

He kneels.

Sir Carados, the Guv'nor, shuffles forward. His smell is rather overpowering. Like ripened cheese and something that's been dead too long down in a ditch. Plus cooked chicken.

'My sword?'

'Here, lord.'

The flat of the blade lands on Kay's shoulder. He tries not to wince. The sword rises. The Guv'nor's hands are not the steadiest. The sword descends again, touches Kay lightly on the other shoulder, then withdraws.

'Rise, Sir Kay,' the Guv'nor says.

Kay rises. Everyone cheers. Suddenly he's surrounded by well-wishers, clapping him on the back, shaking his hand in the manner of the Greeks, voicing congratulations. The Guv'nor sits back with a grunt. Waves his hand – it is done.

Kay finds Arthur. The boy is always so still. They hug.

'Sir Kay,' Arthur says.

Kay grins.

Servants bring in food. The knights descend on the offerings like starved orphans. There's chicken and pheasant and boar. There's wine and beer, breads, cheeses. There's asparagus and radishes and plenty of fish.

On the other side of the court, Kay catches Bors the Younger's eye. Bors gives the tiniest nod.

Arthur and Kay slip into the shadows. They find themselves next to that curious rock with the sword in the stone. Kay, on a whim, tries to pull it out, but it's stuck fast.

'Well?' Arthur says.

Kay says, 'Day after tomorrow.'

Arthur nods. They watch the assembled dignitaries gnawing at the food. The music crescendos and grows wild. Dancing girls emerge into the courtyard in flimsy robes. The robes fall down. Kay blushes. The knights and lords reach for the girls with greasy hands. Wine amphorae crash to the ground. The air is filled with the smell of spilled wine, bad breath, men's sweat, women's perfumes. The knights copulate with the whores like pigs in a litter. Kay watches Arthur.

'Look at them,' Arthur says. 'They are like dogs tied to a cart, and compelled to go wherever it goes.'

It occurs to Kay that his friend is quoting Cleanthes, the Stoic. It is not that Arthur is entirely free of the passions of the body. But rather that mere animal sex is not enough to arouse him. He lusts not for women but for naked power. Sharing room and bed together as they do, Kay knows his friend does not even perform self-release on himself. And Kay thinks he must be wound so tight, it can't be healthy, not to let out your seed. Sir Hector's always mocking Arthur, he once sent his wenches to try and seduce him, but Arthur politely turned them away.

So Arthur only watches, with distaste, the other knights. Kay knows he thinks them weak. And as for Kay, there's nothing here he wants. His interests lie elsewhere.

They slip away. No one will miss them. Outside the palace it is night, the witching hour. But Kay's a knight now. He's not afraid, for once he's not afraid of puckles or cutties or nickers or trolls.

And so he doesn't even notice, in the shadow of a wall, the figure watching them, a youth wrapped in the silver haze of moonlight, with eyes like a lizard's. Merlin, the watcher, hisses, and his tongue darts out and he tastes for something nebulous, like a Greek wine taster at court. And whatever it is Merlin finds, he finds it well, for he smiles.

It is the real thing, he thinks.

He walks inside the governor's palace. The guardsmen start, yet move aside for him. Merlin's not unknown here, at the court of Sir Carados. He helps himself to a piece of fruit from the food tables, and skins it half-heartedly with a small silver knife. He watches the fornication. It makes him miss his old master, how fond Uther was of fucking. It was his downfall.

There's power here, in this room, but it's hard to taste over the stench of body odour and semen. These men are like humping dogs, they're quickly spent. It's not much of an orgy, Merlin thinks. A young man stumbles past him and pukes onto the ground, just missing Merlin's feet. Merlin kneels and gently pulls his head so he could throw up more comfortably.

'You're Bors the Younger, aren't you,' he says.

'I know you?'

'I know you,' Merlin says, with unassailable logic.

'Get your fucking hands off me, man,' Bors says. Then he retches again. Merlin takes a step back, looking at this young knight crouched naked on the ground, his bare back shining with sweat. The short-cropped hair, the wicked arms, that flaring temper. He nods.

Then he goes and finds the Guv'nor, who has fallen asleep in his stone throne. He shakes him awake, none too gently this time.

'What? What!' Carados says. 'Oh, it's you.'

'Did you tell them?'

'About your stupid stone?' A look of cold amusement suffuses the Guv'nor's eyes. 'Not yet.'

Merlin scans the courtyard. Notices the new wood cross erected in the earth. He shudders.

'What's that?' he says.'

'It's a cross, Merlin. What does it fucking look like?'

'*Why* do you have a cross, Carados?'

'Had some fellows over here a couple years back, wine merchants from the old country. You still get traders willing to make the passage even out here to the back of beyond. Christians, apparently that's the height of fashion in the Empire these days. Figured, what's the harm, right? Do as the Romans do, and all that. What! Don't look at me like that. They said this Jesus of theirs came here, of all places, after he died.'

'Well, that's a likely story,' Merlin says. He claps his hands. One last knight gives a shuddering thrust and the rest are already pulling up their pants and reaching for drinks.

'Listen up!' Merlin says. 'Listen up you fucking degenerates.'

'What did you just call us?' one of the Frankish mob shouts, confused.

'I said listen up, good sirs and knights,' Merlin says. There's something so calming in his voice, like a murmuring brook in your memories of childhood. Like Mother's voice as she lulls you to sleep. Like the chirping of birds in an enchanted forest, full of light.

It works. They all calm down, turn expectant eyes on him. For just a moment, these ruthless, savage men are vulnerable like children.

And so he delivers it upon them: the prophecy. It is the oldest grift in the book, and still one of the best. He thinks of that Hebrew wizard, Moses, who learned his magic in the temples of Anubis and Ra. Those Egyptians, he thinks, had a neat line in sorcery, like the old staff-to-snake transformation routine.

Merlin would have loved to go there.

Yet Merlins are not great travellers, as a rule. Too much binds them in place, to the land and its memories, like some sort of spiritus loci.

But this Moses, anyhow, had the whole prophecy gig down pat; and as a kid being shunned and tormented by his peers, had not the power of prophecy rescued Merlin, allowed him to become the king's own man?

So he lays it on them, and he lays it on thick.

'The Empire has fallen,' Merlin says. 'And for too long have the people of this land fought each other, like rats scrabbling for scraps at their dead master's table. Now a new threat is coming, from beyond the sea. Foreigners coming to take our land, our livelihoods – our wives!'

'Our whores!' someone shouts. Merlin ignores him. He

scans the crowd. They're listening, he sees. They're nodding in agreement. They're starting to mutter.

It occurs to him that this sort of patter will never quite fail. Perhaps in centuries hence, a millennium from now, this sort of crap would still light up people's hearts. Hatred, after all, is so very comforting to have.

'Foreigners!' he says, savouring the words and their effect on his captive audience. 'Angles and Saxons, coming over here, to fight and pillage and – and rape!'

Even the Frankish mob guys are nodding. They may have been Germanic originally but by Nodens these guys are Londinium born and bred.

'I was King Uther's wizard,' Merlin says, and he can see them exchanging looks, can see them shifting, these half-denarius strongmen. They know power, he thinks. They know Uther.

'He died. He died nobly—'

Died shitting himself, what other way was there to die, Merlin thinks but doesn't say.

'Died nobly to unify this land, to bring it back to – glory! I had seen this, I had delivered this very same prophecy onto King Vortigern, the usurper – yes, I see you nod, yes, I see you know the truth of what I say. I had told him a *true* king will be born. A true and royal king will rise, to unify this warring land, one king for all of Britain!'

He has their full attention, now. One guy had not even remembered to shove his cock all the way back in his trousers. It still drips a little bit of cum. Merlin magics light, a little ignis fatuus or will-o'-the-wisp, and it floats over the enraptured audience to the rock with the sword in it.

He watches them, how they follow the foolish fire. Like a conjurer he turns their attention where he wants. Good, good, he thinks. For all the while they'll be busy here, while the real magic trick takes place elsewhere.

'Behold!' he bellows. 'Behold the sword! Behold the sword in the stone!'

'What make is it?' someone asks.

'Is it a gladius?'

'The workmanship is very nice on the grip,' someone says.

'Why is there a bloody sword stuck in a bloody stone?' someone else says, one of the Bors boys, he thinks.

'This is the true king's sword!' Merlin bellows. He has to sell it. This is the hard part, now. 'For so it has been prophesied—'

By me, he thinks, but doesn't say.

'It has been prophesied, that only the true king shall have the power to pull the sword, and in so doing, declare himself to one and all the king!'

He looks at them. He watches them closely. And he knows that they *want* to believe him. This is how true magic is made, in letting people see what they want to see.

In the shadows, under the crumbling arches of the old palace, a street cat watches him with cold, amused eyes. She licks a paw, delicately. She sticks her tongue out at him.

Fucking Morgana, he thinks, but doesn't say. Don't spoil this right now for me.

'But... but who's the king?' a knight shouts. One of Sir Hector's crew.

'It sure ain't you, Lucan!' one of the Frankish mob says, and someone sniggers.

'Only one way to find out!' this Lucan says. Emboldened by drink or the crowd's attention he strides to the stone and lays his hands on the pommel of the sword. He pulls. Then pulls again, harder this time, then grips with two hands and strains against the rock, one foot against the stone, pulling so hard that he ends up flat on his ass.

And *that's* how it's done, Merlin thinks. Then they're all at it, each trying their luck, and when Merlin next looks to the shadows, the watching street cat is gone.

He kneels beside Sir Carados' throne. The old fat man shakes his head.

'A sword in a stone,' he says. 'That is the dumbest fucking thing I've ever heard, Merlin.'

Then he grins, and pats Merlin's hand.

'Nice one,' he says.

21

The night the deal goes down the boys go out of town. They slip away like eels in moonlight, swarming through unspoiled seas. They leave the safety of the walls behind them. They cross the bridge over Tamesis to the south side. This area, once the fort the Romans built, is now under the rule of the Frankish mob, nominally at least. A Roman road leads out to the distant sea. There's still grain storage here, and sheds, and taverns, but mostly the Frankish knights run brothels and theatres and the occasional unlicensed gladiatorial fight. They ship in bears from the countryside and set them against debtors while people shout and drink and gamble over who will win. There's good money in the bookmaking business, and decent cash in running whores, but the theatre's a bit of a risky proposition. The Frankish mob also hire out as armed escorts for traders venturing out of Londinium, for the roads are full of ruffians and vagabonds, that is, men much like the Frankish knights themselves.

But the boys slip like a blade through the dark night, past the Greek-style hot baths where men congregate for Greek-style matters of the heart, past the dimly lit theatres where painted actors and actresses perform rowdy comic mimed escapades – sometimes live sex acts, at times, for the discerning clientele, a real execution.

Absque argento omnia vana, the Romans said. Without money all is in vain.

Kay's heart is beating fast, the blood is in his ears. They move swiftly, silently, they cross the south side and vanish into the wild lands until there is no more city. The sky is so full of stars, it almost hurts to look at them. They swirl in all that deep infinite black. Kay's not familiar with open country. There're sounds in the night, the call of birds, the tread of deer; he fears wolves, though they do not usually come near the city. Kay's heard of the wild untamed forests beyond Londinium, they say the primal forest covers much of this land, dark, impenetrable in places, where only animals and fae creatures dwell. Trolls and such like... Aurochs, with horns as large and twisted as gnarled old trees. He'd heard of them. Giant creatures, with eyes of flame. Shit, he hates being out in the open. He's sure this has all been a terrible mistake.

They find the place. In truth it's not far from the city and the path is well-trodden, and by a pool of water there's even a little wooden hut that must have been standing there for years, and they hide inside it. There's not much there but some sacks of grain and a few hoeing tools. They keep their swords at the ready and wait.

An hour or so, then they hear the approach. The Knights of Bors don't even bother to be stealthy. They obviously have no expectation of an ambush. Bors the Elder whistles and the whistle cuts the night. From out in the distance comes a whistled reply. The knights' contact approaches, he and Bors the Elder hug, they seem to have an easy camaraderie born of long association.

'You have the stuff?'

'You have the cash?'

They laugh.

'All the way from Rome itself,' the contact says, 'it's prima stuff.'

The deal is going down.

Arthur gives the signal.

The boys burst out of the hut, swords at the ready.

'What the fuck—'

'Shut the fuck up and nobody fucking *move*!' Arthur screams. The boys tackle the knights, drop them to the ground, hold swords to their throats. Kay kneels over Bors the Younger. He can feel his heat, his warmth.

Bors the Elder turns with a furious roar.

'Don't fucking move or your boy gets it.'

At that the half-giant calms. The contact tries to flee but Arthur's after him, and the sword flashes, once, twice, and the man is fallen, and there's blood on the ground. Kay steals a glance. For a moment he thinks he sees something rather disconcerting, in the pool of water nearby he thinks he sees a woman rising out of the lake, naked and silvery like a fish, watching them. He thinks there's cold amusement in her eyes.

But when he looks again she's gone.

'You won't get away with this,' Bors the Elder says. He's very calm. Somehow he's more terrifying that way, when he speaks softly.

'Already did,' Arthur says. He picks up the drugs. Nods to Elyan the White, who picks up the money.

'Pleasure doing business with you,' he says.

Kay looks at Bors the Younger. It has to be convincing, he knows. He whispers, 'I'm sorry—' and hits him over the head with the hilt of the sword, knocking him out. It is an ugly wound in Bors' scalp.

It's over so very quickly. The ones they don't knock out they push into the pool. Then they are gone, running like crazy, hooting and laughing at the night and the stars. All the way back to Londinium. Fog falls on the ground, obscuring them from pursuers, but none of the boys think to question it.

*

The Goblin Fruit heist *makes* them. That night on their return to the safe house they count the money and realise just how much they'd got. Gold, hard cash, so much of it that it must have been everything the Knights of Bors had and more – they must have borrowed just to make the payment. The Goblin Fruit's two sacks full, enough to dominate the trade completely. The boys want to celebrate. They want to hit the town, get blind drunk and get blown.

'Look at all this *gold*!' Geraint says. He picks a handful of denarii and Persian darics. 'We're going to be *kings*!'

Arthur coldly stares him down. He picks up a Greek obol, with the head of Alexander the Great on its side.

'Now *there* was a king,' he says softly. The boys quieten down. Arthur says, 'Kay, count it up and make a record. Elyan, Geraint, Owain, you cut the merch and get it ready for distribution.'

'Sir, yes, sir.'

Arthur sits himself down at their small round table. He looks at each of them in turn. His eyes are so calm.

'We're not safe here anymore,' he says. 'We hit them today, and we hit them hard. They'll come for us. I want everything moved to the new locations. I want you to go out tonight and sell the first batch, make it primo stuff, and set the price high. We need more. More of everything. Tomorrow, at first light, we start to build.'

'Build?' Owain, the Bastard, says.

'We need more men. We need more arms. It's time for us to take our rightful place here in this city. Build and expand. I don't want anyone out alone. Go in pairs, and go armed. Draw no attention. Buy nothing new for yourselves, not yet. Whatever we want, we will *take* – but later. To do what must be done now, we need an army.'

The word sits there between them on the table.

'But Arthur, we can't take them *all*,' Owain says. Protests. Arthur turns his eyes on him.

'They will come to us,' he says. 'And those who don't, well—' He makes a cutting gesture on the throat. 'You understand?'

'We understand, Arthur...'

'Good. Then go!'

They do. Kay and Arthur divvy up the loot, Kay faithfully transcribes figures and types of currency, and to what use to put them.

'Use Bors,' Arthur says.

'What?'

'He can defect to us, but I don't want him on his own. Work on him. Get him to talk some sense into his father's thick skull. I want the Knights of Bors to come to us.'

'Are you fucking insane?' Kay says. 'We just robbed them! Bors the Elder is going to want to kill you, and by kill you I mean, kill you very, very slowly. And if he finds about his son and me he's going to kill both of us twice over.'

Arthur nods, but Kay knows he's not really listening. Arthur has made up his mind.

Arthur says, 'Kay, things are going to change round here. I want whoever is willing to accept this change to come over to us. I won't hold their past loyalties against them. As for those who can't accept the change, we'll deal with them. Do you understand?'

'I do, but—'

'They're like a pack of dogs,' Arthur says. 'They'll roll over and submit to whoever holds the power. Bors will come crawling to *us*, and he'll ask for permission just to take a piss. Do you understand?'

'I do.'

'You're a knight now, Kay. You're one of *them*. They can't touch you, and they'll listen to you. I want you to be my go-between. You're my consiliarius, man. I trust you.'

Arthur leans over, grasps Kay's arm. Pulls him to himself, until their foreheads touch.

'I love you, Kay. You know that, right?'

'I love you too, Arthur.'

'We're brothers, Kay!'

'Yes,' Kay says. 'Brothers.'

Arthur smiles. And Kay knows, at that moment, that he's lost him. That the Arthur he'd known is gone forever now, had perhaps never existed in the first place. This new Arthur's nobody's friend, and nobody's brother. He is alone.

He pulls away. Stands up to go.

'Sir, yes, sir,' he says softly.

22

'Oww!' Carados says. He rubs his skin. It's cold and white as Greek marble. 'That hurt.'

'Sorry,' Merlin says. The Guv'nor's sitting naked in the examination chair. It doesn't take a doctor to know that he is dying. 'You've got cancer. I could try bloodletting or purgatives as recommended by Celsus in *De Medicina*, but—'

'Yes, yes, don't you think I've done all that?' Carados says. 'I have my own physicians, thank you very much.'

'Then what...'

'I need something for the pain.'

Merlin looks him over. The man has a crab in his body, crawling, tearing up his insides. Cancer, from the Greek karkinos, meaning crayfish or crab. It's no way for a warrior to die, and Carados knows it.

'I have some poppy juice from Cyprus where they grow the plant,' Merlin says. He'd scored it from his contacts on the docks, but it is rare. He dreams of having his very own botanical gardens, where he could experiment with Nature and its bounty, but life since Uther's fall has been... erratic, and he'd been forced to move around a lot. Just at the moment he is renting a two-room abode near Cripplegate, from an irate landlady, but it won't do to advertise this fact.

Carados looks at him with awful hope in his eyes. 'Is it magical?' he says.

'It will ease your pain.'

Merlin fetches the bottle and lets out drops of the precious liquid, and mixes it into a glass. He gives it to the Guv'nor to drink.

'How goes it with the sword?' he asks.

The Guv'nor grins. 'It worked much as you said it would,' he says. 'It draws them to itself like flies to a corpse.'

'The knights?'

'All of them, sure. I have one of my boys take admissions on the door. To help with costs, you understand. Also the concession stands for drinks and snacks and the performers, well, you can see for yourself when you go. It's a bit of a Saturnalia out there. See, you never specified it had to be a knight, did you? So everyone now wants to have a go. And why not? It's democracy, I say, like they had in Greece. A democracy of the sword. And anyone can try their luck for a few shekels.'

The poppy juice is doing its job. The Guv'nor looks more animated, his eyes brighter, the smile – the smile of a man who'd eaten and fucked his share in life, and then murdered some others so he could eat and fuck all *their* share in life – widens. He moistens his lips with his tongue. He reminds Merlin of a great big toad.

'You may leave me now, Merlin...' he says.

Merlin nods. He turns to leave. There is power still around this Sir Carados, but the taste of it is sour, spoiled – it makes Merlin want to heave. He says, 'Have you?'

'Have I what, Merlin?'

'Have *you* tried it?'

The Guv'nor smiles.

'Get the fuck out of here,' he says.

On his way out he passes the sword in the stone. The courtyard's full. Musicians play. Jugglers juggle flames. Whores leer at passers-by, flashing pale thighs. Vendors sell mutton, bread, honey and apples. Merlin thinks he sees a Pan – a fucking *Pan?* – dancing on cloven hooves with a gaggle of young maidens. There's beer and mead on sale in all four corners, and a jakes set up for the crowd to go and do their bit for a handful of coppers. Rooms, too, for hire for as much time as it takes a small sandglass to empty. It's like the Guv'nor said – it's fucking Saturnalia.

The cross Sir Carados erected stands forlorn. There's no one to pray kneeling beside it, but a couple too poor or too in a hurry to pay for a room begin to fuck against it as the crowd cheers them on, until the Guv'nor's men pull them roughly away with a beating.

But Merlin's attention's not on the cross, nor on the festivities, but on the sword in the stone.

It stands apart from the festivities, and the sunlight falls down on it in just the right way to make it seem special somehow, it dapples around the hilt and the exposed metal of the blade, over the weathered old stone and the dark green moss that grows in the cracks. It's a lovely effect, and only took a little bit of magic.

The townsfolk queue. The queue snakes around the court-yard and all the way to the entrance and continues beyond. One of the Guv'nor's burly men stands guard to collect the fee, but even he seems subdued, as though the bloody thing is genuine.

And Merlin thinks, Christ, is that how *he* felt, back in Judea, how you put a little charm on and mouth a few homilies and suddenly people just... *buy* it? For all he knows, in centuries to come, people will whisper of this miracle and tell the tale over and over again, of the sword, and the stone, and the king who came to claim his birth right.

While Merlin knows, just as the Guv'nor does, just as these men should know, if they only stopped to think about it, that there is no magic to being a king. There's no birth right but the one that is bought with blood. And still they come, and queue in patience, and take their turn at the hilt of the sword. Some heave, some pull gently, some struggle with their feet against the stone. Some curse and some sob and some shrug and move on – and many merely return to the back of the queue, ready to part with their coppers again, to try once more, just one more time, maybe this time they'll get lucky.

And Merlin thinks, old Sir Carados, bless his black soul, must be making a *killing* in profit here.

While he, Merlin, still has to live in that shitty two-room hellhole by Cripplegate.

But patience, Merlin, he thinks. Patience. And he watches the good citizens of Londinium queue for their chance at becoming magical kings, and there's a power here, real power of a kind he'd not seen before. And he finds it nourishing.

He walks out of the gates. This was not in his plan. But it's something, and he makes a note of it, in his mind.

Then he turns into a cat and scuttles away.

He follows the smell of her piss all through the town. It's marked on corners, on a fallen arch, on a clump of weeds by a butcher's shop, in an alleyway next to a place where a rat was killed, near the entry way to an underground mithraeum, past a gladiatorial steam baths with the smell of semen and blood lingering not unpleasantly, down the market and past a money changers', and alongside Tamesis with the smell of frying fish from the nearby stalls in the air. He steals a fish and gnaws its flesh and bones under a statue to Magnus Maximus, the Pretender. A feral cat hisses at him and Merlin shows his claws, and the cat slinks away.

The stink of her piss is everywhere, she has marked this town for her own. And he resents her that. For all that he has temporarily made his home here, in the big city, Merlin is a country boy at heart. He knows the village green and the rolling hills and the clear clean brooks and the call of birds, while she is of the city and the city is of her. She knows its dark dank alleyways and endless commerce and the coming and going of traders and ships. She was there when the Romans came (or so she claims), when Boudicca rose, when the city was razed to the ground, when it was built up again. She will be there (so she claims) when the city shall fall again, and when it shall rise, and for as long as the occult stone of Londinium still stands in the street of the candle-makers.

He follows the scent of her piss until he finds her at last in a maze of tenements a stone's throw away from the White Hill, and he joins her under the arches of a shop. She licks a paw and bares her teeth at him.

'Took you long enough,' she says.

'Morgan.'

'Been enjoying your handiwork?' she says.

'It hasn't gone exactly as I thought it would,' he says.

She purrs a laugh. 'And the boy?' Morgan says.

'You keep your paws off him.'

'Fat chance of that, little Merlin,' she says. He does his best to ignore her.

'Is he here?' he says instead.

'He is,' she says. 'Arrived two nights ago, at the witching hour. He wasn't easy to find.'

'He has his own spell makers.'

'So it would seem. But no one comes and goes in my town without me finding out about it,' Morgan says.

'So... *here*?' Merlin says. He peers across the road. It's a hovel worse than where he himself is staying. A maze of old Roman-built streets, low-ceiling rooms in crumbling masonry, no sunlight, trash everywhere... 'This is no place for a king.'

It's Leir, of course. The clever old man of the ridings, lord of the Brigantes, the man whose claim to power goes all the way to Imperial Rome. A real king, and they say despite his age he's ageless. Has he really been lured all the way to Londinium because of a sword in a stone?

'He's not stupid, Merlin,' Morgan says. Reading his thoughts. 'If he's here it's because he smells something. He smells a rat.' She swipes at him with her claws. 'No offence.'

'None taken. And well done on finding him. Are the others here, too?'

'Word is Outham the Old's on his estates outside the city,' Morgan says. 'And Conan Meriadoc's on the southside with the Frankish mob. But don't be fooled, Merlin. They won't go down easy. They know the score. They have their men and their protections.'

'Whatever, Morgan. Any gossip?'

'They say Outham's got a pet bishop with him, from that new Christian church. It's all the rage over on the continent. I fear they're here to stay.'

'Christianity's just a fad, surely,' Merlin says.

'I'm not so certain.'

Something whistles through the air. Merlin reacts lightning-quick. He pounces on Morgan, throwing her out of harm's way, landing on her. The missile whistles past and hits the wall behind them with a nasty bang.

'What the fuck?'

Their cat bodies are intertwined. She pushes him away. They peer around the corner. A brutish Briganti stands there with a catapult and another rock at the ready. He leers at them as he cocks another missile.

'Mother*fucker*!' Morgan screams.

The man fires. The cats draw back in time. Morgan le Fay takes a deep breath and begins cursing.

'May your eyes boil in your head and may your tongue shrivel and die in your mouth, may your penis fall off and your testicles explode, may your gut rot and your teeth fall out and your hair wither and you get boils on your ass, may you—'

'Morgan, stop!'

When Merlin peers around the corner again he sees the

Brigantes man on his knees, holding his head in his hands. The man retches a black foul liquid onto the squalid stone floor.

'There are covenants in place,' Merlin says, 'there are *understandings*.'

'Then let him understand this,' Morgan says, 'no one fires on *me* in *my* town.'

'Now Leir knows we're watching him.'

'You think he didn't know before?'

'I love you, Morgan,' Merlin says, 'but you're a fucking liability.'

'I love you too, pet wizard,' Morgan says. 'Now, have you seen enough?'

'I have.'

'Then fuck off back to your wank pad, darling,' Morgan says; with affection.

23

The Goblin Fruit heist *made* them. The word's out. Merlin watches the boys' new compound from across the road. A month later, they have men and boys positively *queuing* to sign up.

Kay and Arthur, sitting behind that same shitty old round table they'd lugged over from the safe house:

'Name?'

'Agravain. Of the Hard Hand, sir!'

'Let's see them, then.'

Agravain shows his fists. Kay whistles. Arthur nods.

'Good at bashing heads, then?'

'Very good, sir!'

'Can you handle a sword?'

'I can handle any blade, sir!'

'Pay's two coppers a day, plus bread allowance, meat on Tuesdays and fish on Thursdays, plus a one-tenth of whatever spoils you catch. And a roof over your head.'

'Sign me up, sir!'

'Can you read or write?'

'No, sir!'

'Good enough. Go see Elyan over there, he'll sort you out.'

Agravain goes off. Arthur says, 'Make sure they know bedding and gear will be deducted from pay.'

'Elyan will sort it out,' Kay says. 'Stop fussing.'

'I'm not.' Arthur rubs his hands as though cold. 'How did we get to this?' he says.

Kay says, 'We won,' and Arthur smiles. Then the smile fades.

'Not yet we haven't.'

Kay sighs. Kay shouts, 'Next!'

A new wannabe shuffles forward.

'Name?'

'Ulfius, sir.'

'Can you handle a sword?'

The boy grins. 'Wasn't born yesterday, Sir Kay, was I?' he says.

'Dunno, was you?'

'No, sir!'

'Pay's two coppers a day, plus—'

'Bread allowance, I know, sir, we all know, all the boys, we want to serve, don't we? We know what you guys did and we want in.'

He looks at Arthur, who looks back at him levelly.

'You're the Guv'nor now, ain't you, Sir Arthur. Begging your pardon, but it's true, innit? It's true?'

Arthur says, 'We'll make it true, Ulfius,' and the boy near blushes, so delighted to be called by name. 'Go see Elyan,' Arthur says. 'He'll sort you out.'

'Sir, yes, sir!'

'Next!'

And so it goes. The boys have arms now, swords, knives, shields, some fucking *battering rams* Owain, the Bastard, got half-price from some dealer. Half the city's trying to get a place with their gang. And the others are keeping a wary distance – for now. Kay knows it's not over, not by a long shot. They have to stay vigilant.

'Name?'

'Merlin.'

'You!' Kay says. He stares at this interloper, who seems not much older than they are. Pale, almost silvery skin, long black hair and those unsettling eyes, like a fish's or a lizard's, not quite human at any rate.

'You know him?' Arthur says.

'He *talked* to me,' Kay says. Somehow the very memory of Merlin approaching him on the steps of the Temple of Apollo is unsettling. The very nature of the memory doesn't feel quite right. It's out of focus, the details smudged.

'He *talked* to you?' Arthur says, laughing.

This Merlin licks his lips, as though the very sight of Arthur is a meal for him. There's nothing sexual about it, Kay thinks. That he could understand, at least. Arthur's a handsome lad, more than one girl or one boy would be glad for the chance to fuck him. But this is something different. It's wrong, somehow. Like Arthur is a kind of *food*.

'I did meet and briefly converse with him, yes,' Merlin says. 'It was a most illuminating chat.'

'He's a... he must be a *spy* or something!'

'A spy? For whom?'

'For, I don't know...'

Merlin kneels before Arthur. He raises his head and looks him in the eye.

'I wish only to serve,' he says.

Arthur laughs, as though the very presence of the creature delights him. 'And can you use a sword?' he says.

'Goodness, no,' Merlin says. 'I abhor naked steel.'

Arthur looks at him, still amused. 'No swords? Then what can you do, pray tell?'

'I can do magic.'

'Cups and balls? You'd make a denarius disappear?'

'No, lord. I mean, I could, if it pleased you, lord. But no. I mean, like—'

Merlin clicks his fingers, spouting a colourless flame. He sends it dancing above them.

'A will-o'-the-wisp?'

'An ignis fatuus, or foolish fire, lord. It's but a trifle, of course, but...'

'So you are what, a fae?'

'A wizard, sir.'

'We do not have a wizard, Kay,' Arthur says.

'With good reason, Arthur! We shouldn't truck with such as these.'

'Such as what, please?' Merlin says.

'The fae! Boggarts and that.'

'I am no boggart or bogie,' Merlin says reproachfully. 'My mother was mortal, just like your own.'

'I never met my mother,' Arthur says.

I have, Merlin thinks, but doesn't say. Gods, but it's hard standing so close to him now. What a fat little baby he was. There's such an innocence to babies, before the world takes them and shapes them as it will. This Arthur, he is like a blade. He could be great, Merlin thinks. He's so proud of him. It's like watching Uther again, but Uther in youth, in bloom, an Uther with all of the world still before him, ready for the taking.

He says, 'I wish only to serve.'

'Pay's two coppers a day, plus bread allowance—'

'I don't eat much, my lord. This will more than suffice.'

Kay glares. But Merlin knows that Arthur sees him for what he truly is, and that he approves of him. A monarch needs a wizard like a wizard needs a staff.

Which reminds him he should really get one. Oak or something. It looks more formidable, somehow.

'Then go see Elyan, he will sort you out.'

Merlin rises. Bows. 'My lord.'

'I like this guy,' Arthur says.

Kay buries his head in his hands.

'Well?' Kay says.

Sir Daniel von dem blühenden Tal is the head of the Frankish mob. They're sitting in a riverside establishment on the south side of Tamesis. This is the Frankish mob's domain. No one is armed. They'd left their weapons at the door. Merlin's with Kay – Arthur had insisted.

The leader of the Frankish mob drums bejewelled fingers on the tabletop.

'If you don't mind me saying, but he's a fucking little upstart,' he says. 'No offence.'

'None taken.'

'I have my own good thing going here,' Sir Daniel complains. 'The south side's always been independent.'

'You pay the one-tenth tax to Sir Carados,' Kay reminds him. 'You owe him fealty.'

'I owe him dick!' von dem blühenden Tal says, affronted.

Kay shrugs, conciliatory. Merlin's silent beside him.

Kay says, 'The times are changing.'

'What does that even mean?'

Merlin leans over. His quiet voice carries. 'It means that, for too long, this nation was divided. Small outfits like yours could operate at ease. This will no longer be the case, von dem blühenden Tal. This is a time of... consolidation.'

'I beg your pardon?'

'Small outfits just won't survive,' Merlin says simply. 'You have to join up or go under. This isn't personal, it's business. This is the nature of the world.'

Sir Daniel broods. Merlin watches him. Kay had told him this would be the easier pitch. The Frankish mob, for all their claims to independence, are really small-fry operators, all too aware of their recent arrival into this world. They are not much more than dockyard thieves and petty criminals, the sons of sailors and traders who settled in Britannia before the fall.

He says, 'Were you not, yourself, just such a leader as Arthur? Rising from your humble beginnings on the south side to form one of the most fearful gangs in all of Londinium?'

'I was.'

'You owe no debt of loyalty to Sir Carados. You've been maligned, tolerated only because you're on the wrong side of the water. Join up, and you'll be one of us, an equal. No one sits at the head of a round table.'

'And besides,' Kay adds, 'Arthur has bigger aspirations than Londinium. There are fortunes to be made, Sir Daniel. There's a kingdom to be won!'

'I did hear you kids are building up an army.' Sir Daniel mulls it over, but Merlin knows: he knows his mind's already been made up.

'What if I say no?'

'Why would you say no?' Kay asks. 'Arthur has the utmost respect for you, Sir Daniel.'

'Yet he didn't come himself.'

'We are his voice, Sir Daniel.'

'So I see.' He turns his frown on Merlin. 'You,' he says. 'Of you I've heard, and not good things.'

'And I heard Conan Meriadoc's staying with your lot.'

'And so? You want him as the price of joining?'

Merlin's smile's a thin line. 'Whatever for? All are welcome of their own volition in Arthur's coalition of knights.'

'A coalition now, is it?'

'He'll need wise counsel, and experienced men such as yourself.'

'Enough. What do I get?'

'A kingdom of your own. Say... the whole of the south side from here unto Silchester?'

'That's Atrebates land,' Sir Daniel says.

'So?'

Slowly, Sir Daniel smiles. 'I like the cut of your jib,' he says.

'Do we have a deal?'

Sir Daniel nods. 'Tell Arthur that he's got himself a partner,' he says.

★

'You trust him?' Merlin asks.

'I think he'll hedge his bets until he sees which way the die falls,' Kay says.

'You think it will be our side?'

Kay sighs. 'We have the soldiers, but they are hardly tested. The other gangs have hardened men, and arms to match ours. What Aristotle called *politics* will only take us so far.'

'You expect bloodshed.'

'Don't you?'

Merlin shrugs. 'I am only the hired help,' he says.

'I know what you are, wizard. Everybody's heard the stories.'

'And Arthur?'

'What Arthur knows or Arthur thinks is known only to Arthur.'

'I swore to serve him,' Merlin says.

'And I don't doubt you on that score. I just don't trust you, or your motives.'

'...That's fair,' Merlin allows, and makes Kay laugh.

'Where next, then?' Merlin says.

'The Knights of Bors.'

Bors the Elder towers over Kay, his giant fist raised to strike him.

'Give me *one* good fucking reason why I shouldn't bash your brains out right now, you fucking rat!' he says.

'Dad!' Bors the Younger says pleadingly.

'You stay out of it!'

'I am a knight and Sir Hector's son,' Kay says. 'And I was assured safe passage.'

'Safe passage my *ass*.'

'Dad!'

'You stay out of it.'

Merlin, with his arms crossed, watches the proceedings. They're in Sir Bors' hall, but really it's more like an old Roman military encampment, with training posts and trading stores and Bors' men at practice with their weapons. And Merlin thinks, this Bors has missed his true calling, a hundred years earlier he would have served the Emperor with pride and gone to see the world and fought the Gauls or Libyans. The man was born to be a prefect.

'I know it was you little shits,' Bors says. 'You think I'm a fucking idiot? I'm going to hunt down Arthur and split his skull and roast his brains on a stick and eat them.'

'Arthur holds you in the highest regard...' Kay starts.

'One more word, motherfucker! One more word and I'll—'

'Perhaps I may interject,' Merlin says.

Bors the Elder turns and frowns at him in irritation. 'The pet wizard,' he says. 'I've heard of you.'

'Then you know what master I served before Arthur.'

The frown deepens. 'I knew Uther from the old days. He was a good fighter.' This seems the highest compliment Bors can bestow. 'Why you serve that fucking cur Arthur I am sure I have no idea.'

'No?' Merlin says quietly.

'What are you getting at, wizard? My beef is not with you.'

'Your beef is not with Arthur, either. He did only what you would yourself do, what any of you would, in similar circumstances. Arthur wants to make amends. He sees you for what you truly are, Sir Bors. A knight, a warrior, a leader of men. He has a need of you.'

'A need.' Bors snorts. 'He wouldn't last five minutes out in the real world.'

'I wouldn't be too sure.'

'You really think...' But he simmers down. 'The bet you're placing is a hefty one,' he says.

'I know.'

'You gamble with your life?'

'I am a soldier too, if of a different sort.'

'A different sort indeed...' A note of amusement crops into Bors' speech. His fist drops. Kay scuttles from underneath him.

'Did I say you could move!' Bors roars.

'Dad!'

'You stay out of it.'

'I'm just saying, Dad. We should listen to them.'

'You think so, do you?'

'An alliance, Dad.'

'Shut the fuck up, Younger.'

'Dad...'

'Arthur would make you commander of an army,' Merlin says.

'An army!' Bors says. 'You call that gaggle of riffraff he's hiring an army?'

'Not yet,' Merlin says. 'But I will.'

He watches Bors. The man might be a brute, but he isn't stupid. Bors can sense the way the wind is blowing.

'...With your help,' Merlin says.

'You want *me* to command *them*?'

Merlin shrugs. 'They need a real officer in charge,' he says.

'You ever been off the island, wizard? You ever visit the continent?'

'I've been to Bath once,' Merlin says.

'You don't *know* what a real army is,' Bors says. 'I saw them, when I was young I fought in Gaul and Jutland. A young hired sword I was, same as Uther. That boy always had dreams beyond his station...' He looks thoughtful. 'I saw the last of the Fifth Legion, and even diminished as they already were, they were incredible. The discipline, wizard. An army is nothing without discipline.'

'Then join us. *Teach* them. You could *make* them soldiers.'

'Dad, I think we should—'

'You stay out of it.'

'Think about it,' Merlin says. 'Just don't think too long.'

Bors nods.

Kay and Merlin leave.

'You think we got him?'

'I think you made a compelling case, Merlin. But he'll wait and see where the die falls.'

'Where to next, then?'

Kay sighs. Massages the bridge of his nose.

'The White Hill Gang,' he says, without enthusiasm.

'So, what do you fuckers want?' says the Black Knight of the White Hill Gang.

Kay and Merlin stand before him in the white marble opulence of the gang's seat of power. Rich, powerful and vicious.

Kay snaps his fingers. Two of the boys bring in a wooden chest.

'Gift,' he says.

He snaps his fingers again. The boys open the chest.

Inside are jewels, coins, arms, wine amphorae. A small treasure, or a rather large bribe.

'Nice,' the Black Knight says.

'More where that came from.'

'Alright, then.'

'Are we good?'

'We're good.'

They leave.

'That was brief,' Merlin says.

'They only speak one language,' Kay says Shrugs.

Merlin says, 'You think they'll go for it?'

Kay says, 'I think they'll wait and see—'
'Where the die falls. Alright, I get it. Where to next, then?'
Kay sighs.
'There's one last man to pitch,' he says.

24

They leave Merlin behind, but he changes into a crow and follows them. He perches on the windowsill.

'Father,' Kay says.

'Sir Hector,' Arthur says.

They stand before him, like truant children.

Sir Hector perches on the bed and scratches at his belly. His men stand by. Cynric, the Welshman, who taught Arthur the use of the bow and the knife. Escanor the Large, whose father was a giant and his mother was a witch, and who taught the boys bare knuckle boxing. Gareth, who was Sir Hector's best thief.

'You are *my* ward, Arthur,' Sir Hector says. 'I have raised you like my own child.'

Arthur bows his head, acceding the point.

'And I am forever grateful, Sir Hector,' he says.

'My *ward*, Arthur!' Sir Hector fingers the jewelled hilt of a knife. 'Now look at the mess you've made,' he complains.

'Sir Hector?'

'They want your *blood*, Arthur!' He glares at him. 'I told them, he is but a boy. I told them, he is like a son to me. I told them, I could not abide losing a single lock of his hair, let alone a finger or his life. I spoke for you, Arthur. I would have made you a *knight*!'

'You made Kay a knight,' Arthur says quietly.

'Kay is *blood*!'

That word hangs between them.

'And I am not.'

'What blood you have I'm sure I couldn't say.'

'You don't know? You can't even tell me who my father is?'

Sir Hector waves a jewelled hand. 'You were the price I had to pay on a debt,' he says. 'I was given no choice in the matter. But I always treated you well, did I not? I treated you like a *son*!'

'Sir Hector,' Arthur says, 'I do not question the debt I owe you.'

'Then what is it, Arthur? Do I look like a sheep?'

'What?' A momentary look of genuine confusion suffuses Arthur's face.

'I said, do I look like a sheep?'

'A sheep? No, but why—'

'Then are you trying to fuck me like a sheep!' Sir Hector screams.

'Why would I want to fuck a shee—'

Cynric and Escanor look away.

'Look,' Arthur says. 'You know why I'm here. I respect you, Sir Hector. But I am no longer a child. And a man must make his own way in this world. Join me. Together, we could—'

The bird Merlin watches from the windowsill. Sir Hector rises. He waddles to Kay, wraps his arm around his son's shoulders.

'I love you, boy,' he says.

'I love you too, Father.'

Sir Hector kisses him on the top of the head. 'You're a good boy, Kay.'

He releases him, shuffles over to Arthur. Stands before him, looks him in the eye.

'No hard feelings,' he says. He extends his hand for a shake.

Arthur looks relieved. He reaches to shake Hector's hand.

The crow Merlin feels a sudden, blinding white pain. The Welshman, Cynric, with lightning-fast reflexes, threw a hard sharp stone at him. Merlin totters on the windowsill on tiny bird feet. He blinks his crow's eyes.

Sees Kay dragged back by Gareth and Cynric. Sees Arthur felled by Escanor the Large.

Merlin tries to hold on to consciousness, to shift back, but his crow's head feels so sore and the darkness seems so welcoming.

The last thing he sees before he falls to the ground is the prone body of young Arthur on the floor, and the half-giant Escanor reaching for a rope.

Merlin wakes up to a bird's worst nightmare. An alley cat towers above him, her claws extended. She bares her teeth and hisses. A delicate pink tongue darts out to taste his face, a prelude, no doubt, to chomping his head off next.

He crows, 'Get off of me! Get off of me!'

The cat laughs.

That mouth reaches down. The teeth clamp on his tiny body.

Gently, she lifts him up. He's powerless to resist. He sees the Welshman, Cynric, emerging from the house with a catapult. The Welshman grins when he sees the crow's fate.

'Was going to step on your fucking skull, wizard, but this is even better,' he says. He bends down and strokes the cat's head. 'Enjoy your dinner!' he says, and cackles.

The cat purrs.

Then she bounds away, swift as a starling, and takes the wounded crow with her.

'It is for the best, lad,' Sir Hector says. His men hold Kay, but he has stopped resisting. He stares mutely at his father.

'It is out of my hands,' Sir Hector says. 'I would have warned him, but he never did listen, did Arthur. You must have known it couldn't be, Kay. You're not a fool. Such a naked power grab would never be tolerated. He is not even blood.'

'What have you *done?*' Kay says. 'What will happen to him?'

'What I should have done a long time ago,' Sir Hector says. 'My debt is paid, and a reckoning is due. You will learn this, Kay. Sooner or later you will learn: there must always be an account.'

'Oh, for *fuck's* sake, Morgan!' Merlin says.

The cat, transformed back into a woman, laughs.

'Little birds get their little wings clipped,' she says.

Merlin, transformed back into a man, lies on the ground. His clothes are torn. His face is bloody. He says, 'You *knew?*'

'Oh, fuck off, Merlin. You think he's yours? If I can't have him, then no one will.'

'By God, I want to kill you.'

'Which god? This Jesus?'

He ignores it. Throws a lightning bolt at her head. She inches it away and the lightning hits the wall behind her with a loud explosion.

'Oh, stop it,' she says.

'You sold him out?'

'I did nothing,' she says, laughing at him now. 'Sir Hector did no more than do as you bid him all those years back. He looked after the brat like it were his own. When Arthur robbed the Knights of Bors, it was Arthur who broke the rules. Sir Hector had no choice but to give him up. His debt was paid.'

'And you didn't think to tell me?'

'All I did was not intervene.'

'I can still save him,' Merlin says. He changes back into a bird and flaps his wings. He rises stiffly. Hovers at the window.

Morgan le Fay looks at him with that fondness cats have for their prey.

'Fly away, little birdie,' she says. 'Fly away.'

The Guv'nor watches as the boy comes slowly back to consciousness.

Arthur lies on the ground at the ruined old governor's palace courtyard. There is still that rock with the useless sword in it, but no punters for the day, the courtyard's closed for a private function. There is still the cross nailed into the hard ground, but no worshippers for that wild-eyed messiah from the distant Galilee.

There is only the boy. He is the centrepiece of this tableau.

The boy blinks bloodied eyes. They'd worked him over, some, Sir Hector's men, so that by the time he arrived he was already a little worse for wear. Then the Guv'nor's men had their fun. He doesn't look so good now, this boy, this Arthur.

He should stay down. He's naked, bloodied, bruised and broken-ribbed. He's dog meat now, perhaps he just doesn't realise it yet.

The Guv'nor stands. Sir Carados of old Londinium, the boss of bosses. Sure, he's sick and he's old and he's, well, he's dying, but then, isn't everyone, from the very moment of their birth, dying, if you really think about it? Sir Carados is not dead *yet*, is what he means. It is a message that his audience cannot fail to receive.

They stand all around the courtyard. The sun is down and the night is dark and torches burn and the shadows dance. The air smells of burning wood and men's stench, of blood.

They are all here. They are assembled. The Frankish Mob and the White Hill Gang and the Knights of Bors and Sir Hector and his son Sir Kay. In the shadows stand the grim old men of the outside, the quiet kings: Leir and Outham the Old and Conan Meriadoc.

It is a body of men, a silent mob. All watching. All waiting. Sir Carados steps forward. He is impeccably dressed today. He wears his oldest sword. He raises his huge fists and slips on iron knuckles.

This will be settled the old-fashioned way.

He takes a step, and then another.

Stay down, boy, and this will all be over quickly.

Stay down, boy.

Racing desperately through the night across Londinium, a lonely crow beats wings against the hostile winds.

On the ground under the light from the burning torches, the boy, Arthur, stirs.

He opens his eyes. He sees Sir Carados.

He spits blood.

Pulls himself up on his knees.

Stay there, boy. Stay kneeling.

Stay down, boy.

Sir Carados bears down on him. His fist, with those nasty metal knuckles on it, connects with the side of Arthur's face. It smashes it good. It smashes it hard. The punch sends Arthur flying back.

The crowd murmurs. Eager, excited. They love the smell of blood. This is the court and I am the king, those are the words the watching men hear.

Sir Carados advances. The boy, Arthur, opens his eyes. Spits blood. Scrambles back. Scrambles, but no one will help him. Kay watches, helpless to intervene. High above the city, the crow, Merlin, dives towards the palace.

Late, he thinks. *Too late.*

Sir Carados swings a fist. The metal casing gouges Arthur's skin, it breaks a bone, it slams him to the ground again.

Sir Carados towers over him, breathing heavily. He coughs. His body shakes. He hawks up dirty phlegm and gobs a load on Arthur's face.

Stay down, boy. Stay down and this will all be over soon.

The crowd murmurs appreciatively. Money, furtively, changes hands.

On the ground, the beaten naked boy opens his eyes.

Kay watches, helpless.

A crow dives down from the skies, but he is still too far, too far.

Sir Carados reaches for his sword. It's time to end this.

The boy scrabbles back, desperate to live.

And hits an obstacle.

He stops.

He's hit a rock.

There's nowhere else to go.

Stay down, boy.

Stay down.

Carados advances. The boy slams one palm into the ground. Pushes himself upright, holding on to the stone. The useless sword's still stuck in it.

He looks. You can see him thinking.

In the audience, all those knights and kings had tried their turn and wrote it off as just another goof.

Carados advances. He raises his sword. He is breathing heavily. His forehead is beaded with sweat. He is not a well man, is Sir Carados.

Arthur's fingers close on the hilt of the sword in the stone. He tries a tug.

To the onlookers' dismayed surprise, there's no resistance.

The blade slides out smooth.

It is at that moment when his fingers close on the hilt of the sword and he pulls it out of the stone that he knows he would be king. Not by divine right or by line of descent.

By force alone.

★

As Sir Carados raises his blade for the fatal strike, Arthur falls forward, and the sword in the stone slides out and swings and strikes true.

It slides deep into the Guv'nor's belly, up to the hilt, and stays there.

Sir Carados looks down with an expression of faint surprise on his face. The torch fire casts angry shadows on the floor. A crow falls down from overhead, and a cat tiptoes in between the feet of the rapt crowd.

'...Oh,' Sir Carados says.

He sits down heavily.

He clutches his belly. A look of confusion, or perhaps relief, suffocates his bloated features. He grasps the hilt of the sword and tries to pull it out of himself, but he has not the strength to do it.

Arthur, beaten and bloodied, crawls to Sir Carados. He barely looks at the man. He reaches for the sword – *his* sword. He pulls it out of the man's belly.

Sir Carados' blood jets up, hits Arthur's face, drips down his chest and arms. Sir Carados sinks back with a soft, sad *whoomph*.

His eyes close. In death, he shits himself.

Arthur pushes himself upright. The crowd take a step back, involuntarily. Arthur turns to face them. He is half-blinded by the torchlight and the blood in his eyes, but he marks their faces.

He raises the sword high up in the air.

He stares defiance.

He screams.

'*Come and have a go if you think you're hard enough!*'

PART THREE

THE COUNCIL OF SIX

25

And Ulfius remembers that night, one year ago now.

They were summoned to the old governor's palace by Sir Kay. How silent it was, when they arrived. How pale the faces of the men who stood there in the torchlight.

He saw the king, then. Arthur, naked and bloodied, holding a sword.

How savagely he grinned, and the sword, it had been the one in the stone, even Ulfius had paid his copper and had a go at trying to pull it out, a harmless thing it had seemed then, an amusement at a fair.

But Arthur pulled out the sword, and he had slain the old Guv'nor; and the other men, those fearsome knights, stood and watched him and they were helpless before him.

He was the boss of bosses now.

And how they'd cheered, his boys, Ulfius and Agravain of the Hard Hand, and Elyan the White, and Owain, the Bastard. Arthur's boys. Arthur's knights. And the others fell from them; and they lifted Arthur up and carried him away back to barracks, and in the morning the whole of Londinium knew that the game had changed.

The king was dead. Long live the king.

That was a glorious time.

But now, running through the black night, his right side

aflame in agony from the sword that pierced him, Ulfius is scared, more scared than he has ever been.

'Eli, eli, lama sabachthani?' he murmurs. He staggers on the uneven terrain. His mind is filled with the flames of the burning castle and the sound of clashing swords and the screams of dying men. Some unfamiliar bird crows overhead and makes him start. Though he's been running for a long time he has the uncanny sense of being followed silently.

There are no cities. There are no towns. The stars are hidden behind clouds.

This is no place for a God-fearing Christian to be. There are too many... *things* that walk and crawl and hop and fly on a night such as this, when the devil rides out and all his creatures are loose. So much death.

And he wonders if his king, Arthur, is still alive.

The night sounds frighten him. The pain in his side is so bad. Oh, Lord Jesus, some say that after you died and were reborn you came here, to this fair land, and if so perhaps you could spare a moment for your poor follower, humble Ulfius, who is in rather considerable pain and does not, most devoutly does not wish to die on this night. Not after all the death he was already witness to.

His heart races. He hears running water, the soft murmur of a nearby brook. The ground rises. He stumbles over roots and stones.

'God!' he cries, in anguish. He kneels in the dirt. Surely he can go no more.

And so Ulfius prays in the words he was taught. 'Infinitely merciful as You are, it is Your will that we should learn to know You. You made heaven and earth, You rule supreme over all that is. You are the true, the only God; there is no other god above You.'

And for a moment, it is as though his God has heard. For a soft light shines ahead, and it illuminates a path! And Ulfius pushes himself up, and he staggers up the slope, and he comes to the mouth of a cave, carefully hidden in the mountain. And he smells fresh, soft grass and the air seems scented with beautiful flowers, and with a glad heart he enters.

'Sit the fuck down, Ulfius,' a voice says.

This is clearly not the word of the Lord.

Ulfius starts, for the light hurts his eyes after the darkness. A small fire burns within a circle of stones on the cave's floor, and next to the fire sits the king's wizard, Merlin.

He raises those pale and disconcerting eyes and examines Ulfius much as a frog might examine a fly.

'Why are you not at your king's side, Ulfius?'

Ulfius collapses heavily to the ground. He is so glad to be still, and for the warmth of the fire, and even, he realises with some surprise, for the wizard's presence.

'...It's a long story,' he says.

The wizard stirs the firewood with a stick, and sparks fly into the air.

'You're wounded,' he says.

'You're very observant.'

'Is the king alive?'

'...I do not know.'

Ulfius feels so very tired. He wants to close his eyes and sleep. To sleep forever – would that be such a bad thing? The priest, Father Matthew, spoke to him of Heaven, but will he be allowed inside its gates, all things considered? Or will he be sent... to that other place?

He reaches for the small iron cross round his neck, and the wizard turns from it sharply.

'Put that damned thing away!'

'Is it the cross that bothers you, or the iron?'

He doesn't much like the wizard, it has to be said.

'That shit isn't gonna heal you, Ulfius. But I will.'

The wizard checks Ulfius.

'Does it hurt here? Here? Here?'

'Ow! Ouch! Stop that!' Ulfius says.

'It looks like you've been cut by a sword.'

'I *have* been cut by a sword, you fucking unnatural *thing*!'

'Tut, tut,' the wizard says. 'Do you want me to help you or not?'

'Yes,' Ulfius says reluctantly. The Wizard pinches his skin along the open cut. Ulfius screams. The wizard brings the two folds of skin together and mutters something. He runs a finger along the join and it is like a burning blade, and Ulfius screams again, but the skin seals with a sort of burning smell.

'You'll have an ugly scar to match your ugly face,' Merlin says.

'Thanks. I guess...'

The wizard sits back down. Stirs the fire. Stares into the flames.

'*Why* weren't you there?' Ulfius says. There might be just the tiniest hint of reproach.

'I was called away.'

'At *this* time?'

'I was on the king's business!'

They both settle down into silence and staring at the flames.

'Do you happen to have some food?' Ulfius says.

'I don't eat much.'

'But *do* you have some f—'

The wizard tosses him a pouch. Ulfius opens it, extracts half a loaf of bread, a small hard cheese, a wizened apple. He doesn't complain. He eats.

'So it did not go well?' the wizard says.

'Not really.'

'Things got... messy?'

'You could say that again,' Ulfius says, with feeling.

They sit and stare at the fire.

'So are you going to tell me?'

'Where do I even start?'

'In the beginning,' Merlin says. 'That's usually good.'

'...Alright.'

Ulfius takes a deep breath.

'As far back as I can remember,' he says, 'I always wanted to be a knight.'

'You have to understand what it was like, Merlin. Growing up in Londinium like we did. We had nothing. My father was a fisherman, he died on the river. My mother took in washing and, when that didn't pay, men. You had to make a living. We boys learned to fish and catch game on the south side, and we kept a garden and some sheep. But there were too many of us and we were always hungry, and I never did have a taste for fish.

'My father, he had Roman blood. Back when he was alive he always spoke about the Old Country, like it'd meant something. He'd never even been farther than the Fleet. Then he drowned, drunk on his boat one time.

'So I learned there was an easier way to live. The local knights were the White Hill Gang. I used to see them every day, sitting outside their *popina*, drinking watered wine and nibbling on olives like they were back on the Aventine. That's in Rome. Even before I went over there one day to ask for a job, I always knew I wanted to be one of them. To me, being a knight was better than anything else in the world, better than being Caesar.

'To be a knight meant to *be* somebody! They had the swords and they had the attitude and they offered protection. There was no one you could turn to if you had problems – not the sad excuse of what was left of the Watch, not the king because we didn't have one. The knights provided order in a world that no longer had any. They weren't like anybody else. They did whatever they wanted, because they could.

'I wanted some of that for myself.

'The Black Knight of the White Hill Gang liked me. I was big and strong and I could use my fists. He had me do the occasional job for them, carrying stuff or bashing heads, whatever they needed. You have to understand, they were good Romans! They were from the Old Country, they did things the Old Country way. One time, my mother was crossing the road and a couple of the lads from down the street came and gave her a chicken. A whole chicken! You know why they did that, Merlin? It was out of respect.

'Anyhow, that's how I grew up. Then word spread around about Arthur – King Arthur, I mean, only he still wasn't king then – and the Goblin Fruit heist. I wasn't a made guy, I wasn't a knight and I knew the White Hill Gang wasn't going to make me any time soon. They were older guys and they did things the old way and they still believed in the Empire – they still believed in Rome. I knew there was no Caesar going to come back to Britain, there wasn't going to be no new governor in Londinium, no legions coming over to fight any more wars. It was just us, here.

'So I went to Arthur. I was one of the first to sign up. I wanted to be in *his* gang. *I* wanted to sit at the Round Table. He told us we were all equal sitting round it – it had no head, see.

'Then he pulled that stunt with the sword in the stone and killed the old Guv'nor... well, that's when I *knew* this was all going to happen for real.

'What?

'The cross? What about it?

'Brought up that way. It's not that unusual. Came over from the Old Country with the missionaries. They're all doing it back over there. Had a priest, Father Matthew, he taught me my letters, well, much as he could, anyway. I'm better at remembering things than writing them down. Handy with a sword, too.

'See, that's the thing. It ain't like the old days, when it was each knight to himself. I'm *serving* the Lord, doing this. This is God's work. I'm sure Arthur will see the light of truth, for it cannot be hidden under a bushel, as the Christ said.

'Blessed are those who hunger and thirst for righteousness, for they shall be satisfied. The Christ said that, too. Don't you see? That means *us*! It's alright to fight and murder as long as it's in the name of a higher power, as long as it's in the name of the Lord.

'You laugh at me, wizard. But your kind cannot know the true love of Christ.

'Anyway. All this you know already. The following few months were busy, of course. Arthur consolidated his power – much, I may add, with you whispering in his ear – and the other gangs all came under his domain. How quickly they bowed down to him! And most of all that loathsome Sir Hector.

'Arthur was now, truly, the new Guv'nor. He was the lord of Londinium.

'And were he content to be just that, all would be well. But of course Arthur wanted – deserved – more than that. He was king!

'I was there when you told him. How proudly you proclaimed his true inheritance! The long lost son of Uther Pendragon, and the child of Queen Igraine of Land's End! The hall was packed for your great reveal, and all the lords and ladies in attendance. Oh, they knew already, didn't they. They knew you of old, and all of your tricks, wizard. I see you do not deny it. Yet it is one thing to *know*, and another to *acknowledge*.

'His face! I will never forget his face. To know his mother was still alive! That he could see her! That longing, I believed, was genuine. But all the kings and lords assembled jeered and made a ruckus. So what if he were Uther's bastard child? they said. They were masters of their own domains. Arthur must respect the code. He has won Londinium – well, fair game to him. Let him rule Londinium. But they had made it very clear that any claim he may wish to make beyond was not to be discussed.

'Well... you know how that went with Arthur. Not well. Not well at all. So for the next few months we were doing drills and training – that Bors the Elder is a harsh master-at-arms, I can tell you that, wizard! – and then, at last, we were off.

'We were a proper army by then. At least, I think so. Most of us had been in plenty of brawls and what not, at least. But we weren't tested in real battle. Anyway. Arthur left Sir Kay to be his steward in Londinium, and his little pet wizard went off to – well, I'm sure I couldn't say. Perhaps you'd care to enlighten me, Merlin? Where *have* you been all this time?

'No? Alright, then. Keep your secrets, wizard. I won't pry. So what can I tell you? It was a glorious day when we set off, banners waving high, a company of men marching out of the gates and into history. Or so Kay told us. The truth was, Merlin, none of us really knew what was out *there*. Beyond the city, I mean. And it *was* strange, to begin with. All that open space, and the stars overhead each night, and, well, *birds*. I guess I had expected forests, thick and dark, but all we got to begin with were lovely, rolling hills, green with grass and pasture, and well-kept villages with children fat as geese running around, and maidens lovely beyond compare smiling shyly at us soldiers. I tell you true, wizard – more than one child will be born in these places who could claim a knight for his father in the coming months.

'The hunting was plentiful and the road pleasant. If there were brigands they kept clear of our company, and with good reason. Everywhere we went the king's banner led, and the villagers assembled to point and stare, and more than once we heard a voice raised in a cry of old – "Pendragon! Pendragon!"

'They remember, still, you see. They know a true king when they see one. And Arthur sat with their elders and their witches and spoke with and to them, and he must have been compelling, that or it was the number of our swords, for all swore their allegiance to him.

'So it went for some time, and perhaps we became a little lax. One night, crossing a brook, we were fired at. It happened in total silence, flaming arrows arching through the sky. The man beside me fell down dead with an arrow through his eye. We turned and turned, but we could see no enemy. Arthur became enraged, and screamed defiance at the sky, but only more arrows came and we had no choice but to run for it.

'We came back the next day and the corpses of our comrades were gone as though they had never set foot in that part of the world. Arthur's face told us nothing. Calmly he ordered us about our task, and it was only when we'd finished that I realised what he had done.

'First he had us pile stones and mud into the river. Laborious it was, and hot work besides, but at last it was done. We had made a good job of it, too. We had dammed the river and it would not flow through there again.

'Next we chopped down the trees. We tore out the flowers. The sound of hammers and axes rang that day under the clear blue sky. When it was done nothing remained of that place, yet still it was not enough for him. "Set it on fire," he said. "Burn it all."

'And burn it all we did.

'The flames rose high, wizard. They licked the sky itself, and the cloud of smoke and ash dispersed to all corners. Oh, they saw it alright, the pixies and lubberkins of the forest. And the rest, too. The fire marked our passing through that place.

'I see you know of which I speak. Very well. The rest of the journey was uneventful until we reached Monnow-mouth. The old Roman roads in truth were decent, all in all. And there in the town in the old fort of Blestium – I see you nod, wizard.

'Well, there were still men there loyal to his father. Once more the banner of Pendragon stood atop the fort. And once more a Pendragon climbed to the top, and there...

'I see you nod. You knew, didn't you.

'The decapitated head of Duke Gorlois.

'For near two decades it stood there on a spike. The wind lashed it and the rain pissed down on it and nature in all her glory did her best to reduce it to nothing. And still it sat there, glaring down on the land its owner tried to steal, and there is skin still on its skull and lips still with which to speak. And speak it does. Oh, how it speaks!

'It's maddened by now, that is certain. It is unnatural, wizard, no – it is ungodly.

'You laugh. But it's obscene to keep the spirit of a man locked up like that inside its rotting head. It screams at night. The screams kept us awake, and no birds fly above the fort of Blestium.

'It is wrong to keep a man from ascending to the Kingdom of Heaven. So I believe.

'You laugh at me. You mock, wizard. But the lord Jesus said that whoever wishes to slap you, turn also the other cheek to him. As I do now. But regardless. The king, Arthur, rose to the top of the fort and spoke long with the head of dead Gorlois. He let none of us come near, but I and some others were detailed to him and though we were far away we heard Gorlois' voice, for it carried. And this is what he said:

'"I see white sails and dark clouds, a storm on the horizon. Sea spray and crying birds, and a single boat, sailing on the sea towards a distant shore. I see your death, Arthur, son of Uther, son of filth and scum, born of rape and violence and lies. And I see worse for you. I see you *disappointed*. Uneasy lies the head that wears the crown. I see you jilted, boy. Does that surprise you? I see you cuckolded and betrayed by those you love, if you could ever be said to know love. Love has died inside you, I think, boy. And know this, too. You will die as you have lived, in empty violence. And you will rule, but only over this godforsaken island, this speck of dirt in a cold and filthy sea, far from the world stage, the poetry of Greece and the oratory of Rome, a savage king to rule a savage land. So fuck you, Arthur, just as I fucked your mother—"

'Here Arthur raised his sword, and silenced the head of Gorlois once and for all. Which is all the mad dead duke ever wanted, I reckon. The rotten old head split in two and burst like an overripe plum, and the stench of it was awful. I saw Arthur then. He leaned on his sword and he stared at the spike that held the head, and the skin was drawn tight on his skull. I had never seen so much hatred before, and it scared me, wizard. It scared me. For I knew then that he would be the true king, the one to rule over all of Britannia. It was the dead look in his eyes that day. I knew then he would let no one and nothing get in his way.

'We ate roasted pigeons that night, and they made the men sick. By then our numbers had swelled considerably. In every village we passed there were young men eager to join, and less eager to look after sheep. Can't say I blamed them, either. So by the time we'd arrived in Blestium we had over five hundred with us, plus camp followers of all sorts, petty traders coat-tailing for security, working girls and sweethearts picked along the way. I tell you, wizard, it takes all sorts to make a world, but it is hard to feed them.

'To tell you the truth, the king didn't seem to mind. He *wanted* them following. Wanted them on his side. He knew, you see. He knew what was ahead. Where we, foolishly, thought we'd already won, Arthur knew the war hadn't even *begun*.

'We were about to find out, though, weren't we, wizard. We were.

'On we rode, until we came at last to the castle.

'Dinas Emrys, of which it is spoken in legend and song. Where the clouds lie low over the rolling hills like the breath of a dragon. Where the nights are cold and clear like a king's purpose. Man. It must have been strange for him to arrive there where his father sat. But if so he did not show it.

'There was much to prepare. The steward was summoned, a Sir Fergus – you know of him, wizard? A minor character, by all accounts, yet the accounts he kept meticulously. Two working silver mines, he said, and a gold mine still about producing. One chest of coinage, eleven serving girls, a herd of sheep, and problems. He listed *those*, I tell you, Merlin. Brigands upon the roads and the tax collectors, one by one, assassinated. The mines still working skimmed the profits ruthlessly. Giants stole the sheep. The serving girls were past their best, the treasury's been depleted, the mice had eaten half the books – "Enough!" shouted Arthur. He ordered that his men be fed. We rode out to the hunt. The local men had tried to hide their sheep from us. Wizard, I'm afraid we did them an unkindness, but we were wary and the road was hard. That night the blood of animals ran all down the sides of the ancient hill in great rivulets and campfires burned again in Dinas Emrys. We drank late into the night and feasted merrily, the knights on choice cuts of the meat, the entourage on the entrails and leftovers. In truth, we all got disgustingly drunk. I tried some wine from Greece stored in the cellars, but it had gone bad long ago. The morning came, the sun rose true, we were a sorry mess.

'He put us right to work. The king had come to claim his kingdom. We did what we do best, wizard. We rode out with our swords and robbed the fuckers blind. We had to. For two decades they had got away without a tax, without a king's protection. We raided stores of grain and food, snatched maidens to replace the ones who still remained from Uther's time. We took their coin and jewels and then offered them payment if they came and worked for us. Arthur had stonemasons and carpenters brought in to fix the castle. The local boys and girls were welcomed in to hunt the rats and mice, and the new cooks were kept busy skinning and gutting the animals for supper. You should have seen it, wizard! The castle was alive again, bustling with the king and his knights and the assembled entourage grew larger every day. All sought the king's favour. His banner flew over the castle once again, and all the land around it was subservient to his will. The weavers worked tirelessly until their fingers bled, but new tapestries were hung, new lights burned, the old dungeon – ah, but I see you wince, Merlin! – the old dungeon was cleaned up, and gold and silver shone everywhere.

'It was beautiful, man. Though it was strange, too, I grant you, being this far from the city, with all that *land* around, and all that mist, and the people strange and surly, and the smell of the far sea in the air like the smell of bewitchment – a cold coming we had of it, in truth.

'But we had to make ready. We had to make due.

'For they were coming.'

26

'We were *prepared*,' Ulfius says. He stares with angry bewilderment at the wizard. The small fire hisses as Merlin adds damp logs onto the flames. The wind keens outside, and it seems to Ulfius that there are other voices lost within its sound. Sometimes he thinks he hears the cries of comrades, pleading mercy, begging to be shown the way. At other times he imagines something more unearthly, the cackle of mormos and baying of Gabriel hounds. He tries to shut the sounds away.

He thinks of clashing swords, the screams of dying men. The fire. He's cold. His side still hurts. He shifts in place and the pain flares up and he lets out a small cry.

'Quiet,' Merlin says.

He listens too, Ulfius sees. He listens to the wind.

'All manner of things are abroad tonight, and none of them friendly,' Merlin says.

'The king,' Ulfius says, 'I do not know if he's alive or dead.'

'Oh, he's alive,' Merlin says. 'He'd better be, or I'll kill him myself.'

That sudden fury in the wizard shocks Ulfius. He tries to make himself comfortable but the pain remains. He thinks suddenly that for sure he's dying. That Merlin's nursing witchery was but a trick.

'I don't feel well,' he says.

'You'll live.'

They listen to the wind. Bugaboos and Tom-pokers and witches and nisses. All manner of things are abroad on this night.

Ulfius touches the cross on his neck. 'All this will vanish, in time,' he says, his savagery startling even himself – a cold fury to match Merlin's. 'All this charmery and abomination, they will be wiped off the face of the earth as the word of Jesus rises. Brimstone and salt, and a fire burning, so that their seeds will no longer be sown nor grow again, like in the overthrow of Sodom and Gomorrah.'

He feels so *righteous* speaking these words. He wants them to hurt.

But the wizard sits back. His boyish face, so pale in the light of the fire, his skin drawn tight over his delicate bones, stares at him, and there's a spark in those unsettling eyes, as though now, and only now, Ulfius has finally, somehow, fully engaged the wizard's attention.

'I had heard these names,' Merlin says. 'The cities of the plain, they were called, were they not? It was said the god of the Hebrews sent down destruction from the heavens upon them.'

His mind is shrouded to Ulfius, but some dark design seems to be behind the question.

'Imagine such a weapon...' the wizard says.

'It was the will of God!'

'Aristotle argues that we are at the centre of the universe and all about us matter moves in uniform circular motions that are eternal. Yet the Stoics say the universe is an infinite non-physical void, the cosmos a gigantic oscillating sphere. And Empedocles specified that the universe shifts between the forces of philia and neikos, love and strife. I think I know enough of strife to know it is a powerful force. Don't you agree, Ulfius?'

'Yet what of love?' Ulfius says. He stares into the fire as though under a spell. What is he *doing* here, in this cave, how has it come to this? 'John the Apostle said that God is love, and whoever abides in love abides in God, and God abides in him.'

'I see no God here,' Merlin says. He moves his hand between the fire and the wall. The shadows dance and shift, become a rabbit, spider, wolf in quick succession. 'I see only nature. Can you say that you – and I don't mean this as a way to cause offence, Ulfius – but you as a dumb-as-shit city boy who until recently's not been farther than the fucking Cripplegate, *you* know all of nature and its secrets? You'd believe in a cameleopard or an elephantus, but not in magic? What *is* magic, after all, but the understanding and manipulating of nature?'

Ulfius can sense the wizard's anger, underneath the calmness of his voice. Another man, he'd nut right there and then, but not the wizard. He's like the one small boy no one would ever fuck with cause you knew he was crazy. He'd known boys like that, as small and meek as anything, who'd knife you in the eye and walk away still whistling. The cold ones were always the ones you had to watch out for.

He says, 'You twist your words to suit you.'

Merlin: 'That isn't magic, that's called *speech*.'

'Accept God's love or you will go to Hell!'

Merlin sits back. Smiles. 'So that's the catch?' he says.

'Say what you will, I know the truth of it. Accept the word of God or perish.'

'Everything *perishes*. We are but organised systems of atoms—'

'Spare me your *atoms*!'

They're at an impasse.

A howl tears the night.

The scream would curdle milk, it is a howl straight out of nightmare. Ulfius clutches the cross and begins to mutter a prayer. Merlin stands, as sinuous as a cat in motion. Goes to the cave's mouth and peers out. The howl comes again, closer.

Ulfius rises. He reaches for his sword. He is a knight and a Christian.

'Our Father who art in heaven, hallowed be thy name...' he whispers.

He goes to the mouth of the cave.

Peers out into the dark.

That howl again, tearing through the wind. The rain beats down. Far in the distance, lightning flashes. In its light Ulfius sees a hideous form, some vast and ungainly *thing* shambles past, screaming. It has too many mouths, too many tongues, too many lips.

Behind it comes a rider on a dark horse.

'Please,' the rider cries, 'come back to me, come back, come b—'

The lightning flashes. The two figures, like mimers, go past. The light fades. The howl fades.

In the next flash of lightning, they're gone.

'What was that?' Ulfius says.

Merlin says, 'One of my rare mistakes.'

They return to the fire. They sit wordlessly now. Ulfius' mind drifts. How glorious the castle had seemed, when they were done. A new dawn had broken over Dinas Emrys and the hills seemed washed afresh like laundry after the rain. Birds sang in the trees. They were ready.

When he begins to speak again, he isn't sure if it is to the wizard he is talking or merely to himself. He feels so drowsy.

He says, 'The first one to arrive was Conan Meriadoc.'

'It was three days to the council and the first king had just arrived. He rode into the castle like he fucking *owned* the place. Three hundred men in his retinue, and his banner flying high. He rode bare-chested, did Conan Meriadoc. His chest was tanned and glistened with his sweat. His hair was long. His teeth were rotten. Climbed off his horse with booted feet thumping on the ground of the courtyard.

"'I am here, you fuckers," he said, "now bring me something to drink!"

'So there was that. Towards evening the second arrived. Urien of the Old North, and a more savage fucker you would never wish to see. One-eyed he was, as thin as a snake and as leathery. He had but fifty men with him but each of them a backstreet hardened killer, the sort of footpads with smiles like slit throats. He had a raven with him, and more flew overhead. They came and settled on the gate posts and the towers, and none dared shoo them away.

'He didn't speak. He had a man to speak for him, and they asked for nothing, but camped outside the gates and made their own fires and chanted late into the night, and their fires smelled of damp leaves and bad magic. They took only bread and water from the kitchens.

'The next day Outham the Old, accompanied by a company of Franks. He was wrapped heavily in fur, and was cowled, and no man saw his face. He, too, spoke little, and he moved with care, but you could feel his eyes roam, checking out the battlements, the number of our men, the stores supplies, as though already calculating how long to starve us in a siege. I did not like him.

'Then Yder, with a hundred men and two giants in his retinue. Then Lot. At last the council was all but ready to begin. Arthur welcomed each of the kings personally, but otherwise kept to himself. All we were missing was Leir.

'I was in the new library when it happened. It was your order, wasn't it, Merlin? A king to be a proper king must have a library? And so we were sent out into the adjacent towns to raid their stores of manuscripts. A heap of trash! Roman romances and Greek pornography, bestiaries and grimoires. All to satisfy your lust for words! And nary a Testament to be found. Regardless. We had swelled the number of manuscripts and scrolls considerably, until an entire room that used to be a pantry was reserved for it. I was there, taking a moment alone, for I liked to pray, when he appeared, right out of nowhere. I swear it, it is true. The door was closed and there were no windows or hidden entrances and I was alone. Yet I turned, and there he was, a man browsing the manuscripts without a care. He turned to face me.

'"Plutarch's *Lives*," he said, "is really most excellent. Have you read it?"

'"No," I said.

'"A shame," he said. "You should. You are...?"

'"Ulfius."

'He nodded pleasantly. Replaced the scrolls back on their perch. "Well, shall we?" he said. "We might as well get this over with."

'"Excuse me?"

'"Oh, no," he said. "There is nothing to excuse."

'"Who the hell are you?" I said. "And how did you—"

'"Get in here?" He shrugged. "I just walked in."

'"No, you didn't," I said. "I'd have seen you."

'He smiled at that. "People usually see what they want to see," he said. "It's easy, really. You just have to follow in the margins, where they aren't looking. Now, let's go get this meeting over with. They *are* expecting me."

'"You're Leir," I said.

'"So now you're looking properly," he said. "Well done."

'And he threaded his arm through mine and out we went, as if for a pleasant stroll along the stream. He knew the way, too. Went down the corridors like he had a map of the castle all stored up in his head. Marched us right up to the throne room, where everyone was already waiting. Oh, how they turned when the doors opened and we came in. He took his place among them. Three to one side they sat, and three to the other across the long table, and Arthur on the old throne facing them all.

'Well, wizard, we all knew what was what. No one carried weapons, that was one. They left them at the door. For another, there wasn't a retinue. This was a high-level council, bosses only. Between the six of them and Arthur, they had the vast majority of Britain under their control.

'And so.

'No retinue, but that didn't mean no men. Security, see? Everything above board and proper. Yder had one of his giants. Outham two of his Franks. Urien had two nasty Northmen – well, you get the gist of it. Only Leir was alone. He looked amused, even a little bored, maybe. Like this was a game he'd stopped playing long ago. Like he could take every single fucker in that room *personally*, if he'd only wanted to. Giant included. He's a strange one, that Leir.

'So. As it happened I was assigned to guard duty, me and Agravain of the Hard Hand to act for Arthur. We all kept a respectful distance from the table, stood with our backs to the walls. Eyed each other. There were more than a few hands itching for a sword, I can tell you that. But business is business, and pleasure is pleasure, you know what they say.

'Arthur began. He looked good on that throne. Looked like it fit him. No jewellery on him, no rings, not even a crown. He was as you see him. He was what he was. And they all knew it. He said, "Welcome."

'They all murmured politely. Eyed each other, too, like we did on their behest. They were none of them friends, Merlin. Power does not have friends, and these men were power.

'"I won't waste your time," he said. "Some of you I know. Some of you I know of. You each of you control a significant territory. You each of you run protection, brothels, wine and Goblin Fruit – but so much more than that. Each of you control countless *lives*. You have farms and villages and fields and produce, roads and mines and workshops and goods. *Nothing* moves in your territory without you knowing about it. A child's not *born* unless you say, *It is so.*

'"I respect that. You got to where you are today by being smart, by being strong, by knowing when to kill a guy and when to make him happy. You know who you are.

'"And you know who I am.

'"Leir, you hold the ridings. The Brigantes answer to you. Urien, you control the Hen Ogledd, the whole north is yours before the wall. Well, you know who you are – and some of you knew my father.

'"My father's dead. I hold his lands now. I hold this castle and these parts and I claim Land's End. I rule Londinium. Do you contest this?"

'There were looks exchanged. Some mutters. But they nodded, every man of them. Accepting Arthur's claim. Accepting, thus, his right to sit at the table. But they did not look easy as they sat. They did not *trust* him.

'"Each of you, alone, is strong. But each of you *is* alone. And lone is *weak*. The world is *changing*, gentlemen!" His voice rose then, and his full fury hit them for the first time. They were not prepared for it. "The world is *changing*," he repeated, more softly this time. "Foreigners come. Angles and Saxons. Jutes. Rome was here. It had more power than any of you could ever dream of. It offered stability and trade. And it is gone. Forget Rome. Rome is dying. And a thousand lawless tribes beyond that thin strip of water that separates us from Europa are no longer waiting for their chance but *taking* it. They're crossing over. They want our land. They want our wealth. They want our women and our fields and our mines. And each of us, alone, will fall before them. Each of us, alone."

'He has a way with him, he has, Arthur, doesn't he? He knew their minds, you see. He knew just where they felt vulnerable. He stuck in the knife as you would in an oyster, and then, when he had their attention, he twisted. He wanted their pearls. He wanted *all* of their great big fucking pearls.

'"I want you to join me," he told them. Oh, that got their attention alright! Those heads whipped up fast and furious.

'"Alone, each of us is weak. But together we can be strong! Together, there can be no one to oppose us! Let them come *then*, and try to take us! For I tell you true, friends. As I look ahead, I am filled with foreboding. Like the Roman, I seem to see the River Tiber foaming with much blood." He was quoting Virgil, I think. Then he said, "Well, let them come! We'll drive them off the cliffs and let the sea wash away their blood! Join me, in a syndicatus, all of us, in it together! What do you say, gentlemen? I ask you, what do you say!"

'Oh, there were many looks exchanged. They knew, they must have known it was coming. But no one wanted to speak first. At last it was Leir. He looked up at Arthur, nodded. "Each of us here is a boss of bosses," he said. "Beholden to no man. Yes, there is wisdom in your speech, Arthur. Yes, our territories are threatened by the new arrivals. Though some of us see opportunity, not threat, in those. New markets, new ways. Some of us see profit. But regardless of that notion. It was the Roman, Gaius Sallustius Crispus, who said, concordia res parvae crescent. Small things flourish by concord. There is logic in your words, but, Arthur, is this to be a syndicate of equals? For even in Republican Rome, where the people were ruled by the vote of the bosses, there nevertheless had to be someone to sit at the head of the table. Much as, indeed, you sit now, as our host. So I shall ask you, Arthur. Is that your intention? Do you wish to be first among equals? Or do you wish even more? Your father—"

'"I am not my father!" Arthur said. "And I know nothing of Republican Rome, and I care even less. The Romans came, they went, they ate shit and they *died*. I am speaking to you of a syndicate of equals, with me at the head of the table, yes. You've had your time, Leir, you and the others, growing bloated and fat in your old dispensations. And you did nothing. You're old and you're weak and, without me, you'll die." He spoke with true venom then, and they scowled, and Conan Meriadoc slammed his fist on the table, but they were quiet when he spoke. "Choose life. Choose a home. Choose a great big fat palace to stuff all your money in. Choose a wench, any wench you please, to stick your old men's dicks in. Choose a sword, choose a horse, choose blood, because if you are not warriors you're nothing. Choose death. Choose life. Choose the fucking *future*."

'There was a silence then. And Conan Meriadoc raised that great big head of his and said, "And *you're* the fucking future?"

'But they already knew it. And Arthur did not need to answer.

'So there it was. The kings had been summoned – and they came. They had expected an offer – and he'd made it to them. It was the sort of offer you couldn't refuse.

'"Are you with me?" Arthur said. And one by one the bosses nodded, and one by one they stood up from the table, and left the room, their men on their heels.

'That night a feast was held in the castle grounds. Ewes and lambs were slaughtered, dormice were stuffed, pigeons were roasted, and the fires burned so bright that night became day over Dinas Emrys.'

27

'm cold,' Ulfius complains. The wizard stares at him across the dying fire. The first rays of dawn stain the sky outside their cave. Ulfius can hear strange little sounds in the deeps of the cave, like tiny rodents chattering to each other, and it makes him nauseous. They sound excitable, and hungry.

'You'll be fine,' the wizard says. He seems more energetic now, more full of life, as though the very act of hearing Ulfius' story has invigorated him somehow. 'So what went wrong?' he says now. Holds a small stick in his fingers and breaks off pieces one by one.

Ulfius stares at him in suspicion. 'You look like you already know, somehow.'

'Tell me. Consider me your... confessor. Did not your apostle, James, say, "Confess your sins to one another and pray for one another that you may be healed?"'

Ulfius' suspicion grows. 'I did not *sin*,' he says.

'So, what?'

'It was a ruse.'

'How so?'

And Ulfius remembers. The light of the flames. The clash of swords. That surprise attack, from within, from without. Remembers Yder's giants smashing in through the wall. Lifting people up like rag dolls and tossing them against the stones, bashing their brains in. Remembers the Northern men firing arrows, the whistle of arrows like deadly birds overhead. Remembers Conan Meriadoc's savages streaming in with their faces painted and blood lust in their hearts. Remembers the shouts – 'Fall back! Fall back!' – remembers rushing to the aid of his king.

'The six had made their plans in advance,' he says. 'They'd seen which way the wind would blow and formed a syndicatus of their own. They'd never have accepted a snot-nosed boy at the head of the table. They saw the logic of it – Leir spoke true. They *knew* that, alone, they'd fall. They knew they were better together. So they had hatched their plan, and came in peace to make war. I guess when you're a king no one tells you they're going to kill you, it doesn't happen that way. Your murderers come with smiles.'

'It was always a probability,' Merlin says.

'That's *it*? That's all you have to say?'

Merlin shrugs. 'You don't become a king by being honest,' he said. 'You come to the throne by force alone.' He licks his lips. 'And so?' he says.

'And so…'

'Fall back! Fall back! Protect the king!'

And the arrows coming down, and Elyan the White jumping on the back of one of the giants and slitting his throat with a sword that seemed as small as a dagger, and the Northern men silent like ghosts slaughtering everything in their sight, and a fire burning where the king's banner flew.

Ulfius ran. He ran to the castle, fighting his way through men who'd never see the light of the Christ, whose death meant nothing but dust and being forgotten. In a thousand years if people came and dug on the grounds of this castle, what would they find? Not even bones, perhaps. His sword flashed and he erased whole lives in mere seconds, fighting through the melee, falling back to serve his king. He saw Owain, the Bastard, and Agravain vanish down the long corridor to the throne room. But his own path was blocked. Conan Meriadoc's savages stood in his way, grinning with their awful, filed-down teeth. They were too many to fight.

Ulfius fled.

He would not tell the wizard that. What *could* he do? The fix was in. The king would live – or not. He whispered, 'Eli, eli, lama sabachthani?'

'This way, you fool!'

A door, open just a crack. A hand reached out and grabbed him, threw him inside and slammed the door. Then a knife was at Ulfius' throat.

'Be quiet and you'll live.'

'*Leir*,' he said.

The old man of the ridings cackled.

'I've had my eye on you, boy. You're not as stupid as the others. The Nazarene said, "I am the light of the world. Whoever follows me will not walk in darkness."'

'Sir?'

The pressure of the knife at his throat eased.

'I am saying, follow me, boy. The path you walk now leads to only one place, and it is down below.'

'You – a Christian?'

'I am… not unsympathetic.'

'Sir, I could never betray my king.'

'And I am not asking you. I am merely offering you a way out of here. Or I could take your life right now and be done with it. Have I got you wrong, boy?'

'My name is Ulfius.'

'And my name is legion.'

'You dare quote scripture?'

'Yes – or no, Ulfius? Think quickly and speak true.'

'…Yes.'

The knife left his throat.

'Then come! I tried to reach the throne room stealthily to end the little fucker earlier, but someone else had set... protections on the place. Another time, then! Now let's get out of this shithole.'

He followed King Leir. It was as though he'd been enchanted. The fear – and shame of his betrayal. Abandoning the king. Yet he could do nothing! The throne room was barricaded, and outside the door waited only his doom.

He followed Leir.

'Oh, God!' he said.

'Hold your nose if you're so squeamish,' Leir said.

Into the shitter they went.

It overflowed with crap and piss and – blood now, from above. Ulfius threw up. Leir grimaced, but said nothing. Down into the aqueduct they went.

'Roman engineering!' Leir said. 'Say what you want about the Romans, they knew how to build.'

Crouched low, they followed the ancient tunnel. Swimming in the shit. Ulfius could not breathe. He could not think. He could not pray.

He would die down there in the shit, in the blood.

He would die down there, and his soul would be lost forever.

He would d—

Then came light, and fresh air. He emerged after Leir, choking and wheezing, into a night lit in the distance by flames.

Dinas Emrys was on fire.

Ulfius threw up what was left in his stomach. A thin drizzle of bile. He stared about him, a lost soul.

'Give yourself a wash in the first stream you come to,' Leir said. 'You'll be alright after that.'

Ulfius turned to him. How old was Leir? How many decades had he ruled his manor? It was impossible to tell.

'Remember this night, Ulfius,' Leir said. 'And remember who gave you your life. There is a debt now.'

'And you my creditor?'

'Did you ever think it was going to be different?' Leir said. He almost sounded sad. 'This is the life we choose, Ulfius. And you chose life.'

With that he turned and, in moments, he was gone into the dark. Ulfius stood there alone, blinking after him. Leir had an uncanny knack for disappearing.

But there was no use dwelling. He wasn't safe yet.

And so he ran.

'I could not reach Arthur in the frenzy of the battle,' he says now. 'I led a force of knights against Outham's Franks but we got separated and my comrades were slaughtered. I tried to find my way back and got lost. As I wandered away, searching for help, I was set upon by two of the Northern men.'

He touches the wound at his side, and winces. This part is true.

'I killed them both, but I thought surely I would die now. How long I wandered I do not know. Then you found me.'

The wizard's pale eyes are disconcerting. The fire's dead. Outside, dawn breaks at last.

'...Alright,' Merlin says. He stirs himself. 'Well, you did all you could, and no one could ask more of you, I'm sure, Ulfius. Now get some rest. The battle's past and the day is newly born. I'll stand guard and wait for news.'

'Are you sure?'

But he is so very tired, he does not wait for the wizard's reply. Ulfius curls up on the cave floor. In moments he's asleep.

Merlin watches him. In the shadows, at the back of the cave, the same chitinous sound begins again. He'd heard them all night, and he knows that they are hungry.

He waits.

The creatures creep out of the shadows, some forgotten abominations out of an age that knew not man. With pinchers and mandibles they click their way to the prone Ulfius. They're a little like crabs and a little like rats. They begin to lap at the psychic spillage from the sleeping knight.

So much there to feed on, Merlin thinks. Holy faith, ugly betrayal, the philia and neikos of a thousand bad choices.

Love and strife, to make the world go round.

PART FOUR

THE SUMMER COUNTRY

28

But where is Merlin in all that time?

I did as you asked, my lord. I followed the fairy paths to the barrows of the fucking elves. I jumped off the end of a rainbow and plunged into the icy water of Puck's puckered pool. And all for a weapon.

The wizard stares out of the cave mouth.

Dirty dawn smears the skies.

Are you alive yet, my lord? Or did the six dispatch you to the ghost roads?

A shining isle out of a blackened sea, and a small boat, and white sails.

A terrible silence.

No, the wizard thinks. It's not your time.

Well, then.

At first, Londinium.

There is a place where these kind of things tend to congregate. It's out just beyond the city walls, perched on the water by a muddy bank. A shack of clay and straw, sitting on stilts, a sign swings from a beam and says, *The Grindylow*.

No one goes there. When people pass it they avert their eyes and spit three times, and no one whistles till they're well clear of it. There are no windows and a single chimney coughs out black-lung smoke.

Merlin slides in.

He perches on the bar. A deer woman by the fire stirs a pot and scratches at her antlers. She glances over, nods.

'What will it be, Merlin? Got Water of Lethe or Dionysian wine.'

'...A beer.'

He sits there sipping from his cup and thinking mathematics. The six kings are ranged against his lord and they have numbers on their side. More men, more arms, more territory. To live, his master must wage war. To *win*, he has need of a weapon.

It's never early and it's never shut at The Grindylow but there's not many people about just at this moment. Three boggarts at a table playing dice and drinking sour milk; a shug shelling hazelnuts by himself in a corner; an ogre feeding angrily on... Well, it is better not to look too closely at the smallish corpse. It gauges out eyes and pops them like a delicacy, it rips off an arm and gnaws on the fatty tissue.

Things of the dark, these creatures of men's mind. They have no place out in the sun. Merlin sips his beer, nibbles on a plate of fungal dead man's fingers from the deep forests of Rutland.

A ferryman slides into The Grindylow and onto a seat and chooses Water of Lethe. He places his lantern on the bar and stares into its steady flame. From somewhere, the Seikilos epitaph begins to play, an old Greek melody played on hidden strings, and Merlin whispers along with the tune, 'While you live, shine, have no grief at all, life exists only for a short while and time takes its toll.'

'What brings you in here, Merlin?' the ferryman asks. He doesn't take his eyes off the flame in his glass. 'You hate the night creatures even more than you hate yourself.'

'They are nothing but shadows,' Merlin says, 'when the sun rises again over the West it shall burn them away into nothing.'

'Superstition is merely the child of fear,' the ferryman says. 'And fear is a condition of being human. If you expect an Enlightenment to occur centuries hence you are sure to be disappointed, wizard.'

'Haros, why do you drink?'

'I drink,' Haros says, 'to forget.'

'Forget what?'

'Forget that I'm drinking.'

Haros smiles a thin-lipped smile at his own joke. Merlin looks at him sideways. He thinks of a vision he saw nearly two decades past. A fireball flaming low on the horizon, falling down to earth, a cloud the shape of a mushroom on impact. Others saw a dragon, he saw a star, or something else, he knew not what. That year there was no summer. In the years since he has searched for the site of the meteorite strike without luck.

He dares not ask for it openly.

Instead he says, 'Have you had word of Nimue recently?'

'The Lady of the Lake can usually be found where water is,' Haros says.

'You could say the same fucking thing about ferrymen.'

'Ah, but for us it's a job,' Haros says. 'For the lady it's her nature.'

Merlin accedes the ferryman's point.

'So, where?' he asks.

'Am I the lady's keeper?'

'You are a ferryman and ferrymen know water like your mother knew dicks, which is to say, intimately.'

'You really are a rude little cunt,' Haros says, but he says it without malice.

'Is she still dealing arms?'

'Do boggarts eat shit in the woods?'

A sudden silence in the bar. From the corner – 'What did you say, ferryman?'

'You heard me.'

The three boggarts rise. They flash dull copper knives.

'You sure you want to make a thing of it?' Merlin says calmly.

The ferryman doesn't stir from his seat and his gaze remains fixed on the light held captive in his lantern. But his shadow grows around him, and its outline is not entirely human. The shadow lengthens and becomes a darkened pool, and waves lap at the shore where the three boggarts stand as on a precipice, about to fall.

The boggarts stare.

'Ain't worth the fucking trouble,' one says at last, and spits. 'Let's split, boys.'

'It's like they let just anyone in here nowadays.'

'Really gone downhill, The Grindylow. Let's go steal some spoons and hobble dogs.'

'Fucking ferrymen.'

The boggarts vanish. Haros smiles that little tight-lipped smile. Motions the deer woman to refill his glass.

'Fucking boggarts,' he says.

'Nimue,' Merlin says patiently.

'Oh, I don't know, Merlin. Caledonia, last I heard, in some freezing backwater lake, trading swords with the local hicks. Didn't she lock you up in a crystal cave once?'

'That was a long time ago.'

'Patch it up since, then?'

'We have an understanding.'

'Well, good luck.' Haros downs his drink and stands. 'I'll be seeing you round, Merlin.'

'See you, Haros.'

Then he, too, is gone. The ogre's finished his meal and left earlier, leaving behind him a small pile of bones and a tip. The shug in the corner's asleep. The bar's quiet.

'Nimue, Merlin?' the deer woman says. She polishes a mug with a piece of dirty cloth. 'If you ask a ferryman all you get is gossip and lies. By this time tomorrow word will be everywhere.'

'So?'

'I thought you conducted your business in a more circumspect way.'

Merlin sighs. 'I just want to know where she is.'

'Fairyland,' the deer woman says.

'Oh for fuck's sake,' Merlin says. 'Really?'

The deer woman shrugs.

'I hate that fucking place.'

'Well, then you're out of luck, wizard.'

'Why did it have to be Elfland?'

The Summer Country. It has so many names for a place that isn't even *real*. It's just a twilight world, conjured up by humans when they're dreaming. *People* cannot go there consciously. It's but a glimpse, sometimes, when they're asleep or close to death. The place where bogies live and wills-o'-the-wisp light the way. It's where ferrymen ferry their barges.

People can't go but Merlins can.

It's just that this Merlin doesn't really want to.

'Why there?' he says at last.

'A convocation of the ladies of the lakes and streams,' the deer woman says. 'You know what they're like when they get going.'

'And you are sure? Nimue is there?'

'Just what I heard, wizard. Take it or not, it is up to you.'

Merlin tosses a handful of porthmeion coins on the bar. Burial money, death coins that serve as the fee for ferrying. Regular coins don't count in this particular bar.

He says, 'For services rendered.'

'Bring your master sometimes,' the deer woman says.

'Thought you didn't serve mortal-kind.'

'For a king I will make an exception.' She gives him a leer. 'Besides, they say he's hung like a Greek war elephant.'

'A dick's a dick, when all is said and done. One is much like another.'

'Oh, Merlin. I think you really do *worry* about him, don't you?' the deer woman says. 'That's sweet. I heard he's off to council with the kings. Word to the wise – those boys play dirty.'

'No shit, Serena.'

'Well, good luck,' Serena says. 'Come back sometimes, why don't you.'

'I will.' He reconsiders. 'You hear a lot, don't you?'

'This and that.'

'You ever hear of a falling star? It would be somewhere on this island.'

Her face closes. 'One shouldn't meddle with the stars.'

'I'm only asking.'

'Be careful what you ask, then.'

'Is that a warning?'

'Take it as you will.'

She tries to tell him something without saying. He nods.

'Thanks, Serena.'

Gets up to leave.

'See you, Merlin.'

The deer woman returns to her scarab stew.

Merlin departs. He just needs to find a temple.

29

'You've *got* to be shitting me,' Merlin says.

He's found a temple to old Moccus, the god of pigs. It is beyond the great bend in the river, east of Londinium. A wild land with wild horses running in the marshes, and no people for miles, nothing but a great barren silence, and reeds, and mud, and larks or whatever birds they are.

He likes it.

The temple's been abandoned for a century at least. It's really nothing more than a stone altar that, in all honesty, could have been just a rock.

But Merlin can sense it. The residue of worship in the old stone and the trees. People had come here. They had prayed. They poured their hopes and fears and dreams into this air, they murdered pigs here and the hot blood spilled and stained the ground. It's in the roots and in the bark. Its faith. He *smells* it.

The way to Fairyland is easy. Just walk around the temple widdershins three times. Only he's done it, now – and nothing happened.

'Come *on*!' Merlin says.

He tries it again but the road, stubbornly, refuses to open. Usually there'd be a soft suffused glow, some reddish outline, the sky would flatten and his ears would pop but... nothing.

He tries it again and now he can *feel* the resistance, like something or someone fighting to keep the doors closed against his transgressing.

'What the fuck!' Merlin says. He lifts a yew branch and knocks heavily, making an ungodly racket in that other place.

'What!' a voice says. A Jenny Greenteeth emerges out of the canopy of the tree and crawls head first down the trunk. She stops at head height and hisses at him. A spider flops out of her hair, starts to fall, then stops on the end of a rope of silk and starts climbing back up.

'I was asleep,' the Jenny says. Her hair is mussed. Her eyes are puffy.

'Apologies, mistress. But the road is blocked.'

'A Merlin, are you? Such a dainty little creature. Climb up to my tree and you can be my supper.'

'I do not think so,' Merlin says.

'My, my. So touchy. Well, what is it you want?'

'The road, Mistress Greenteeth. It's blocked.'

The Jenny hisses. She twists her neck and sticks her head up in the canopy. She rummages. Returns.

'Not to me it ain't,' she says.

'What does that mean!'

'It means fuck off, you little weasel. The road is closed. Begone with you. Shoo. Shoo!'

The spider trembles on the end of its rope. The Jenny Greenteeth flicks her tongue and catches it. She chews and swallows.

'Well? Are you still here?'

Merlin stares at her, perplexed. He tries again. The Jenny watches. Cackles. Merlin can feel the road resisting him. The path remains blocked. He shrugs.

'Who doesn't want me going?' he says.

'Who does!' the Jenny says, and farts. She starts to laugh.

'I'll just have to go the long way,' Merlin says.

'Stubborn little thing, aren't you,' the Jenny says. She sticks her tongue out at him, then climbs back up the tree and disappears. He hears her rustling up there, then a silence.

Fine.

He'll do this the hard way.

Transformed into a crow he flies across a darkening skies. Merlin speeds away from Londinium until the city vanishes from sight, and the island spreads out before him.

His home. The contours of its coasts are the walls of his existence. Merlin is bound to the land, the sea around it is his gaoler and womb. He dreams, sometimes. He dreams of Constantinople where they say a thousand thousand books are held in the Imperial Library, where they say the Emperor's palace has fabulous automatons of hummingbirds and flowering trees. Merlin dreams of mechanics and artifice. He dreams of sunny Athens where mathematicians congregate like flies. 'I wish everything was mathematics,' said Marinus of Neapolis. Merlin dreams of prime numbers, which are infinite and mysterious; their correlation, if it exists, might reveal a deeper underlying reality.

This is what they don't understand, these people among whom he lives. Mathematics *is* magic. And he, a man of learning, cannot leave this island – but why must he, when in contemplating the infinite he is truly free. He could be anywhere, even locked up in a crystal cave, like that shithole Nimue once trapped him in, when they'd had that disagreement – she was fucking him at the time in exchange for his teaching her Greek mathematics. Ancient history, anyway. He had no beef with her now. She knew her Euclid.

He just wishes sometimes he'd been born in a different time and in a different place. He often thinks about the future and what it might look like. More of the same, perhaps. Strongmen and warlords with the might of the sword, holding on to power, by force alone.

Perhaps. But Merlin likes to imagine impossible things, machines that can fly and medicines that heal, tall buildings that reach for the skies, pictures that move and talk by themselves and tell *stories* – it's *all* magic, man! he thinks to himself. But that's not to say it's impossible.

Now he flies as the sun sets over Britannia, and down below he can see the world in the twilight of its cycle. The fairy roads shine white as they criss-cross the land and fade into the distance that is that other place. He sees the hill figures come alive then, their ghostly geoglyphs outlined in chalk – the naked giant on a hill with his erect penis, the wild man with his staves, and all the white horses, and the stags and giants. Who put them there, who carved them into hillsides far and wide, he doesn't know, but they have magic in them too, or maybe you could call it art. He's not sure what's the difference.

He needs something old, to start with. Something old and something new, something borrowed, something blue. The crow flies fast, the sun goes down, a flight of goshawks swoops high in the distance, notice him – give chase.

Merlin dives, the goshawks follow, their talons flash, their plumage startles, the fuckers have the blood lust and Merlin is their quarry.

He swoops, dives, rises, but you cannot outfly a goshawk, and the fucks are *sticky*. They don't let go of prey.

Then he spots it, low on the horizon – an ancient long barrow from some vanished tribe, half-hidden with the grass growing around it, but distinct enough, and old, and he can *taste* it. People died and were buried in the stones and there's a path that opens there if you have eyes to see it.

He swoops, he dives – the fucking goshawks follow, close on his tail. They're so silent and all he can hear is the wind. He dives to the old barrow where people have died and were buried long before Romans came. The goshawks are so close, a talon slices at his wing and Merlin tumbles. He rights himself but spirals, falling. Down and down towards the ancient tomb, something old and something new—

'Oh, fuck this,' the crow says. He twists mid-air and grabs the nearest goshawk in a hug and pummels down onto stone, the goshawk first, its skull bashed in, new blood on old stone—

Merlin falls through into the other place.

He turns back into a man in the ruins of the temple. Not ruins, exactly, and not a temple, either – it's nothing but a folly, the fae love nothing more than old and ruined things, they litter Fairyland with faux-antiquity and garish architecture. They have no class, the wizard thinks. Fairyland is peopled by the creatures of man's imagination and, as such, they have no imagination of their own.

He looks around. A blood moon peers down from behind a shroud of clouds. *Cheesy* is the word that comes to mind. He's somewhere on the outskirts of Fairyland, he thinks. A shining path emerges through the thicket, leading further on. The branches of the trees screech-scratch against each other like bony fingers. An owl hoots. He hears the sound of bubbling water in the distance. It's cold and damp and dismal.

Fucking Fairyland, he thinks.

30

There is always a Fairyland. There has been one around for as long as there have been people. It is the twilight realm where dreamers go in dreams, the place that children see when they awaken in the dead of night. It is the place where ghosts and ghoulies come from.

In this place the ghosts of vanished hominids still roam, the early nomads who predate humanity, who for a time lived with modern humans and interbred with them, and died. In this place the spirits of stoneworkers still chase megaherbivores and giant birds they'd since hunted into extinction in the other place, the one that people live in. The world of Fairyland is but a dull reflection of the real world, containing all its ghosts and echoes, the shards of memories and dreams.

It is a shithole, Merlin thinks. But he shrugs his shoulders and he marches onto the road, figuring whoever's tried to block his entry might have forgotten about this one.

An enormous wooden club with studded iron spikes swings at his head. He ducks – it whooshes over and a stench he should have noticed explodes in his nose.

Two giant figures step out of the foliage and block the road. Two ugly mountain-creatures, knobbly and hairy, their skin like melted wax, their eyes like nasty little blackbirds' eyes. They grin. Their teeth could grind a femur into dust.

'Merlin.'

'Fancy running into you here.'

Fucking trolls. How much he hates the fucking trolls.

'Grendel,' he says, 'and Mami Grendel – what brings you both this far into the sticks?'

'What do you think, magician?'

'Care to venture a guess?'

They leer. Their clubs are deadly, and so are they. Two nasty trolls-for-hire, but they are not usually found this far from the court.

He measures out his options. They block the road. He knows their strength. He says, 'Who sent you, then?'

'You know we never divulge the name of a client.'

'And we always carry a job through.'

'I'm hungry, Mami. Can I eat him?'

'Wizards are bad for your digestion, Grendi.'

'But Mami!'

'Besides, we like our Merlin, don't we, boo? We have no wish to hurt him.'

The trolls smile. There is nothing, Merlin thinks, as ugly as a smiling troll.

'Was it Morgan?'

He thinks it must be. Morgan has her own designs on Arthur. She hungers for the power, same as him. She thinks Londinium is hers and doesn't like that Merlin's gaining influence. With Merlin out of the way she could have Arthur for herself.

'I'm sure I couldn't say—' from Mami Grendel.

'How goes it in the world of mortal men?' asks Grendel.

'Same old, same old. You should visit sometimes.'

Grendel frowns. 'I don't like them,' he complains. 'They're always trying to fight me and Mami.'

'Mami and *I*,' his mother corrects him.

'I'm not sure that's...' Merlin says, and then gives up. He reconsiders. 'I could use a couple of goombahs like you,' he says. 'If you seek employment.'

'We have a job,' Mami Grendel says.

'*You're* the job,' Grendel says. 'Now, do we bash your head in, or will you be sensible and fuck off back to England?'

Mother and son grin at each other.

'You're in my way,' Merlin says. 'And I fucking hate trolls.'

When Mami Grendel moves it's like a mountain shaking. The smiles drop and the clubs come out in force. They swing at him and Merlin turns into a mouse and skitters between their legs and onto the road.

You can't *fight* trolls, he thinks, but they *are* dumb as shit.

'Where did he go, Mami? He was here a moment ago.'

'Fucking wizards,' Mami Grendel says.

The trolls turn this way and that.

But Merlin's already far away.

The road crosses boggy marshes where small dead bodies float – a stoat, a vole, a brace of rodents, all lying gutted on their backs, their empty eye sockets staring at the sky. The stars rise over Fairyland, the constellations are unlike the ones above the earthly plane. Merlin sees the Swift, Old Lady Death, The Dice and Gallows and the Hummingbird. He wishes he was closer to the centre. The air smells foetid, dank with rot and reeds, to turn from the road is to be left behind. In Fairyland there is no real death, you just become part of the scenery.

It's proper cold and shitty here. By all the gods who ever lived and died he hates this fucking place.

Crows and ravens cry overhead. Shooting stars fall, far in the distance, a shower of sparks. The moon leers down on Merlin.

At last he comes to the edge of a forest. Here the road peters out into the dark and its light fades. Merlin steps, uneasily, into the trees.

This is the Weald.

Its ancientness is misleading. The Weald is timeless. Its trees were never born and never die. Its darkness is as thick as that black viscous rock oil the Greeks call petraoleum. The mosquitoes and bloated black flies that haunt its air are creatures of necromancy and all its thorns are poisoned.

Merlin curses, but quietly. He has very little actual power in this place. The enchantment of the Weald is young as time and old as human dreams, and it predates him.

He'll have to step carefully, he thinks, and hope not to be seen.

Whoever set him up, he thinks, they've been doing a good job of it.

He wonders how long it's been, and how King Arthur's faring. He did not mean to be away so long, the king is on his way to council and time flows differently in Fairyland. It could be months, or years if he's not careful.

The Weald surrounds the heart of Fairyland like a crown of thorns. As Merlin walks through the trees he tries to make marks of his passing. A dropped pebble, a piece of string tied to a branch, a sigil scratched into the bark. But it's no real use. The Weald erases everything, he could be walking in an endless circle.

The ratio of a circle's circumference to its diameter is a universal constant.

The Egyptians and Babylonians knew this, the Greeks called it Archimedes' Constant.

Merlin tries to think. These numbers do not, cannot change. Such things have power here. The square root of two is an irrational number. The Babylonians first recorded a calculation of it. The followers of Pythagoras the Greek discovered the number's irrationality and for a time kept it a closely guarded secret. They say Hippasus was murdered for divulging it.

Merlin whispers, 'One plus twenty-four over sixty plus fifty-one over sixty to the power of two—'

Is it his imagination or do the trees spread out, is it getting lighter, far ahead?

'Ten over sixty to the power of three—'

It has to be Morgan, he thinks. *She's always been a jealous bitch. What is she up to now?*

He treads so softly. Branches catch his clothes, tear at his face. The forest whispers, hungry.

There! Something moving in the trees. A flash of white. He loses caution, gives it chase. The roots attempt to trip him.

Gone. He finds himself again in darkness. Turns round and round.

'Boo!' a voice says.

Merlin jumps.

A woman comes floating into his bubble, holding a lantern with a captive will-o'-the-wisp. The will snarls inside its cage of glass, in Fairyland its true shape is revealed, a nasty little creature full of claws and teeth. It hisses at the wizard.

The woman has no face. It's just a smooth and featureless skin mask, and she doesn't walk but floats above the ground. It's just another Woman in White, the damn Weald is filled with the infernal creatures.

'Did I startle you, Merlin?'

How she talks without a mouth. It's like a particularly upsetting ventriloquist act. They say the priestess of Apollo in Delphi spoke in this way. *Gastromancy*, its practitioners call it. Nothing wrong with a bit of stage magic, Merlin thinks with only slight distaste.

'Do I know you?'

'I know of you,' the White Lady says. It's said they are the ghosts of jilted lovers, or – well, who knows. The Lady shimmers close, she runs her bloodless fingers through his hair. He jerks away.

'Word spreads,' the Lady whispers. 'The great magician in the world of mortal men, who has the ear of kings. Is it true what they say about Arthur?'

'I don't know, what do they say?'

'That he is hung like a Greek war elephant.'

'What is it with you fiends!'

The Lady laughs. 'Take me with you back to that other world,' she says, 'and I could help you.'

'Help me how?'

'I could show you the way. All you have to do is turn back.'

'Then what the fuck do I need you for?'

The Woman in White gives a growl of rage.

'Then fuck you, wizard!'

She swings the lantern in an arc and hits him in the face. The tiny door opens and the will springs out. It jumps on Merlin's face, hissing and snarling, gouging out skin. The Lady laughs.

'He's over here!' she cries. 'He's over here!'

'Shut *up*!'

He grabs the will and smashes it against a root until its tiny brains spill out. Merlin tries to stand but the roots twist and try to grab him. He kicks and staggers like a drunk. This fucking place! he thinks.

The White Lady starts to laugh. It is the sort of sound to make dogs howl and babies cry and grown men piss themselves.

'Fuck you, Merlin,' she says. And then she's gone, like that.

And then he hears it.

Far away, but moving fast.

A hunting horn.

He says, 'Oh, *fuck*.'

Merlin runs. He stumbles on gnarly roots. Branches tear at his hair and clothes. Mosquitoes buzz. A blood-red moon shaped like no earthly moon shines down yet illuminates no path. Far in the distance, the hunting horn again.

Followed by the baying of hounds.

He hears them coming. The hounds streaking through the forest. The ghost-men fanning out on their steeds. He hears them crunch through broken twigs, he hears their calls, he hears the barking of the dogs.

It is the Wild Hunt.

Merlin mutters pi. Pi is an irrational number, only such numbers hold power in an irrational place. and it is transcendental, which seems appropriate. And it is infinite, just like the Weald.

Archimedes the Greek developed a formula for calculating an approximation of pi. Merlin whispers, 'Three point one four one five nine—'

The moon loses its red aspect, for a moment ordinary white light shines through. The trees are revealed for the tawdry fakes they are, this simulacrum, this backdrop to a mummers' play.

A giant horse leaps over Merlin, and in the moonlight he sees its rider's face. Herne the Hunter, with his head bearing twisted stag's antlers, his shout of triumph at having startled his prey.

'Fuck off, Herne, not now!' Merlin screams. Then the dogs are upon him, and he screams curses at them. Ahmes the Egyptian was the first mathematician to put his name to paper. Merlin screams Egyptian fractions at the dogs. The dogs lose their substance and become as thin as ghosts. A road appears, a road of moonlight, and he steps onto it.

Herne the Hunter blocks his way.

'Merlin, Merlin, Merlin…' he says. 'You always were a stubborn little shit.'

'Who sent you, Herne? Just give me a name!'

The hunter shrugs.

'Was it Morgan?'

'Does it matter, wizard? The way is closed. Go back or…' Herne the Hunter shrugs again, almost apologetically. 'The dogs are hungry,' he says.

'The dogs,' Merlin says, 'are fucking ghosts.'

'That is unkind, if not untrue,' the hunter says.

'Come on, man. Just step aside. I need to get through.' Merlin feels so terribly tired.

'You know I can't do that.'

'Two,' Merlin says. 'Three. Five. Seven.'

'What are you doing?'

'Eleven. Thirteen. Seventeen.'

'Stop it!'

The stag-headed hunter shudders. The dogs bray beyond the road. The light strengthens. The hunter and the forest lose definition.

'Give me a name.'

'Fuck off, Merlin.'

The hunter reaches for his bow. Merlin smiles, nastily.

'Nineteen, twenty-three, twenty-nine,' he says. Prime numbers *are* magic, to understand their correlation would be to understand creation itself. 'Thirty-one. Thirty-seven.'

'Stop!'

'Never fuck with a wizard, you stag-headed prick.'

The hunter's little more than fog and mist now. The arrow that he nocks and shoots does little harm.

'Forty-one,' Merlin says.

He blows.

The whisper of air from his lips disperses the Wild Hunt and the Weald. It erases the forest, the road, the dogs and Herne the Hunter.

They're all gone.

The sun shines down.

At last, he is through.

31

Not that the real Summer Country's much of an improvement.

The sun is small and its light lacks warmth and it is freezing there. The plants are stunted and the trees are bare, their branches black and twisted, and it rains a lot. There are puddles everywhere and no good roads. What Fairyland needed was the Romans, but the Romans never had much time for other people's make-believe. They just stuck their own temples where other people's temples were, co-opted rituals and renamed local gods and that was that – welcome to the Empire. In truth it mostly worked for everyone, other than the druids and the Christians.

And, well, he supposes, the Jews. He wonders if the Jews have their own version of this place.

But he can't muster much enthusiasm for theological considerations right at this moment. He stops and takes a piss against an ancient ash tree. As he finishes a tiny gnome leers at him from underneath a flower, sticks out her tits and roars with laughter. He kicks, half-heartedly, and she vanishes.

Lizards scuttle under rocks as he walks past. A raven caws. Everywhere in the distance are ruined buildings. The fae love ruins like a pimp loves whores and wolves like blood.

From somewhere in the distance, the sound of hand bells and bone flutes.

Great.

Another bloody party.

He wends his way through the debris of dreams to the palace of night.

It towers out of the marshy ground. Crooked towers with curious extensions, like several types of fungus growing out of a rotting tree. The whole edifice wrapped carefully in mist, and somewhere a bell peals, and somewhere a raven cries, and somewhere a door opens and a voice says, 'Oh, Merlin, it's you.'

He stands there on the threshold of the castellum of the fae. This is the House of High Dudgeon. This is the seat of power, hosting the Unseemly Court.

A tiny fairy buzzes by his shoulder and tries to bite him and he shoos her away. Looks at the servant.

A young man, like all the servants here. Some fool who fell in love with a creature of this land and followed her. Or some fool who fell asleep on a cold hill's side. Or some dying soldier who woke to see the most beautiful face he'd ever seen, and would have followed its owner everywhere, even unto the spirit roads.

Merlin tries to remember if this one has a name.

'Rodarchus?' he tries.

'So you remember,' the boy says.

'Sure, sure,' Merlin says. Did they fuck? He has no idea.

'Well, I suppose you want to come in.'

'That I do, Rodarchus.'

'Are you expected, Merlin?'

'Expected? I rather think not.'

'Well... I suppose you could come in regardless.'

'I suppose I could. Are the ladies in session?'

'They are.'

'Been at it long?'

'A while.'

'Know which of them tried to get me barred from Fairyland?'

'I am sure I couldn't say. A beverage?'

'Excuse me?'

'Would you like a beverage.'

'I don't know,' Merlin says. 'What have you got?'

'Mulled wine, honeyed wine, watered wine, beer?'

'I don't know...'

'A nice cup of hot water infused with medicinal herbs, perhaps? Mint is nice.'

'Do I look sick to you?'

'I could put some cow milk in it...'

'What the fuck?'

'No? I've got some Goblin Fruit somewhere...'

'Got any fish?' Merlin says.

'Sure,' Rodarchus says. 'Fish.'

'Then get me some. I'll be in the solarium.'

'But—'

'Just fucking do it,' Merlin says. 'It's not my fault you fucked a fae and now you're stuck here.'

'I *like* it here,' Rodarchus says.

'Sure, sure,' says Merlin. 'Whatever helps you sleep at night. Now go.'

He enters the House of High Dudgeon. He's not even sure who rules here now. Mab, Titania, maybe Gwen. Who cares. The floor is hard and on the walls hang tapestries and paintings of fantastical scenes: griffins fighting unicorns, a phoenix rising from the ashes, attack ships on fire off the coast of Smyrna, a bearded Merlin imprisoned in that crystal cave—

'Haha, good one,' he mutters sourly. The house knows its occupants, remembers everything. Merlin skirts the way to the main hall or the gardens and takes the spiral stairs to the solarium.

The sun room is encased in glass. It's dark now, and all Merlin can see are the stars above Fairyland. Littered around the room are sky disks and astrolabes, celestial globes, star charts and maps of the constellations. Merlin checks the log and is not surprised to see Morgan's clear handwriting. He checks her chart and sees a note:

Merlin. Checking up on me? For shame.

'What are you up to, Morgan?' he mutters.

The stars are favourable to your boy. But Mars is rising, and with the Sun in Cancer there's a wide conjunction to the sixth house of alliance—

'What the fuck, Morgan!'

So watch out for him. Remember, I want my share. Love, Morgan.

'Love you too...'

'Your fish.'

Rodarchus.

Merlin says, 'You move quiet, now.'

'I adapt.'

'You're more house than human, now.' He'd seen it happen before. The house uses people like people use pigs. It consumes them. Soon all that'd remain of the mortal man would be a sofa leg, a bit of curtain, perhaps some crockery of bones.

'Not while she keeps me vital.'

'She who? Is your mistress not bored with you yet?'

Rodarchus tries to smirk prowess but it sits badly on his tightly drawn face. He is so faded.

'Just give me the fish,' Merlin says, taking pity on him.

Merlin takes the plate. Two living pike and an eel, and he is *famished*. He picks a pike and bites through scales and skin into the raw intestines. He chews and swallows.

That's better.

He can hear them talking when he goes back down the stairs.

Treads softly on the hard floor, to the wide doors that open onto the hall.

Peers inside.

The hall opens onto the gardens. Outside are water features and plants as cannot be found in England – fairladies and delphiniums, angel wing begonias, blood lilies and bleeding heartwine.

Inside the hall the Unseemly Court's in session.

The Nine Sisters sit sedately on both sides of a long table. Merlin's stomach rumbles at all this concentrated power. The fae are to the mortal realm what kings are to their commoners.

They're dressed in white. Their eyes are red. Their nails are blunt. They sip mint leaves in boiled water.

They have no need for swords or knives.

'I will not have him trespass north of the wall,' says Cailleach, the Queen of Winter.

'Hadrian's Wall lies in ruins, and your precious Picts can go fuck themselves, dear,' says Morgan pleasantly. She spots the hovering Merlin and gives him a lascivious wink.

'We are the last of the free!' the Queen of Winter says, quoting Calgacus. Her general against the Romans, he died at Agricola's hands five centuries ago. It's but a moment to the Queen of Winter. In time she'll no doubt find some other Pictish champion. For now, she mourns.

'The Angles and the Saxons' growing influence will never tolerate the boy's ambition,' Morgause says. Merlin stares sharply. He'd never trusted Morgause, honour to her is what money is to thieves. She spots him too. Was that expression on her face surprise?

'No,' Tyronoe says, 'I side with Morgan. It's time this shithole of a land was unified to serve us. And I am sick and tired of the pirates coming in from Eire-land. We need a human who could rein them in.'

'Who gives a shit about Hibernia?' Thitis demands. 'These people scrabble in the mud like pigs and their druids smell of dog shit.'

'You only say that seeing as they wouldn't serve you,' says Morgause.

Merlin sees Nimue, by the windows. She stares at the garden outside. So she is not committed yet, he thinks. He knows now what is happening. Just as the Council of Six is meeting Arthur to discuss arrangements, so does the Unseemly Court.

It's *all* about power. It's *always* about power.

He knows now why he's been barred from this place.

They are deciding what to do about Arthur.

'I don't see what's wrong with the current arrangement,' Thitis says. The others look at her askance. She's sided with the new arrivals, Hengist and Horsa. 'Each to their own, and land enough for all. Sisters, we each of us have power. It's good to share.'

'You lying cunt,' Morgause says, 'we all know what you're planning. To use your foreigners to conquer all the land.'

'I thought you were against this Arthur!' Thitis says.

'The boy's the bastard child of a worthless shit!' Morgause explodes. 'I will not have a son of Uther ruling Britain.'

'Oh, fuck off, Morgause, you're as plain as day,' says Thitis. 'You just want power for yourself and think King Lot or someone else may serve you better.'

Morgan smiles. 'Sisters, sisters,' she says. 'We *all* want power. We are here to discuss how best to share it.'

'You never liked sharing, Morgan,' Thitis says.

The others laugh.

'More minty water, ladies?'

'Why not. And an incense burner please, Rodarchus darling. Do we still have that cannabis from Scythia?'

'Yes, my lady.'

'It's primo stuff, sisters.'

'Shall we adjourn, then?'

'Let's light up this shit.'

'Oh, Merlin...'

'Yes?' He turns. It's Morgan, materialising beside him.

'You know you're not allowed in the Sanctum Sanctorum.'

'No men!' someone shouts – Glitonea, maybe.

'He's hardly a man,' someone says, and the others laugh.

'You reek of fish,' Morgan says. 'Come on. We'll talk, now you are here.'

She threads her arm through his. Out of doors and to the garden where it's humid and the plants are odd. A giant centipede slithers underfoot and rubs itself against Merlin's skin. He picks it up and strokes it. He's missed the fauna found in Fairyland.

'Put that disgusting thing down,' Morgan says. She looks around, to check they're undisturbed. 'What happened?'

'Someone tried to block my access,' Merlin says. 'They even sent that Grendel and his mum.'

'Those fucking trolls.'

'And Herne the Hunter.'

'Has a tiny penis,' Morgan says.

'Yeah?'

'Honest.'

'He's a dick. Anyway. Does our deal still stand? The court is yours and Arthur's mine.'

'Right now his "court" is spotty boys who scratch their balls and don't smell right.'

'And when they rule Britannia? Come on, Morgan. We have to lay the table before we're served the feast.'

'It must have been Morgause.'

'What?'

'Who sent them after you.'

'What's *her* game?'

'She sees where things are heading and she wants to have the lot, not you or me.'

'Well, she can fuck right off.'

Morgan frowns. 'Don't underestimate her. She's a nasty piece of work and worse, she's patient. She could be real trouble, now or down the road.'

'Look, forget about her for a moment. None of this will matter if I can't get Arthur arms to fight with.'

'What were you thinking?'

'I was thinking Nimue and her Lord of War show.'

'I see...'

'Morgan?'

'Yes?'

'You know anything about a star that fell from heaven?'

'The Lapis Exilis? There is power in star stones... Is that why you ask?'

'There was a comet in the skies years ago, when I was with Uther.' He's not sure he should tell her his suspicions. 'It fell somewhere far, and all my searches came back empty.'

'I don't, but I will try to find out.'

He isn't sure he should have told her. Now she knows what he suspects, what he hopes for. A source of power.

He doesn't trust her and perhaps she'll be a problem later down the road and, if so, he will deal with her then. For now they are allies – and he *does* need help.

'I'll speak to Nimue. But it will cost, both you and him.'

'Doesn't it always?'

'I have to get back. The Unseemly Court's about to get even more unseemly.'

'Do you know how the decision will go?'

'Merlin, darling. It's every woman for herself in there, same as it ever was.'

'Well, tell them our side will win.'

Morgan laughs. 'I keep forgetting you're half-human, Merlin. You're always so *invested*. Haven't you got it yet? The game's the game! Let men war and murder for king and throne. But the land's ours. Their souls are ours. Men come and go but we remain.'

'By what right, Morgan?'

She laughs openly in his face. 'No right,' she says softly. 'By force alone.'

'Morgan—'

'No, hush. It's time for you to scoot, darling. I'll send a raven with the time and place to meet. Till then, your boy-king needs you.'

She turns. She is so dazzling in that cold, cold land.

'Mo—'

She clicks her fingers, and the world is gone.

He is standing in a drizzle, at the entrance to a cave.

Far in the distance, the screams of dying men, the clash of steel on steel in battle.

He sighs.

After a while he goes into the cave and starts to build a fire.

PART FIVE

THE LADY IN THE LAKE

32

No fires burn over the Castle Perilous where the lady Nimue makes her abode.

The castle towers over its barrier island. The island is black and tall, volcanic rock perhaps, some fire long ago quenched by the salt water. The castle *looms* against the sky, all tall and craggy and austere, the moon behind it shining so dramatically.

Beyond the lagoon lies the sea. The monstrous fish-cat, Cath Palug, stalks up on the black rocks to the castle. Her tale is a tragic one, she would tell anyone who'd listen; but there is no one here to care. She was once a black kitten who was drowned at sea; there she became half-fish and grew nightmarish; then she returned to land and massacred all the peoples of the isle of Mona until the shallows of the ocean ran red with their blood. Now she is old. That is her story in short.

She stalks up to the castle.

The cat sees many things. She purrs as she passes the silent guards, these spirits of once-fearsome warriors who vanished down the fairy paths. They stand erect and tall like statues, black helmets, black armour, black swords. Cath Palug slinks inside and down the whispering humid corridors where the hum of water is always present, where the drip-drip-drip of drops is always there. The Castle Perilous *sings* of water and its many forms. There is a storm forever present, raging over the castle and its island, and lightning flashes and provides illumination for the castle through the open windows. The cat hisses and tastes the air, electric, humid: a perfect storm.

'Ah, there you are, pussycat,' her mistress says. Nimue lifts her up and cuddles her. Cath Palug purrs and butts her head into her mistress's armpit. The lady laughs.

'Where are you going, little kitty, pretty kitty?' she says. 'Come, see my new toy!'

Her mistress's voice is so full of excitement and hope that the cat, for all that she desires the quiet and the dark of the seeing pools, relents. Nimue lowers her down and the cat follows the Lady of the Lake through the corridors of the Castle Perilous to the treasure room. There, there is a wide and deep pool with walls of marble, and ivy growing on the vanity Doric columns, which stand up holding nothing. The roof is artfully caved in and the moon, Sister Moon, shines down through it and casts the scene in a bewitching glow.

'What is it, mistress?' the cat says.

The mermaids rise up from the depths and frolic in the pool. They call to Cath Palug, 'Hello, little kitten! My, haven't you grown!' and she yowls at them until they laugh.

The mermaids shout into the depths and Cath Palug can see dark shapes move lithely in the water, rising, carrying a present for Nimue. At last it breaks the surface and the mermaids hand it over. Nimue places the device lovingly on the floor and runs her fingers over it.

'It's magnificent!' she says.

'The sirenia of Greece found it for you, mistress,' one mermaid says. 'In a shipwreck off the coast of the isle of Antikythera. They swam across the Syrian Sea and traded it to the Gorgona who live beyond the Pillars of Hercules, who traded it to the fish-folk of the Sea of Atlantis, who traded it to us.'

'But what *is* it?' the cat says. She yawns. The nights are long in the Castle Perilous, and she craves the dark, and fish, and the glittering visions of the seeing pools.

Nimue crouches by the mechanism. It is a heavy piece of machine equipment, cogwheels and gears. Nimue runs her fingers over it, brushes mud from the intricate, interlocking wheels.

'It is a sort of calculating engine,' she says. 'It calculates the moon's motion across the skies. An astronomical device. Just think, cat! How useful it would be in war.'

'In *war*, mistress?'

'With this device one could call with accuracy the conditions of light and dark and when best to launch an attack. It even predicts eclipses! Oh, wouldn't the little Merlin love this? He's always going on about Greek science this and Greek science that.'

'But why do you need a machine to predict the moon,' says Cath Palug, confused, 'when you can just talk to her?'

Her mistress laughs and strokes her scales and fur.

'That magic is for us, cat, not for the men who shed blood in our honour. Oh, they think they do it for themselves, for pride and honour. But there is no honour and no pride in war. Just death and dying men shitting themselves, and entrails – you do like entrails, don't you?'

Cath Palug licks her lips.

'I thought as much. Their leaders know this – the ones who are drawn to power. This Arthur knows it. You think he cares *who* sheds the blood, who lives and dies at his command? He cares only that it is *his* commands that are obeyed, that on *his* word men live or die. It is a terrible drug, power, yet oh so wonderful...' Nimue sighs. 'Once you taste it you can never truly go back.'

The cat yawns. Nimue moves the mechanism, wheels interlock and spin, the moon above smiles down on the mermaids in the pool and on the Lady of the Lake and on her cat.

Cath Palug butts her head against her mistress's shin, then slinks away. She follows the whisper of water along a canal and through more dark corridors hewn into the stone, where moisture coats the walls, until she comes into the Hall of Seeing.

No one usually comes here but her. Nimue, sometimes. But she grows bored more easily. Not Cath Palug. She could spend hours here, days sometimes.

The hall is very big and deep into the mountain. The floor is cool and wet and made of marble. Scattered all across the hall are pools of water, some shallow, some deep. As the cat prowls, blue lightning fizzles overhead as salamanders crawl along the ceiling. It lights the visions in the pools. The cat moves slowly, savouring the flickering images in each. At last she chooses, drawn to one or merely sleepy. She lies on her belly and lets her paw dangle into the pool. She stirs the water.

There.

Something is coming.

Horses and men.

Clippety-clippety-clippety-clopping, going round the bend.

33

The ravens sit on a branch together, chatting as the convoy passes down below.

One squawks, then falls, dead instantly, a polished rock smashed through his skull. The other ravens take flight in fright and anger.

Down below on the dirt road, Merlin chuckles.

'Aren't you a bit old for throwing rocks?' Kay says.

Merlin, weighing a pocket full of stones, still smiles. 'If you see a raven, kill it,' he says. 'They're nothing if they aren't natural spies.'

'I *like* ravens,' Kay says. 'They're highly intelligent, very social, and can even mimic the human voice.'

'Well aren't you a natural philosopher,' Merlin says sourly.

The cat watches them go. How they bicker! And their king, he's little more than a boy! In her time, so many of their ilk had come to try and claim her head and she had bested them all.

Well, not the wizard, perhaps. She had seen *him* before. Nasty, nasty! She hisses and the water eddies for a moment and the figures grow faint. At last the water's still and she watches. It is later in the day (time flows differently here, in the Castle Perilous, which lies in the hinterland of the mortal world and the fae) and the men sit round a fire. Their horses graze nearby. The king has a retinue of young knights with him who sit apart, and clean their blades and stare into the dark beyond the trees and mutter to themselves and scratch and fart. They're nothing but cheap hoodlums, country boys who tired of a future tilling earth and planting grain, back-breaking labour, the same meagre food day in, day out, the same tired faces, a drink of mead and beating up the wife on Saturn's Day, and growing old, and weak, and dying back into the dirt from whence they came. They gave it up without a moment's thought and joined the war to take the king's coin.

In this Britannia, first you get the money, then you get the power, then you get the women – this is what they say, and laugh, and dream of big-bosomed girls and whisper of the Castle Perilous and mermaids – 'Oh, I would fuck a mermaid!' someone says, and laughs, and the cat hisses, 'Fool! A mermaid's like a shark, she grins to kill and she will chew you up to pulp and shit you out before you know you're dead.'

But they do not hear Cath Palug, and she turns away from them in disgust.

'The Six must pay,' King Arthur says.

'And pay they will,' says Kay.

'It won't be easy—' Merlin, and he turns his head from side to side, uncomfortably, as though there is a buzzing in his ears.

'What is it, Merlin?'

'I have the oddest feeling something's listening.'

'You always think someone is listening or watching,' Kay says irritably, 'it's like a curse with you.'

'Just because you think they do, it doesn't mean they *don't*,' Merlin says, with unassailable logic.

'Let them listen,' Arthur says. 'I want their heads, all six of them.'

'And they want yours.'

'I want their lands, their wives, their cattle and their fields.'

'And I'd like one of those Egyptian staffs that turn into a snake, but we can't always have what we want,' Merlin says.

'You're in a funny mood,' the king says, and gives him a dirty look.

'We cannot attack the north beyond the Pictish wall without an army. And we cannot shake Leir loose of his ridings *with* one. This will be a long campaign, my king.'

'Tell me something I *don't* know.'

They fall to silence. The burning wood crackles in the fire. The night's quiet is broken by an ungodly sound. The men startle.

'What *is* that?'

It is an awful keening sound of loss and fury and despair. A monstrous call.

'Oh, not *again*!' says Merlin.

'What *is* that, Merlin?'

Then they see it. Cath Palug leans over, interested. The creature bursts through the trees – hideous! Deformed! – it has too many mouths, too many tongues and teeth, and it is yowling, crying, warbling out an insane stream of wordless pain. Oh, Cath Palug *likes* this! She speaks this creature's language, she *knows* what is it like to have been born unwanted and to be thrown away.

'The Questing Beast,' says Merlin sourly. The creature flails too many arms, the hoodlum knights reach for their swords but the creature swats them away and vanishes into the trees again. Behind it there's a human cry, 'Come back!'

A knight comes to their fire through the trees. He is bedraggled and unkempt, with long dirty locks of hair and a long dirty beard, and nails chewed down to the quick. He stares at them in confusion as Arthur's young bodyguards finally draw their swords.

'Err, hello,' he says.

'Pellinore,' Merlin says. 'It's been a while.'

The knight turns to the wizard. 'You?' he says.

'Me. The beast is gone, for now. Will you stay with us a while?'

Pellinore looks longingly at the fire. 'You have sausages?'

Kay and Arthur exchange an amused glance. 'We saw you

once before, Sir Knight,' King Arthur says. 'I think we did, in passing.'

'I do get around,' Pellinore says. 'It is the beast, you see. It keeps me busy. What *sort* of sausages?'

'Auroch, and wild boar,' Kay says. 'With herbs and seasoning. They're good.'

'I could stay a *little* while...'

He sits beside the fire. Arthur motions to the guards. They step away and, cursing, return to their own encampment.

The knight feeds ferociously, like he's not eaten in weeks. The juice runs down his cheeks and into his beard, where there are also twigs and leaves and what looks like a dead bee or two. His eyes are sunken, and he is a far cry from the hopeful young man Merlin remembers.

Merlin picks delicately at a small hard roll. He nibbles crumbs. Kay and Arthur each eat a sausage, and Kay adds more onto the flames. The sausages hiss and sizzle. Cath Palug licks her lips. She loves her mistress dearly but the fae for sustenance are drawn to power, not sausages.

'Your name is Pellinore?'

'It is.'

'I'm Arthur.'

'A pleasure, I'm sure.'

'Sir Pellinore was Uther's page,' says Merlin. 'Your father's, Arthur.'

At this Pellinore goes still. 'This is the boy?'

'It is.'

'Has it really been that long?'

'It has.'

Pellinore examines Arthur's face. The king bears with the scrutiny.

'You have something of his, for sure,' he says. 'It's in the eyes.'

'I never knew my father.'

The words must hurt the king, Cath Palug thinks. There's

something so hard inside him, some cold unfathomed core, but still. He is a boy and boys do hurt. Boys need their fathers.

Cath Palug yawns, feeling sad. She strokes the face of water. The image shimmers, breaks. She'd had a mother and a father once. So many deaths, she thinks. They stay with you. Even if you didn't know them – especially then, perhaps.

The picture shifts and changes. A castle room, high in the air, a queen sits by the window. Her long hair is like a dark waterfall. She gazes out at the moon, Sister Moon. The queen turns and sees the cat.

'Hello there, Cath Palug,' she says, and smiles a gentle smile.

'My Lady Igraine,' the cat says, and bows her head respectfully.

'Stalking the dreams and the what-could-have-beens again, cat?'

'I grow old and fat, my Lady Igraine, and I find watching the world from a distance more soothing than action.'

The lady nods. 'Only the lucky grow old, Cath Palug,' she says.

The cat hisses. 'The game's the game, my lady.'

'The game's the game.' The lady smiles. 'And what have you seen in your night-time wanderings?'

'I saw a boy who would be king.'

At that the lady's face turns sad. It makes the cat sad, too, though she does not know why it should be so.

'Is he well, Cath Palug? Does he eat?'

'He is well. He is eating sausages.'

This makes the lady smile, and for that the cat is happy.

'Sausages? But that's ridiculous, cat.'

'I like sausages,' the cat says. 'And he looks like he is in need of fattening.'

'Is he too thin?' the lady says in worry.

'He's like a sapling, who might yet grow into a tree.'

'Is he handsome? Does he yet have a wife?'

'He is no cat, so I'm sure I couldn't say, my lady. But he has a wizard with him.'

At this the lady's face twists in hate. 'He is alive still, that one?'

'And scheming in that way that wizards have.'

'I wish him dead.'

'You do not like him?'

'He took from me a thing I loved.'

The cat nods. Her paw trails in the water. 'Perhaps he meant well...' she says, but the water's disturbed and the Lady Igraine vanishes.

The cat naps a while. When she awakes the scene is once again the forest, but the fire in the circle's dead and the sun's out, and Arthur and Merlin are rising.

'Where did he go?' King Arthur says.

Merlin shrugs. 'You cannot keep him long in place, my lord. Sir Pellinore alone among the strong has given up his power. He would have been a king unto himself, your father knew it.'

'What makes him go, then?' Arthur says.

A look of bewilderment steals on the wizard's face. 'I think it love, my lord.'

'For that, that *thing*?' Kay says.

'When Pellinore looks on the Questing Beast it is no *thing* he sees,' says Merlin. 'It is a child. Vulnerable and hurt, too easily perhaps. Yet not unloved.'

Arthur says nothing to that. But he grips the hilt of his sword, and his knuckles are white with the strain.

At last he lets go.

'I wish him well,' he says.

'We have a long way still to go, sire,' Merlin says.

'Then let's be about our business.'

And so they mount and ride back on the road.

The water ebbs.

The picture, for a time, is gone.

34

When she's awake again and watching it's another landscape and another day, she's almost sure of it. Those boys on their horses look a little more tired, but still like boys playing with swords, out on the glens or by the stream; like boys are wont to do and girls too, until they're stopped from dreaming in this way.

'We can stop here.'

'It's pretty.'

'It's too cold,' Kay complains.

They're up a hill somewhere and it is north, the cat thinks they are getting closer. They set up camp against the side of the hill and the wizard lights a fire and prepares water to boil. Sir Kay skins a hare. Arthur rises, stretches, looks up at the horizon where the sun, gloriously, is yet to set. The sky is blue and dotted with white clouds, and the sun paints it with strokes of reds and swirling violets.

Merlin glances up. 'Don't wander too far,' he says.

'This is my land, Merlin. I shall go where I please.'

'The land does not yet know it, sire...' Merlin mutters, but too quietly for the king to catch.

He watches as Arthur bounds up the hill. Gestures to the bodyguards. 'Follow him.'

The cat leans over the pool, interested now. She smells something in there, a familiar scent.

Eye of newt and toe of frog, wool of bat and tongue of dog, that sort of thing, in a simmering stew. Witchcraft. Sorcery. The cat's tummy rumbles.

Arthur strolls through this green and pleasant land. Purple thistles and bright yellow gorse, and heather and bluebells and primrose. He breathes in the fresh air. Somewhere nearby, the sound of running water, and he finds the brook and follows it downhill on the other side, until he comes to a small waterfall.

Oh... The cat thinks, and she places her head on her paws and stares. Oh...

He comes to the ledge above the waterfall. The stream falls over the edge and down to a small rock pool.

Under the waterfall, quite naked, stands a woman.

She looks up at Arthur and smiles. Her black hair is wet and long and clings to her back.

The boy, Arthur, seems quite drawn to her heavy bosoms.

Or perhaps it is the triangle of coarse black hair below.

'Hello,' the woman says. She's cast in glamour, Cath Palug realises. When she smiles her teeth are like a shark's, but the boy king cannot see it. Her eyes are like a fish-hawk's but the boy sees nothing but two dreamy pools in which to drown.

Now, what are you playing at, Morgause? the cat thinks.

'Hello,' the boy says.

His voice sounds thick, the cat thinks. Strangely uncertain.

'Come down,' the woman says. 'The water's nice.'

The boy, almost comically, looks from side to side. *Me?* his face seems to say.

'Yes, you!' the woman says, laughing.

Arthur takes a step and then another and soon enough he's sliding down to the bank. He stops there, staring. Transfixed.

It makes Cath Palug think of being on heat. A weird, uncomfortable feeling, an urge cats cannot fight. When it comes upon you, you are helpless in its thrust. The body wants what the body wants.

But still. The boy can't be *this* dumb?

'Take off that heavy sword,' the woman says. She rises from the water and the drops glint on her body. She comes to him. With expert fingers she undresses him. He stands there naked as the day he was birthed, but his blade is fully grown.

'My, my,' Morgause says. Her fingers trail down his stomach, find his hardness, *squeeze*.

The boy gives a gasp of surprise or something like pain.

She leads him by his sword into the pool.

My, my, the cat thinks.

What then transpires is the sort of thing that humans often engage in. It involves swords and sheaths, and so on, and there's thrusting and counter-thrusting and lots of grabbing and grunting and pulling and heaving and, well—

'There he is!' comes a shout. Up on the hill, three men silhouetted against the setting sun. They pull out weapons and start to clumsily run. One stumbles on a rock and falls. Cath Palug almost feels sorry for him.

In the water, the Lady Morgause smiles and she bites the boy's neck and he shudders and *heaves* and then *it* is, apparently, over. The boy stands there looking a little confused and a little bit pleased with himself, his sword drooping now, and dripping too, and the lady looks *very* pleased with herself for some reason. Then the men finally make it down but tumble over the edge and fall into the water and the lady flicks her fingers and they turn into voles.

They stare around themselves in some bemusement.

Then a crack of lightning out of nowhere, and Merlin materialises on the bank. He stares accusingly at the two in the pool.

'I *told* you not to wander off by yourself!'

'Well, hello again, Merlin.'

'Morgause. I see you've had your fun.'

'One must get it where one can.'

'You didn't bleed him dry?'

'A little taste is all, Merlinus. He really is a meal and no mistake.'

'Arthur, can you even hear me? Arthur!'

'*What*,' the boy says irritably.

'Put your clothes on.'

Morgause smiles wide. 'No second round?'

Merlin thunders, 'Begone, witch!'

'Fuck you too, Merlin. I'll see you soon.'

She turns into a fish and swims away, vanishing down the brook with the setting sun glancing off her silver scales.

'What in all the worlds possessed you, Arthur!'

The boy smiles goofily and doesn't answer.

'Oh, for fuck's sake.'

Merlin waits as Arthur dresses. He snaps his fingers as an afterthought and the voles transform to men again.

'You lot are useless,' Merlin says.

The men are wiser than to reply.

'This escapade will cost you dearly,' Merlin says.

'How so?'

'The seeds of one's inevitable destruction lie always in the family,' Merlin says. But he does not elaborate, and Arthur doesn't ask. Perhaps, the cat thinks, he simply doesn't care.

She yawns. The picture shimmers, fades. The Hall of Seeing's dark and quiet and the pools cast their shimmering images onto the ceiling silently. It's rather beautiful.

Far in the distance she can hear the mermaids singing, each to each.

35

When she awakes again the song is gone and the hall is quiet and she tiptoes from pool to pool in search of something interesting to watch. There in the light of roaring flames in a grove dance Northern men, white savages inked with tribal scars as a druid chants into the flames and throws dried roots and dried dead things into the fire, evoking some nameless, dreadful deity in search of ancient power—

Oh well, she's bored. She moves in search of something else. There, a battle between Arthur's knights and Outham's men, somewhere in the boggy marshes of the Tamesis estuary. Outham's Franks are grizzled and experienced, but Arthur's knights are reckless and they are too dumb or too poor to fear death. Agravain of the Hard Hand leads them.

Cath Palug watches for a while, but the sight of dying men no longer excites her much. For what it's worth, Arthur's men appear to be winning. Well, good luck to them and all that. She tunes it off and searches, but a worthy scene, annoyingly, eludes her.

For a moment, something, somewhere. An innocent young woman by a stream, and the sun lights up her hair, reflecting in her eyes, as the girl sits in the meadow and it is like an eternal spring, and perhaps, Cath Palug thinks, it's always spring when we are innocent and young. The girl holds a daisy, a beautiful yellow-and-white daisy, and as she tears the florets off one by one she chants softly, 'He loves me, he loves me not, he loves me little, he loves me a lot. He loves me to passion, he loves me to folly, he loves me not at all.' And she repeats, 'He loves me, he loves me not...' until all the florets are torn and strewn upon the ground and the girl, laughing, twirls the yellow disc of the flower head on its stem until it rises in the air, for just a moment, and seems to fly.

This girl, so new to womanhood, she must be someone, the cat thinks.

'Now, *that* is interesting,' her mistress says, turning up behind her.

The cat purrs. The lady strokes her scales and fur.

'And how *has* my little kitty been occupying herself?'

'I watch the world beyond the walls of sleep,' the cat tells her.

'And what do men and their affairs concern you?'

'They concern me little,' the cat says. Beside her mistress she truly does feel herself a kitten, still. The little black kitten who was once loved, who had parents, before all the deaths, before she was drowned in the sea. Perhaps that's why the girl in the pool-image captivates her. She is like Cath Palug once was. An innocent.

'No one's *innocent*,' her mistress says, reading her mind. 'This girl bears watching. Yes. You have done well, my kitty cat. Here, a little treat.'

She gives the cat her favourite snack. Cath Palug chews on sailor's fingers, sucks out juice and crunches bone around the knuckles. She loves knuckles. Some fingers are white and some fingers are black and some are blue, from some merman off the Sea of Atlantis, perhaps. The world is big and it contains multitudes.

Then it is night-time again in the outside world, and her mistress is gone, and at the cat's feet is a small pile of bones. Which is all that men ever are, when all is said and done.

She stares into the nearest seeing pool. It's dark. A blackness that is pure. Then lights, the stars, not as they are seen from Earth but out in the place beyond. So many stars, that she must conclude that the Greek, Anaximander, was right when he postulated that the universe is infinite. And did not Aristotle write, in his *Physics*, that 'It is always possible to think of a larger number: for the number of times a magnitude can be bisected is infinite. Hence the infinite is potential, never actual; the number of parts that can be taken always surpasses any assigned number.'

What. She knows her Greek and Latin. Her mistress has a most extensive library of scrolls and clay tablets and codices, all rescued from the bottom of the sea. Nimue has stores of ancient knowledge, for all that her interest lies almost exclusively in the destructive arts.

As for the cat, she likes to watch the stars.

There, the world, blue and white, and its grey pockmarked moon, Sister Moon, smiling. There Venus of the storms, there red Mars going past, and there the belt of rocks that circle the sun beyond it. Then mighty Jupiter, with raging storms, a giant in the heavens, surrounded by moons. There Saturn with her gorgeous rings. And on, and on. The cat sees what people cannot see, for she has magic, while they are yet to figure out a way to look to the beyond. Perhaps some sort of seeing glass, if they had the techne, but they don't. So Cath Palug, alone, gazes on the planets.

She's swept away on the solar wind. Then it's days or hours later. The hall is quiet. The hall is *always* quiet. She waddles to a pool and stirs the water.

Morgause, in a grove, weaving a figure out of leaves. She looks up, smiles, says, 'Hello, cat.'

'Mistress Morgause,' the cat says politely.

'Abroad on your dream quest again, my dear?'

'I watch,' the cat says. 'I watch and I listen.'

'And what a wonderful watcher you *are*!' Morgause says,

with that insincere sweetness the cat hates. She remembers Morgause from the Summer Country, and she had never much liked the false bitch.

'These men you are trying to hurt,' the cat says, and there is the sound of unsheathed claws in her voice, 'they are my mistress's guests.'

'And I would not *dream* to cause them harm!' Morgause says, still with that radiant, unstable smile. 'Not while they are under *your* protection.' The peals of laughter in her voice mock Cath Palug. 'In fact I think on our last encounter the sapling of a boy king rather enjoyed himself. Don't you?'

She weaves leaves and vines and twines them all together. She claps her hands and *breathes* on the thing, and it comes alive.

'Why did you fuck him?'

Morgause shrugs. 'Why not? Besides, I want his seed.'

'For what?'

'What do *you* think, cat?'

'I... I see.'

'A king's a king, and a throne's a throne,' the sorceress says. 'And when one's indisposed, the other needs filling. Now fuck off, cat.'

Cath Palug hisses. Her claws strike the water. The image is broken into a thousand pieces, then gone.

Fine.

She'll watch.

It passes the time until dying.

36

The Green Knight stalks the forest roads, his lance of thorns raised up against his enemies. The Green Knight has only a rudimentary intelligence in that thick skull of bark and sapwood, but he has deep roots, and the roots *know* things.

The Green Knight knows, for instance, that the Nine Sisters are abroad again, and scheming their endless schemes. He knows the land is being fought on, for blood soaks deep into the earth. And he knows that somewhere, far away, there is a great wound in the earth, and it is slowly poisoning all that is around it. But where it lies he doesn't know.

The Green Knight doesn't have a name, but he casts about him and decides that 'Bercilak' has a nice ring to it, for all that it is a pretty silly name.

The Green Knight also knows it is his job and duty to await the arrival of three men, and kill the runty one, who thinks himself a king.

The Green Knight is a king himself. In many ways, he thinks, he *is* the forest, the one that's always been there on this island, primordial and dark. A forest where things lived and died, namelessly, for generations. When humans first came to this land they cut down trees and cleared farmland and built houses and roads. And that was long, long before the Romans came. And he remembers them all, for the land remembers what people forget. He remembers how big and strong he was, before the people came. And he hates the people for it.

Bits come to him as he stalks the forest. Looking for the intruders. Sniffing them out. Memory, hazy at first and then bits of it more, from the roots and the leaves and the whispers of fungus. Fungus is *weird*, the knight thinks, with some understandable distaste. Not quite plant, not quite animal, but a third thing, a different thing. The humans are all the same and yet they have endless divisions, and they're always fighting, like right now with this king – Arthur, the name comes to him from the howl of wolves far away – and these Angles and Saxons who keep coming over. There's a whole *world* beyond Britain, the Green Knight knows, for the land was once linked to the continent by the Doggerland, which now lies underwater. It had flooded after the last Great Winter, when the glaciers melted away. The Green Knight remembers the glaciers, remembers when this island was merely an offshoot off the great continent, and he does not understand how people act. In the primordial forest all had a purpose, lives that were lived in a complex web of need and usage. But humans just disrupted everything, killing just for killing's sake, destroying without thinking, disturbing the delicate natural balance of things. Angles, Saxons, Celts – what the fuck is the *difference*? the Green Knight thinks, and flexes his muscles.

The witch, Morgause, may think she'd made him, but she ought to know better. He is merely the embodiment of an idea, given shape.

Yet shape follows purpose. And finding himself in this humanoid form the Green Knight also, increasingly, finds himself… *being* a little, well…

There's no easy way to put it, he thinks as he urinates into the bushes. That feels good, pissing. Do they call it pissing? He'd seen wolves and foxes do it. Mice. But to experience, as a male human – well, that's something else, he thinks. Standing on two legs with that thing dangling between your legs, facing up to the sky and the world and just saying, you know what? Fuck it!

Feels good.

It feels strangely, horribly *good* to be, well, human. To have that thing between his legs. Male.

And there's something else he wants to do with it, he realises in some alarm. He kind of ends up holding it in his hand after he'd finished peeing. Feels good, too. He can make it bigger. Well, he'd seen *that* before, too. Even snails do it. Though snails have both male and female parts. Snails don't care. They just do it. They like to do it after it rains. They love to just come out after the rain and just do it. They can even just fuck themselves! The Green Knight has to admit that's impressive. Not *that* many creatures in the animal kingdom can do *that*. He thinks that as he strokes the thing. It gets big and it gets hard. He thinks about the snails.

Snails fucking.

Those tentacles of theirs, rubbing against each other.

All that slime—

The Green Knight jerks and the thing erupts and there's something mucus-like and sticky in his palm. He tries to wipe it off on a leaf but it sticks to his palm. The thing between his legs start to deflate. He looks around him uncomfortably, and that's when he sees them, coming along the path.

They stop on their horses and sit there and watch him.

Cath Palug watches in the seeing pool.

'What the *fuck*?' Kay says.

'Put that thing away, man, for crying out loud!' says Merlin.

Arthur doesn't say anything. He just takes it in. His eyes move. Smart, the cat thinks. He is checking for weapons.

'I think I'm supposed to… I'm supposed to *fight* you,' the Green Knight says, pulling his underclothes back on, reaching for the bits of bark and heartwood that make up his armour.

'With *that* thing?' Merlin says.

'No, I have a lance...'

He casts around for it. Arthur, on his horse, draws his sword.

'Oh, I don't know,' the Green Knight says. He scratches the weird fold of skin under the two balls that dangle below the thing. Feels good, to scratch. 'I'm kinda sleepy.'

'Do you have a name, Sir Knight?'

'A *name*? Wait, yes, I do. It's Bercilak.' He looks at them expectantly. He'd never had a name before. The eternal living force of the primordial forest does not have a *name*.

'You're very green.'

'I am the Green Knight.' He stands tall and proud. 'The voice of vanished mammoths and sabre-toothed tigers roars through me. The thunder of aurochs calls out of me! The cry of the hawk and the raven and the whisper of snails are in me! The rattling of branches and the shaking of leaves come from me. The insane muttering of the fungal beings speaks from within me—'

'Yes, al*right*,' Merlin says testily. 'I swear he didn't exist an hour ago,' he mutters under his breath.

'Merlin?'

'He seems harmless enough,' Kay says.

Merlin gives him a withering glance. 'Seen the size of his cock, have you?' he says.

'Fuck off, wizard.'

'Fuck you, *steward*!'

'Stop it, both of you,' Arthur says. He turns to the knight. 'I will fight you, if you wish, Sir Knight,' he says. He climbs down from the horse and extends the sword. 'I have never fought a thing such as you.'

'On, go on, then,' the Green Knight says. 'Take your best shot.'

'I would hate to kill you,' Arthur says.

The Green Knight shrugs. 'And I would hate to die.'

He draws his own sword of wood. Lunges at the king.

The king swipes with his sword and with one fell swoop he neatly lops off the Green Knight's head.

'Well, that is that, then,' Merlin says.

The head just sits there on the ground.

The body stands.

The head opens its eyes and blinks and looks up at the king and his men.

'That was fun,' it says.

'What is this?' Arthur says. He turns to his wizard irritably. 'Is this magic?'

'What do *you* think?'

'Can't you make it stop, then? I can't be expected to deal with magic, Merlin. I can't do *everything* around here.'

Merlin shrugs. 'Try, I don't know, kicking the head.'

'I am not going to *kick* the *head*!'

The body kneels. The Green Knight picks up his head and screws it back on, and tiny shoots spring and reattach. He blinks again.

'Was that death?' he says. 'It didn't feel like much.'

'You know what death is,' Merlin says. 'You more than most—' and he says a name, an ancient one, and in a language that was lost.

The Green Knight shrugs. 'Now it's my turn,' he says. He lifts his sword and makes for Arthur.

'Oh, no you don't!' Merlin says. He interposes himself between them, and his own staff is raised. 'Go back from whence you came, Bercilak, or whatever you call yourself these days. Go back to ancient woodland, where the mulch is rich and dark, where dandelion seeds fly in the thick air, where the deer give birth and birds go to die. Go back, Bercilak, for you will not harm a single hair on Arthur's head.'

The Green Knight looks at him without expression. He scratches at the leaves on his head.

'So what do you guys like, *do*?' he says.

'Do? He is the king.'

'But, like, on a day to day basis.'

Merlin shakes his head. 'You don't *want* to go back, do you?' he says.

'I kinda like it out here.'

Arthur looks at him. He motions to Merlin and the wizard moves out of the way. Arthur walks up to the knight. Looks him in the eyes, which are very green.

Lays out his pitch.

'Do you like to fuck?' he says.

'I think so.'

'Do you like to fight?'

'I think that, too.'

'Then join me,' Arthur says. 'And there'll be more than enough of both for you, Sir Bercilak. What do you say?'

The Green Knight thinks.

'Sounds good,' he rumbles. 'You got anything to eat?'

'There's still some sausage left,' Kay says, and Merlin smirks.

The weather turns cool and the clouds amass black and pregnant with rain on the horizon, and lightning flashes periodically and the earth shakes with the rumble of thunderous applause. It rains, and their journey is slow and miserable, and only the Green Knight delights in the rain for it makes him grow bigger and stronger, and his green eyes shine, and he finds everything delightful.

In a copse of trees on the edge of the forest they huddle together against the rain, chewing on meagre rations.

'Not far now,' Merlin says, and sniffs the air. Tastes of wizardry and elderberries, with a hint of Persian lime.

'It's so fucking wet,' complains one of the bodyguards.

'It'll get wetter,' Merlin says.

Kay isn't there. The Green Knight, too, is missing. Cath Palug watches, interested. She swirls the water with her paw.

There, in the forest, Kay on his knees and the Green Knight with his green cock hanging out.

Man, she thinks. He's really taking to this being human stuff.

'What do we do when we get there?' Arthur asks.

Merlin says, 'We negotiate.'

And that is that.

37

The men arrive at the Castle Perilous on a day when thunderclouds choke the sky and lightning beats it black and blue, black and blue. They come on foot, and what had happened to their horses Cath Palug doesn't know. They come bone-sore and weary, in a torrential downpour of rain, not like a king and retinue but as supplicants.

Cath Palug tiptoes out to see them. She leaves the Hall of Seeing and its pools, and skulks through corridors and out to the lagoon. She lies on the black rocks and tastes the air, which is so rich in oxygen and magnetic charge.

The knights stand on the shore.

Behold the Castle Perilous!

It rises stark and ancient into the heavens and the lightning wreathes it in a crown of blue fire. The water runs down the sheer cliff and the imposing black façade and down, down to the lagoon.

Beyond, the sea rages, waves batter the shore, white foam flies like spittle. The trees shake in the storm.

But the men are resolute. They stand. They wait.

Well, let them wait, thinks Cath Palug.

Out on the open sea the mermaids open song, and a whale rises from the depths, enchanted by their singing. The mermaids stroke the whale and sing to it before they savagely murder it with their tridents, and with its spilled blood a feeding frenzy of sea creatures occurs.

A sacrifice, Cath Palug thinks, and shudders in delicious anticipation. There must always be a sacrifice.

And besides, she is partial to the taste of whale meat.

Then she sees her.

Her mistress.

Nimue, the Lady of the Lake.

She of the Nine Sisters, she of the fae who are the dreams and greed and vanity of humankind made manifest.

She rises from the deeps.

The men watch.

Arthur's breath is caught. He's got a taste for the ladies of water now.

The Green Knight is still. He revels in the rain and in the storm, for he is ferae naturae, that is, of the wild.

Merlin stands stoically, he's been to this parlour show before.

Kay just stands there needing a piss.

Then she comes.

Like a ray of moonlight breaking through the clouds, illuminating a path across the lake.

She rises.

The point of a sword pierces the water.

A blade, emerging, painted silver in the moonlight.

A white hand, gripping the hilt of the sword.

Nimue rises.

She moves almost lazily through the water towards them. Arthur can't take his eyes off of her. She rises, her face illuminated in the moonbeams. Her pale breasts, her long black hair, wet and clinging to her back and shoulders. She rises and Arthur gives a startled little bark at the wet triangle of black hair, and at that startling white belly, like the belly of a shark.

What need has she for clothes? She is Nimue, the Lady of the Lake, and this is her domain and all who come here must bow before her.

Then she is there, among them. Standing still and smiling faintly, and she places the sword horizontally in her palms, one under the hilt and one under the naked blade.

She proffers the sword to Arthur without words.

He takes it. The sword lights up with blue fire. The air crackles. Arthur grins in boyish delight. He swoops and swooshes it through the air.

'A little taste,' Nimue says, still smiling. 'Her name's Excalibur. She was forged of ancient star-stone metal, in the volcanic fires of the Venomous Mountain, Beinn Nibheis, in the days before men, when its flames still spoke out from the ground. It cannot be broken, nor will it ever leave your side.'

She's laying it on a bit thick, Cath Palug thinks. But the punters like that sort of thing.

'She is magnificent!' Arthur declares. He's like a child with a toy. And did he ever play with toys? wonders the cat. What were his birthdays like? He never had a father of his own to give him gruff advice or hold his little hands and guide them with the practice weapon, nor did he know a mother to kiss a wounded knee or let him cry. *Did* Arthur ever cry? He must have, once. But perhaps there had never been anyone to hear it.

She feels sad for him. Oh, cat, she thinks. You've grown soft and mushy in your old age! She yawns, and a fish jumps out of the dark water and she grabs it and bites off its head and rips its belly. She nibbles on the flesh.

'It's good to see you again, Nimue,' Merlin says.

'Likewise, little Merlin.'

'May we go inside?'

'Be welcome in my castle.'

She swipes her hand, and stepping stones appear. They pop up one by one and lead up to the castle.

'Be careful not to slip,' she says, and sweetly smiles.

She leads. And like the boys they truly are, they follow.

★

'And this is the Poisons Room,' Nimue says as they pass through a full apothecary, complete with labelled bottles, flowering plants, instruments of measurements, vials and other, more arcane devices. 'Mithridates VI of Persia used to test his poisons on criminals facing execution. He was a great pioneer. Was deadly afraid of being poisoned, hence the search for cures. Finally he invented a concoction that he called Mithridatium. Supposedly it had over sixty-five ingredients and could cure almost anything. Lost now. I can do you a good deal on belladonna, if you're in the market for that. Extremely toxic. No? Then maybe henbane? Deadly nightshade? Oh, I know. There is a distillation one can make from the Strychnos nux-vomica tree. Odourless, tasteless, and deadly, you really can't go wrong for the price. No? Well, then. This way, gentlemen.'

Cath Palug slinks besides her mistress, butting her legs from time to time. The king and retinue are quiet, focused. The water drips down the black stone walls.

'Here we have assorted magics – nothing of much use for wide-scale military engagement, I'm afraid. Rings of invisibility, rings for producing gold, a ring from Judea that can supposedly imprison demons... Trinkets, really.'

'Invisibility,' Kay says. 'That sounds useful in a battle.'

Nimue shrugs. 'In all honesty, they have a one in ten chance of failing just when you don't need them to. Now, here we have anti-poison jewels, flaming pearls and mermaid's tears, what else... Urim and Thummim seeing-stones replicas, also from Judea... Thor's belt, some cloud-stepping boots from Qin... None of it much use to you either, I suspect. Magic stuff is usually bespoke, there's not much call for bulk... Through here, please.'

The next room's long and narrow. Armour hangs on faceless dummies. The cat grows bored with all the weapons talk, but the men are excited now, and Arthur is tense and paying close attention. He asks all manners of questions as they go through types of armour, Roman, Persian, an unfamiliar style to him from distant Qin, and they discuss quantities and availability.

Cath Palug yawns.

Then they go into the giant sword room, which is really a warehouse, because here is the thing. Here is the racket, such as it is.

Nimue gets her supplies from water. Rivers, lakes, the sea. Some were thrown in as offerings. Some were lost by successive army crossings. Some were drowned, are found in ships and military transports. The bottom line is, there's *lots* of them buried underwater, collected over centuries. Some of this stuff's *old*. She's got thousands of swords in the warehouse and thousands more stored off-site. It's not like Arthur can get his hands on this kind of quantity anywhere else. Not unless he trains and hires smiths, builds foundries, opens mines. The *logistics* of arms manufacture are complex. It just goes to show how interconnected everything is. You need resources, skills, an *infrastructure*.

So this is Arthur's shortcut.

If he can make a deal.

The cat is bored. The men speak intensely among themselves. They talk of troop numbers and enemy holds and the costs of a siege and expected number of casualties in open space warfare. They speak shipping logistics and fortifications and acceptable losses and expected returns.

Then there are just Merlin and Arthur and the Lady in a room; and the cat at her mistress's feet.

'And the cost?' Arthur says quietly. Beside him, Merlin is still.

The Lady says nothing.

'I can offer you gold,' Arthur says. 'Previous stones, coin—'

'Perhaps you misunderstood what this *is*,' the Lady says. 'I have all of these, and more. All that falls into water falls into my hands.'

'I can offer you men,' Arthur says, a note of quiet desperation. Beside him, Merlin is still.

And the cat thinks, this is what it comes down to. There is always a price, and it is always more than you can afford to pay.

Only the desperate strike deals with the fae.

And the Lady says nothing.

'What do you *want*?' Arthur says.

The cat thinks she can hear his heartbeat. It is so strong, so vital. There is so much *life* in him, and so much *power*, or the potential for power still. *This* is what the Lady wants, this is why Merlin serves him. They feed on power like leeches feed on blood.

The Lady and Merlin exchange glances. She cannot have him, not now, the cat knows. The little Merlin has staked out his claim long ago. The boy is his, for life.

The Merlin nods. The Lady looks at Arthur.

Her smile is sad.

'I want your death,' she says.

What has transpired in that room is for them alone. And perhaps the king thinks he has got the bargain he had come to seek. What is death to a young man, anyway? Well, he is promised now. They'll say no more about it, till the very end.

When he comes out of the room his men are jubilant. They have the arms they sought. The battles from here on will go their way. They'll vanquish Yder of the savage north, and Outham the Old and all the others. They'll unify this island and rule over all. They'll grow stinking rich with power.

That night there is a feast to seal the deal and the mermaids come out of the depths to sing, and the shadows dance in the torchlight and the wine from sunken ships from the sea of Hispania flows like water.

In the morning the men are gone.

Cath Palug watches their departure, the knights clutching their heads in the dawn's early light, and Arthur stepping with a new weight on his shoulders, and Merlin beside him is mute.

Then they vanish into the mist, back on the road. The arms they had bargained for will be delivered by water.

They're gone, and she will not inquire further.

In the afternoon her mistress calls her to her rooms. Cath Palug sees a familiar figure taking wine with the Lady.

'Oh, *cat*!' the Lady Morgause says in false surprise. 'What a *delight* to see you once again!'

'Lady Morgause,' the cat says politely, with barely disguised loathing. 'What brings *you* here?'

'I have business with your mistress, cat,' Morgause says. 'If that's alright with you?'

'Business, Lady?'

'I'm in the market for a weapon,' Morgause says, and smiles a smile that bares her teeth. 'Who better than the Lady of the Lake to sell me one?'

'You need a magic sword, my lady?'

'In a way, cat. In a way...'

That smile she has. Those awful teeth so white and sharp.

'So, Sister Nimue?' Morgause says.

The Lady of the Lake smiles politely back. Takes a sip of her hot flavoured water.

'It's thanks to Cath Palug I found it, really,' she says. 'She's most astute in her use of the seeing pools.'

'Indeed...' Morgause murmurs.

'Here,' Nimue says.

She hands over a woodcut.

The cat cranes her neck to try and see.

Morgause smiles. The cat jumps on the table and slinks

around her mistress, peering into the woodcut in Morgause's hands.

A pretty girl is carved into the picture. She's by a stream, and looking up and smiling, with eyes so full of hope.

She looks familiar. The cat has seen her once before, in scrying.

'Her name is Guinevere,' the Lady says.

Morgause says: 'She's *perfect*.'

PART SIX

THE CHOIR OF ANGELS

38

'**G**uinevere's coming! Guinevere's coming!'
Running footsteps. They hear her before they
see her. A shadow, moving softly, whistling. 'Let All
Mortal Flesh Keep Silence', some melody she'd picked up from
the traders on the Tyne, some Christist ditty out of Greece or
somewhere. She smiles and her teeth are sharp and the night is
cool and the night is dark.

She sings.

'Let all mortal flesh keep silence, and with fear and trembling
stand...'

They hear her before they see her.

They run.

'Guinevere's coming! Guinevere's—'

Behind her, the twang of a bow, the whistle of an arrow
overhead. One of the men ahead pitches face forward in the
dust and doesn't rise. She steps over his corpse.

'For the King of kings and Lord of lords comes forth to
be sacrificed, and given as food to the believers; and there go
before Him the choir of Angels—'

'Choir of *Angels*, mother*fuckers*!' Laudine screams behind
her. She lights a torch and it bursts into flame. In its shuddering
light the young woman is briefly visible, her face a painted war
mask, her eyeballs as white as imported ivory.

She tosses the torch high in the air.

It arcs overhead, hits a thatched roof, and the flames burst to life. In the light of the fire Guinevere can see the silent outpost's packed earth tracks, the few houses and, ahead of her, her destination: the local thane's counting house.

They're out and about in the new Bernicia, far from home. The local thane's men are in the counting house getting drunk. The Choir of Angels have been watching the camp all day. Now men come out to face her. Angles, holding swords. The flames light their faces, their reddened eyes. They charge her.

She turns her javelin, a Roman pilum, and stabs once, twice in one flowing motion. Two men drop to the ground with their intestines spilling. From within the shadows Isolde, 'The Blonde', fires knives.

Guinevere steps over the bodies and enters the counting room. The thane's not there, only some weaselly accountant of his. He cowers from her. Guinevere looks around the room and gives an appreciative whistle.

'Tax collecting's been good, then?' she says conversationally.

The accountant wields a knife, for all that his hand's shaking. 'Get away, witch!'

'No witch, good sir,' she tells him. 'Merely an honest woman doing an honest day's work.'

'Please,' he says. 'Please.'

She reaches for an open, half-full bottle of barley wine. She lifts it up and takes a swig and makes a face.

'Put the knife down,' she says, not unkindly.

Screams outside, then silence. The rest of her choir step into the hall. Isolde, 'the Blonde', and Enid 'the Knife', and Laudine and Luned, 'the Sapphic Assassins', who follow the teachings of the ancient Greek poet.

'Well lookie here,' Isolde says. The accountant makes a mad, desperate dash for the door and Enid buries a knife in his neck. She jumps neatly out of the path of the blood spray and it catches Laudine full on.

'Bitch!'

Enid laughs.

Guinevere looks at the loot. The Angles have been around for the past twenty years or so. A generation. They came up the Tyne or over the coast, some as small traders, some as farmers seeking land, others as soldiers-for-hire, for the kings of Bernicia and Deira were always at each other's throats. Before you knew it the Angles built villages of their own, raised livestock, ploughed fields, established small businesses such as weavers and carpenters, potters and jewellers; and they also executed the old kings of Deira and Bernicia and their strongmen took over the thrones for their own.

In the counting room she sees bars of iron; gold jewellery; Roman coins, and Rhone wine from the continent; good firewood, and sacks of flour, and a pair of lovely gold earrings in a wooden box, and good cloth, and jars of honey, and pickled fish, and the remnants of a feast on the long table.

The girls sit down and finish off the goose and the bread and some apples and cheese, and they drink cider until they are quite drunk. Then they take whatever's portable, the coins and the jewellery and the pieces of cloth, and Enid helps herself to the pickled fish for she has a predilection for the stuff, and then they scoot.

They set fire to the rest of the outpost before they ride into the night, and the flames cast the sky into a false dawn.

Guinevere sits by the stream tearing the petals of a daisy, yellow and white.

She smiles a secret smile, and chants the words to herself.

'He loves me, he loves me not, he loves me little, he loves me a lot. He loves me to passion, he loves me to folly, he loves me not at all.'

Of course I love you, the worm says, far away, and the girl shudders with delight.

Then she straightens up and forgets about the flower. She

whistles, and her girls come to her from across the isolated meadow where they'd made their camp.

Isolde, 'The Blonde', rises from behind the bushes and shakes her shift back over her thighs. 'Can't a girl take a piss in peace anymore, Guinevere?' she says in annoyance.

'Isolde, *dearest*,' Guinevere says. 'Is there ever a time when you *don't* take the piss?'

'You should get yourself checked by the herb woman, Isolde,' Laudine calls from the bank. She climbs out of the water, a fish and a knife in her hands. 'You piss too much, you probably caught something from that Angle you were fucking back in Mercia.'

The other girls laugh. 'Fuck off,' Isolde mutters, but Guinevere can see she's thinking it over.

'You don't know *where* they stick their dicks,' Luned says sagely. 'A watermelon or a sheep it's all the same to men.'

'What in fuck's name is a watermelon?'

'A Jute trader told me about it. It's a sort of Egyptian fruit, I think. It's big and round and red inside.'

'Like your ass, then, Luned!'

'Fuck off, Enid!'

'You can't catch herpes from a watermelon, anyway... Whatever it is.'

Guinevere lets their conversation drift over her. She scratches herself idly.

I'm hungry, the worm says. It has longing in its voice.

'They'll be coming after us hard after that last score,' Laudine says. 'I say we head back to Pons Aelius. We've got us more than enough for the winter.'

'And miss out on all the fun? I hardly think so,' Isolde says.

'You hardly think at all, and that's your problem,' Laudine says.

Guinevere heads to the copse of trees where they'd stashed the loot. She checks it over – the iron bars the Angles often use for barter, and sacks of salt, and the usual assortment of jewellery and coins and weapons. They *could* go back to Pons Aelius, she thinks. The Romans' once-new castle on the Tyne's mostly avoided by the Angles, who do not, apparently, trust Roman architecture. There are still independent Britons there.

'Fuck that,' she says. 'Let's send a message. I want to rob the Aetheling of Deira.'

'Rob him? Rob him how?'

Guinevere's smile widens. 'We kidnap him and then demand his ransom.'

The girls erupt in shouts. 'Are you mad!'

'His weregild's set at what, ten thousand tremissis? We will be set for life.'

'A fucking *short* life!'

Hungry... the worm growls, far away.

Soon... Guinevere promises.

'Besides, no one has this much gold lying around, not even the Aetheling. Not even the whole Kingdom of fucking Deira,' Laudine says.

'So what will you do, run off to the castle and take up sewing?' Guinevere says. 'The game's out there, bitches. The game's the *game*.'

'No *doubt*!' Isolde says, then blushes when the others stare at her. 'I mean... One more big score, then we'd all be land owners and respectable, like. Right?'

'Right,' Enid says dubiously.

'Right...' Laudine says, but she does not sound convinced.

'Luned?' Guinevere says.

'Hmmm?'

'Are you in?'

Luned turns around and slowly smiles. 'Can't win if you don't play, can you?' she says.

So that's that.

'Guinevere's coming! Guinevere's coming!'

They ride down a dirt track with fields on both sides. Children run in the mud, waving and shouting, and Guinevere and the rest of the Choir of Angels toss them little bags of honey cakes, dusted with precious cinnamon spice. They'd scored some at the thane's counting room. Where it came from remained a mystery. It is said giant cinnamon birds collected the sticks from trees that grew in some faraway land and used them to construct their nests, which brave traders then robbed.

Along the fields the farmers, too, straighten from their labour and wave and smile. To them, the Choir of Angels throw bags with precious salt, and here and there a small chunk of iron ore, which the Angles and the Saxons prize. This is why Guinevere and her girls can operate as they do. No villager would turn them in, and when the thane's men come asking they are helpfully and politely pointed in the wrong direction.

They ride to the chief's hall.

'Maggs!' Guinevere says. She hugs the old woman who comes out to welcome them. Maggs gives her a toothless grin and enfolds her in strong wiry arms.

'My, my, but you look ripe for the plucking,' she says.

'Maggs!'

The old woman leers. 'I'm just saying.'

'I'm not looking for a man.'

'It's when you don't look...' She frowns. 'Haven't I taught you better? You must always look to see what's ahead.'

'I mostly look behind me, these days. Besides, I do not have your vision.'

They go inside. The chief, Aldwyn, is grateful for the gifts they bring. A feast is ordered. Guinevere says, 'Who runs Deira these days?'

'Fellow by the name of Pelles,' Maggs says. 'Came from the continent to take over the local racket. The clan chiefs back home want to make sure their... investments are taken care of.'

'He's the Aetheling?'

Maggs says, 'The omnium ducibus dux, the boss of bosses,' and cackles.

'What's he like?'

A shrug. 'Alright, I suppose, as long as you don't fuck with him.'

Guinevere: 'I think it's too late for that.'

Maggs: 'So I've heard. You girls been keeping busy.'

'Girls gotta eat.'

'I raised you well…'

'Do you think he'll come after us, Maggs?'

The old woman looks at her levelly. 'He already has, fool. His men have been scouring the land from half across the Roman Wall to the sea. If they find you…'

She leaves the thought unsaid.

Guinevere, with a lightness she doesn't quite feel, says, 'Well, we'll just have to make sure he doesn't.'

'You can't run forever, girl.'

'I don't intend to.'

'Then what?'

'Tell me, Maggs. Where can this new Aetheling be found?'

The old woman goes still. 'Why?'

'Call it curiosity.'

'Curiosity killed the cat…'

'I ain't no cat.'

'Well, that's debatable.'

'So?'

'He inhabits a hill fort to the north of here. Wild country, out there you can run into anything, even Picts and giants, all sorts of things. New place, heavily fortified, mostly Angle soldiers, some hired Jutes. Not people to fuck with. Called the Dolorous Tor, it's near the Wansbeck River. From what I've seen in my scrying, they have been landing men there for some time, as though building up an army. But for what or against whom I couldn't tell you.'

'They say there's a new king in the south,' Guinevere says.

Maggs shrugs. 'A king's a king and a rat's a rat, and if one dies there's always another one right behind on its tail.'

'The Dolorous Tor, eh?'

Hungry... the worm whispers, far away.

Maggs cocks her head quizzically. Perhaps she alone beside Guinevere can hear it.

'You know why I never kept a pet?' she says.

'Why?'

'Sooner or later they shit in your home.'

'Alright...'

'Come. There is time before the feast. I see your girl Isolde's getting busy with the boys already.'

Guinevere looks over. Isolde's got her hands on a young hunter's chest and is urgently murmuring in his ear.

'Dumb as two planks, that boy,' Maggs says.

Guinevere says, complacently: 'That's how she likes them.'

Maggs' house is cool and dark and quiet. A fire smoulders in a ring of stones. The house is untidy. There are chicken bones on the ground and garments thrown about, and a collection of dried herbs and an assortment of oddly shaped rocks and metals, and a small thin knife made of flint, which must be very old.

'Sit, sit. Let's scry. It's been forever since I've had a good scry. How about you, Guinevere?' Maggs leers. 'Got any good scrying recently?'

'I'm sure I don't know what you mean.'

'Well, well, I'm sure you don't, I'm sure you don't,' Maggs says. 'Now, where's my glass ball, where did I put it... Ah, here it is.'

It's impossible to say just what Maggs *is*. She is not a native Briton nor an Angle or a Saxon or a Jute. She speaks bad Latin and worse Anglisc and whatever it is Jutes speak. She has been old for as long as Guinevere has known her, which is her entire life. She is what the continental newcomers call a haegtesse, and like their wise old women she, too, can use a glass ball to sometimes see that which is unseen. She'd brought up Guinevere after her father died.

'So what do you see, Maggs?'

'I see white sails, and a black sea, and an island in the distance... But this is far in the future still, I think.'

She peers into the glass ball and mutters to herself. Her index finger moves, as though swiping through images only she can see.

'I see a group of men moving furtively through this land,' she says at last, thoughtfully. 'One of whom is a fish and the other a tree.'

'That doesn't make much sense, Maggs,' Guinevere says.

'Yes, well.' She coughs. 'I see... I see a man in your future. He's handsome, if you like them that way.'

'Handsome how?'

'Skinny as a chicken bone, and with a killer's eyes...'

'He doesn't sound very appealing. Don't you have anything else for me?'

'So impatient, you are. Always were.' But she keeps scrolling, and her lips move without sound, until—

'I see gold,' she says, and her eyes grow large, for Maggs, as Guinevere well knows, is a greedy old woman and no mistake. 'I see so much gold that the shine it gives is blinding – no!' she cries, and she throws the glass ball away and covers her eyes, and Guinevere sees a flash of burning light burst out of the glass and sear the wall, for just a moment before the glass smashes into bits.

'Maggs!'

But Maggs is huddled on the floor, hiding her face. 'Beware, Guinevere!' she says. 'Not all that glitters is gold.'

'What?'

'Beware that which is false, and beware, most of all, the attentions of kings.'

And she says no more. And Guinevere cannot rouse her. And so, at last, she leaves her there, and ventures outside to see her girls.

That night they feast in that little safe haven, but they take little of the mead and beer and, in the night, they slip away and watch, and wait. And Guinevere is not entirely surprised to see a force of men creep up on the village, until they stand surrounding the chief's hall.

Nasty, brutish men in metal helmets, armed with swords.

'Betrayed,' Enid says, with loathing.

Guinevere calms her with a touch of the hand. 'We can bribe them all we want with cinnamon and salt,' she says. 'But an argument of kings is only ever settled with a sword.'

'I will burn their houses down and dance upon their graves,' Enid says; but she lacks conviction.

'Come, sisters, we have the information that we need. So while they hunt us here we will journey north, and strike them where they least expect it.'

'What did the madwoman say?' asks Laudine.

'She isn't a madw—' Guinevere reconsiders. 'She said she saw gold. Lots and lots of gold.'

'Gold is good,' Isolde says.

'Yes...'

'Let's just go,' Luned says.

They mount their horses.

'To the Dolorous Tor!' Isolde says.

They ride out of there.

Behind them, the sky is aflame with fire; the Aetheling's men, having failed to find the Choir of Angels, have carried out the same punishment on the villagers as Enid had wished.

'Goodbye, Maggs...' Guinevere says; but softly.

39

The kingdoms of Deira and Bernicia lie on opposite sides of the River Tyne, and in truth there is not much difference between them now to when they were ruled over by Britons. They are still mostly farmland, inhabited by farmers, trappers, fisherfolk and small craftworkers, it's just that now some villages are native and some are of the newcomers.

There is also, in truth, plenty of space for everyone, for the island is big and its population is somewhat sparse.

The newcomers arrived in stages. They are a tribal peoples from Germania on the continent, and some arrived with Hengist and Horsa as mercenaries, or so Guinevere was told, while others came as farmers speaking of an apocalypse, that is to say, an uncovering, for their lands have been invaded by floods and the sea until their peoples starved and they were forced to migrate. These boat people have been fleeing Europa to these shores for the past two decades, where they have mostly formed colonies of their own. Some of their colonies war with the native population, and some war with each other, and some just try to get along.

They work hard, on the whole. And they keep themselves to themselves.

They do not speak the common tongue but their own harsh *Anglisc*, a language truly of demons and half-men, a language so barbaric no one should ever have to speak it or, worse, write a story in it.

It doesn't even have an alphabet. To write in it they steal the Latin script of Rome. It is an awful thing, to have to think in Anglisc. One may as well speak in the tongue of dogs.

Or so they say. But Guinevere has grown in Pons Aelius, which is situated on the Tyne between the two spheres of influence, and for all that she has her Latin and the common tongue she also knows her Anglisc and the manners and customs of these newcomers, for she was raised in their midst. Perhaps, she sometimes thinks, one day all of this land will speak in Anglisc, and they'll resurface the old Roman roads and ride down them in horseless chariots, like dragons belching smoke, and somehow sit inside the belly of the beasts while voices in the air sing for them in many voices.

Sometimes she thinks she has the gift of sight, like Maggs. But then again, perhaps she's crazy.

But I love you, the worm whispers, far away.

The Choir of Angels ride down track roads and skirt the villages. They sleep under the stars, build small fires, catch hares for their supper. They pass through woodland, over hills, until one day they reach the Tyne and cross it.

Growing up in Pons Aelius, Guinevere had seen what seemed like a certain present become a horrifyingly unknown future. She never knew her mother, who died giving birth to her. Her father vanished on a sea journey when she was three. She has only one memory of him still, of strong arms lifting her up, a scratchy beard, the smell of smoke and sweat, and something like love. She was raised by the nurse-woman, Maggs, while her uncle Cador ruled from the castle. For a time she knew the world and the world made sense. Then the newcomers began to come, a few at first up the Tyne, then overland from the southern shores, and more and more, and when Cador died the newcomers' man was in place to take over.

How Cador died wasn't entirely clear. A hunting accident,

some said. Others muttered darkly that it was no accident, and that a Saxon wizard turned him into a wild boar, slit his throat with a scythe and bled him into the earth until the grass and flowers all around the body shrivelled and died and nothing ever lived in that spot again. Guinevere had gone riding into the woods once where they said the black spot was, but she never found it. Still. There might have been some truth in it.

So Guinevere... adapted. She learned Anglisc, and she watched the Angle women, some of whom were *fierce*. They taught her knife work and the sword and how to gut a rabbit and how to slaughter pigs and how to sew a wound. And one moonless night she rode out into the forest, into the deepest part where no light broke and the creatures that moved in the mulch were nameless, and there she channelled all her rage and her despair, for the mother she never knew and the father who vanished at sea, for a family and a kingdom lost, for a language and a way of life slipping away, forever – she took it all and *fed* it, into a wordless scream.

She also cut herself, but she'd been doing that a lot back then. A way of, somehow, asserting control, in a world where she had none.

Her blood fell on the black, fertile ground.

Her scream vanished into the thickness of the trees. It fed into the roots and soils.

And out of the darkness, something came back.

A small, helpless little animal slithered out of the dark and came to rest by her feet.

Guinevere knelt there in the dark. The thing glowed white. She cupped it in her bloodied hands and lifted it up and stared at it, entranced.

I love you, the worm said.

And Guinevere said, 'I love you too.'

★

I love you… the worm says.

'I love you too,' Guinevere murmurs. Too many days on a horse, and the land had changed once they crossed the Tyne, became a wilderness of feral forest, routes that led nowhere and roots that tripped the animals and branches that lashed at the Choir of Angels as though the land itself, somehow, rose against them.

'What does it look like?' she whispers.

Many nasty men… Fires that burn in many colours, and evil smoke… A terrible stench.

'You're really not selling me on this, are you, worm?'

Eat them?

A note of hope, and longing.

'Not a good idea…' She mulls it over. 'Not after last time.'

Hungry… Miss you.

'I miss you too, worm.'

'Who are you talking to, Guinevere?'

'What? No one.'

'Talking to yourself again?'

The other girls laugh.

She pays them no mind. As they crossed the Tyne she peered into the water and saw something impossible: a troupe of pale women swimming in the depths, carrying swords. They looked up at her and waved and smiled, and mouthed the words, *Hello, sister.*

Now they ride through a land that is green and yet shows signs of sudden, failing health. Dirty bogs where once clear pools of water stood. Blackened trees with twisted branches drooping to the ground, scattered here and there amidst the healthy ones. Some sort of a selective plague had touched them, maybe. And here and there the bodies of birds that fell from the skies.

The air, too, is hazy with something that is not quite smoke, too thick and too sweet. As they ride they begin to notice, and avoid, the patrols and the watchmen who guard the approach to the Dolorous Tor. It is easy enough for the girls at first, but then they pass through the last of the forest, suddenly, and see the hill fort rise overhead.

The Dolorous Tor is a black mass against the sky. It is built as though multiple architects have got together, taken a bunch of Goblin Fruit and then each designed a section of the fort without paying any consideration to the others or, indeed, to the rules of common sense or Euclidean geometry. It is like a black hole punched through reality, distorting the air around it, like a wound that pulsates, both repelling and drawing the eye.

Smoke rises high into the air and the fires below burn in many colours, and a weird chanting emanates from that high place, and Isolde says, 'Maybe this isn't such a good idea.'

'It's a terrible idea,' Laudine says firmly. 'But it's the only one we've got.'

They see the patrols, then. Men in chainmail riding dark horses, their faces obscure.

Guinevere scans the approach. The hill is steep and the only path leading up is guarded at several checkpoints. There is little vegetation to offer cover and the ground is burned black and there are evil sharp rocks everywhere.

Luned says, 'Unless you can turn into a bird and *fly* there, I don't see how else we can get in.'

'Oh, we can get in,' Guinevere says darkly. 'Now, take off your clothes.'

'You what?'

The others exchange amused glances.

The naked woman runs screaming towards the approaching patrolmen through the forest. They rein their horses, and two of them even climb down to assist her, and this is their undoing. Laudine's arrows whistle through the air and the other girls fall on the men from the high branches and stick their knives through the eye holes in the helmets and toss the screaming men from their horses.

Then the remaining men charge and it is each girl for herself, and Enid gets a nasty gash on her arm but they all have swords now and, what's more, they know how to handle them. One of the men, horseless, turns to run, but no one can be allowed to get away and warn them up on the hill and, on the horses now, they catch up to him and string him like a fish.

They bury the corpses in a shallow grave under an oak, and keep the one prisoner tied up as Enid nurses her wound and Laudine builds a small fire and heats up her knives. The forest is dark, and small blind things crawl in the earth and there is just something so *wrong* about the air. Guinevere kneels besides the soldier. He is not so scary now, but it is hard to look scary when you're nude and your shrivelled junk is dangling between your legs and your balls are trying hard to crawl all the way up back inside you. Besides, he's young. And Guinevere takes one of the hot knives and holds it close to him, just enough to feel the heat it's putting out.

'What's your name?' she says, in Anglisc.

'S... Selwyn,' he says. He stares at her with what he thinks is defiance. It just makes him look more scared and small.

'Listen, Selwyn,' Guinevere says gently. 'It doesn't have to go down bad. It can be over quick, quick as you like.' She makes one motion with her hand across her throat. 'Won't even feel a thing. I promise.'

Then she shows him the hot knife. 'Or it can go down slow. It can go down hard. I don't want it to. You don't, either. But it's your choice. I just need you to tell me the password for the checkpoints, and the way things are up there. Simple stuff. One way or the other it won't matter to you anymore.' She strokes his short-cropped hair. 'What do you say, Selwyn? The fast road, or the slow?'

He stares at her in bewilderment and hate. 'F... Fuck you, you witch!' he says.

So Guinevere applies the knife.

They bury him with the others and dress for the part. Five patrolmen on five horses depart the forest and start up the road to the Dolorous Tor. Guinevere marvels at the workmanship on the helmet, all anyone can see of her is her eyes. They reach the first checkpoint and give the password and pass through. The road winds up the hill and black clouds amass at the top but it never rains, and the air feels suffocating and heavy.

'This is going smoothly so far,' Laudine says dubiously.

'Keep your eyes open and your hand on your sword,' Guinevere says. 'I don't like the smell of this place.'

'Yeah, it's kind of...'

'Dolorous?' Luned says.

'*Melancholic*,' Laudine adds, in Latin. 'What?' she says, to their looks. 'Everyone knows the melas kholé or black bile in the balance of the humours leads to feelings of fears and despondencies and unreasonable torpor. It's all in Galen.'

'If you say so...' Isolde says.

'It's all in Galen...' Enid says, and they all laugh.

They're hailed at the last checkpoint before the castle by a burly captain. 'Hey, Edwyn! You're a few men short!'

Guinevere, thickening her voice: 'They're down hunting a trespasser, captain. Some crazy woman, possibly a witch.'

'A witch? The lord will not be pleased. You sound strange, Edwyn. What happened to your voice?'

'I feel a cold coming upon me, good captain. It is nothing, really. We better hurry up to see the lord.'

The captain frowns.

'You don't seem quite yourself today, Edwyn.'

'I must hurry,' Guinevere says. 'The lord will want the news.'

She waits; still on the horse, forcing her hand to remain steady and not creep to the hilt of the sword. Trying to work out how many they could kill before the soldiers got them. The others waiting too, the horses neighing, the guards watching, not yet suspicious, perhaps, but ready to act on order.

'...True,' the captain allows. He waves them to pass. Guinevere sighs inwardly with relief. As they ride up to the tor she risks a glance back. The captain's frowning, looking after them.

Guinevere raises her fist in salute.

The Dolorous Tor is even more foreboding up close. Those walls are hewn out of black rock not native to the area. The towers rise misshapen high into the air. The fires burn with a smell like cannabis and opium. Rare medicines, imported from across the water. She doesn't know what's happening here, only that she doesn't like it.

They ride into the courtyard...

The gates close behind them.

She looks around her.

Archers stand overhead with their bows at the ready.

Warriors emerge out of the shadows and ring them with swords.

A small, black-clad figure emerges out of the doorway. It is a man of unremarkable features but for a scar across his face, thinning hair, a pleasant smile.

He nods.

'Guinevere's coming...' he says mockingly.

She thinks – Oh, shit.

She removes her helmet. The others follow her lead. They stare at this man – this Aetheling.

'Lord Pelles, I presume,' she says.

'Lady Guinevere. You honour my halls.'

'I've come to kill you.'

He shakes his head. 'A fool's errand, surely.'

'I'm not so sure.'

He regards her quizzically. 'Well, I would like to think you an honoured guest. Please. Dismount and come inside. I shall have food prepared, and hot water for you to bathe – it must have been a while since you'd had a shower, no offence.'

'None taken, I'm sure,' she says coldly.

But she has no choice. It is a trap, has always been a trap. It must have been. She dismounts from her horse and surrenders her sword and her weapons. The others follow suit. They go inside. Black halls, cold stone, the whisper of steel. They are shown to quarters that are lavish enough, but a jail cell all the same.

'What do we do now?' Isolde says.

'If he had wanted us dead, we would be dead by now.'

'This is ignominious,' Laudine says.

Enid washes and cleans her wound, her face tight.

'He wants something.'

'Sure, but what?'

Guinevere shrugs.

'I'm starving,' Luned says.

A clear bell rings. A guard shows up at the door.

'The Aetheling of Deira will see you now,' he says.

He unlocks the door and they follow him to the king's hall.

40

A harpist plays soft, beautiful music. Four musicians play the bone flute. It sounds like birds chasing each other in the wind.

A table is laid with food. Boar and hares, apples and cheese, bread, beer. Guards watch them impassively. The Choir of Angels fall on the food. It's been a while, and a girl is better ready when she's full, or so Enid is fond of saying. Guinevere stuffs her face until grease runs down her chin.

'Enjoy,' the Aetheling says.

He's sitting with another man. A Briton, and kingly with it. A fire burns and herbs burn in the fire and the flames have many colours and the shadows dance queerly on the walls. Guinevere palms a paring knife, then notices the man watching her. He smiles.

'Who the fuck are you?' Guinevere says.

'My name,' he says, 'is Leir.'

She knows the name and she grows still. He rules the ridings from the old Roman town of Eboracum on the River Ouse. He's nothing much to look at, but for his eyes, which burn with power.

'I did not know Angles and Britons ran together,' she says.

'Running, not so much,' Leir says, and smiles. 'A measured walk, perhaps. The Aetheling and I have an understanding.'

'Why fight,' Pelles says, 'when two can profit?'

Guinevere looks from one to the other. She likes nothing about what is going on. She still intends to do harm to this Pelles. And now she's added this Leir to her list. But these two wank stains clearly have something in mind for her, or she'd long be dead by now. She gnaws on a chicken drumstick.

'Profit how?' she says.

'Ah...'

The two men exchange amused glances.

'The usual, really, dear Guinevere. A tax on all that can be taxed, control of the waterways and imports from the continent and exports to same, some Goblin Fruit, the beer concessions, a bit of slavery, metalwork, hire out mercenaries to protect the merchants, gold...'

'Gold? What gold?'

She senses something important in the way he'd casually dropped in that last one. There are no gold mines in this area. The two kings exchange glances but do not reply directly.

'You understand the benefit of neighbours cooperating in this manner, don't you? Besides, there's always someone keen to steal your shit.'

'Me, you mean?'

'Oh, precious thing! You and your girls are like the mosquitoes that irritate by biting, but can always be swatted away. No, I mean the one in the south. A lean young wolf, who thinks us fucking lambs he can devour at will.'

'Yes,' Leir says, 'this Arthur has proven quite a taxing obstacle. We almost rid ourselves of him a while back but he... prevailed.' He shrugs. 'But that's a problem for another time.'

'Yes,' Pelles says. He claps his hands. 'Bring out the leprechaun,' he says.

The other girls perk up at that. It's not the sort of line you hear every day. Enid even puts down the slice of bread she'd been dipping in the fat, though not before taking a healthy bite.

'What the fuck's a leprechaun?' Isolde says.

A small creature is brought into the hall in chains. Guinevere watches it. Him. It's a male, and though he's the size of a child he is clearly adult, even old. His clothes are a dirty green and he has a bushy red beard and sad, haunted eyes. She watches his hands. They are dirty and scarred, and the nails are broken.

As though he had been made to dig in some pit for too long.

'*That's* a leprechaun,' Pelles says.

'Top o' the mornin' to y—' the leprechaun starts, then gives up. 'Please,' he says. 'Please. Just let me go.'

Pelles removes a small pouch from his belt and opens it. He takes out a round, shiny object and tosses it to Guinevere. She snatches it out of the air.

Stares at the gold coin in her palm.

Wrong...! whispers the worm in her mind. *Poison!*

It feels strange in her hand. It is a plain coin, it is not imprinted with anyone's visage. She scratches the face with a nail and the gold comes off and a strange, silvery metal is underneath that feels almost crumbly.

'What *is* it?' she says.

'Leprechaun gold,' Leir says. 'Wash your hands now that you've handled it. I believe the material to be poisonous.'

'I have never seen this kind of metal before.'

The Lord Pelles yanks on the leprechaun's chains savagely, and the small creature stumbles and falls.

'Please,' he says. 'Please. It is not my doing.'

'Tell them,' the Lord Pelles says.

'The grail...' the creature whispers.

'The what?' says Guinevere.

'It streaked across the sky, perhaps three decades ago, in the time of Uther it were.' The leprechaun's eyes are wide and haunted. 'A dragon...' he says.

'A star stone,' Leir says. 'A Lapis Exilis, that fell from the heavens. It did not fall straight down but at an angle from the skies, descending until its path led it at last through this land. Mutilating it in the process with its burning flame.'

'A stone from the sky?'

'This happens. You may see them in the night sky, sometimes. Like fireflies, flashes of brightness that just as quickly vanish. Not this one, though. This one was big.'

'As the dragon flew,' the leprechaun said, ignoring Leir, 'it laid an egg. The egg fell, to the north of here. The dragon flew further on, and where it fell nobody knows or, if they know, they aren't telling.'

'An egg,' Guinevere says flatly. She makes sure to put the false gold down and to wash her hands carefully in the basin, like the king said. She cleans under her fingernails. Enid, a hen's egg half up to her mouth, lowers it.

'I believe,' Leir says, 'that a fragment of the heavenly rock broke apart from the main body and fell not far from here.'

'And it has, what, gold? This isn't gold.'

'This is a metal seldom seen upon this Earth,' Leir says. 'And what's more, I want it.'

'Why?'

'That is not your concern.'

'Well, can't you go and get it?' Guinevere says.

Leir nods to the leprechaun. The creature nods nervously.

'No, no. I mean, yes. I mean, no. It is far beyond the wall, you see. It belongs to *him*...' He shudders.

'Who?'

'Urien of the Hen Ogledd,' Lord Pelles says. 'That sneaky fuck. It's in his territory and the bastard's mining star stone for all it's worth. And passing it as gold to all and sundry! I do not care, myself, for this tale of dragons or what have you. I just want the counterfeiting done with. Leprechaun?'

'Yes, yes. I mean, no. I mean, he had enslaved us in service of the mining, lady. It is a dismal operation in a dismal place where nothing grows and nothing lives. We sickened there. Look at me!' The leprechaun watches her with its sad deformed eyes. 'I am dying, lady. We are all dying there.'

Guinevere finds an apple. Takes a bite. She stares at them all. Shrugs.

'So?' she says. 'What the fuck has any of this got to do with *me*?'

Pelles smiles.

Leir smiles.

The leprechaun moves its mouth in a ghastly pained grimace that must be an attempt at a smile.

'Well, seeing as you're here...' Pelles says.

'Yes...?'

'I'd like you to solve this problem for me, Lady Guinevere.'

'Excuse me?'

'I'd like you,' the Aetheling says patiently, 'to go to this accursed place where the false gold is minted, bring the operation to an end and liberate the metals mined there.'

'You what?'

'To put it plainly, I want you to rob them of their gold.'

Guinevere stares at him. Knows this is a fool's errand. Knows this is an execution in waiting. Knows, too, that she doesn't really have a choice.

'And if I refuse?' she says.

'Lady, if you do,' the Aetheling says, 'then I shall slit your throat and bury you and your women with all due ceremony in a barrow, with all your possessions intact – you know how us Angles take our burial rites seriously. And you will be left to rot and your bones to bleach for centuries, for curious grave robbers to eventually come, and dig your sorry carcass up, and puzzle over your garments and all your assorted crap to try and figure out questions such as what roles did women play in this society. But they will come to few good answers, and you'll be dead and buried all the same. So?'

'...I'll take the job,' Guinevere says.

41

'That fucking fuck,' Laudine says.

'Oh, I will deal with *him* in due course,' Guinevere says darkly.

They ride out of the Dolorous Tor at daybreak. The sky overhead is bleak. This smog in the air is bewitched with dark sorcery. Guinevere thinks of star stones and poisoned metal. She thinks of devastation.

Perhaps from the air you can see it, she thinks. A dark path cutting across the landscape. The route of fire plotted by the fallen star.

All through that day and the next the sun is hidden behind the smog. They'd entered a land of mist. Shapes move in the fog, and coloured lights, and she can hear sobs and screams. Footsteps come and go. She hears the neigh of horses. She hears the ghostly clash of steel. The tang of sulphur in the air, the stench of coal, the burned taste of mistletoe. The smoke gets in her eyes and into her mind and makes her see fantastical shapes, all bursting stars and ghostly apparitions. There are no maps in this land beyond the wall. The Angels travel blind.

At night it gets colder and there are no stars and distant fires glow behind the wall of smoke. The night is restless with the tread of troubled spirits. The Angels stop, exhausted, make camp beside a giant oak. They come to realise too late it is a gibbet. The mutilated corpses of some hideous beings hang from thick ropes. She'd seen nobody like them. They are mutatio, transformed. Human shapes but made deformed and awful, some with arms like trunks and some with skins all green and covered in boils. One has three eyes. The girls have not the energy to even cut them down. They huddle by the ancient tree and fall into uneasy sleep. They do not build a fire.

In the night a beast passes questing through their camp. Guinevere wakens. The creature moves stealthily, almost sadly. It has many mouths and tongues. It looks at Guinevere out of multiple sad eyes. It stops and stares.

'Hello,' Guinevere says.

The creature warbles at her. It cannot form coherent words, but she can sense the need behind it, the desperate aloneness, the fear and pain. She says, 'You are a girl,' in mild surprise. The creature warbles. Guinevere strokes her fur.

Footsteps in the fog. A knight appears. Bedraggled, thin. The creature turns and faces him. The knight looks on at her. A look of longing, and despair.

'My girl,' he says. 'My girl.'

The creature shrieks in wordless love and pain. The sound's awful, it cuts the night. The Choir of Angels awaken, they stand guard, instinctively, knives drawn, siding with this questing beast.

'I mean her no harm,' the knight says tiredly. 'She is of me. My daughter.'

The creature keens.

'Then let her be.'

'I can't.' The anguish in his voice seems real. 'It's like a part of me and if I go too far I die, or she does, or we both.'

They seem frozen there, staring at each other.

'Where do you come from, knight?' Luned says.

'Far away from here. This land's not right. Do you not feel it? There's poison in the earth and in the air.'

'A star stone, we were told,' Isolde tells him.

The knight considers. 'Perhaps, yes. It is true I saw one

fall, once, long ago, with my master Uther. They say there's radiance in them, strong enough to heal or kill or both. I know no more. You should be careful. I have seen the dwellers in the fog and they are many of them crazed and altered, like these poor corpses overhead. And others dwell here who would use the weak and powerless. Beware, my ladies.'

'We can take care of ourselves, if it is all the same to you, good knight.'

The knight acknowledges the rebuke. 'Forgive me, I did not mean to offend.'

'What is your name?' Guinevere says.

'It is Pellinore, my lady.'

'And where do you venture?'

'Wherever she goes.'

Guinevere turns to the questing beast. 'Where *do* you go?' she says, and very gently.

The creature keens. The arms reach out and stroke her face.

Images come, unbidden, into Guinevere's mind. She sees a castle rising in the fog, above a great precipice. She sees great mounds of earth, and fires burning and a great radiance, and slaves digging deep in the ground, and she sees the rudimentary use of Roman mining techniques.

But these are no Romans.

Why there? she whispers into the questing beast's mind.

The reply is wordless. A sense of shelter, freedom, peace. The beast's confused. It turns from Guinevere abruptly. Screams at the knight. The sounds that she makes are terrifying. Love and hate and longing. Then the arms like tentacles swing round and round and she is gone, bounding with superhuman speed into the mist.

The knight just stands there, looking all forlorn.

'Perhaps we'll meet again,' he says. 'My ladies.' He steps into the fog and then he too is gone.

They sleep in shifts. When morning comes it is no clearer. They ride through peaty bogs and over twisted branches rising out of the ground, under trees where swinging corpses dangle. Mute faces stare at them behind the trees and from the water. The girls all stink, they dare not wash, their hair is matted, the knives or bows are always in their hands. But they are not attacked.

They come one day at dusk to a village on the edge of the fog. The houses are small and lean-to, the thatched roofs grey and the walls made of mud and sticks. All men, all stooped and hopeless-looking. They welcome them in. They build a small fire and cook soup. The girls sip politely.

'They took them,' the chief of the village explains. Confiding.

'Took who?'

'The womenfolk. They stole them away.'

'Who did?'

'*She* did.'

He nods, as if that explains everything. The girls exchange glances.

'Took them where?'

'To Maiden's Castle.'

Laudine farts. She looks vaguely surprised. Their diet has been meagre, their farts are as rare as hope, in this place.

'We tried to plead with the mistress of that place, but we were ignored.'

'Mistress?' Guinevere says. 'We were told the lord Urien rules in this land.'

The chief shrugs bony shoulders. 'Perhaps.'

'You don't know?'

'We know little, lady. We were prosperous once, and at peace. Then came the blight on the land and we sickened. Then they came to take the womenfolk away, for the work they are doing.'

'What work are they doing?'

He just shrugs. 'We'd lost hope,' he says. 'Then, one day, knights appeared from the fog. Outsiders. *Welsch*. They were unaffected by the blight. Strong and lean. They had been travelling for some time, they said. They had wandered far along the fairy path and on their return to the world became lost. They wanted to go south, but we pleaded with them to help us. To go rescue our women from Maiden's Castle and from the clutches of the queen who dwells there. At last they accepted.'

'And did they return?'

'They did not.'

The girls sleep uneasily that night, in that village of doom. In the morning they mount their horses and ride into the fog again. There are people living, even here. They meet them on their travels. Wanderers in carts, and small hidden villages amidst the ferns and even fields of boggy weeds where farmers bend to pluck ill-smelling plants – but they have *gold*. The girls have never seen so much gold as this. Wary of the coins, they do not handle them. All these people are sick with a plague that has no earthly origin. In a clearing one night they see a unicorn emerge out of the trees.

They are rare. Julius Caesar had reported seeing one deep in the forests of Germania. It is stag-like, huge, and with a single horn protruding from its forehead, with branches growing out of the tip.

The girls are still. The creature stands there. Moonlight filters through the fog.

Guinevere dismounts. She tiptoes to the unicorn. It stirs. It huffs. It shakes its mane.

'There's a good unicorn, there, there...'

The creature stares at her. Its eyes are very bright. It sniffs the air. A stream of piss hits the ground and steams into the air.

'Well there's a big boy, no mistake,' Isolde says, staring.

The unicorn shakes its head. It neighs again.

'I think he wants us to follow him.'

They do.

The unicorn leads them through the trees. It leads them over a brook with foul-smelling waters. It leads them on a trodden footpath and over a fairy bridge and past a lost Roman cemetery from some forgotten military campaign, and then they're through the fog and the castle looms out of the earth.

It's night. The moon is out. The moon is red. The castle's black. It stands atop a giant precipice. Hot fires burn in the enormous pit. They hear the sound of chains and grunts and cries of pain. They hear the sound of whips. The unicorn whinnies, once, and vanishes into the trees and fog. The Choir of Angels are alone again.

The girls stare at the castle. The place is definitely spooky.

'Well?' Isolde says at last.

Guinevere shrugs.

'You only live once,' Guinevere says.

They turn their horses.

They ride up to the castle.

42

'Welcome, *welcome*, ladies!'

The reception committee's a bit of a surprise.

A beaming major-domo extends her arms to the travellers. Guinevere, on her horse, sags with tiredness. They'd expected a fight and got a ceremony instead.

Soldiers stand to attention. Women, all, helmeted and breastplated, holding spears. Their armour gleams. There's gold woven into everything.

'Welcome to Maiden's Castle. I shall have rooms prepared.' The major-domo claps her hands. 'Water! Baths! Garments for our guests! Prepare the feast!'

'This is somewhat unexpected,' Guinevere says.

'Why?' the major-domo asks. 'What did you expect?'

Guinevere considers. 'I'm sure I couldn't say.'

'I shall inform the lady of the house of your arrival. Please, follow me.'

The girls dismount. They hand over their tired horses, and surrender blades and bows. They follow meekly, the castle broods upon its mound of dug-up earth. Its halls are cavernous, its corridors are hewn of strange black stone. But there are carpets on the floor and torches set at intervals along the walls. The air is scented with crushed sage and marjoram.

It's like a repetition of a thing already seen. They're given rooms, hot baths are readied, the girls bathe and clean their hair, the soap is scented. The air is bright and clear with candlelight. Soft music plays. It's very pleasant. The Angels gather to discuss.

'This is a trap, it must be.'

'I do not care, I'm tired.'

'And I'm so hungry I could eat a horse.'

'Which horse? Not mine.'

'Perhaps a sausage.'

'Girls, focus. We have a job to do.'

'We're guests here, Guinevere,' Isolde says.

'By guests I'm sure you mean to say we're prisoners.'

'Hush, Laudine. It's nice here.'

'It's very nice—' from Enid. She yawns. 'I like it here.'

'Well, don't get comfortable.'

'Why in Woden's name not? We travelled days to get here and deserve a rest.'

'It is a trap.'

'You said already.'

They break the convocation, undecided.

'Just keep your eyes and ears open and your mouths closed.'

'Not if there's food,' Isolde says.

'We know what *you* like to stuff in your mouth,' Laudine says, and they all laugh.

'Fuck off!'

The tread of footsteps, soft, assured. A chambermaid appears. 'You're called to supper, ladies,' she informs them.

Coiffed and perfumed, in soft silks and cotton – imported gods know how and where from – the Choir of Angels follow the servant to the feast.

There are a few things Guinevere notices about the dining hall straight away.

It isn't necessarily the immaculate preparation of the long tables, how everything is so neatly and beautifully arranged.

It isn't the beautiful fresh flowers artistically placed (and where did they even *get* such flowers, in such a place?).

It isn't the silver cutlery or the gleam of gold on the walls, where objects of great beauty are beautifully displayed. It isn't the tapestries, which are enchanting, nor the music the musicians play, which is also enchanting, nor the smells of the food, which are intoxicating, nor the sound of conversation, which seems invigorating—

It isn't even, so much, the sight of the beaten naked man chained to the wall.

He is a one-eyed man, thin as a snake and leathery, with old battle scars across his arms and abdomen. He must have been a savage leader, once. A Northern man who might have been a king. Guinevere accepts a goblet from a passing server. She sips the wine. It is exquisite, of course. Everything in this place is done with great taste and deliberation. She walks to the chained man and examines him curiously.

The man's one good eye stares at her. His lips open, move, but no sound emerges.

'Urien of the Old North, I presume?' Guinevere says.

The man closes his eye, defeated.

'Leader of the Hen Ogledd. I thought this was your land. I thought this was your castle.'

'Perhaps it was, once.' A smiling woman joins her. She is very beautiful, with a brooch of gold holding her hair. She sips her wine and looks at the display. 'Who can remember? Men come and go, but women stay.' She turns to Guinevere. She alone draws the eye in this place, at this time. She says, 'I am Elaine of Corbenic.'

'Is this your castle, lady?'

The smile widens. 'So it is.'

'And this?'

'This thing? It's but a man. I like to keep him there as a reminder.'

'A reminder of what?'

The woman laughs. 'I forget,' she says. She turns away from Urien. He's been forgotten long ago, it seems. 'You must be Guinevere,' she says. 'Your name precedes you.'

'I see.'

'Please, come. Eat. Drink. Be merry. Did Pelles send you?'

She tries to catch her by surprise.

Guinevere smiles back instead. 'He did,' she says. 'You're well informed.'

Elaine waves a hand. 'It is my business.'

'What *is* your business, mistress?'

That smile again. She's like a cat and Guinevere's a pigeon. 'Come. Eat,' she says. 'You must be starving.'

Guinevere accepts gracefully.

Dinner that evening is a lively affair. They sit at the long table and Elaine of Corbenic sits at its head.

Guinevere is introduced to her table mates.

There is Legate Marcus Aurelius Agrippa, of Byzantium, a stately Eastern Roman with a military bearing and a spotless tunic, who speaks three languages but says relatively little and listens a lot. Guinevere has never met a Roman. What one is doing here, so far from home, is a mystery to her. But when prompted the Legate brightens. He speaks softly of Byzantium, or Constantinople as it's called now. Of its majestic palaces and churches, its wide avenues, its beautiful climate, the wealth of its produce and artisans.

There is Bahram of Persia, part-roving ambassador, part-trader, part-spy, with a twinkle in his eye, and he speaks fondly of the great trading cities of Bukhara and Samarkand, of silks from Qin and spices from India, and he paints to Guinevere a picture of a world that is vast and glorious, somewhere distant, so far away from this rainy island that she is incapable of even imagining it.

'And what do you do here, Sir Bahram?' she inquires.

'Gold, dear lady, gold!' he says. 'What else is there?'

The Legate from Constantinople frowns at this but says

nothing. The food is served. Toads stuffed with herbs and dormice stuffed with cheese and wild turtles shelled and served in soup. Guinevere's stomach growls but she dare not eat this tainted food. This whole land's poisoned, and the enchanted air feels like a bad miasma, the music cloying, the lights too bright, the gold too fake. There is a wrongness here, she thinks. She finds a bread roll and nibbles on it.

It's just a play, she thinks. It is an act put on, for all she knows it's put on nightly. She sips the wine for it's imported and therefore should be safe to drink, but then she feels light-headed. Eels and water snakes are served, and honey with the bees dead in it.

Legate and Persian ambassador both eat like starved children. The more they eat the more they seem to crave. Their brows shine with sweat. Their stomachs bulge. The more they eat the hungrier they get. Their eyes are glazed. Their speech deteriorates into incomprehensible mutterings. They grunt like pigs. Guinevere glances at the head of the table. Elaine of Corbenic smiles faintly at her and shrugs.

'We heard talk of leprechauns and gold,' Guinevere says.

'I see no leprechauns.'

'And on our journey we came upon a village where only men dwell.'

'So?'

'They claim their womenfolk were stolen away to Maiden's Castle.'

'Nothing but tales,' Elaine says.

'I am sure you are right.'

'Tittle tattle. One mustn't set store by the tall tales of the people in the fog. Their minds are weak.'

'I am sure you're right.'

Elaine of Corbenic smiles. She is beatific. On the wall in his chains, Urien of the Old North, king of the Hen Ogledd, sags in defeat.

At last dinner is over. The musicians fall silent. Guinevere is hungry, as hungry as she's ever been.

They're escorted back to their rooms. They are not prisoners. There are no guards set on their doors.

'This is bullshit,' Isolde says. 'What are we supposed to do now?'

'Kill the good mistress Elaine and take hold of her castle?'

'Did you *see* the fate of Urien?' Isolde shudders. 'We are highwaywomen, not a Roman legion. And she has magic on her side.'

'How do you know?'

'How can you not? Do you not smell it? The whole air's tainted with its stench.'

They argue, but in vain. There's something wrong in Maiden's Castle, but is the castle the cause of the wrongness, or merely a part of it? The Choir of Angels settle at last. Yet Guinevere is restless.

She rises. Bites on an apple. The castle's never silent, there are far cries and sounds going on behind the walls. She steals out to the corridor. There are no guards that she can see but that is not to say they are not there.

'Pssst! Over here!'

She turns. There is a huddled shadow hiding behind a monstrous Roman marble bust of some dead emperor. It is gaudily painted. Where Elaine sourced it is a mystery, like so much about this place.

'Pssst! You!'

Guinevere kneels. The figure steps out of the shadow. It is a little leprechaun girl, soot-stained, grimy, with wild red hair and miner's clothes that are dull green.

'Yes?' Guinevere says.

'Come with me,' the leprechaun says.

Guinevere, curious – the little girl vanishes behind the statue's dais. A shadow there – Guinevere sees a hidden opening. She crawls behind the Roman emperor and into a narrow space.

'Come on!'

She follows the girl into the little crawlspace. They are behind the walls. The shaft angles down. Guinevere slides. She bumps into the leprechaun girl, who gives a squeak of alarm. Then they come crashing down into a stone-hewn corridor and land in an ungainly pile.

'Oww!'

'Sorry.'

What is she doing here? She disentangles from the girl. They're in some sort of mining tunnel. Wooden beams support the ceiling, torches burn at intervals. No one around.

'My name's Ulla,' the leprechaun girl says. 'Are you the magical princess who came to save us?'

'Am I?' Guinevere starts. 'I hardly think so.'

'Well, you're all there is,' Ulla says. 'So you will do or...'

'Or what?'

Ulla shrugs. 'Or you will die,' she says, 'I suppose.'

'Well, that's cheering,' Guinevere says.

'Come on. I'll show you where they're held imprisoned.'

'*Who* is held imprisoned? What?'

'The men.'

'What men?'

'The knights who came to help us.'

'And did they? Help you?'

'No. I told you. They're held in prison.'

'So much for men,' Guinevere says, and the leprechaun girl, unexpectedly, smiles.

They walk down mine tunnels and round twisting turns. There's no one there.

'These are the early sections,' the girl explains. 'The gold's been mined here long ago.'

'The gold?'

'And other metals. From the star stone. They say they have a special radiance and are not found in nature.'

'I'd heard the same...'

'It's killing us.'

It's said matter-of-factly, and somehow chilling all the more for that.

They reach the cells. They hide behind a wall and watch. Two guards look bored. A lone prisoner's behind bars.

'This was the old storage unit,' Ulla whispers. 'When this section was still being mined.'

'And now? Where are we?'

'Somewhere under the palace. I don't know why she keeps them. I think she took a fancy to their leader.'

'Their leader? Who—?'

Then she sees him.

43

He is young, he must be her age or a year or so older at most. He is thin, there is no fat on him. He's muscled in the way a swordsman's muscled, but he has no sword in his captivity. He has some scars on him. His hair is short. His eyes are bright. He prowls the cage with restless energy. She thinks he's handsome. He reminds her somewhat of a blade.

'His name's Arthur.'

'Where are the others? You said there were others.'

'I don't know,' Ulla says. 'Perhaps she's moved them. There is a Merlin, I think that's a kind of wizard or some such. He's locked up in the tower, in a room he can't escape. The other knights – one's green and big, one's small and unremarkable, and a few underlings.'

'So what do you want from me?' Guinevere says. 'And how come you can wander round as you do?'

'I hide and they don't see me. They don't think we're a threat because we're not. We just work in the – you know.'

'I don't.'

'I'll show you, if you like. But you'd have to be quiet, so they don't catch you.'

'Oh, fuck it,' Guinevere says – which is as good an attitude to have as any. She marches out of the hiding place directly at the guards.

'Excuse me…'

They turn. She doesn't give them a chance to reply.

It's over quickly. The guards are on the floor and now Guinevere is armed.

She walks to the cage. The boy, this Arthur, stands still, watching her. He really does have eyes so very bright…

She looks at him. Considers. He doesn't beg.

She reaches a decision.

'Come on,' she says. 'Before they come around or someone comes to check.'

She unlocks the cage with the keys from the guards. He follows her swiftly.

'Thank you,' he says. His voice is rough with disuse.

'Don't mention it.'

'I'm Arthur,' he says.

'I'm Guinevere.'

Unexpectedly, he smiles. 'Thank you, Guinevere.'

She smiles back. 'Been here long?'

'Longer than I'd care to.'

'Bit careless, getting caught.'

'Yeah.' He runs a hand through his short hair. 'They caught us unprepared and under-manned. And my wizard's useless here, there's something in the earth that nullifies what power he has.'

'Why did you come here in the first place?'

'We were on our way south when we came on this village in the fog. They told us of the castle. I thought… I thought I should see it for myself. And I was right to. There's power here. There's real power.'

She looks at him curiously. 'Is power what you crave?'

He looks back at her levelly. 'Don't you?'

And she thinks to herself – I can see the attraction.

'Yes, perhaps…'

'Will you two hurry up?'

They glance – guiltily – at the leprechaun girl.

'Hello, Ulla,' Arthur says.

To Guinevere's surprise the little leprechaun blushes.

'Sir Arthur.' She tries a curtsy. Guinevere hides a smile.

He helps himself to a sword from a fallen guard. Tries it, swings it about. Nods. 'It will do.'

'Do for what?'

'He's come to save us,' Ulla says, with utter trust.

'Have you really...' Guinevere says.

Arthur has the decency to look sheepish.

'Well, let's go, then,' Guinevere says. She looks to Arthur. 'Let's go save everyone.'

She hefts up her sword. Arthur grins at her. She stares. Yes, she thinks. I can see the attraction.

They follow the leprechaun girl.

Down and down and down they go, through twisting winding tunnels too numerous to recall. It is a huge enterprise, Guinevere realises. The mine must have been started even before she was born, back when the star stone fell. Perhaps by Urien, perhaps even earlier. This keep has been here long before – and she realises that either Leir and Pelles lied or, worse, had no idea of its scope. For all this while the Angles came to Britain someone out here was building up a store of power all its own...

No wonder Arthur came here.

She steals a glance at him. She'd heard his name before. So he's that southern king with dreams of glory and consolidation. He doesn't look like much. But there's a hardness to him. There is that.

He takes it in. His eyes miss little. Yes, she thinks. He's drawn to power like a fly to honey. He wants to *take*, and this, here, is worth taking.

He sees her look. What does he see when he looks at her? Why does she wonder this, now? And yet it's not uncomfortable.

Worm? Worm, are you there?

But there is no answer. Her pet is mute, something in this place, perhaps, blocks their communication. A deadly radiance, she thinks. What does it mean?

'There,' the leprechaun girl, Ulla, says.

They have come to a precipice. They crouch low. The tunnel ends here and the pit begins.

Guinevere steals a look.

The pit lies down below.

Flames flicker down there. Huge figures move through haze of smoke. Trolls, she thinks. Pulling on chains and shifting mounds of earth. And tiny figures darting everywhere, the womenfolk of a hundred villages, and the leprechauns, miners, diggers, with pickaxes or bare hands fumbling at the rock. Somewhere near the furnaces a pile of what she realises are tiny corpses.

She looks at Arthur. His lips move. He sees her looking.

'I wonder what the expenditure on miners' lives is on a daily basis,' he says softly.

'We lose one in four in the first week,' Ulla says. 'And four in five over a six-month period.'

'A high turnover.'

'It's why she keeps sending out for more. Only a few of us survive this long exposure to the metals in the earth.'

She says it simply. Arthur accepts it as such.

'And the yield?' he says.

'It was rich at first. Gold seams as thick as your arms. But mixed in with these other, stranger metals. The likes of which I'd never seen. It's said they mustn't be brought together in close proximity. Lady Elaine has calculating-wizards working for her—'

'You mean mathematicians?' says Guinevere.

Ulla shrugs. 'I suppose. Some from the Old World she had shipped over secretly, with her gold. They've been conducting experiments. We hear explosions, from time to time. There are boreholes out in the wastelands beyond the keep, too vast and deep to have been dug by any human hand, where the very sand has been fused into glass by enormous heat.' She shudders. 'And there is worse,' she says. 'For those who do survive are changed beyond recall.'

'Mutatio,' Guinevere says.

Ulla looks at her in surprise.

'I saw evidence of them on our way here.'

'They are the lucky ones,' Ulla says. 'It is better to die free out there than live in here.'

They stare at the giant pit where the fires burn. At the thousands of slaves moving to and fro. At the piles of rocks.

A mountain hollowed.

And Guinevere thinks, uneasily – Leir had said this was only a fragment that fell off the larger star stone.

The thought fills her with nameless horror. She reaches blindly, realises with surprise she's found a hand, warm and dry. Arthur's. He holds her hand, wordlessly. There's comfort in the touch.

She says, 'We have to get out of here.'

But there's no getting out. There is a rumble overhead. There is the sound of a landslide, of rocks in motion, crashing, crushing. There are screams, cut short.

Then she sees it's not a rock slide. It's mountain trolls.

Gigantic, rock-formed, malignant shapes. Their teeth are gold. Their eyes are moss-green. Thin strands of grey metal run through their stony bodies. That invisible radiance, what the Romans in their tongue call *radium*.

Those strips of radium and such. The miners cower from the trolls. Between the giant creatures steps the queen. The lady Elaine in all her splendour. She too is radiant. And she alone is smiling.

'I do not like the looks of this at all,' says Guinevere.

But Arthur's hand is warm and dry in hers. Their shoulders touch. And there's a warmth in Guinevere she hadn't felt before. Or not like this.

It's fucking disconcerting, is what it is.

Behind the queen, dragged on a chain, are people she knows well.

'Oh, fuck.'

There's Laudine, there's Enid, there's Luned and Isolde. Looking furious, and beat up, and weaponless, hands and feet bound by the slaver's chains.

'Your women?'

'Yeah.'

He nods at the advancing prisoners. 'My men.'

She sees them. There's a slithery little prick – 'Merlin. My wizard.' He points out a giant green man. 'The Green Knight. We call him Bercilak. That small guy next to him, that's my foster-brother, Kay. He is my steward.'

'And the others?'

'Soldiers.'

And she knows he means, *expendable.*

There is a ramp in the heart of the pit and the procession moves towards it slowly. Heaps of old stones have been thrown there in times past until it became a compacted tor, and now the queen is raised up there by her minions, and torches are set and lit, and a ring of flames rises, and the prisoners are placed to kneel at the queen's feet.

She raises her arms. Turns and turns. They can see her perfectly. That beautiful face. That savage grin. This woman is in full control of her domain.

'Come out, come out, wherever you are!'

Her voice carries. Arthur clutches Guinevere's hand.

'I know you're there! Did you really think to evade me?'

Elaine of Corbenic is amused, serene. To her this is a game, Guinevere realises. There is no outcome she can see that isn't in her favour.

'King Arthur!' She spits that word, *king*, with such contempt that Guinevere flinches.

'You could have been great, serving beside me, my consort! I would have given you power beyond mortal ken!'

'If I wanted to be someone's fuck toy I may as well have stayed with Morgause,' Arthur mutters.

'Who?'

He shakes his head. 'There are too many women in my life recently.'

But he glances at her and smiles when he says it.

'And you, Guinevere! You could have served as my lieutenant! Word of your deeds has reached even here. Together we would be magnificent. Join me! Both of you. Come claim your rightful places by my side.'

'At her feet, she means,' Guinevere says, and Arthur surprises her by laughing. It's such a childish sound, and it's clear he's not used to it.

'Or else!' Elaine screams.

The queen gestures. A sword is placed into her hands. A shining sword, of gold and radium, for all that it must have a core of steel.

Guinevere sees Merlin. The little wizard's swaying, looking ill. He's drenched in sweat. But she has no time to feel sorry for him. The Choir of Angels fight in vain against their chains. Elaine of Corbenic brings up the sword.

'A single cut is poison in the blood,' says Arthur.

Guinevere watches in horror. 'We have to stop her.'

'Yes.'

He lets go of her hand. She's strangely disappointed. He turns to Ulla. She's been standing there, as quiet as a mouse.

'Can you get us down there?'

The little leprechaun girl makes a face at him. 'She'll kill us all,' she says.

'I have a plan.'

'*Really…*' Guinevere murmurs. But she knows they have no choice.

'Come out, come out, wherever you are!' the queen screams. Then the sword swings, and Guinevere is mute in fear and revulsion. The sword slices through air and hits Luned in the neck. The Green Knight, with a roar of hatred, throws one enormous fist and brings the whole chain up with him. He lashes at the queen.

'Down, you abomination! Down!'

'Luned!'

'Don't look,' says Arthur. He takes her hand away. Guinevere looks for Ulla, but Ulla is gone.

Together and alone, Arthur and Guinevere follow the mountain path down into the pit.

44

'**S**top!'

The crowd parts for them. Guinevere looks at them now, the puckered, pussing skin, the wounds, the hollow eyes. A sickness of radiance, she thinks. She and Arthur make their way through the throng to the dais of the queen of Maiden's Castle.

The mountain trolls glare down on them. Leprechauns dart in the dim light. And Guinevere thinks, we are lost.

They climb up to where she awaits them. The prisoners in chains, and poor Luned with that awful wound in her neck, the cut had not been clean. There is a lot of blood.

Elaine of Corbenic smiles at them in radiance. She's glowing. The golden sword is in her hand.

'A shame,' she says. 'I would have started on your Merlin.'

'It's Merlin,' says the wizard – pale and sweating, with the shakes. 'It's a *name*, it's a—oh, forget it.' He sags to the ground.

'Please,' Arthur says. 'I'd like to keep him. For sentimental reasons.'

'He is part fae, and such as his have no place in my new world order,' says the queen.

Guinevere: 'Excuse me?'

Arthur, in an aside: 'Don't get her started. It's her thing.'

'They're nothing but mere superstition,' says Elaine of

Corbenic. 'You wouldn't understand, not yet, at least. But the time of legends is coming to an end. This much I have seen, this much is clear to me. So much is clearer now, in the light of the star stone. Its true nature is not yet manifest to you. But it is to me. In the new world I shall create, logic will flourish. Pure mathematics! I shall build a perfect world, to rival and surpass the empires of Greece, Persia and Rome. With the power of the star stone I shall prevail! I am become Death, the Destroyer of Worlds!'

'You're mad,' Guinevere says involuntarily.

'Mad?' Elaine laughs. Her laugh echoes in the pit. 'You call me mad? Look around you!' She spreads her arms wide, encompassing the spluttering torches, the enslaved workers, the seams of silver and gold in the walls. 'You don't have to be mad to work here, but it helps!'

'What the *fuck* are you on about?'

Elaine gestures. Arthur, as though moonstruck, walks to her. His hand when it leaves Guinevere's gives a little squeeze. A promise of some sort, perhaps. Just before he turns, he pops something in his mouth.

Elaine draws him to her. At that moment her power seems absolute. This really *is* her world, what the Greeks might have call a eu-topia, a good place. It's *her* good place. Made in her twisted image. She glows.

She pulls Arthur to her.

He comes without resisting.

She grabs his chin. She pulls him roughly to her, leans in for a kiss.

Their lips meet. Their mouths open hungrily. Arthur holds her, dips her back. His mouth opens wide. And something passes, from his mouth to hers.

She chokes and swallows.

She pushes him away.

'What?' she says. 'What!'

She spreads her arms. She shines – she burns. She stares

around her in outraged confusion. She is so hot she glows. The light begins inside her, shines through her skin, her pores. Fine lines of light appear along her arms and face. She's made of gold. She is enchanted and enchanting both at once.

The lines of light become cracks opening onto a sun.

The light that shines forth is blinding.

Arthur screams, 'Run!'

Guinevere pivots. Down below she sees a tiny figure appear. Ulla, holding a man's sword in her small arms. She grins up at Guinevere and tosses the sword.

Guinevere catches it, swings. The blade hits the prisoners' chain, cuts through the metal with a terrible screech. The prisoners scramble up, turn to flee. Behind them all, Elaine of Corbenic is a golden statue of flame.

She roars.

They run.

They jump over the edge just as Elaine of Corbenic explodes.

The Angels curse. They're filled with righteous rage. Isolde headbutts one of the maiden's soldiers, grabs her sword. She roars with glee. She leads the charge. They flee.

'Hey, that sword is mine,' says Arthur.

'It's nice.'

'Her name's Excalibur.'

'Of *course* it's a she.'

Why *do* men always do that? She swishes the sword, stabs another soldier through the heart, helps her down, takes her sword for her own. She hands Excalibur back to Arthur.

'What the fuck did you do to Elaine of Corbenic?'

He looks sheepish. 'I ate a piece of the star stone.'

Guinevere stares at him in horror. 'It's poison!'

'I hid it in my mouth and passed it to her in the kiss. I didn't know what to expect but not... that...'

'Are you alright?'

'I don't feel so well, but I'll worry about that later. We have to get out of here.'

The Merlin's pretty useless. The Green Knight roars and hits with bare fists, and people fly away from the giant. The steward helps the wizard along. The Choir of Angels lead the way, slashing and stabbing, and people flee. There is total disorder.

Far ahead, a tunnel mouth. There has to be an exit. They slash and fight their way towards it. They stab and kill. They almost reach it.

Out of the tunnel mouth emerge two figures.

Legate Agrippa, of Byzantium.

Ambassador Bahram, of Persia.

With eyes glazed, with hands outstretched.

With foam in their mouths.

Showing sharp teeth.

'Fucking *kill* them!'

'Grrrr!'

The swords flash. The two crazed men duck the swords, somehow. They reach for the party. They bite.

'Fucking get him off me! Fucking get him off of me!' Enid screams.

Legate Agrippa has his mouth fastened on her unarmoured arm. He tears chunks of flesh.

'It burns! It burns!'

Guinevere can only watch in horror. Isolde stabs the Legate. He grunts and lets go but the wound seems not to disturb him. He turns on Isolde. Enid slumps to the ground. She keens, an awful sound of pain and sorrow. Her eyes grow glazed. Her mouth foams.

Some sort of sickness, Guinevere thinks. Again. Isolde backs away from the Legate. She doesn't see how Enid rises stealthily, how she attempts to steal on Isolde, how her mouth opens to bite.

Guinevere's sword slashes. Enid's head detaches.

Her headless body sags to the ground, and she is at peace.
'Mother*fucker*!' Guinevere screams.
The remaining Angels attack.
They stab and slash and hack and bash.
Legate and ambassador are pushed back.
They lose chunks of themselves.
They roar wordlessly. Their lips foam.
They are reduced to piles of organs. They are destroyed.
At last they're done.
There's nothing left worth fighting.
Behind the party there's a roar. Those mountain trolls have found their purpose. And behind them come the others, mutatio, with arms outstretched and murder etched on their ruined faces.
'Run!'
They flee down the tunnel. It slopes sharply down. Guinevere skids and slides. She finds Arthur beside her. He reaches for her hand. Together they fly down the shaft, down and down—

They emerge into empty air.
A dirty river down below, and they fall into the water, which is cold and bitter to the touch. Guinevere and Arthur cling to each other.
A voice in her head, one that has been silent for too long.
I love you... the worm says.
It is close. She can feel it.
Hungry... the worm says.
'Now!' Guinevere says.
'Now?' Arthur says, in bemusement.
Now... the worm whispers, in her mind.

Everything happens kind of fast after that.

★

Behind the bedraggled travellers, an army of mutatio emerges from the pit.

Arthur and Guinevere wash onto a ruined shore.

On the hill overhead, the sound of horns. The silhouette of an army on horseback.

Guinevere and Arthur, facing each other on the bank in the light of a silvery moon. Their faces close together.

'I'm no good, you know,' he tells her. 'I think I could have been once but that path is closed.'

She nestles closer into him. 'I'm bad all over and inside,' she says, 'And I keep killing people.'

'I suppose we are about to die anyway,' he says. 'But I was thinking, if we don't, perhaps you'd like to come with me.'

She stares at this stranger.

'Go where?' she says.

'Anywhere. I mean,' he gestures at the ruined bank and the approaching armies and the fog. 'You could stay in this shithole, or you could come with me.'

'So valiant,' she says.

He laughs.

They kiss.

That quickening of her heart, could it be love? His lips are rough, his hands are gentle. That heat inside her, like a star about to burst.

Hungry... the worm says.

Then it appears. High overhead. Descending. It's like a bird, if birds were reptiles. The worm is hot. It breathes fire.

The army of mutatio scatter. Over the hill comes the other army, and she can see it is her enemy. It is Sir Pelles and his men.

Guinevere growls with hatred.

'What the—' Arthur says.

The worm is white and huge and gormless.

I love you! the worm says.

'I love you too…' Guinevere whispers.

'I love you too,' Arthur says.

But Guinevere isn't listening. And anyway, what is love for such as them? Two broken things, shaped into weapons. A sword does not feel love.

She pulls her sword. The worm flies over Pelles and his army. Guinevere scrambles up the hill.

The army lies in tatters. Men burned, their horses dead or fled into the mist. She finds Sir Pelles. He stands, yet.

'*You*,' he says, with hatred.

'We merely did your bidding, lord.'

Their swords meet, clash. She slashes downwards.

He screams.

An awful, ugly wound runs through his groin and all down his thigh.

'I dipped the blade in the dust of the star stone,' she tells him. 'May your wound never heal, lord.'

She leaves him there, alive, a wounded king.

The worm is gone when she returns to her party.

From far-away: *I love you…*

'I love you too, worm.'

Not hungry…

She smiles.

The survivors band together on the riverbank.

'I think I'll take up farming,' Isolde says, 'it must be less harmful to your health.'

Laudine tries for a smile and fails. Her eyes are full of sorrow. The wizard, Merlin, rubs his hands together as though trying to stay warm. He looks used up and haggard. They are a sorry sight.

'Well?' Arthur says.

Guinevere looks away from him, to the river. A small figure

comes floating down the stream like so much garbage, and she sees with sorrow that it is Ulla. In death, at least, she seems at peace. She watches as the little corpse floats down and down until it vanishes beyond the distant rapids.

Guinevere turns back to Arthur.

'Alright,' she says.

PART SEVEN

KNIGHT-ERRANT

45

The barge from the north slides softly across the water into the docks of Londinium.

There are arrow holes in the sides and the sail had caught fire at least once. The men who sail her look half-dead as they clamber out.

The knights wait patiently for the cargo. Well-equipped, heavily armed, young and trained. They speak in low voices.

'From the north, Agravain.'

'From the king.'

'What says he?'

The captain hands the knight a rough parchment. Agravain scans it, lips moving as he reads.

'He is alive, then.'

'Was there ever any doubt?'

'And Urien of the North is dead.'

The men cheer softly.

They offload a heavy trunk. Agravain opens it.

Lancelot, in the shadows, watches.

Well, well, he thinks. Isn't this interesting.

The contents of the trunk glow bold. They're heavy objects made of gold. The men, with avarice, reach for the gold. Agravain barks an order.

'Don't. The king says they are poisoned.'

'Poisoned? Poisoned how?'

He shrugs.

Well, well, thinks Lancelot.

He shadows the men as they escort the treasure. He needs to get closer, he thinks. He needs to have a proper look.

He steps into the street. Bold as you please, before the company of knights.

They stop and stare.

'Do you not value your head, stranger? Get the fuck out of the way.'

'The contents of your trunk,' he says. 'I'd like a rummage, if you please, good sirs.'

They stare at him, incredulous. They draw their swords.

'May I enquire your name, sir?' Agravain says. 'So I should know what moniker to give Tamesis as I offer her your corpse?'

'It is Lancelot.' He considers. 'Latterly of Judea.'

'You are a long way from home.'

The men snigger.

'There will be no one to sing your burial song. Or whatever custom is of your peoples.'

'That's alright,' Lancelot says. 'I hadn't planned on dying.'

'Then you're a fool.'

They charge him.

The flying sword, Secace, is out of her scabbard before they take a single step. It whistles through the air. Chops off the sword arm of one attacker, swings in a parabola and returns to Lancelot's hand. The men move warily, surrounding him.

'Pharaoh's Chariot!' Lancelot says. He is a blur of motion, rising through the air, the sword sending sparks as he barrels through the enemy. He doesn't wish to kill. Aims for their sword hands. They drop the metal, one by one.

'Solomon's Tent!'

He moves in a circle around them, as fast as thunder, and he draws the darkness round them until they can see no more.

Swordless, confused, they stumble and curse him. He steals to the trunk. He opens it.

A chalice, made of gold. He scratches the surface, finds the grey metal underneath.

Yes, he thinks. It is as his old master told him.

Excitement grips his heart, for this is, at long last, a clue.

More objects, looted who knows where. Bowls and plates, an altar decoration of some local god. He wonders that they should be placed so close together in one place. His old master had warned him that such objects should best be placed apart.

The darkness ebbs. The men see him.

He turns, mockingly, and bows. 'Gentlemen.'

'Thief!'

They charge him. He tosses the sword Secace in the air above their heads and leaps. He lands on the flat of the blade and sails beyond them, over the low roofs, and jumps again, grabbing the sword by the hilt as he lands on the ground. He sheathes the sword.

Well, well, he thinks.

It is high time to get out of town.

So that's why Lancelot, the Knight of the Cart, Initiate of the Inner Circle of the Venerated Secret Brotherhood of the Seekers of the Grail, Master of the Flying Sword, the Auroch's Charge, and the Judean Lightning Strike, travelling swordsman and powerful practitioner of the ancient art of gongfu, now sits alone in the dark recesses of the Cameleopard's Head drinking establishment and roadside inn and warily watches the door.

He is also disconcertingly low on funds.

The inn is on the great Roman North Road leading out of Londinium. Lancelot sips warm beer from an earthenware mug and watches the door with one hand on the hilt of his sword.

He also watches the other patrons.

It is an interesting time to be on this island, he reflects. The ship from the continent had dropped him off on the eastern shore of the Severn sea, and from there he made his way by foot to Glastonbury. It was where his old master had come, and where, before him, it was said, that the secretive Saviour from the Galilee had come after faking his own death in Jerusalem, and before he went to distant Qin, where he became a wushu master.

He'd searched for clues in Glastonbury but found none. In learning the lie of the land, he learned of the new king, Arthur, and the gang war brewing with the Six Kings.

Which made things potentially... interesting, Lancelot thought. And also, potentially, lucrative, since he'd need to take on work to keep him going during his quest.

Ascertain. Assimilate. Infiltrate. Engage. How many times has he had the field operative tenets drilled into him back in Arimathea? At least they still spoke Latin here, at least in the southern parts.

What a shithole, he thought. What a colossal fucking shithole this place was.

Still.

He asked around and heard the stories of the dragon that appeared in the sky during the reign of Uther, him who they called Pendragon. He tracked the journey of the dragon northwards and that decided Lancelot's direction.

He made his way up to Londinium, taking on small jobs, monster hunting and the like. He slew a brace of giants outside Sorviodūnum but, in truth, there was hardly a fight in them. They were big and slow and seemed mostly confused, and malnourished. He kept his eyes open for anything out of place but he'd seen no trace of that which he was seeking.

The town, when he got there, was a let-down. Lancelot, in his time, had seen the great pyramids of Cairo, where the ancients buried their kings. He had trained with the magus, Simon of Samaria, in the seclusion of the Mount of Olives above Jerusalem, that fair city of white stone, and seen its new churches being built. He had fought bandits across the desert beyond the great salt sea of Palestine to reach Petra, that fabled city of red rock hewn into the mountains themselves. In the disguise of a beggar he wandered the Aventine and the Capitoline Hill, there to seek a boon from the mysterious Lord of the Guild of Beggars, whose eyes and ears, it is said, are everywhere.

He's been around, Lancelot. And Londinium, frankly, in his not so humble opinion, was a – well, yeah. A shithole.

It is a word Lancelot is exceedingly fond of.

Oh, there was no doubt Londinium was Roman enough... in parts. You could see where once someone half-competent had drawn the streets, where army engineers constructed a river bridge, houses, even a governor's palace. There was still a forum, of a sort. But what had once been a competent if unglamorous military town in a minor and distant part of the Roman Empire was now, well, an unglamorous and still military town in what was most definitely no longer a part of the Roman Empire, and moreover clearly had no decent engineers or architects to hand. Oh, there were fresh coats of paint on some of the houses, and some form of primitive rubbish collection still took place, and the local warlord had even made some half-hearted attempt to keep the public baths going, though they were dirty and the water lukewarm at best.

Lancelot liked things clean, for all that his work was often dirty. He liked things neat, for all that his work was often messy. He hired a room in a dosshouse near the White Hill and from there he did what he always did. Ascertain. Assimilate. Infiltrate. Engage. And all that nonsense they drilled into him back in Arimathea, when he still had his people and he still had his clan. When his old master was still alive.

But that was then. And that was a lifetime ago.

Now he was all alone. Homeless. Clanless. Masterless.

Rogue.

But the objective was still the same. The mission was the mission, and Lancelot would stick to it, like a drowning man holding on to the sides of a boat.

He had nothing else.

He just hoped it was worth it.

Whatever *it* really was.

So he observed Londinium. The town was a hive of activity. It had been near impossible to get a room. There were young men travelling everywhere from the countryside into the city, in search of employment, and in their wake they brought merchants and sweethearts and working ladies and pickpockets and jugglers and thieves. The jianghu, as his old master called it.

Those who lived outside the existing law.

Though as much as Lancelot could make out, this island and its people barely *had* law.

The young men streaming into the city were hired, if they were able-bodied and capable of handling a sword. Arms shipments came in by river, where from, he didn't know. He hid one night near the bridge and watched a shipment come in, and saw a barge towed from the north but no one pulling it. Until he looked down, into the water of the great Tamesis, and saw pale bodies swim through the murk, women with gills and fins, and he smelled the stench of enchantment. He had seen mermaids before, had once nearly drowned when the ship he was travelling on from Paphos was attacked by water demons, what the Romans called orcus. He had nearly drowned, but they saved him, and carried him to shore, half-dead, and one had kissed him, blowing air into his lungs. He had never forgotten that kiss, though he never knew her name...

But if the arms merchants had this whiff of enchantment about them, the swords were very real, and some of them quite old. He saw the blades distributed to the new recruits, saw the training camps established beyond the city walls.

This new warlord, Arthur, was building himself an army.

Lancelot considered enlisting, if only as a way to earn some money, but he sensed that Londinium and its meagre charms did not hold what he was seeking.

What *did* catch his ear, however, were the dockside tales of where the young warlord and his close circle were. Which, as it turned out, no one knew.

He'd gone north on the fairy paths, they said.

He'd struck a deadly bargain with a stunningly beautiful enchantress, they said.

He was captured by Picts, or pixies, or leprechauns, and held imprisoned in a black prison in a land where the earth itself was poison.

Whatever he did or didn't do, his men were preparing for war, and the shipments of arms kept coming.

'What's up north?' Lancelot asked Mirabelle. She was a little Frankish woman he'd met at the dosshouse, her mind half-gone, usually, on Goblin Fruit.

Mirabelle curled her hair and stuck her tongue out at him. 'Picts,' she said. 'That sort of thing. They say there's a wall the Romans built to keep them out, but it's been falling apart. Old Uther, the Pendragon, fought there. Why?'

'Just wondering,' Lancelot said, and he drew her to him and she laughed.

Then, one night, he saw the shipment of false gold, and knew his quest was true.

Then he got the hell out of town.

46

So this is how Lancelot ends up at the Cameleopard's Head drinking watered beer. He scans the patrons. He notices the clink of old coins, and the other things the locals use for currency now that the Romans are all but gone. Some trader earlier had deposited a heavy bag of onions on the floor by the door and loudly proclaimed a round of drinks for the house.

No one cheered – it isn't that kind of place. A fire burns nearby but fails to warm the room. Earlier some young tough desperate for a drink deposited his sword behind the counter, on the account. This is how society operates when there isn't a central authority issuing currency, Lancelot thinks. It runs on debt, not barter.

Everybody owes and everybody pays, as the poet said.

He watches for the shine of gold. It's been growing more common, he has come to find. Leprechaun gold, they call it. Trickling into Londinium along the old North Road. So this is where he'll go, too. North.

Try to find the source of it.

He watches the door as a cat comes slinking in. A queen cat, an alley cat he thinks – a city cat. She has the scars of battle on her.

She passes under tables, rubs up against the drinkers' legs, steals a slice of liver off a plate without anybody noticing.

She passes him. She glances with that special disinterest cats have.

'Hello, kitty,' Lancelot says.

The ancient Egyptians worshipped cats, he remembers. His master, Joseph, had trained for a time with the Egyptian magi, learning forbidden arts long forgotten elsewhere. For a long time he had thought the grail could be found there, deep in the deserts. There were drawings in the forbidden tombs of the pharaohs...

They broke into the Khufu's great pyramid one starless night, he and the master and Iblis. It had not ended well, and they had to leave Egypt in something of a hurry...

The cat purrs. Those eyes that are so inhuman watch him. He feeds her a slice of beef. She meows and takes her prize under a chair.

Perhaps he is distracted.

The door bangs open and a troop of men barge in.

They kick the tables and the patrons run. They know what's coming. In moments the room's empty. There's only Lancelot and the knights facing up to him, blocking the only door.

A rough and ready bunch.

Agravain of the Hard Hand steps into the room.

Extends his sword, then lets it drop. The knights make room around them. Agravain raises his bare hands, palms open. Assumes a fighting stance. Of the minor Sons of Zebedee School, if Lancelot has it right.

Well, well.

Agravain extends one hand in a gesturing motion.

Says, 'Fight, motherfucker.'

Lancelot sighs.

'Not *again*,' he says.

In Smyrna when things went south he found himself, alone, facing up to some forty holy assassins of Mithras, the bull-headed god. It had come towards the end of a long and frustrating year that saw their master leading them all through the Decapolis and further – this was after Egypt and the debacle there. In Smyrna in a newly built church to the Christ the master believed an artefact could be found, but in the end it had turned out to be a trap. Iblis and the master made it out but Lancelot was trapped. That time, that fight, he thought he was done for. The assassins were well-trained, versed in the Eastern arts. They fell on him from all sides, jumping from the rafters, lighter than air, their blades like light.

He countered with the Tears of Demeter, flying throwing stars fashioned by the master's personal smith. He killed five before they threw a net and caught him, then doused him in something potent that sent him into an enchanted sleep.

When he awoke he was in the dungeons deep under the city, in a stone-hewn cell where no one could hear his screams. They bound him in irons and tortured him until his mind fled from his body and wandered in another world, under an alien sky.

Later, when he woke again, the details were fuzzy. A purple sky, and red-and-purple storms raging far on the horizon. The land itself was made of black tar and ice, and all manner of mechanical things moved about it. He saw yellow flowers as tall as trees, and met, in their shadows, natives of that world, who greeted him in some sing-song language he could almost understand, but didn't.

Locked in his cell for that long and cold duration, shivering, talking to the rats beyond the walls, he thought of the words of his master. It had been long ago, only recently after finding Lancelot. They were camped under stars in the Galilee, and the master pointed to the heavens.

'The sky thou seest above is Infinite,' he said. 'It is the abode of persons crowned with ascetic success and of divine beings. It is delightful, and consists of various regions. Its limits cannot be ascertained.'

Lancelot looked at him without comprehension and the

master smiled. 'These words are from the Mahabharata, which travelled back to us along the roads from India.' The master looked up, and his eyes softened. 'I want to believe...' he said.

But all through the long winter in Smyrna, abandoned, forgotten, Lancelot could think of nothing but the walls of his cage.

'We are all caged,' his master said, in his mind. 'It just so happens that for some of us the bars of the prison are bigger.'

His master never made a lot of sense, in truth. His true faith was perhaps unknown even to himself. In his travels with the master Lancelot had seen churches being built and synagogues and temples being destroyed. He saw ancient oracles burned down and groves of sacred trees set aflame. He saw the statues of ancient gods broken and ground to dust. His master was tolerant of religions old and new, but he had his own dark faith.

Once a year, the master undertook a pilgrimage to Carthage, where members of his order gathered. They followed a strain of Gnosticism, believing, so the master told him, that the earthly world was merely a prison, that the demiurge – a sort of jailer-god – had thrown them into.

The members of the Venerated Secret Brotherhood of the Seekers of the Grail sought to escape that prison.

All through that long winter in Smyrna Lancelot raged against his absent master. The master had learned secret arts from the East. He could kill a man instantly with the touch of his palm. He could speak the language of Jinn. He could summon elementals and leap from treetop to treetop, and hold his breath for almost five minutes when diving underwater. The master was, quite possibly, insane, but he was Lancelot's master all the same.

He had found him, wandering, dazed, lost, out in the Arabian desert one night under cold bright stars. Lancelot's memories of the time before the master found him were hazy. He preferred to keep them that way. The master found him, and fed him, and drew him to his fire. The master trained him. Lancelot owed him everything – his loyalty, his love, his life.

And yet he raged.

It was Iblis who came, in the end. Iblis of the black eyes and the silken assassin's cord and the hidden knives – oh, how she loved her knives! She came like the wind down the corridors of that sunless prison, and the guards fell like leaves. She unlocked his cell and stepped in and said, 'It stinks in here.'

'It's good to see you too,' Lancelot said.

'Here,' she said. She tossed him a sword. 'If you still remember how to use it.'

'It will come back to me, I'm sure.'

She smiled, but only with her teeth. Iblis had the coldest eyes that Lancelot had ever seen.

He followed her meekly out of the cell.

That night on their escape they slaughtered the followers of the bull-headed god until the blood flooded down the corridors. They emerged into sunrise, leaped up over the wall of that temple, and Lancelot stumbled. Iblis grabbed his arm and pulled him straight.

'Can you manage?'

'Let go,' he said. But he knew she was right. He was weak after months of imprisonment.

The master waited for them in a grove beyond the city. He embraced Lancelot, briefly, then outlined the plan. It was as though the entire thing, their assault on the temple, Lancelot's long imprisonment, none of it had mattered at all.

It was always on to the next clue and the next, with the master.

Searching for…

Something.

The Lapis Exilis, he called it.

Or sometimes, more simply, the grail.

Something that fell down from the heavens, and into the prison of mortal men.

★

So this is, in a roundabout way, how Lancelot ends up in Britain.

'Fight, motherfucker,' Agravain says.

Lancelot rises. He assumes the Stance of the Weeping Willow.

Agravain launches at him with the Strike of the Grass Snake.

Lancelot merely sways. The attack passes harmlessly. Agravain, with a roar of rage, launches head kicks and face strikes, but Lancelot is a shaking curtain of branches, the knight's attacks pass harmlessly through empty air. Lancelot expands little energy. He moves only enough to let the strikes miss. Agravain works himself up to a sweat. Lancelot sways on the balls of his feet like a dancer. The onlookers look on.

Money changes hands as they bet on the outcome.

'Parting of the Red Sea!' Agravain announces. This attack, from the School of the Sons of Zebedee, catches Lancelot by surprise. Where did the knight *learn* this? He is unable to avoid the strike, merely parries it back, and he and the knight face each other again.

Agravain grins.

'Wasn't expecting that, were you,' he says. A statement of fact.

'You are crude,' Lancelot says. 'With but rudimentary skills. Who was your master?'

Agravain's smile widens and Lancelot doesn't like the implication at all. Could another master have beaten him to this land and gone before him? Agravain, having had enough of talking, launches into Elijah's Fist – the same technique that, it was said, the prophet had used to destroy the priests of Ba'al.

Lancelot counters with Ishtar's Snare. He traps Agravain in a headlock and kicks his knee into the other man's back.

'Who trained you!' he says. 'These arts are not native to your country, knight.'

'Go fuck yourself, foreigner!'

The cat watches them from under a chair, chewing on her slice of beef. Lancelot releases Agravain. The man, in rage, launches Apollo's Fury and the kick sends Lancelot flying against the wall. He hits it with his back and drops to the floor.

This is ridiculous, he thinks.

But Agravain is already flying overhead, coming down to finish him with what looks like some twist on Solomon's Cut of the Infant.

It's time to finish this.

Lancelot twists sideways. He swipes his leg and catches Agravain on the way down. He spins round and locks onto the knight. He grabs him by the head and prepares to break his neck. There's no art to this. It's simple butchery.

He hesitates.

'I have no cause to fight you,' he says.

'Arghghh!'

'I could let you go.'

Cheers and curses among the onlookers. More money changes hands.

'Kill him!' someone shouts. They must have money riding on this particular outcome.

'This is demeaning,' Lancelot complains.

'Arghahrg!'

He reaches a decision. He wraps his arm around the knight's throat and squeezes hard, and Agravain's body flops to the ground. Lancelot stands.

'Is he dead?'

'Just resting.'

'Come on!' someone says. The onlookers, having been denied their satisfaction, go back to their drinks.

Lancelot looks at Agravain's waiting men. They shy away from him. He walks to his table, lifts up his mug, downs the rest of the beer. The cat comes slinking up to him and rubs against his shin. He picks her up, strokes her fur.

'Here, kitty kitty,' he says.

The cat purrs.

Lancelot leaves a handful of coins on the table and walks out of the door.

No one, he's glad to notice, tries to stop him this time.

47

He makes camp a day's ride north of Londinium. The cat had taken a liking to him. She'd purred and rubbed against him until he gave in to her unspoken demand and lifted her up to ride with him on the horse.

Now the cat curls by the fire. Earlier she went into the wood and came back with a water rat in her jaws. She offered to share but Lancelot politely declined.

He chews miserably on a piece of hard cheese and thinks perhaps he was too hasty in turning down the offer.

He'd spent the last of his money paying for the shitty beer at the Cameleopard's Head.

What a fucking stinking shithole of an island, he thinks.

How had it come to that!

After Smyrna the master took them to summer amidst the ruins of Nineveh. The locals shunned the place, which they said was cursed. Lancelot found it peaceful.

The master and Iblis trained in the arts of gongfu as Lancelot recuperated. He could hear the sound of their sparring as he fished in the Tigris. The river was wide and fast-flowing, and strange fish lived in its waters. As he grew stronger Lancelot took to diving barebacked into the wild current, battling with giant barbels and wily catfish. There were eels, too, swimming to the sea, slippery and numerous, and they parted around him as they passed.

He wished to learn the secret languages of eels. Their yearning for the distant sea moved him. Lancelot was loyal to his master and he would follow Joseph of Arimathea anywhere, and to the very ends of the Earth itself, but he could not find it in him to share the master's obsession with the grail.

'In the time of King Jabin of Hazor,' the master told him, 'a battle took place in which the Jewish sages say the stars themselves rebelled against the king's general, Sisera. It is written that the stars in their course fought against Sisera. All but the inhabitants of Meroz, which the rabbis in the Midrash, some centuries later, explicitly identify as a star in the sky. Do you not see, Lancelot?'

His voice shook with passion when he spoke. The master was a passionate man. 'And is it not said that in the earliest of days the Nephilim and the Sons of God walked freely on the Earth and intermarried with mortal kind? And furthermore—'

But Lancelot usually stopped actively listening at that point. It was all nonsense, anyway – he was pretty sure of it. Besides, as he pointed out to the master one time, if these sons of God were beings from another world, what did it make Jesus, he who they called the Christ?

At that the master huffed up somewhat, for he had a blind spot where Christians were concerned.

'Keep watching the skies,' he said ominously; and he would be drawn no further on the subject.

All through that hot long summer Lancelot recuperated. As his body healed he began to practise again, hesitant and weak at first, but then with new enthusiasm. Iblis was always there, fashioned by the master into a weapon. He'd called her the Lightning Sword, for she was as fast and as brutal as both blade and heavenly bolt. Together they sparred against each other, leaping from the top of one palm tree to the next, meeting in mid-air, using each other as ruthlessly as anything they ever did.

All through that long hot summer, members of their master's order would arrive, in ones and twos, and always unexpectedly. They stole into the dead city of Nineveh like thieves, which many of them indeed were.

Grave robbers, Iblis called them. Creepy little men – they mostly *were* men – with dirty broken fingernails from digging in the dirt. They loved the abandoned old places of lost civilisations. According to the master, Nineveh was once the capital of one such empire. Supposedly it had once been as grand as Rome, if not grander, and its gardens were a marvel to behold.

To Lancelot the lost city just seemed desolate. When he wasn't at practice with Iblis or serving the master and his guests, he took to wandering the ancient streets of the city. Not much remained of proud Nineveh. Its foundations had sunk into the ground and only the faint outline of what had once been avenues and houses remained. The wilderness had claimed Nineveh for its own. Trees and wild plants grew in abundance, and camels and goats roamed in search of feed. From time to time he'd see tigers, too, but he and they gave each other a wide, respectable space.

Once, he came upon what must have once been a palace of some sort. Columns half-buried in the earth even after centuries, the brickwork exquisite. An artist had chiselled bearded men fighting lions, soldiers on their horses holding spears. In a collapsed inner room Lancelot found a rotting chest, inside which were hundreds of coins, silver and copper and gold, bearing the profiles of nameless monarchs lost to the dust of time. Perhaps it had been a bank, once, he reflected.

He sat there, cross-legged in the vault, if that's what it was, until the shadows of the evening fell and lengthened, and the darkness swallowed the city whole. At last he rose, and walked in the light of the moon, trespassing under the stars of that old, dead city.

Back in their camp the master was in a rare good humour. He had two members of his order with him: Tiberius, a burly ex-tribune from the legions and now, as far as Lancelot could tell, a roving bandit; and Leviticus, a scholar from the Imperial Library of Constantinople, a thin tall man with the nervous manner of a praying mantis. The men drank cups of rough red wine and sat around the campfire like soldiers planning their next campaign. Though mostly what they did was swap old war stories that were as improbable as anything Lancelot had ever heard. The men considered themselves scholars and learned, busy with unlocking the secrets of creation itself. In the pursuit of this unearthly knowledge they robbed graves and took on shady jobs; they lied and schemed and profited from war; they were unscrupulous, arrogant, immoral and fanatical.

In other words, as Iblis once said to him, dismissively – they were men.

'Remember the black pyramids of Punt?' Leviticus said. He rubbed his hands by the fire as though he could never get warm. Red wine stained his scholar's tunic.

'The fabled lost land of Punt!' Tiberius exclaimed. 'We were so young and handsome, were we not, Joseph?'

The master gave him a tolerant smile.

'It was the Pharaoh Hatshepsut who first sent an expedition to Puntland,' he explained to Lancelot. 'The Foremost of Noble Ladies she was, and she ruled over a thousand years ago, before a Roman ever took a shit in a latrine or a Christian preacher ever bored a crowd. She sent her chancellor, Nehsi, a Nubian like you, Lancelot. With a fleet of ships they sailed across the Red Sea. They wished to lay claim to Punt but the Puntians told them where to stick it, didn't they, boys?'

'So say the ancient records,' Leviticus agreed solemnly.

Tiberius waved an impatient hand bejewelled with fat rings. 'For weeks we trudged,' he said, returning to his story, 'with only our slaves to carry our load. No ships for us, master Lancelot. And that land has long been lost, and its exact location forever unknown.'

'But we had the map,' Leviticus said. He puffed his chest up importantly. 'Which I myself discovered, at no great cost, in the antiquities market of Thessalonica. A single sheet of papyrus from the great library in Alexandria itself. Snatched from the very fire!'

'We all thought it a fake, of course,' Tiberius said. 'A special convocation of the order was summoned in Beirut. Our master then was Simon of Ararat, The Pigeon Fancier and Keeper of the Sailcloth Tatters of Noah's Ark—'

'Which I held once, I remember,' Leviticus said. 'Old and dirty it was.'

'Because of the elephants,' Tiberius said.

'What elephants?'

'The elephants on the ark.'

'If the tatters really came from the ark,' Lancelot's master interjected gently. 'I had always taken the story to be a distorted account of the vehicles of visitors from another world.'

'Of course, Joseph. Of course,' Tiberius said. '*Anyway*. There we were, in Beirut, the master poring over the precious map, and at last he pronounced himself satisfied as to its authenticity. And he selected us. We were young, then, and strong and handsome. We were mere boys! We felt we could do anything, back then.'

'Anything,' Leviticus said, nodding his head vigorously.

'So onwards we went, across the sea, first by ship to Egypt and then in boats up the Nile for a while, and then we rode on camels. We tried to stay close to the Red Sea shores, but the sandstorms and the dust, and the heat – the cursed heat!'

'And the camel men cursing and grumbling and running away—'

'And nothing strong to drink for miles around, if you know what I mean—'

'The villagers dirty and charging high prices—'

'It was shit.'

'No two ways about it.'

'A cold bloody coming we had of it.'

'Anyway.'

'Anyway.'

'We found it.'

'But why?' Lancelot said.

'Why what, boy?'

'What was so important about Punt?'

'Ah...'

It was his master who intervened then. He leaned close to the fire and his face shone in its light. 'Gold,' he said, with quiet command.

'Gold, master?'

'It is the belief of our order that gold is extra-terrestris,' the master said.

'I'm sorry?'

'Gold is exceedingly rare on this earthly realm,' the master said. 'It is my belief that it is not natural to this world but is deposited here, in minute quantities, by falling star stones.'

'I see.'

'Punt was famously wealthy in gold,' the master said. Explaining, as he always did. 'Therefore...?'

'Therefore you surmised it may be the site of a Lapis Exilis,' Lancelot said.

'Excellent,' the master said. 'Quite. Or...?'

'A fallen sky chariot, master?'

He saw how Tiberius and Leviticus exchanged glances then. It was the master's secret obsession. For had it not been said that the Hebrew prophet, Elijah, rose up to the heavens on a chariot of fire? For if things could come *down* from the sky, could not something or, perhaps, even some*one* go *up* the same way? And what might such a person *see* up there, in the heavens?

It was folly, Lancelot thought. But he never spoke the thought out loud.

'Yes,' the master said. 'Well, it was worth a try, anyway.'

'And did you find it? Anything?'

He saw the other two men exchange glances again.

'Whatever we found was inconclusive,' the master said. It was another of his favourite terms. He used it often. To Lancelot it seemed clear that the master would never find what he sought. That it was in the realm of make-believe and story-telling, not reality. The world was the world, and that was all there was to it.

Perhaps it was then that the first seeds of what transpired were planted, or perhaps they began long before. Tiberius emptied his wine and burped. 'We *did* find gold,' he said. 'Lots of gold.'

To him, it seemed to Lancelot, their mission therefore *had* been a success.

'In those black pyramids,' Leviticus said. 'Smaller than the Egyptian ones, you see. But filled with precious artefacts for the afterlife which we, well, liberated, as it were. For our troubles.'

'To finance the quest,' the master said quietly.

'Right, right. Exactly.'

'There were a lot of corpses,' Leviticus said.

'Mummies,' the master said.

'Fucking mummies!' Tiberius said. Then his head dropped on his chest and he began to snore.

Now he sits and stares at the fire. The pussy cat yawns. Lancelot turns a rabbit on a stick over the coals. He'd broken down earlier and gone hunting, though he doesn't trust these foreign forests and their traps.

But now it's good. He sits and listens to the quiet. Leaves rustling in the wind. Breathes in the sweet smell of wood smoke. The smell of roasting rabbit. His stomach growls. Go north tomorrow. Try and find some clues. Stick to the plan. Somewhere out there, there's gold.

He tears a strip of meat. The fat burns his fingers. He sucks it off his fingers. It's good, but the animal's so bony. The cat yawns. He passes her a morsel and she swallows it whole. He smiles at her. He listens to the quiet. The rustling of falling leaves.

The sound of a horse's hooves, approaching. He cleans his hands. He reaches for the sword. The horse stops in the trees. He hears a rider dismount. Footsteps. Lancelot rises and turns in one smooth motion, the sword Secace in his hand.

Sees Agravain, standing half in shadow.

Says, 'Surely, not *again*!'

48

'm sorry, master.' Agravain is bare-handed. He stands submissive. He says, 'May I approach?'

'I don't see why you should.'

The knight reaches slowly for a side bag. Holds it up. 'I brought sausages,' he says.

'...Then you may come.'

He watches Agravain. The man comes timidly. A brutish lad, a city rat of fair Londinium.

'Stop.'

He searches him, but the boy's clean.

'Sit.'

'Thank you.'

Agravain sits. He sees the cat. His eyes widen slightly.

'Mistress,' he says.

The cat purrs.

'Well?' Lancelot says.

The boy reaches into the bag. Brings out sausages, bread, small pickled onions, a side of ham, half a roast chicken.

Lancelot nods.

They eat.

The boy shares in the food but leaves the most of it for Lancelot. Lancelot offers more morsels to the cat. The cat licks the tips of his fingers, her tongue rough on his skin. She purrs.

'What do you want, then?'

'I never saw a man fight like you do.'

'It was barely a fight,' Lancelot says. 'And someone, I presume, gave you some basic training in the arts. Who was it? I had asked you once before.'

The boy, of all things, blushes. 'A traveller, from beyond the sea. She passed through Londinium—'

'*She?*'

The boy nods.

Lancelot broods, but surely it is impossible.

'Did she give you her name?' he says at last.

'She called herself Sebile,' the boy says.

Lancelot stares at the fire. But surely it's impossible, he thinks.

'How long ago?'

'Two, three months back.'

'Where did she go?'

'North, lord,' the boy says.

Lancelot is shook. But he won't think about this now.

'So what do you want?' he says.

'Lord, I brought some cannabis, too,' the boy says, eager to please. 'Grown in the king's own new fields outside the city.'

'Alright.'

The boy extracts the buds from a small string bag. Places them on a hot stone by the fire. The smell takes Lancelot back. His old master and the Order of the Seekers in their meetings liked to use it, just as the ancient Greek oracles were said to do. He breathes in. The cat blinks at him and settles head on paws.

Lancelot likes the smell. The air released is soothing.

'Well?' he says.

'Lord?'

'I am no lord. And I won't ask again. What is it you want?'

'You are travelling north?'

'So it would seem.'

'Take me with you.'

'Excuse me?'

The boy stares into the fire. 'My king is there. I would go to him.'

'So?'

The boy raises dark eyes. He stares intently at Lancelot. 'My king has need of men. Good men. Men like you.'

'There are no good men,' Lancelot says.

'Sir. I would have you teach me.'

'Excuse me?'

'I would that you were... I mean... If it pleases you to learn me—'

'Boy!' Lancelot says, shocked out of his stupor. The fumes of the cannabis really are most refreshing on the mind. He feels a pleasant heaviness in his limbs and his mind seeks flight in flights of fancy.

'Of course, you're right, it wouldn't do,' the boy says, abashed. 'Only, master – I have never seen one fight as you did.'

'What of this Sebile you mentioned?'

The boy blushes. 'Sir, we did more fighting of the other kind, if you take my meaning.'

'She fucked you and she left you? Well good for Sebile. What did you give her that she needed?'

'Sir?'

Lancelot sighs. 'She must have wanted something from you.'

Thinks – she always did.

'This is bullshit,' Iblis said. She and Lancelot had gone off on their own in the night as the master and his guests slumbered in drunken sleep.

'What is it this time?' Lancelot said grumpily. He and Iblis were both raised and trained by the master. They were like brother and sister – but siblings did not necessarily have to *like* each other. He thought she was a cold, nasty piece of work, who'd torture a man with hot blades just to see him cry.

She thought he was a useless limp dick who couldn't throw a punch to save his life.

They both competed for the master's good grace against each other – which was no doubt as the master intended.

'He's after another star stone again.'

'Well, when wasn't he?' Lancelot said, yawning.

'Some years back,' Iblis said, ignoring him, 'there was a year with no summer.'

'Before my time.'

'And mine. But nonetheless. It got very cold and a dense dry fog fell on the lands hereby.'

'So? I've heard the master bring the subject up a couple of times already.'

'More than a couple. It is high on Order's list of Incognita Natura.'

'Iblis, will you get to the fucking point already? Who gives a shit about something that happened before you were even born?'

'While you were... *incapacitated* on your little winter retreat in Smyrna,' she said, and he winced at the venom in her voice, 'the master and I heeded the urgent summons of that prune-faced fuck-weasel over there.'

'Leviticus?'

'Yeah. Come quick, he said. Important news, he said. So we drop everything and schlepp half across Byzantium to New Rome, where they do a good line in Christianity and the emperor has a magical garden full of automaton trees and bird simulacra. We snuck in there one night to see it. It's a shame you missed it.'

'I was busy,' Lancelot said. 'You know how it is, when you're having a good time in prison.'

'Yes, well. Would have come for you sooner, only... Anyway, they have the Imperial Library and a whole culture dedicated to collecting shit. They have the Crown of Thorns and a piece of the True Cross and, if you go down to the market, there'd be half a dozen touts offering to sell you a shard of Jesus's bone, a thumb or a locket of hair, with prices to suit all pockets. I swear, if you put all those pieces of Jesus together in one place you'd get a four-armed giant with seven fingers on each hand, five eyes and ten dicks of differing sizes. Which, you know...'

'A girl can dream,' Lancelot said.

'Fuck you. Anyway, where was I?'

'Constantinople.'

'Right. New Rome my *ass*. And the hotels are extortionate. Still, it's kind of impressive, if you're visiting.'

'You know, I *have* been there before,' Lancelot said.

'Right. When we robbed the vaults of the Bank of Justinus.'

'Right.'

'Well that was a shitshow.'

'That it was,' Lancelot said, wincing. They'd come up against David's Gibborim, an independent outfit of Jewish exiles, paramilitaries who were – as it turned out – in charge of the bank's security. They'd managed to get away, and Lancelot got a slash on his arm and Iblis couldn't walk for a month, but the master got what he'd come for – whatever it was. Another artefact, something to prove definitively that some tribe beyond the Sahara was in communication with the Dog Star, or some such shit.

'So what was the summons all about?' Lancelot said.

'Right, yeah. So this *asshole* Leviticus pulls another fast one on the master. A *witness*. Some dim-witted Brittonic slave that Leviticus acquired somewhere off some Germans. Saxons are all over that fucking island now, apparently. So off we trudge to fucking Constantinople. And out comes this *eyewitness*. Who tells the master, oh, that weather thing, that must have been the dragon what done it. So the master says, what dragon. And the man says, why, the dragon what flew over Britain that year. So the master gets all excited and he starts questioning the slave, and before you know it the man is drawing weird clouds, and

Leviticus brings out an atlas and old maps of Britain when it was still at least partially civilised by the Romans, and they're working out the angle of the sun and the direction of the wind and fuck knows what – I was surprised they didn't call a fortune teller to augur the omens of success or otherwise in the entrails of chickens. And so.'

'So?'

'Don't you get it?' Iblis said. 'He wants to *go* there.'

Lancelot laughed.

Like the fool he was! He *laughed*.

'Go *where*?' he said.

'To that island. Britain.'

'*Britain*?' He still couldn't take it seriously. 'But there's nothing there! No one's even been there for, well, years! It's just some backwater shithole former colony the legions left just as soon as they could. I bet there isn't even a decent toilet.'

'Do you have any idea what it's *like*, there?' Iblis said. 'Cold! Damp. Miserable. The natives are half-savages, the Germans are overrunning half the coastal areas, the native warlords are scrabbling like dogs over a rat, the roads are in disrepair, there are no working hot baths and there isn't even a *library*.'

Lancelot winced.

'*And* it lies beyond the back of the fucking beyond,' she said. 'To get there we'd have to leave everything we know, cross savage Germania and Gaul, filled with ghost-chocked forests, warring pig-men, rain and snow, and if by some miracle we've done *that* we still have a sea crossing just to *get* to the fucking place. And who knows what's actually out there.'

'What's your *point*, Iblis?' Lancelot said. He felt a headache coming on.

'My *point*, you stupid *fuck*, is that if you go there, you ain't never coming back.'

He thinks about it now. Doesn't want to, but does. That fateful conversation and its consequences. He strokes the cat. She purrs. Agravain is silent by the fire.

'I have never taken on an apprentice before,' Lancelot says.

The boy speaks not.

'One cannot serve two masters,' Lancelot says.

'Sir... My king has need of men such as yourself.'

'So you keep saying.'

'There's work to do,' the boy insists. 'The king has enemies, and those enemies have hefty bounties on their heads.'

'The Six Kings?'

'Five, now. They say Urien is no more.'

Lancelot considers.

'Whose is the heftiest?' he says.

'Leir. He is the most dangerous.'

'I've taken bounty work before,' Lancelot says.

'I rather thought you might have.'

'Still. I have my own quest.'

'But your pockets are empty, sir,' the boy says shrewdly. 'And a job's a job.' He looks sideways at Lancelot. 'And two swords on the road are better than one. The north's a savage place. Let me serve you, master.'

Lancelot nods. But whether in assent or no he doesn't say. He gets up from the fire and goes to his bedding under an ash.

Bounty hunting, he thinks.

And he thinks – *fucking* Germania.

49

His name was Parzival and the local chieftain, for whatever reason, wanted him dead.

Germania. It really was as bad as Iblis had made it sound back in Nineveh. The forests were dark and there was snow on the ground and the maidens all had wrestlers' arms. There was all kind of death magic in those forests and the trees were decorated with the swastika symbols of the Saxons.

Fucking Germania. It was a miracle they'd made it out of there alive.

What transpired after Nineveh was just as Iblis had predicted. The master had decreed one last voyage. One last attempt, he said, to find the grail. He had gathered them one day, in the ruined temple of Tiamat, and laid out his plan. He had maps and charts from the Imperial Library in Constantinople, and small treasure provided by the Order. He showed them the path they would need to follow.

'From the coast there,' he stabbed a finger at the map, 'we can charter a ship to the island. The Germans have been raiding that part of the world for years – from what I hear they've even started establishing colonies. Once we get there we'll track the original crash path of the star stone.'

'But master,' Lancelot protested, 'we'd never make it there. This whole part of the world's fallen to barbarity. It's filled with hostile tribes. There's no more Roman safety, no legions to keep the peace, the roads must be full of robbers, and you know the Germans' reputation for mass murder.'

'Nonsense,' the master said. 'They were merely protecting their lands against the Romans. And we are but humble travellers, boy. We've done this a hundred times and more. Why, in my youth, I had—'

But before he could launch into yet another story, Iblis interrupted.

'Master, is this wise?' she said. She used her most reasonable voice. She could be many things to many people, when she wanted to. 'The cold is bad for your bones, you know it is. And the road is long, and dangerous, and the climate inauspicious. Besides, didn't you say you have always wanted to investigate the old sites of Sodom and Gomorrah? They are a far likelier site of a falling star stone, seeing as how they perished in flame from the heavens, and besides, the air of the great salt sea and the heat of the desert will do wonders for your lungs. Why don't we—'

The master looked at her coldly.

'Are you calling me *old*, Iblis?' he said.

'No, master, I merely suggest—'

'Suggest nothing!'

It was the closest Lancelot had ever seen the master come to open fury.

'I am Joseph of Arimathea, third of that name, Commander of the Inner Circle of the Venerated Secret Brotherhood of the Seekers of the Grail, Master of the Death Palm, Answerer of the Sphinx's Riddle, Finder of Lost Punt, and all around fucking *bad*-ass. And you tell me I am too *old*? I will cross Germania if I have to tear the throat of every hearthweru and foederati between here and Colonia, if I have to fucking *swim* the sea to reach Britannia, and if I have to crawl through flame to find the fucking *grail*! So children, are you coming with me? Or will you be left behind, to wonder forever at the mysteries not solved, at the riddle not answered? For if you do not have loyalty, children, then you have nothing in this world, and I may as well kill you now, and spare you the agony of living without honour. So what will it be, Iblis? What will it fucking be!'

Lancelot cringed. But Iblis stayed cool. 'I am sorry, master. My worry for you has made me forget your awesome powers. We will follow you, gladly. Of course we will. And to the ends of the Earth itself.'

'To the ends of the Earth itself, and *beyond*,' the master said, and his eyes gleamed.

'Beyond, of course.'

'The heavens!'

'Yes, master.'

'Yes, master!'

'Shut up! Now, both of you, go pack up your shit. I'm going to take a nap.'

'Yes, master.'

'Yes, master.'

The master stormed off to his bedding.

Lancelot and Iblis stared at each other.

'I t—'

'Don't say it,' Lancelot said.

'I t—'

'Don't say it!'

'I told you so.'

'Well, *fuck*,' Lancelot said; with feeling.

Why this Parzival fellow deserved to be hunted was anyone's guess. His mother died of heartache – some said poison – and his father ran off to marry some Nubian princess in a land called Zazamanc. This Parzival grew up in court and fancied himself a sort of knight. That seemed to mostly involve the usual highway robbery and protection racket. He married, but his betrothed, Condwiramurs, was left shortly after the nuptials with a child quickening in her womb and no husband to be found. As to what he actually *did* to piss anyone off, Lancelot truly didn't know. Whatever it was, the chieftain in this part of the world really hated Parzival, and was offering a handsome reward for anyone who brought him back the man's head.

At this point of their voyage the master was rather poorly, and all three of them were short on funds. Iblis had taken to throwing knives at the trees. Lancelot, meanwhile, fostered closer inter-cultural relations between Byzantium and the lands of the Saxons, by making the acquaintance of a maiden named Orgeluse. There were places she expected him to put his tongue that he'd never even known you could *go*.

'Shit eater,' Iblis said.

'Fuck you,' Lancelot said.

'If only,' Iblis said. 'Everyone here's a pig.'

'Your standards are too high.'

'And you don't have any.'

'Silence!' the master said. 'This Parzival should be an easy job. Easy enough that even you two nincompoops can manage not to fuck it up. Hopefully. So go. According to the locals he's holed up in something called the Red Castle, on the way to the coast. Which is where we should be heading anyway. I'll follow you when I've... recuperated.'

He coughed. He was not a well man anymore. Exposure to various dangerous metals on his many voyages had left Joseph of Arimathea with a skin as yellow as cheap parchment, no hair – not even eyebrows – and an increasing reliance on poppy juice. Which he was running low on. He was sweating now, and his hands shook. Lancelot felt sorry for him.

'Yes, master,' he said.

'Gladly, master,' Iblis said.

She collected her knives, throwing stars and spear. Lancelot got his sword and his daggers. There was no point to using horses in the thick forests. He paid a quick goodbye call on Orgeluse, and left her with lingering regret, his clothes in disarray, a small food hamper and two bottles of decent red wine.

'Alright?' Iblis said acidly.

'Lead the way,' Lancelot said.

Iblis melted quietly into the dark of the trees.

Lancelot followed.

They moved like shadows, and not even the wild forest animals of those primordial woods noted their passing. They moved with an exhilarating rush of speed, leaping between trunks and from treetop to treetop, as wild as birds. Lancelot never felt more alive than when he was doing this, with no need for conscious thought, no reason beyond the pursuit of speed. As they fled through the dawn and into day and through to night again, all the ridiculous, deadly forces that had shaped his life melted away. For that brief time, he had no master.

He was free.

Lancelot and Iblis moved as one. They were perfectly coordinated, wordless in their communication, knowing each other's minds by subtle clues in the shift of a toe hold, in the turn of an eye. They did not speak, they merely *were*. In that and that alone they were perfectly matched, entirely at peace with each other. They may hate each other, he thought, but they also made each other complete.

The master and Iblis. They were the only family Lancelot knew.

They sped through the dark of the forest, unwilling to slow down, unwilling to stop. They saw many strange things in the forest. A herd of aurochs, stealing through a clearing in the moonlight. A giant bear, fighting off a pack of wolves in deadly silence. A unicorn lapping at a spring. They saw witches dance around a fire, saw hunters with their faces masked in blood, stalking human prey. They did not stop. They were addicted to the rush of passing.

At last they did have to stop, however. They found themselves on a precipice, under the awning of an ancient oak, with bats nesting in its branches. Sweat dripped down Lancelot's face. Iblis, beside him, was breathing heavily. They had run until day and night blended into one.

Below them was the castle.

It was not, in truth, a castle. The Saxons' architectural leanings did not go in the direction of Roman-style fortifications. What it *was* was—

'A fucking *burial mound*?' Iblis said. 'You've got to be fucking kidding me.'

The Red Castle was a series of nestled, vast barrows. It lumbered towards the horizon, mounds built on top of mounds, made out of some unnatural red earth, with stone archways leading into the dark inside at bizarre angles. No grass grew over the barren hills and swastikas decorated the stones and timber that could be seen.

Above the castle, bats fled across the falling sun.

'Well, this is fucking pleasant,' Lancelot said.

'No shit.'

'Sausage?'

'Sure.'

So they sat down under the oak and ate the food Orgeluse had packed them, and shared the strong red wine the people of Germania are so fond of. They watched the castle for any comings or goings.

'I'll take first shift,' Lancelot offered.

'Alright.' Iblis was already nestled between the roots. She yawned. 'Wake me up when it's time.'

'Sure.'

But she was already asleep.

Lancelot watched the castle. As night fell completely, burning torches were lit among the barrows, and he thought he could see silent, shadowy processions moving in between the tombs, but he could make out no features and no details.

Past midnight a witch flew over the castle, cackling. Shortly thereafter three bears lumbered in from out of the wood, shook the frost from their furs in the moonlight, and transformed into men, then vanished into the openings in the artificial hills. As the moon dipped low in the skies a silent procession emerged out of the wood, men carrying between them a glass coffin. They halted before the barrows until some signal was given. Then they, too, vanished inside.

When it was time to wake up Iblis it was nearly dawn. She stole awake and glanced at the castle.

'Anything?'

Lancelot shrugged. 'General witchery,' he said.

'Figures.'

He yawned and slipped into the same dip in the earth that Iblis had occupied before. The ground was warm from her sleep. He closed his eyes.

How many more nights like this? he wondered. He was tired of sleeping in the roots of trees, tired of keeping watch over dismal, most likely cursed castles, tired of breaking in and out of places, of following orders, of scrabbling for his next meal. He could have really been somebody, he thought. There had to be something better than this.

Dimly in the back of his mind he replayed a conversation with the master about star stones. How gold wasn't native to this Earth but fell from the sky. How it was dug up from the ancient craters of these fallen rocks.

Gold.

With gold you could buy anything, he thought. You could *be* anything.

But it was just a thought, as yet.

He fell asleep, dreaming of summer palaces on slopes, and silken girls bringing sherbet.

When Lancelot wakes up, the boy Agravain is standing over him with a drawn assassin's knife, and the cat is hissing furiously.

50

'**M**other*fucker*!' Lancelot screams. He raises his foot to perform the Leper's Leap, with a follow-up of Yael's Hammer to the temple, thus eliminating the pain-in-the-ass Agravain once and for all. But the boy is strangely still; he seems transfixed in the position, the knife hovering over Lancelot, one foot raised awkwardly to stomp or simply step; only his eyes are alive, and they dart wildly from side to side, as though searching for an escape.

The cat has transposed herself between them. Her fur is raised and her hiss turns soft and plain menacing. As Lancelot pushes himself upright the cat transforms into a woman. She takes the knife from the unresisting knight and puts two fingers on his neck. Agravain drops to the floor. The woman drops the knife on top of him and turns, smiling. Lancelot notices she isn't wearing any clothes.

'I'm Morgan la Fey,' she says.

Lancelot says, 'Charmed, I'm sure.'

'And I have heard so much about you.'

'You have?'

The woman smiles. He'd met enchantresses before. The world is full of magic and its ungodly practitioners. She wraps her arms around his neck and purrs.

'I was curious enough to come look you up in person, at least.'

'Curiosity killed the cat,' Lancelot says.

'What a silly expression.'

She feels him up. He hardens, he can't help it. He feels her smile against his neck. Small sharp teeth nibble on his skin. She bites him playfully. He yelps. She laughs.

'Want to fuck?' she says.

'Look, lady...'

But she can tell the truth of his desire. He's just a man. He's weak like mortal men are weak.

Her nails rake his back. Then she's on top of him, mounting him, and she does something unspeakable on top of him and he cries out and she laughs.

'It's called Bast's Entrapment,' she tells him.

'Is that so, mistress?'

He understands now. He twists and scissors, throwing her off him. She flies through the air and hits a tree, bounces back and flips twice while airborne. She lands softly, facing him, and smiles, showing teeth.

'Jerubbaal's Well!' Lancelot cries. He stomps on the ground with funnelled energy. The ground shakes and sinks into a borehole. Morgan loses her balance and tumbles in, but at the last minute flips up, catches a branch and loops around it, aiming a double kick that hits Lancelot in the chest and sends him flying back.

'Mab's Fury!' Morgan sings, and then she's a whirlwind of flame rushing at him, and he throws himself sideways. He swipes a leg and tackles her, bringing her down on top of him. For a moment their faces are close; so close. She inhales him.

'Yes...' she says. 'Merlin *was* right.' She shudders, as though Lancelot's scent is intoxicating to her. He feels it draining him, somehow. He's weak beneath her.

'So heady...' she says. 'You could be the greatest of them, yet. Perhaps Merlin's backed the wrong horse after all...'

'Mistress? I don't understand you.'

Her hand grasps him – painfully, pleasantly! – between the legs.

'Do you understand this?'

'Yes,' he says. His voice is hoarse. 'Yes...'

'Then shut your fucking mouth and fuck me.'

'Yes, mistress,' he says. 'Yes...'

Then he lets go entirely as the enchantress has her way with him; and all the while, the body of the unconscious Agravain lies nearby.

'Wake up, fuckwit,' Iblis said. Lancelot was shaken from a nightmare into life. In his dream he was being chased by—

'Argh, get it off of me!'

There was a bat lying on his face. He fumbled helplessly. Iblis laughed and pulled the creature gently by a wing. It flew back into the canopy of the trees.

'It's only a fruit bat, you idiot.'

'I don't like bats.'

'Well, they seem to like you.'

It was dusk again. How long had he slept? He felt groggy, as though the air itself was perfumed with some potion of sleep. Which it probably was, he thought. Hidden defences. It was the sort of lair he and Iblis had had to penetrate before. There had been that cave in Endor... He shuddered.

'Any movement?'

Iblis suppressed a yawn. 'Very few comings and goings,' she said. 'So what do you want to do?'

'You got a plan?'

'Sure,' Iblis said. 'Go in, kill everyone until we find Parzival, then kill him too... Same as we always do.'

'Think there's gold in there?'

'Probably. Split it fifty-fifty?'

'Same as we always do.' He rose, stretched, fetched his sword. 'Ready?'

'When am I not?'

He felt so bone-weary then. How many more castles? he wondered. How many more senseless assaults on bewitched barrows filled with who knew what monstrosities, how many more murders of people who meant nothing to him beyond the price on their heads? He followed Iblis down the hill, silently, the sword drawn: two tiny shadows trespassing under the rising moon. They found the entrance and went in.

There were no guards to stop them.

Lancelot didn't like it. He *liked* guards. You knew where you were, with guards. Not having them on the door meant somebody was being *confident*. It meant they didn't think they *needed* guards.

Meant they thought whoever was coming in was a sucker.

He didn't like it at all.

The barrow was well lit. He couldn't tell where the light came from. The walls were blood-red, adorned with swastikas. Their feet made no noise on the stone ground. The air smelled fresh and clean. They went deeper and deeper down the tunnel. It curved and split. They kept following, side by side now, weapons drawn, breathing in tandem. The master had fashioned them into weapons. They worked as one, like gears in one of those calculating machines the Greeks had built back in Antikythera or wherever it was.

Side by side, their faces stern, they advanced into the Red Castle.

And still they met no one and nothing. The whole place was silent, seemingly deserted. A clear wind blew. The ground was covered in fresh straw.

Gradually, he began to discern voices. Distant at first, but coming nearer. The clinking of cups and the murmur of conversation. Snatches of song.

At last they emerged onto a cavernous hall. They must have been deep in the centre of the barrow.

A man who must have been Parzival sat on a crude stone.

He was youngish, with yellow hair, and around him stood a guard of knights in full armour, with heavy swords, their visors down, their hands crossed over the hilts of the swords.

Torches burned, secured to the walls. Rich tapestries hung behind the throne. A swastika in a white circle within a cross, against a blood-red background.

'It's quite a theme,' Iblis murmured.

They were clearly visible. But no one paid them the slightest attention.

They watched. Presently a small figure emerged out of the shadows. A page boy, or perhaps it was a girl, it was hard to say. Carrying a large saucer, filled with a dark, viscous liquid.

'What the fuck is that?'

'I'll give you three guesses.'

'Urgh,' Iblis said, and made a face.

The page passed through the rows of attendant knights and brought the saucer to Parzival. The man, with a weary look of resignation on his face, reached for the saucer. He lifted it to his lips and drank. He drank and drank, and the thick red blood fell down round his lips and down his chin and stained his tunic and fell on the throne and on the floor. Parzival drank and drank and drank. The blood never emptied from the saucer and Parzival never seemed fulfilled. He just kept on drinking, until he'd drunk perhaps as much as the blood of two or three men.

At last he lowered the saucer. It was as full as before. He passed it to the page, who carried it away.

'Now?'

'I guess...'

They made their move. They leaped and jumped but no one paid them any mind. The knights with their heavy swords never moved and Parzival on his throne never stirred. Only his eyes were alive, tracking them.

They reached the throne.

Lancelot's sword flashed.

Parzival's head was neatly severed from his neck. It fell into his lap. Surprisingly, there was no blood.

'That it?'

'Huh.'

Presently Parzival's fingers twitched. He reached for his head and lifted it up and placed it back on his neck. He made minor adjustments. He blinked.

'Well, fuck.'

They really went to work on him then. Hacking and slashing with swords and knives. First came off the head and then the hands and then the legs and joints. They carved up his chest like a butcher dismantling a cow.

The ruined organs quivered and were drawn back onto themselves. The body reassembled. Parzival sat on the Red Castle's throne. He blinked.

'I had such high hopes...' he said in a high, reedy voice.

'Mother*fucker!*'

'Poison perhaps?' Parzival suggested helpfully. 'A stake through the heart? How about setting me on fire?'

'Are you,' Iblis said, all but spluttering with indignity, 'are you *enjoying* this?'

'Not at all,' Parzival said. His mournful eyes rotated in the hollows of their sockets. 'Rather the opposite, in fact.'

He stood from the throne. He stretched. The sound was like a thousand tiny bones breaking and re-knitting. Lancelot winced.

Parzival assumed a fighting stance.

'Balder's Spear,' he said, with that same high-pitched, sad-sounding voice.

When he moved he was inhumanly fast. Lancelot felt time slow as Parzival's outstretched palm elongated and came for his throat. He slowed down his breath – the world crawled to a halt – he dodged out of the way in the freezing air of slow time.

'Plague of Moab!' Lancelot screamed, and his hands blurred in motion as he fired tiny, poison-tipped darts at Parzival.

The man did nothing to dodge the attack – nothing! Lancelot watched him in fury. The needle-like arrows struck the man's flesh and quivered. Parzival looked down, began plucking them out, then gave up in boredom.

'I really wished you were better,' he said. 'Your reputation is stellar, Master Lancelot. Mistress Iblis. But I fear it may have been overrated.'

'The Pillar of Fire!' Iblis said. 'You *prick*.' She launched herself up overhead and opened her arms, gathering heat from the stones and the torches and the warmth of the sun in subterranean plants. She flung roaring flame at Parzival.

He screamed as the fire engulfed him. It burned his hair and melted his skin. Then he shook his arms until the fire was flung from him to the ground and he stomped on it. He grimaced, and his skin regrew.

'Ouch,' he said.

'Cocksucker!'

'Plague of locusts!' Lancelot said. He whirled round and fired tiny metal balls at Parzival. They travelled with awful speed, hitting the man across the face, sinking through his skull, bursting his eyes, cutting across his chest and into his heart.

Parzival shuddered. He screamed and raised his arms, and the balls *flew* back out of his body. Lancelot dropped down just in time. They missed him by a thread and embedded themselves in the far wall.

'Rise, knights!' Parzival said. 'Bring them and bind them, bag them and tag them, wrap them and ready them, for the sacrifice!'

'Oh, shit,' Iblis said.

The silent knights who lined the path to the throne all turned as one. They lifted up their heavy swords. They advanced on Lancelot and Iblis.

'Oh shit, oh shit, oh *shit*!'

'Don't panic—'

One knight lifted his sword and tossed it at them as though

it were made of paper. It sliced through the air and narrowly missed decapitating them both with one stroke.

'Alright, panic!'

They tried to run. But the door was suddenly shut and there was no escape. Parzival resumed his throne. He yawned and looked at them sadly. The knights surrounded Iblis and Lancelot. The swords were drawn. The page reappeared from the shadows, carrying the same self-replenishing saucer of blood. Performed the same ritual of marching up to the throne. Parzival took the saucer and drank. The blood gushed down his chin, over his fingers, stained his teeth red. The page accepted the saucer back and carried it to the shadows. The knights, as one, raised their swords. Lancelot and Iblis prepared to die.

'I want to say it's been a blast, but—'

'Yeah,' Iblis said. 'It's been pretty shit, really, all of it, hasn't it, Lance.'

'There were some good parts.'

'Sure,' she said sadly. 'Sure.'

The swords came down.

Something fell from the ceiling. A piece of shadow, detaching from the dark. The master materialised between them, coughed, flung out his arms. A massive burst of what the Greeks called energeia exploded outwards and tossed and scattered the knights across the hall.

'The bowl, you fools!' he screamed. 'The bowl!'

'What fucking b… Oh,' Lancelot said.

The saucer, he realised. The saucer of blood.

'Destroy it!'

Parzival rose from his throne. He threw off the shredded remains of his clothing and faced the master naked as the day he was born. He stretched and with two hands broke his own jaw bone. He adjusted the wound as long new predator teeth grew in his mouth. He smiled, but sadly.

'I really do hope you make it,' he said. 'I had such high hopes, you see.'

His arms grew long and stretched and his chest expanded out. Lines of red, like an infection, shone all across his skin.

'Master Joseph of Arimathea, I presume?' he said.

The master nodded curtly.

'Get the bowl,' he said. 'I'll try and hold him off till then.'

'And I will hope you succeed,' Parzival said.

'How long?' the master said.

'How long, Master Joseph?'

'How long have you been under the thing's curse?'

Parzival shrugged. 'Time has no meaning here,' he said.

'It's got into you, hasn't it.'

'Master, there is more of it than me,' Parzival said. 'If there is anything of me at all.'

'*Parasitos*,' the master said with loathing.

Parzival nodded sadly.

'Sinthgunt's Countenance,' he announced. He almost smiled, then. 'I'll start you off easy.'

'The Breaking of the Ten Commandments,' the master said calmly. He assumed the relevant position. 'Let's see how powerful *it* is.'

'Oh, it is powerful plenty, I'm afraid,' Parzival said.

Then the two men simultaneously attacked.

51

When Lancelot stirs from his post-coital slumber, Morgan la Fey is already dressed and armed. She stands over the still-unconscious Agravain with a stone knife in her hand.

'I think he has a concussion,' she says. 'Should I bleed him?'

'Is that a medical procedure?' Lancelot asks, yawning.

'No, I just like to watch them bleed. Like pigs, you know.'

'I'm a questing knight, not a butcher.'

She snorts. 'Butchers are more useful to society.'

He inches his head, acknowledging the validity of her statement. Could he have been a butcher or a baker? he wonders. Or a candlestick maker. A useful member of society. He knew what he was: a parasite on the body politic – from the Greek: literally, a person supping at another's table.

That's what he is, that's what being a knight *is*. They are like leeches, feasting on the toil of those who can't take the cure, who can't fight them. They bleed the populace, a tenth tithe at a time, just enough not to kill them, just enough to keep them working.

He *knows* what he is. And there's a power in knowing your true self. Lancelot has no illusions, not anymore.

Not after Germania.

'Let the boy be,' he says tiredly. 'He did nothing but try.' And, curiously – 'Are they all like him, here?'

She weighs the question. 'Some are more competent than others,' she says.

'And this king? This Arthur?'

'Yes,' she says. Not really answering his question.

'You have designs on him?'

He knows *her* kind, too. They're parasites of a different order. More similar to the... the *thing* he'd encountered in Germania. They feed on power, the way knights feed on the weak.

'That's none really of your business,' she says, but pleasantly enough.

Fair enough, he thinks. He rises. Kicks the boy Agravain in the ribs just to check. The boy mutters something and shifts.

And something *clicks* in Lancelot's mind, like gears in that ancient Greek engine.

He kneels by the boy. Shakes him roughly awake. The boy opens bleary eyes.

'Why?' Lancelot says.

'Why?' the boy says.

'Why come after me three times?'

'I wanted... To see.'

'See what?'

'How good you were.' The boy almost smiles. 'To see if I could beat you.'

Lancelot stares at him. 'No,' he says.

'No?'

'I don't believe you.'

The boy's eyes dart from side to side. 'So?' he demands. 'So what?'

And Lancelot says, 'Iblis.'

A smile slowly spreads over Agravain of the Hard Hand's face. It lights up his eyes.

'She called herself Sebile...' he says.

'Ah, yes. Yes. Quite.'

'She is the most amazing woman I have ever met...'

'She ain't all that,' Lancelot says sourly.

The boy doesn't reply.

Lancelot, still kneeling. 'So, she sent you to slow me down?'

'Slow you down? I could have killed you!'

'Come on, kid.' He says it gently.

Agravain sighs. 'I guess...'

'What will you do now?'

The boy's eyes have lost their sparkle. 'I don't know. Will you kill me?'

'Would you like me to?'

'There'd be no shame in dying at your hand, master.'

'Oh, fuck off with the flattery you little runt.'

'Sorry.'

'Stand up.'

He has to help Agravain up from the ground. Pulls him by the arm. For a moment they're close.

'...Thanks,' Agravain says.

'Oh, get lost already,' Lancelot says.

The boy smiles. Then he nods to Morgan, says, 'Mistress,' respectfully, and goes to find his horse. In moments they can hear him speeding away through the trees.

'What a pain in the ass,' Lancelot says.

'You like him,' Morgan says.

Lancelot shrugs.

'So?' she says.

'So what?'

'What will you do now?'

'What would you have me do?'

'It seems to me the boy has set you a challenge,' she says.

'Oh?'

'And half-paid you in advance.' She glances pointedly at the bag of coins.

'That king? What was his name – Leir?'

She nods.

'What's he to me?' Lancelot says.

'A job.'

'What's he to *you?*' he says.

She smiles. 'How perceptive of you,' she says.

'Well?'

'I think that bitch Morgause has designs on him.'

'Who?'

'Never you mind. Let us just say I'd like to see you carry the job through. And I could be *most* grateful…'

Lancelot sighs. Another bounty, he thinks. How many more wet nights and smoky fires, how much more bad food or none at all, the long silent roads and the inevitable brigands, how many more empty battles with meaningless moves?

'No, thanks,' he says. 'No offence.'

But Morgan's still smiling.

Like she knows something he doesn't.

Why does he get a bad feeling?

Why, oh why, does he dislike this?

'They say a star stone fell some time back, down in the far, far north,' she says. 'I know nothing of this and care even less, for all that my bay cousin Merlin is obsessed with it. Folks such as us should not go near the radiance of fallen stars, they're bad for our constitution. Nevertheless. So it is said, in recent times. That such a stone did fall, and that prospectors hurry even now to seek their fortune beyond the Roman wall, panning no doubt for celestial gold. And if you believe that claptrap you'll believe anything, I'll wager. But *you*, Lancelot. I see the gleam of greed in your pretty eyes as I say these words. You, too, hunger. Well, King Urien of the North, it is said, is fallen. And Leir controls the boundary into the Zone. Or so they say. I wouldn't know, myself. I do not care for gossip.'

He listens to her but he listens to the silences between the words.

'Oh?' he says.

Her smile widens.

More gears suddenly lock in the device that is Lancelot's mind.

Lancelot says, 'Oh, fuck.'

'Oh fuck, oh fuck, oh *fuck*!'

The page was nowhere to be seen. The master and Parzival in their battle had already half-demolished the throne room. The knights of the blood re-rose, unwounded, and turned upon Lancelot and Iblis once again.

'They're linked to him,' Iblis said, 'to *it*.'

'Fucking Germania!'

Then it happened. Some blast of power, from the titanic battle between Parzival and the master, ripped open the shut doors.

For a moment, escape was possible.

The page came out of the shadows then. And Lancelot looked, and now he saw how puppet-like the page was – not boy, not girl, nor nothing in between but a sort of crudely formed simulacrum. Parzival shifted shapes, one moment a giant wolf, the other an enormous bat, the next a bear. A savage claw lashed at the master and slashed him across the chest and abdomen. The master cried in pain. Lancelot had never heard that sound, before.

It filled the pit of his stomach with ice.

'The grail – get the grail!' the master screamed. His intestines came sliding out of his torn belly like sausages. Lancelot looked to the page, walking with the same jerky, mechanical steps, the saucer of blood filled to the brim, held high. The... *thing* turned and looked at him with empty cut-out eyes.

'No no no no no no no,' Lancelot said.

'Help me!' the master cried.

Lancelot looked to Iblis. And Iblis looked to Lancelot.

And, just like that, it was done.

The way, perhaps, they had always secretly both thought it would be.

'Help me!'

Without a backwards glance they ran to the doors – and out of the hall.

Back up those tunnels.

The screams of Joseph of Arimathea echoing all the way behind them.

Until they stopped.

'*Iblis*,' Lancelot says, with loathing.

'So it would seem,' Morgan says. She scratches herself like a cat. 'She goes by Sebile now?'

'So it would seem,' Lancelot says.

'A friend of yours, I take it?'

'No.'

'That's what I thought, too,' Morgan says. Her ears grow pointy and fur breaks delicately over her arms. 'So, Lancelot, Knight of the Cart? Master of the Flying Sword, the Auroch's Charge, and the Judean Lightning Strike, et cetera, et cetera, as the Romans would say? Will you take the contract?'

'Leir?'

She shrugs. She grows claws. 'The woman's not on the bill.'

'What does she do for him, a bodyguard?'

'How should I know? I do not like gossip.'

The cat purrs at his feet. She butts her head against his calf playfully, and then she turns and without a backwards glance slinks into the woods and vanishes.

Afterwards, when it was over, they stood on the edge of the wood in the dawn's early light.

'Where will you go?'

Iblis shrugged. 'I don't know. Maybe Nubia. You?'

'Maybe back to Judea, for a time.'
'Alright.'
'Alright.'
And with that it was done, and they parted ways.

He stares about him almost blindly before going for his sword and his horse. It was only afterwards, when he got to thinking. What the master had said about gold. How it fell from the stars. And how tired he was of cold nights, smoky fires, the dismal jobs of a sword-for-hire.

How nice it would be, he thought, to be *rich*.

He'd sleep on a bed of feathers and be served orange juice by pale-skinned barbarian maidens with the sun in their hair.

He'd grow fat and wear many rings and wash twice a day in the hot baths and have his own masseur.

He'd read a book. He'd always meant to read one.

Maybe one of those improbable adventure stories the Greeks were so fond of, with monsters and great wars and dangerous women.

So he thought, Oh, fuck it.

And he set off, alone, to the coast.

Taking a few small jobs along the way.

Until he reached the sea, and found a ship.

And thence to Britain.

Oh, fuck it, he thinks.

He picks up his sword and mounts his horse, and begins on the long, slow road to the north.

PART EIGHT

TURNING UP BODIES

52

'What's his name again?' Arthur says. They're sitting in a watering hole on the outskirts of Lindum, near the banks of the Witham. Merlin's drinking something green that might be pond water. Arthur doesn't ask. He's drinking a beer.

'Launcelot or Lancelot, something like that,' Merlin says.

Arthur takes a meditative sip of his beer. 'He sounds like a right tosser,' he says.

'He's supposed to be very good, sire,' Merlin says, almost reproachfully. 'One of the best, really. Trained in Judea, or thereabouts. He knows gung-fu.'

'What?' Arthur says irritably. 'I don't know what that is. Also, I can't honestly say as I give a fuck. Can he do it?'

'...Probably.'

'Then tell him a thousand pieces of gold. In fact, tell them all! Put out the word, far and wide. This shit's gone on long enough. It's time to end it. A thousand pieces of gold to whoever brings me Leir's head.'

'A thousand? But, lord—'

'Can you magic the fucker away, Merlin?'

'...No.'

'No, I didn't fucking think so. So stop moaning. We're going to be rich!'

'Yes, sire,' Merlin says. He sips his greenish concoction. It's really not so bad. Fillet of a fenny snake, tossed with oil and gently flaked, eye of newt and toe of frog, wool of bat and tongue of dog, and, well, so on and so forth. With a bit of blind-worm's sting, which really gives the whole thing a nice, mellow kick.

'We've got most of the south-east and the west up to Land's End,' Arthur says, 'and we'll soon enough have most of the land up to the Pictish Wall as well. We've got the men, and now we have the swords to give them.'

'Yes, sire. And a witch's bargain with the Lady of the Lake, that horrid hag Nimue.'

'That's no way to talk about your own relatives, surely.'

'You didn't have to put up with her for that long,' the wizard mutters, but he lets it go. What's done is done, and Arthur has his bargain and so be it.

There's only the two of them in this hovel of a bar. The lady Guinevere is out somewhere in the night, hunting. And no one knows they're there, not even faithful Kay.

They sip each from their respective drinks and wait.

Till heavy footsteps tread the wooden boards.

He steps in through the back door from the woods. He's tall as he is broad, with a lined face and a wide nose and eyes that are still clear and clean, and the look in them is deadly. He wears a white bearskin robe over his muddy travelling clothes, and a sword and a dagger, and he is every inch a fucking *king*. His boots tread the boards as he comes to the counter.

'What is this shithole?' he says.

'Like it? I got it cheap.'

The man follows Arthur's gaze to a corner of the room, where the previous owner lies slumped in a chair with a knife through his ribs. Pans and skillets hang on the walls. The man grunts and gestures at the bar.

'So?' says Outham the Old.

'It is good of you to parlay,' Arthur says.

'I remember you,' Outham says. Staring at Arthur. '*You*

don't remember this but I've known you all your life. I used to visit Sir Hector in his manor. You and that boy, Kay. You ran around in the nudd, like mutts. Covered in dirt and with your little dingles dangling. It's a wonder you lived to adulthood in that whore's nest. Or did you get the clap?'

Merlin watches Arthur. Arthur's so calm. Only that tiny pulsating beat of blood in his neck. He's coiled so tight.

But Outham's oblivious. He *is* a king. He didn't get to where he is by being timid. He got there by violence and the sword, and thinking he is the toughest motherfucker in any room he walks into. These two pissers mean nothing to him. He smiles. He's enjoying himself.

'Knew your da, too,' he says. 'Back in the old days. That old cuntbucket Uther could fight, I'll give you that, boy.'

'Thank you,' Arthur says. He's not touching his drink. Merlin goes to the edge of the bar, polishes a cup. Neither man pays him any attention. This is between the two of them. A disagreement of kings.

'Say what you came to say,' Arthur says.

'Look, we've had our fun,' Outham says. 'My Franks, your barrow boys. A few skirmishes, enough spilled blood, more than a few spirits sent off to the, well, wherever. I've been thinking, Arthur. There's really no reason why you and I can't get along. I say forget about it. So you took a shot, so what? I say fuck it! You tried to go it alone, against the established order of the bosses, you know what? I say fuck that too. Live and let live, right? Got to give the boy his gumption. Between us we run half the whores of Britain and own a third of the old copper and silver mines. Between us we have enough men to take even the Angles out, maybe even Leir, that cunt. I have a connect on the continent for slaves, and a market in the far north for wool and British brides. We could help each other, you and I.'

Outham the Old stares at Arthur out of those cold, watery blue eyes. He smiles.

'Back when you were a pug I remember Hector's whores taught you how to sew. You once fixed an undershirt for me, with those tiny little fingers, like a girl's.'

Arthur is still.

'No more sewing,' he says.

'Excuse me?'

'I don't sew no more, Outham. Maybe you didn't hear, on account of you're so old.'

'Think what you're saying, boy,' the king says, and *he* isn't smiling anymore.

'Come on, come on, come on,' Merlin interjects. He comes round the bar. 'A drink, to friendship. On the house.'

Arthur relaxes. 'Yes,' he says. 'A drink.'

Merlin pushes two drinks across the bar. He sidles unobtrusively to one side, standing a little behind Outham. The old king doesn't seem to notice. He nods, tight-lipped, and then acquiesces.

'Salutaria!' he says. He raises the drink and downs it in one.

Which is when Merlin bashes him on the back of the head with a frying pan.

The big man sways. He can't believe this is happening, his face seems to say. Not to *him.* he can't believe, when it comes to that, that these two little pissers have the *balls.*

'Motherfu—!'

Then they're on him, with cudgels and kicks. They work him over methodically. Merlin with the little blade he likes, plunging it over and over into the man's stomach, his shoulders, his chest. Merlin licks his lips, feeling all that life force draining. Feeling that fading of *power.* Oh, it makes Merlin feel good. There is no better feast for his kind than the death of a king: and poor Merlin's been *hungry.*

And Arthur, all the while, never says a *fucking* word. He doesn't use a weapon. He kicks and he kicks and he leans down to punch, until Outham the Old's face is a pulped mess, like a squeezed Judean orange.

Bones break and flesh tears and blood spouts; and still the old king won't die. He lies there making strangled noises, blood in his throat and nose. But still his heart beats, and more, *more*, Merlin thinks, so close to climax.

Then Arthur stops. He gets his sword. He looks down at old Outham.

And then he smiles.

'Fuck *you*, you Frankish cunt,' he says. 'You're nothing to me, not even a breath. I would not give you the steam off my piss.'

And he brings down the sword.

The king is dead, Merlin thinks, as he had thought so many times before.

Long live the king.

'...Shall we bury him somewhere?'

'Let's have a drink, Merlin,' the king, *his* king, his Arthur says.

'Yes, sire.'

They sit there at the bar with the dead man on the floor. And Merlin marvels at the death. How a man is so alive one moment, is animated by a spirit, moves and speaks, just *is*. Then, in a moment, there is nothing there, whatever spark had made it walk and talk and think and feel is gone, and all that's left is meat, soon to be rotten.

It isn't in the nature of the fae to think too deeply of the greater mysteries, and yet. What does it mean? he wonders. Are we truly just atoms, as the Greeks have proposed, made up of millions of tiny particles too small to see? What then animates the body, what makes a mind? It just seems so unfair, for death to be an end.

For Outham the Old had well and truly *lived*. Had thought and dreamed and schemed and felt, knew pain, knew joy – perhaps he even loved, for all that kings do not have the luxury of such a thing. But his presence was felt upon the world.

And now he vanished, just like that. And who could say, in years to come, that he had been at all?

'Cheer up, Merlin.'

'Yes, my lord.'

Later, they set the place on fire and walk away. They pause on the edge of the wood. The flames lick the night, and sparks shoot up into the heavens.

'I want the word out,' the king says. 'Outham's dead, and Urien of the Hen Ogledd. I want them all, my wizard. Send out word. Of the Six Kings only four remain. I want them gone.'

And are the Christians right? Merlin wonders. Is there a soul, and does it live on, does it go into the heavens? Or were the Greeks and Romans right instead, and one goes to the underworld? And being of a practical bent of mind, he has to wonder – how does it work, a soul, if such a thing exists? Can it be weighted? Is it located in the body or outside it? Is it an energy like magnets or electricity, of which Thales wrote that they are filled with gods? And had he not been said to have regarded the soul as something endowed with the power of motion, had he not argued that the lodestone has a soul because it moves iron?

But Merlin doesn't know the answers to these questions. No one does, he thinks. No one upon this world.

But there may yet be other worlds than these. Perhaps upon those worlds lived beings who had the answers.

'Yes, my lord,' he says.

'A thousand gold pieces.'

'Yes, my lord.'

'Bring me their fucking *heads*!'

53

The word goes out, and attempts are made.

...They do not always work.

Tor and Lamorak pull the boat up on the jagged rocks. It's night and freezing in these northern climes. The waves are high. The stars above are bright and cold.

'I'm going to be sick,' Lamorak says.

'Hold it in, man, for crying out loud!'

Lamorak throws up on the rocks.

'God damn it!' Tor says.

'It's gods, not God,' Lamorak says. 'You freaking Christian.'

'There's but one true God, and his son is Jesus Christ,' Tor says.

'Where *did* you pick that nonsense up,' Lamorak says. He wipes his mouth with his sleeve.

'I'm cold,' he says.

'Let's get this over with.'

'Yes, let's.'

They draw their knives. Assassins in the night, here in the outer reaches of the Orkney Islands.

Planted in the sandy ground above the beach is a wooden stick with a skull nailed to it. The skull is human. It grins at the two men.

'Motherfucking Picts.'

They go around the skull. They creep along in the dark.

They come to a village. Dogs bark, but they ignore them. Cooking fires smoulder. The village is asleep. The two men circumnavigate the huts. They follow a small packed dirt road.

'It can't be far.'

'There!' Lamorak says. He points. Tor squints. In the dark, under the stars... They see it. A stone house on the cliffs above the sea. The waves pound the shore below. The house is solid and fires burn. They creep along. They melt into the shadows. They are professionals.

Woooohoooo... a passing formless shadow whispers.

'What was that?'

'What was what?'

Tor stares from side to side.

'Just the wind.'

They reach the castle wall. King Lot of Orkney, old geezer that he is, who rules the sea Picts and their northern brood, a man who thinks himself secure here in his wild kingdom, where neither gannets nor great skua tread without his blessing. They say the very land here heeds his word, the Orkney voles obey his every order. The trees don't sway unless the king commands the breeze to make it so.

'That fucker's got it coming.'

His partner nods. They throw a rope and scale the wall. They are professionals.

Woooohoooo...

'What *was* that!'

For just a moment Tor is certain he had seen a ghostly lady pass and smile at him.

'Something I ate, maybe.'

'Don't get sick on me now.'

They speak in whispers. The night here is so quiet and somewhere a sea bird cries and Lamorak flinches. But on they go. They come upon a guard and slit his throat before he even wakes. They tiptoe through the courtyard to the house.

They speak in gestures now.

Upstairs.
They creep with knives. They find a room. The door is open.
They go in.
The door slams shut behind them.
In front of them there is another door.
It opens on to air.
The castle's built along the cliff, and here's a door built into
wind and ocean.
Hello, boys…
And now the ghostly lady, pale as foam, rises in the doorway.
She motions for them, smiling, her long thin fingers ringed in
pearls and seaweed. The two men turn. They hammer on the
door but it is locked and strong. They turn and turn.
The lady smiles. The lady beckons.
Come…
'Our Father, who art in heaven, hallowed be thy name…'
Tor says.
'Jupiter!' Lamorak screams. He runs at the lady with his
knife meant for her heart.
The lady smiles. The lady opens wide her arms, the better
to embrace him. Lamorak screams. Lamorak passes through
her ghostly form. Lamorak falls, a small black spot against the
whiteness of the foam that rises from the waves.
His bones break on the jagged rocks. His body sinks beneath
the waves. A current under sea picks his bones in whispers.
The lady turns. The lady smiles.
'Forgive us our trespasses!' Tor says. 'As we forgive those
who trespass against us!'
'God forgives,' the woman says. 'I don't.'
She takes on solid form. Her bare feet step lightly into the
room from that impossible doorway. She smiles and smiles,
and her teeth are like a shark's, and she is hungry.
Gently, almost lovingly, she takes Tor in her arms. His
useless knife drops to the floor. The lady's lips caress his skin.
Her tongue darts to that pulse of blood under his jaw.

Her mouth opens wide, and then she feeds.

But it only takes one to succeed:

Conan Meriadoc runs through the thick forest on the edge of his estate. His chest is bare and covered in bleeding cuts. His breath heaves. He is barefoot. His eyes are large and the pupils dilated.

Where is it? Where is the thing that hunts the mightiest of all the kings?

He jumps at shadows. He shies away from roots. Strange nameless creatures slither in the dark away from him.

How had it come to this?

Blurred memories. His troop of men, a raid on one of Arthur's villages. They slaughtered the lot of them and burned the place and stole what they could. Drinking later in their meeting place, Conan was merry, a suckling pig cooked on the spit, there was a heavy smoke, it tasted sweet...

There was a woman. Smiling, gesturing. Saying something, but he couldn't really hear.

Then pleasure.

Then pain.

Then darkness.

When he woke it was to the sight of his men dead, and the thing vanished. But he knew it was there. Some sort of shape-shifting demon-knight.

So he ran.

Conan Meriadoc, that mightiest of kings, runs through the dark forest. High overhead the shape of his predator watches. It is some sort of shape-shifting demon. Dressed all in black and wearing a mask on its face. The figure leaps from branch to branch and tree to tree, lightly. It makes no sound. It watches Conan Meriadoc as he stumbles. The king stands blindly in the forest, amidst the trees. He looks from side to side.

The predatory knight nocks an arrow and fires. It whispers through the air. It hits Meriadoc in the thigh.

The king hollers in pain.

He hobbles away. He has his sword in his hand. He won't go down easy. He screams and he curses. 'I've killed babes in their mothers's arms and dragons's brood and things that have no earthly name and I yet live! I am Conan Meriadoc son of Conrad son of Khong, and there is no man alive who can defeat me!'

The knight high in the trees merely nocks another arrow, lets it fly.

Conan falls to the ground, the arrow through his shoulder.

'Show yourself, you coward!'

The knight drops lightly from the tree. It stalks towards the fallen king. It stands above him. Removes its mask.

'*Men*,' Isolde says. She smiles.

'Oh fuck—' from Conan Meriadoc. He tries to crawl away. He can't. 'Oh, fuck, oh fuck, oh fuuuu—'

When it is done there's just another carcass left to rot. It is the fate of men and women both, of rats and snakes and ants and bees, and all that lives on land, in air, or deep under the sea.

Isolde does collect her arrows. 'You piece of shit,' she says, and crouches there, and urinates upon the fallen monarch. She gathers up her garment and departs.

'The king is dead,' she says. The quiet secret creatures of the forest watch her pass.

'Long live the king.'

54

'**W**ell?' Arthur says.

''Tis done, my lord.'

'Give a thousand gold coins to Isolde, then, and my thanks.'

'Yes, my lord.'

'What of Lot?'

'He lives still.'

'That old fucker!'

'He has magical protection, sire.'

'Raise the bounty, Merlin. Fifteen hundred gold on all their heads, and two on Leir. I want them gone and buried.'

'Yes, lord.'

They're standing outside the keep of Tintagel.

Arthur is quiet then.

Merlin keeps a respectful distance.

'She's there?' Arthur says at last. A tone of voice so soft it's hard to bear.

'Yes, lord. And I have not been back since you were born.'

'Merlin, I...'

But he does not complete the thought.

'Wait here,' he says.

'Yes, lord.'

The wizard watches as his king strides to the bridge that links the land to Tintagel. The castle rises on its island much as

he remembers it, for all that last time he went was as a stork –
or was it as some other bird?

He wishes most devoutly to accompany the king. As Arthur's
power grows it produces a delirious effect on Merlin. The taste
of it has gone from smoky beer to fine aged wine from vanished
Rome. It is intoxicating.

And this meeting!

'Oh, Merlin, it's you.'

'Isolde.'

'Is he happy?'

'He is satisfied. There is your coin.'

'And thank you kindly, wizard boy.' She weighs the money
and grins. 'Guess old Isolde can retire now.'

'You will not follow Guinevere?'

The woman shrugs. 'She's made her bargain. I would not
wish to be a queen and put up with that asshole.'

'That asshole is your king.'

'*Your* king, Merlin. Just remember to wash your hands after
you jerk him off.'

She laughs.

'Be well, Isolde, and goodbye.'

'Can't say as I'll miss you. What's in that castle, anyway?'

'A woman.'

'Already he is straying? They haven't even sealed the deal
yet, Guinevere and him.'

But Merlin's barely listening. Remembers that night, so long
ago and yet only a moment past. The woman and the baby, and
how she looked when he gently took the child away.

'Not that kind of woman,' he says; but he does not elaborate,
and mercifully Isolde doesn't ask.

Enjoy your gold, he thinks.

It is late at night when Arthur returns, and the milky-white
moon shines down on the graceful towers and the narrow

curving bridge. He walks alone, and what he thinks nobody knows but him.

His wizard meets him on the land.

'My lord?'

'Yes,' Arthur says. 'Yes.'

But it is clear he isn't listening.

Tomorrow, then, the wizard thinks.

And he remembers the lady Igraine, and how she looked at him, and said not a word when he took her child.

It was for the best, he thinks.

The moon shines down on the black water.

And Merlin sees the vision of a ship with white sails under dark clouds, a storm on the horizon. Sea spray and a bird crying. Sailing towards a distant shore.

'What was my father like, Merlin?'

The question catches the wizard by surprise.

'My lord?'

'My father. What was he like?'

'What would you have me say about him, lord? What? Would you have me say he was a kind man? He was a wise man? He had plans?' Merlin rubs his hands together. He is suddenly cold. 'That he had wisdom? Bullshit, man! He could be terrible. He could be mean. He was a man as men are of this world. He lived and died by force alone.'

'Yes,' Arthur says. He stares across the water at the Castle Tintagel. 'Well, good night, Merlin.'

'Good night, sire.'

Merlin watches the king walk away. He stares at the dark sea, and thinks dark, watery thoughts.

And some slip through the cracks:

'What manner of a thing are you?' King Lot inquires.

'A jester, sir, by name of Dagonet.'

'A clown?'

'My lord, I can perform the ball and cups exquisitely, make coins and scarves appear at will and vanish, I know the dirtiest of jokes in seven languages including Aramaic, and I have mastered both the wet leaf slip and falling on my bottom.'

The king yawns.

'Is that it?'

'I can juggle five balls in the air.'

'I'll have your balls if you don't entertain me.'

The jester looks at the king with a faint smile. Lot is old, and he sits on his hard throne and his women of the water around him. They look at the jester and lick their lips.

'Tell us a joke, then, little man.'

'This is from Greece,' Dagonet says. 'A man goes to the philosopher and says, "Sir, I am ill. I cannot lie down and I cannot stand up. I can't even sit." The philosopher looks at him and says, "Then I guess the only thing left is to hang yourself!"'

Dagonet looks expectantly at the old king. Lot stares at him. His mouth twitches. Then he starts to laugh.

He laughs and he laughs, his beard shakes and his stomach rolls, until tears come to his face. His women of the water smile politely, then fade back into the sea. The king summons the jester, 'Come! Come!' and Dagonet prances to the throne. The king shoves a goblet of wine into the little jester's hand. The jester drinks.

No one sees when the tip of his little finger, smeared with a certain kind of fine powder, trails along the inside of the cup before he hands it back.

The jester prances. The jester juggles. The jester tells lewd jokes. Later, the little man slips away into the night with his pockets heavy.

Later still, the king begins to foam about the mouth.

'Mother*fucker*!' Morgause says.

Morgan le Fay smiles faintly. 'Troubling news, dearest one?'

They are sitting in the solarium of the House of High Dudgeon, in the fairy realm. They're drinking hot mint water and nibble delicately on biscuits.

'They did for Lot, and I was backing him.'

Morgan shrugs. 'The man was old. He was always a long shot.'

'That useless old tosser. That's years of work down the shitter.'

'Language, dear Morgause!'

'Oh, fuck off, Morgan.'

Morgause folds her hands over her stomach. She is heavy with child. She smirks at Morgan, who pretends to ignore her. Let Morgause play the long game if she wants. The babe's not even born yet.

'Is it a g—'

'A boy.'

'You know for certain, then?'

'I have a fairly good idea.'

Morgan mulls this over. Morgause sips her drink. She smacks her lips.

'So who is left, then?' Morgan says.

'Yder and Leir.'

'It would be only a concession,' Morgan says. 'Even if Arthur wins all their territories there are the incumbents to consider.'

'Angles, Saxons, *Jutes*!' Morgause says derisively. 'Their kings are dogs and the rest of them are fleas upon the flesh of Britain. I would not piss on them to put out a fire.'

'Pregnancy has made you ever more pleasant...' Morgan says.

'...Fuck you.'

They sit companionably and sip their drinks while the giant multicoloured caterpillars frolic in the gardens outside under the canopy of plants that have no earthly name.

★

And sometimes the days make for strange bedfellows:

'Ulfius.'

The knight turns, startled. It is night, under the stars, a clearing in a forest, somewhere outside Londinium. He's come alone, and he is armed, for all that arms are useless here where he is bound.

'King Leir. I did not hear you come.'

'I watched you,' he says. 'What news, then?'

Ulfius shrugs, uncomfortable. 'The bounty on your head has been increased again.'

Leir smiles, but tightly. 'How much is it now?'

'Four thousand gold coins, and land.'

'Land, now, is it?' Leir considers. 'Anyone specific?'

'Half the knights in the realm are hunting for you, lord, and every halfwit with a kitchen knife and dreams of glory.'

'Village idiots and Londinium curs I can handle, Ulfius.'

'Then what is it you fear?'

'I fear nothing.'

But Ulfius sees in some surprise that Leir's uncomfortable. The man is rattled, at long last, he realises. He'd underestimated Arthur once again.

'You thought you'd have him at the Council of Six,' he says. 'And you were wrong. You thought you'd have him shortly after, and you were wrong again. If I were you I'd start to think of making peace or running.'

'It is too late for peace,' Leir says, 'and I do not intend to run.'

'Then what, lord?'

But when he looks again, King Leir is gone.

'They will come back at you, and hard,' Merlin says.

'I know that, wizard,' Arthur says in mild irritation.

'Leir has at least one man of ours giving him information.'

'To be expected, really,' Arthur says.

'My lord... this star stone business—'

'It can wait.'

'I worry.'

'You always worry, Merlin. You should eat something.'

The wizard licks his lips. What sustenance he craves cannot be found in bread or cheese or apples. The king must know this.

'Besides, they will have to find me first.'

Merlin looks at his king. Arthur has always been wiry, but now he seems like a taut string, playing a single deep note. They move each night, from place to place, in secret. Visiting their troops and monitoring the battle that's still raging. Consolidating the dead kings' lands will take some doing, there's need for proper administration, census taking, effective tax control. The villagers will always try to hide their extra rations, unlicensed gambling dens and brothels still proliferate, the mines are under constant threat from robbers – damned freelancers!

'It will all work out, Merlin. You worry too much.'

They'll need a proper capital, and soon, the wizard thinks. A central seat of power.

For a moment he lets his mind run wild, imagines a glimmering city to which the brightest minds of the realm are inexorably drawn – scribes, alchemists, natural philosophers! He dreams of a library to rival Alexandria's, dreams of a place where rationality can once more flourish.

Then he looks at his king and the dream dies. Arthur is many things, but he is not inclined to wonder at the wonder of the world.

Well, you've made your choice, he thinks, so stick with it. There's little point in playing games of ifs and could-have-beens. The game's the game – same as it ever was.

'My lord,' he says, in acquiescence.

★

The attack comes three nights later on the shores of the Irish Sea. Three long boats filled with shadowy assassins. The Irish never felt the wrath of Rome and see themselves superior to Britons.

Leir of the Ridings always had an understanding with the savages across the water. Now they come, and steal onto the land. And how did they know where to find King Arthur?

Merlin watches them from the branches of a tree, high above the shore. Leir has his informants, that's not in dispute. The assassins steal towards the camp.

'Now,' Merlin whispers.

On cue, lit arrows flame across the sky. The camp's a dummy and a death trap, it's filled with hay and kindling and wood. The fire takes hold and in an instant blooms to life. It snatches hungrily at the invaders. It hugs their flesh and roasts their bones, it catches playfully in their hair. The men scream. They run like torches. A few die in the sea.

Later, three boats are pushed from shore towards Hibernia. They're piled high with corpses. Away from shore the flaming arrows fly again. Now three long boats on fire sail back towards their source.

Merlin watches from the shore. A warning and a premonition to those devils out in Eire-land.

Your time will come.

And sometimes, they just get the wrong man:

'There he goes! There, d'you see him? It's freaking Leir, Lord of the Ridings!'

'It can't be, Hywel, surely you are mistaken – hello, who's that? I dare say you might be right, for once!'

'Let's get him, boys!'

They stir from their shelter up on the hill. The Llan-fairpwllgwyngyll Lads of Mary's Hollow, rough and ready, mount their horses, grab their swords and thunder down under, giving chase.

The man turns, sees them. He is of middle age, has all his teeth, a good head of hair and wears nice clothes, and he's alone. He spurs his horse and flees.

'After him, boys!'

'String him up!'

'We'll be *rich*!'

The man's horse isn't suited for a long excursion. The men surround him quickly. They grab and pull him off his horse. They stand around him as he lies there on the ground.

'Thought you could get away from *us*, Lord Leir?'

'Nothing passes by the likely lads of Llanfairpwllgwyngyll!'

He stares at them in hurt confusion. 'I don't know what you mean, please, this is a mistake!'

They laugh at him. 'You northern fool! You thought your northern magic would protect you from the Lads? Round here, friend, we are the law!'

'Please, let me go!'

But they do not, of course. They torture him a little, just for fun, and then they chop his head off with their dull-edged swords so that it takes a while for the man to die. But die he does, and that's another for the tally, and it is only when they carry round the disembodied head to those who take the count that it is made clear to them, in no uncertain terms, what bloody idiots they are.

They're lucky to get out with their lives.

This happens more and more, and meanwhile skirmishes continue between Arthur's knights and Conan's holdouts and Outham's remaining Franks and Leir's Brigantes. There are so many tribes fighting so many factions that Merlin's hand-drawn maps keep changing daily.

In truth, he is sick of the whole damn thing.

But months later they're still turning up bodies.

55

A nobody by the name of Tristan improbably gets Yder with a spear to the belly. An inglorious end to an inglorious bastard.

Tristan collects his gold and, when he comes to court, encounters Isolde, who's been hanging round. The two – so Merlin gathers – promptly fall in love, if fucking behind the kitchen counts as love, then pool together their fortune and take off to Gaul to fight giants. At least that's one love story that ends happily, Merlin, the romantic, thinks.

Which leaves only King Leir...

Two months later Arthur narrowly avoids a lone assassin wielding a sort of curved sword of a form unfamiliar in Britannia. Merlin concludes it is of an eastern origin, but who the man was, or how he came here, is unknown. Some hired assassin brought over from beyond the sea at great expense. They bury him in an unmarked grave, but strange stories begin to circulate not long after. A spring erupts in the burial place, and its water is said to heal the sick and wounded. A small temple is built on site and pilgrims start to travel there. Later, the temple is destroyed in a mysterious fire, and a Christian church is built in its place. Small hostelries open to accommodate the travellers. In time, a city flourishes.

★

'How about here?' Merlin says.

They stand in a temperate valley. Surveyors, recruited from the old Dolaucothi mines, are busy taking measures.

'We could run Roman-style sewers all along *here*, public baths *here* and *here*, there's a ready supply of water from the nearby river, good defensive positions on the peaks all round, we could put your palace right over *there*, put a forum over *there*, plenty of access to local produce, we could – Arthur, are you even *listening* to me?'

'What? Yeah, whatever. I suppose.'

'Do you even like the place?'

'I'm not a builder, Merlin.'

'We can't use Londinium indefinitely. Too open, too rebellious. You need a base, lord. A place to call your own.'

'I have Dinas Emrys.'

'Too far.'

'Tintagel, then.'

'And what of your mother?'

'Damn it, Merlin. Then do as you will with this place.'

'Lord, could I—?'

'*No libraries*!'

Merlin sighs.

'My lord,' he says.

Arthur stalks off. He doesn't build, he doesn't read, he wields a sword and kills without compunction and therefore he is king. And he will take this damned forsaken island with its thousands of squabbling tribes and lordlings and make something of it if he has to destroy it in the process.

A shared identity, Merlin thinks. A story to unify all these warring tales, so that Britons now and in centuries to come could tell each other that they share a thing. That they are one. And to be one, as Arthur understands implicitly, you must be defined against an other.

Whether the stories have any truth to them whatsoever matters not in the least.

'I'll call you Camelot,' Merlin says, and he looks fondly on the valley and on his surveyors. Yes... It's empty now, but soon he'll bring in carpenters and diggers and bricklayers. They'll dig the foundations and ensure latrines are built to his exact specifications, and where that clump of trees now stands will soon be the beginning of the castle. They'd need lots of rooms for all the knights – and sparring fields, and stables for the horses, and inns and hostelries and theatres and, and... For a moment he lets himself dare to dream.

'*Camelot...*' he breathes.

Yes. He likes the sound of it. He likes it very much indeed.

A riverboat filled with mercenaries narrowly misses Arthur on his way east and rams the wrong contingent of knights. The would-be assassins are promptly slaughtered by Agravain of the Hard Hand and his men. The few survivors are tortured for information, but they have none that is useful to impart, other than that Leir had sent them.

'Ulfius?'

'Yes?'

'Don't move.'

He feels the cold blade on the skin of his throat.

'Who are you?' he says.

'Name's Lancelot. Could you tell me where to find King Leir? If you wouldn't mind.'

'He'll kill me.'

'That strikes me as less immediate, somehow... Try not to swallow.'

'You're right,' the other concedes.

'Well, then?'

'There is a hidden valley some miles from here, where the stream vanishes underground. I have been there once before. Look for a stunted black tree to mark the passageway. But you will never make it through alive.'

'I'll worry about that, not you.'

'Lancelot?'

'...Yes?'

'Can you loosen the blade? I feel it is cutting into my skin.'

'Is this better?'

'Yes. Thank you.'

'What is it like, serving two masters?'

'...Miserable.'

'What will you do now?'

'It occurs to me a life on the continent might be more suitable for my constitution at present.'

'That might be wise.'

'I will go on pilgrimage. I long to see the Holy Land, and those places where the Saviour stepped on the way of the cross.'

'Jerusalem's a bit of a shithole, you know.'

Lancelot releases him. Ulfius massages his throat. He grimaces.

'Thanks.'

'Go far from here,' Lancelot says. 'One can still purchase passage to Gaul from the occasional trader, maybe even go farther than that. If you make it to Judea... Hell, I don't know. It's swarming with Christians now. You'll be right at home.'

'Thanks,' Ulfius says. But when he glances for his attacker, Lancelot is gone.

The stunted black tree is right there where he told him. Lancelot finds the hidden passage and follows it, through thickets and brambles, until he finds a narrow twisting dirt path that takes him to a hillside. He beholds the valley. Down below, though cunningly disguised, he can see Leir's castle. It appears the ruins of a building, with weeds and blackberry bushes growing from the riverbank to mask the brickwork, but Lancelot's not fooled. It's well maintained in its disguise, and any moment he expects to find the secret guards who must protect this hideout...

He finds one, slumped against a tree. The man's head rests upon his chest. Lancelot gently lifts it up, and sees the throat's been cut neatly.

Oh, shit.

A soft rustling overhead, and something drops behind him, smooth as silk. He turns with his hand on the hilt of Secace.

'Don't even think about it, Lancelot.'

'*Iblis*,' he says, disgusted.

He hates to admit that she always had the better of him.

She smiles. The moonlight wreathes her in white. Her eyes are black. Her hands are bloodied.

'If you're here for the bounty you're a little late.'

'*You?*'

She shrugs. 'Girl gotta eat.'

'You fuck.'

'And I figured you'd be coming round sooner or later.'

'This kill was *mine!*'

She shrugs.

He takes a half step back. Pauses. Raises his hand from his sword, palm open, extended.

'You want to play it like that?' she says.

She crouches. Lancelot moves his hand up and to the side. Iblis raises hers, breathes evenly. They stare at each other. They don't move. This lasts for a minute.

'It's not too late to walk.'

'It's been too late for us for a very long time, Lancelot.'

'Iblis...'

'Hush. Let us do this.'

After another minute she takes a tiny step to the left. Lancelot mirrors her. He lowers his hand. She matches him.

'Really, this is ridic—'

Their blades flash simultaneously.

'Oh.'

'Oh.'

Lancelot looks down with some surprise at the naked blade protruding from his side.

It doesn't hurt. It doesn't hurt at all.

'Huh,' Iblis says. She pulls Secace out of her own side. A trickle of blood emerges from the small, neat wound, and she dams it with her hand.

'You seem to have missed any vital organs.'

'You, too.'

Lancelot pulls Iblis's blade out. It hurts, but he's still alive. The wound, like hers, is neat and contained. He tosses her back the sword. She grimaces and lets go of Secace, which comes flying back into Lancelot's hand.

'Pass me those leaves? They look clean.'

'...Pass that shred of cloth? Should tie it up nicely.'

When they're done and the wounds are bound they look awkwardly at each other.

'Well, do you want to try it again?'

'Not really.'

'Is Leir actually dead?'

'Have you ever known me not to finish a job?'

'I can't say that I have, Iblis.'

'I go by Sebile now, actually.'

'Whatever.'

They stare at each other.

'So?'

'So fuck off, Lancelot. I'm off to get my bounty and then retire.'

'Retire, Iblis? You'll run through the cash in two or three years and be back on the road again before you know it.'

'Dream on, lover boy.'

He shrugs casually. Then winces from the wound. Reaches

into a hidden pocket, and comes out with a much folded piece of parchment, which he holds.

'What's that?'

'Oh, nothing.'

'Lancelot... I don't have patience for your shit.'

'It's a map,' he says.

'A map of what?'

'The grail...'

'Come off it, you ass. You think I care about that? I have a good thing guaranteed, here.'

'Suit yourself. But that's a lot of gold just sitting there...'

'*Supposedly.*'

'The master said all gold comes from the sky.'

'The master said a lot of stupid shit.'

'Aren't you curious?'

'You're grasping, Lancelot.'

'Then walk away,' he says.

She stares at him. And Lancelot remembers once, when he was yet an awkward boy not yet a man, the master took him to the shores of Sheba where they trained, and taught him to catch fish. It was a long and boring afternoon, and nothing happened, and the master taught him how one must wait on the line, wait for a gentle tug, the pull that indicates a fish is nibbling.

But he knew just as well that Iblis had the same knowing as him.

'In good time,' she says; and he tries not to give away that tiny jump of victory he feels.

'So where have you been all this time? I had an inkling you would follow where I went.'

'Don't flatter yourself, Iblis. I went after the grail, same as you.'

'I know plenty of the grail,' she says. 'Leir had his contacts.'

'With the Aetheling of Deira?' Lancelot says. He sees her surprise. 'Oh, I've done my work, Iblis. This map's no fake.

For a year I scouted up and down this dismal island and to the farthest reaches of the north, where things get... *weird*. And I know your Leir never set foot behind the wall.'

'He did like to work through intermediaries,' she concedes.

'I was there,' he says. He doesn't tell her of the things he saw. Mutatio and a land burned black, a pool of green, fused glass, polluted rivers, ailing birds, a coin that spun and spun and broke to poisoned dust in his hand.

Perhaps she sees it in his eyes.

'How bad is it?' she says.

'It's bad.'

She considers.

'Lancelot, you have aroused my curiosity.'

He knows her, better than he knows himself. It's not the lust for gold that drives her, not entirely. Iblis, he knows, has got the questing bug.

And how she'd love to lord it over them! The old fools of the Inner Circle of the Venerated Secret Brotherhood of the Seekers of the Grail! 'Brotherhood', he thinks. It always rankled with Iblis. There were some women members of the order but few and far between and, like the men, all mad. But still.

If she could find the grail she would be *master*.

'I went deep,' he says. 'I mapped as best I could. The landscape's changing. There is a foreign agent of some kind that's altering the world beyond the wall. The animals and plants that survive are... different, somehow. And people. If you can call them people anymore.'

She yawns. 'Why should I listen to you any further? I do not need a treasure, Lancelot, and with the bounty from their scrawny king I could go searching on my own.'

'And how much time would you waste? While I head right through the maze to the prize?'

'Then why don't you, you little shit?' she says.

'Because I'm tired, Iblis. I'm tired of the quest. The grail's not mine to find.'

She looks at him closely, then.

'No,' she says. 'No, I do not believe you.'

'What, then?'

And he tries hard to mask his private thoughts. A memory: a girl with golden hair and killer's eyes, who smiled at him, and said little, all the while standing by her king.

'Besides, I know you. You don't care for the money any more than I do.'

'I wish to join their circle,' he says. Surprising her.

'Their little round table? Whatever for? You'd be a knight? You'd only be a servant once again.'

'If I must.'

'Lancelot...' She sighs. 'You are a fool.'

'I know.'

'I am tempted to accept your offer. Which you have not quite made. So what is it, Lancelot? What's her name?'

'What? Whose?' he says.

'Are you *blushing*?'

'What! No!'

'I can't imagine what floozy you picked up to drool over, unless... No! Say it ain't so, it can't be...'

'Leave it, Iblis!'

'Not that dead-eyed harlot of his, surely? Lancelot, even you... She's killed more men than Locusta of Gaul!'

'So have you!'

'Yes, but darling, I have *style*. She's just *muscle*.'

'I said leave it, Iblis.'

'I'll take that map now,' she says.

'Alright.'

He passes her the parchment. They both stand, their parlay at an end.

'I know you think you played me,' Iblis said. 'But you're a fool, and you will only hurt from following this path of yours. Forget this Guinevere.'

'And do what?' he says.

'Come with me.'

The offer hovers between them.

Slowly, he shakes his head. 'No,' he says. 'I am done with the grail.'

'You just replaced one unattainable object with another,' she tells him. 'Well, I wish I could say it's been fun. I'll see you on the other side, Lancelot.'

And then she's gone.

He stands bereft, and feels that once again she'd got the better of their bargain. And he doesn't understand. After a while, he stirs and follows the path down to the valley and enters the disguised palace.

He finds Leir slumped against a crate of apples in a storage room. The king's throat has been cut. A note's pinned to his chest with a paring knife. It says, 'Enjoy', and there's the imprint of a kiss on the delicate vellum.

'Damn it, Iblis!'

He ransacks the palace from top to bottom but finds nothing of use.

He goes to Leir. Dead, he doesn't look like much. Just another contender.

Lancelot lifts the corpse's head and swings his sword and it is done. He has his bounty.

But Iblis never cared about the bounty, he thinks now. She'd used Leir for what knowledge he had of the Lapis Exilis and then left him like – well, like leftovers, for Lancelot to find.

Well, fuck her, he thinks savagely. And fuck the grail! Let her go to her doom like so many others before her. What does he care for rocks from the sky?

And again he thinks of that blade of a woman with Arthur.

That golden hair and that quizzical smile, and the way she'd looked at him. He wants to hold her like a sword.

Guinevere.

PART NINE

THE WEDDING

56

'How do I look?' she says.

Guinevere adjusts the silver necklace. She touches her hair. She looks in the mirror. In the reflection she sees a man standing patiently in the corner of the room. His perfect stillness. Her would-be husband has set him as her bodyguard.

'You look just fine,' Lancelot says; there's a weight of other, unspoken words between them.

She smiles. Nods. Adjusts the bangles on her wrists. Bends down to check on the hidden knife strapped to her ankle. Straightens and looks one last time.

All the while aware of his presence there. She smiles to check her teeth. Looks alright. There's a packet on the dresser with some small dried mushrooms. She pops one in her mouth, chews. After a while she spits out what's left.

Should be a nice, long trip, she thinks.

Lancelot's there without seeming to have moved. He just materialises. Cloth in hand, to catch the discarded mushroom.

'My lady.'

She shakes her head. There's gold woven in her hair. It twinkles when she moves. She stares at the mirror and sighs.

'Let's do this,' she says.

★

Outside it's a glorious summer day. The bells ring across town, their peals come at her from everywhere, from the towers and the brothels, from the churches and the temples, from the beggars to the lords. The king her betrothed has sent out the bell-ringers to ring all across the city, and the square before the castle is filled with a throng. They have come to see her. They have come to gawk.

Well, let them! she thinks savagely. She takes her place in the procession. Her women are with her. Armed with short swords, crossbows, knives. They wend their way along the path to the raised wooden dais.

The wizard, Merlin, stands there in robes of garish purple, sewn with gold thread. He has made himself up for the occasion, too, she notices without surprise. He's shed youth for more dignified age, has made himself rotund, with balding head and long grey beard, and he leans on a staff. She knows his tricks. He's like a snake replacing skin. Inside he is the same as ever.

'My lady Guinevere,' he says, and bows.

She smiles. She has been doing that so much her lips are hurting.

'Fuck you, too, Merlin,' she whispers, and he smiles back.

'It will all soon be over,' he says.

Hanging overhead are three fat, squealing pigs. They're hoisted up with ropes, and she had watched from her window as they were chased around the court and tied and pulled up by those whose job it is to maintain such facades. Someone had to build the dais and make arrangements for the crowd, and set up the latrines. Already they are hawking celebratory mugs and pouring cheap drinks for the spectators, and soon enough there'll be fights and, with luck, a few corpses to loot, in the evening. There always are, at such events.

She wishes she was out there, picking their fucking pockets.

A hush falls on the crowd. From the opposite direction a second procession approaches. There ride the knights: Bors the Younger, and the Green Knight, and Elyan the White, and

Agravain of the Hard Hand. Ruthless motherfuckers the lot of them, murderers without a saving grace between them. But there you go.

And then there's him. He rides in their midst, moving with a quiet intensity. Arthur, her Arthur. And faithful Kay by his side.

She maintains her perfect posture. Tries to ignore the flies, and the crying of the pigs overhead.

It is as Merlin said. It will soon be over.

She scans the crowd. Notices some faces she knows. Wealthy merchants, an ambassador from the Byzantines, even a few of the Angle and Saxon lordlings have sent their men in respect, though really they are nothing but spies.

She sees the giant, Maelor Gawr.

And that crow, perched on a gatepost, is that Morgan le Fay?

The king and his retinue approach. The knights stop. A horse neighs and shits, a big steaming pile right there on the ground. The king slides from his horse. Strides to the dais and climbs it. He stands with Guinevere.

'We have gathered here together...' the wizard, Merlin, starts.

She barely listens. She nods along at all the right places. She smiles and nods. The king takes her hand. He slips a ring onto her finger. What a strange thing.

'You may kiss the bride,' the wizard says.

The king leans in. She kisses him. His lips are dry.

'My wife,' he says.

'My lord.'

He smiles. The crowd erupts in cheers.

The wizard looks at them and nods. The giant, Maelor Gawr, strides up and lifts his giant blade. He strikes. The blade slices cleanly through the bellies of the pigs.

A rain of blood falls down on the king and queen. The blood is hot. It stains their clothes and stings their eyes and runs into their hair. The blood is everywhere.

The crowd cheers. Guinevere grabs the back of Arthur's head and kisses him hard on the mouth. His lips are hot, now. They taste of pigs' blood. She sticks her tongue in his mouth. The crowd goes wild.

And all this while she's thinking of another.

So it is done, and they are well and truly married.

Down in Love Alley, she knows, they are offering bridal maids dressed up to best resemble her, and for those with different tastes there are young men to look like Arthur. There'll be fucking and drinking and singing all night across town, and now she's tripping balls on mushrooms, and the sky clouds over and the clouds resemble a face.

From afar, forlorn, comes her worm's cry: *I love you...*

Stay hidden, she tells it. *Stay safe.*

The king takes her hand in his. Together they walk through the crowd. Kay and Lancelot follow behind.

She turns her head only once. Lancelot's there, his face as impassive as always.

But it's all in the eyes.

The king and his queen enter the castle. They go to their chambers.

And that's that.

Outside, the first corpse of the day rolls in the gutter, stabbed in the back, and the party carries on unabated.

PART TEN

THE GOLDEN AGE

57

Now come the good times.

Welcome to the Golden Age.

The Six Kings are dead and most of the land is united under the banner of the dragon. Britain has but one ruler, and his name is Arthur. He had nothing but his balls and his sword, they say, and he took those and he made himself a kingdom. His enemies are dead. He built a city. He built himself a throne, and it is his, and his by force alone.

Welcome... to Camelot.

Camelot! The very name sends a shiver down the spine. It seduces. It whispers sweet nothings. And boys and girls all across the land, in villages and shacks, in fields and by rivers, sitting at night by a fire and letting the fire set their dreams aflame, feel its irresistible pull.

A whisper and a promise, and it draws them all, the beautiful girls and the beautiful boys, like a flock of colourful butterflies to their doom.

To Camelot!

Where the parties are bigger and the music louder and the bodies looser and the drink stronger. Where it rains gold, or so they say, and magic blooms as common as red fairy mushrooms by the side of the road.

It is in Camelot where one may run into the famed knight, Lancelot, simply walking down the street or, jumping over a puddle, see through a window in an alleyway the contours of the famed enchantress, Morgan le Fay. It is whispered that the cats in this city are but shape-shifters donning a disguise as one would put on a suit of new clothes. Where the queen, Guinevere, it is said, still picks the pockets of unsuspecting visitors.

Perhaps you'd never visited Gaul, and you'd never seen Rome. But this here town's got everything those continental places have, and more.

It is a seat of power, and the fae, it's whispered, congregate here, for power is to them what rotten fruit is to a bee. It is an irresistible delight.

All roads lead to Camelot, and anyone who's anyone is there, with Merlin the wizard brooding in his tall tower of magic to the north of the castle, and Sir Kay working nightly in the Gilded Cage of which it is whispered even in foreign shores…

Camelot is where the king sits on his throne.

Camelot is where the Knights of his Round Table joust and spar, where they live and sleep in barracks, where they drink and fuck and fight before heading out to all four corners of this island on the king's business.

And it is here that, one autumn day with the leaves just turning, a boy named Galahad comes to seek his fortune.

He is a boy like thousands of other boys, with big dreams and empty heads and even emptier pockets.

As soon as he was old enough to till a field and plough and hoe, he knew he had to get out from that dismal little hamlet where he lived. He slept under the stars more often than not. He ate whatever grew. He rose with the sun and the cockerels, and he broke his back and ate his muck and he drank, but seldom had enough to *get* drunk.

So one day he stole his mother's gold ring that she hid in the secret place she thought only she knew. And he stole the neighbours' stash of old denarii that they hid from the tax collectors. And finally he stole a half-dead horse.

He rode away under the moonlight, and in the distance he could see the fairy paths, shining white, and ghostly knights upon their horses marching down them to the place where all must go. But he took the King's Road, which runs straight and true, and he followed it all the way to Camelot.

Oh, he was robbed along the way, make no mistake. He had his face bashed in and his coins nicked along with his horse, but he kept his mother's ring in a safe place where it hurt, and he has it still. He walked the rest of the way, and begged and stole and turned a trick or two, but finally...

Finally he's here.

He stands by the gates of that great city and looks in awe upon its fortified walls, its towering buildings, its gaily decorated banners, its impeccably armoured guards and the foot and cart traffic going in and out along the King's Road. How smartly they are all dressed! The women all stunning in the reds and greens of the season, the men in their finest garb and with their hair all black and shiny, and little boys darting here and there to scoop the steaming piles of shit the horses leave behind, so that the approach to the city is always clean and without reproach.

And Galahad wants to throw open his arms and engulf the whole city, to embrace it to his bosom. And he is *hungry*, not just from the long road and his severe lack of funds, but from desire. He wants to bite into the city, he wants to eat it whole.

And so he takes a step, and then another and another; until he is past the guards and through the gates; and he takes his first step within Camelot.

'Get out of the way, you fucking mongrel!'

A cart swerves past him, the driver screaming as he waves a giant fist. Galahad sticks up his fingers at the man, shouts 'Fuck you!' and runs past and ducks into an alley. He steals an apple from a nearby stall and wends his way deeper into the city, juice dripping down his chin. A scantily clad lady on the corner holds a giant snake draped over her muscled shoulders. She winks at him.

He passes the public baths and the latrines. Down the Via Mithraea where the hawkers on the doors try to entice him in with offers of the Deeper Mysteries, which give you quite a buzz; along Bear Street where the giant animals are caged before their bloodied fights; into a public square where a garden flourishes and big men walk small dogs while all the while eyeing each other.

He sees a thousand new things: men dressed like women and women carrying swords, an entertainer pulling coloured handkerchiefs out of his nostrils, a dog who can bark yes and no in answer to the spectators' questions, a peacock, and some sort of fruit called figs, a legless man sitting on the shoulders of a blind one, and in one dusty street filled with nervous old men he finds a thing he never saw before: a book. Here on the Via Codices work scribes, who use the tanned hides of beasts or baked earth tablets or thin sheets of wetland plants to make inscriptions on them. They are filled with words he cannot read. And in the back of that makeshift market, behind a stall set in the rear, he sees another form they take.

He stands and stares, transfixed. He'd never seen a thing like this before, had not imagined such a thing *existed*! For there, replicated on clay or in ink, are *women* – in the nude.

He stares at breasts: big, small, rounded, slender, side set, asymmetrical. He stares at vulvas, bottoms, thighs, and finally at faces. They're haughty, proud, shy, nervous, filled with promise. The eyes are captured with such grace.

The women pose. And there are men, too, on these clay urns and these papyri. Men engage in congress with the women; women with women; men with men. Some depict more fantastic scenes. A satyr with a full erection. A minotaur fucking a knight from behind.

Galahad blushes. Galahad hardens.

'Hey buddy, if you use it you pay for it!'

'I didn't mean…'

'I know just what you meant, you little pervert. Show me coin or show me the back of you and scram. This here's high-class erotica, it's primo stuff.'

'But how?' Galahad says. 'How is it *done*?'

The seller mellows. 'You're one of them punters into the practical aspects of the trade? Well, the bosses have a team of scribes and artists and suchlike here in the city, to duplicate the stuff. It's sold by weight. This here's the future of the art of the pornographos. You get your low-cost copies for the masses, and high-end stuff for them what live above. Bespoke, like. The art has its aficionados. You dig?'

He cannot understand half of the man's words, but Galahad is taken.

'But what's it drawn *from*?' he says, and the man smirks.

'From life, what else?'

'How is that possible?'

'You really are a fresh one, ain'tcha. Well, from all sorts. There's plenty models and such like down Love Alley round the corner.' He turns from him to some new buyers, northern by their looks.

'Step this way, gentlemen, we have the finest fuck scenes in all Camelot! You, sir, buy this fine memento to take to the tribe back home! Look at the jugs on this one, drawn from the very leading lady at the Gilded Cage, she has the finest boobs between here and Rome! Or if you like men we have this authentic Greek-themed orgy—'

But Galahad moves on. He's drawn again, the way all these strays and waifs, these boys and girls are drawn, like metal shavings to a lodestone. He passes through Rose Street where men and women piss and shit into troughs dug in the earth, and flowers bloom to try and hide the stench, and at last he comes to Love Alley.

Here the air is heavily perfumed, and the architecture is a

bewildering array of false Greek columns and Egyptian temples, Roman domes and arches, and lights burn red in torches. Here the avenue is wide, the men's faces covered in a sheen of sweat, street sellers offer beer and Minos shields, those thin sheaths of goat's bladder. The doors to the various establishments are guarded by burly men, near naked but for their swords, their muscles oiled for display.

Oh, how he likes it here, does Galahad the Pure! The Pure they called him, for he always puts a sheath upon his sword. He stares transfixed at all around him. And he looks up, for the buildings here have stories, and he had never seen tall houses before. A window high above opens and an old woman empties a bucket onto the street. Galahad jumps back nimbly as a shower of shit comes down, just missing him. The old woman laughs.

'Oh, you're a quick one, ain't ya, little starling! Oh but that I were younger, I would bone you for a bone! Now I could barely pick my teeth with you. What business have you here along the street of love? You're too scrawny for a rent boy and bound to have less money than a drowned rat, so you ain't a client, that's for sure. What is it, boy?'

Galahad nods politely. 'I'm looking for a job, ma'am,' he says.

The woman hoots a laugh. 'Did you hear what he called me! My, my. The name's Maggs. I'm a relation of her majesty the queen, you know.'

'I didn't, ma'am.'

'Oh, isn't he *adorable*?' She whistles down below. The guards on the door look up.

'Fetch him up for me, will you, dears?' Maggs says.

The guards move on Galahad. He stays put. Above the door he sees a discreet little sign in pure gold: *The Gilded Cage*.

The guards escort him inside.

58

Galahad admires himself in the mirror. That soft white shirt, freshly washed. That fetching red coat with the gold buttons. Those fine leather boots.

'You missed a spot,' he says.

'Sorry, sir.'

The boy trembles. He scrubs and scrubs the latrines. The club's about to open.

'What's your name?'

'Gaheris, sir.'

'Well, you listen to me good, Gaheris. You see me now? You see how I stand here before you, in my *fine* plumage, manager of this *fine* establishment, holder of the keys?'

'Sir? I mean, yes, sir.'

'Five years I cleaned this shitter, boy!'

'Sir?' The cleaner looks both afraid and confused.

'Five years I cleaned the bogs. These same ones as you are cleaning now. My first job here in this city. Old Maggs gave it to me, Jupiter bless her shrivelled old heart. And do you know what, Gaheris? I did it with pride. I worked my way up. I *made* something of myself.'

Galahad quite enjoys giving the speech, even if it isn't strictly *true*. Two weeks into the job he stabbed the picker of the glasses after work one night and took his spot the next evening. Six months of that and he poisoned the bartender. After that it was easy, management saw the value in him. As Maggs once told him, good men were hard to find in Camelot.

'You do a good job, Gaheris, in five years you could be working *coats*. Maybe even picking glasses! Think of the tips!'

'Yes, sir! Of course, sir!'

My, but the boy looks dim-witted. Galahad runs a comb through his hair and smiles at his reflection. He finally got the job when the last keeper of the keys fell out of a top-storey window.

Well, accidents happen.

And now the Gilded Cage is all but his.

'Keep up the good work,' he says, and leaves.

Another shit-boy. Another empty-headed kid with dreams large as the moon, too ugly to make much giving blowjobs and too dumb to steal anything good. Perhaps the speech will keep him there another week or two. The turnover's a killer in that job, and it's not like the city's going to run out of shit anytime soon.

You'd think people would be glad for steady pay.

He strides onto the floor. The band starts playing. Ex-druids and drummers washed up on too much Goblin Fruit, runaway slaves from the continent playing the horns, a drunk Roman who came out of nowhere but is a genius on the cithara... The lead singer's a Saxon, of all things, but with a voice like rough wine and cannabis smoke, it sends a shiver down your spine.

The doors open and the punters start filing in.

Galahad clicks his fingers. The beer girls begin to circulate. Galahad gets a take from the door and a take from the bar and a take from the dancers and the show. He gets a taste of everything. He clicks his fingers again. Someone hands him a glass of beer. He raises it high.

'Salutaria!'

And now come the dancing girls onto the stage. Garlanded in flowers. Dressed in leaves. Like wood nymphs out of legends. It's in the eyes, he thinks again. The look they give you even as you undress them with your eyes. The look that says they see right through you. That they know your heart. They understand desire like a banker savvies coin.

The torches burn. the ground is raked and fresh. Muscle boys circle with appetisers on trays.

'Hey, *magister*,' a rough voice says, and Galahad turns to see the twins.

'Balin,' he says. 'Balan.'

Two brickhouse shits with sandy hair and killer's eyes, they run the wholesale copying and distribution of the erotica trade. Just outside the city they have a whole village of sculptors and pot-makers, painters and artisans. Galahad supplies the models, and in exchange he gets a taste. He has his finger in more pots than there were slain Christians in the Roman colosseums, and that's a lot.

'We need a fresh batch,' Balin complains. 'Fresh off the cart. The punters always want new faces.'

'New boobs,' his brother says and leers.

'Same here,' Galahad says. 'And yet we never run out.'

'Anyone good on tonight?'

'Some Angle girls from Magoset, two Jutes from the Wihtwara, and' – he lowers his voice confidentially – 'a Pict, white as snow, and with no trace of a snowline, if you get my meaning.'

The brothers exchange looks. 'No shit?'

'Smooth as a glacier. Look at the house. We're already packed.'

'Well, fuck me, Galahad, why didn't you say?' Balan slaps him on the shoulder. 'You'll make the arrangements?'

'Don't I always?'

'Good man.'

They air-punch at his stomach playfully and scamper to their table.

Galahad mops his brow. Talking to the twins always sets him on edge. He once saw them strangle the waiter just for spilling a drop of their drink. They just did it for fun. They are that sort of guy.

But they're made guys, they are part of a crew. *The* crew.

They are knights of the Round Table.

Fuck but he'd kill to be made. Five fucking years and he hasn't even come close to counting in this town. He's just another dick-and-tits merchant, just some guy out of a bunch. He has no *protection*.

He stalks to the bar and stands there breathing heavily. He hates Balin, Balan, this fucking town. All his good cheer evaporates.

The torches dim. A hush falls on the crowd.

The show's about to start.

Galahad watches without much interest. Which play is it tonight? *Slaves of Passion*? *The Maiden's Touch*? *What the Servants Saw*? He can't keep track. The Gilded Cage keeps several playwrights on rotation and every half-assed literate with a smattering of pig Latin shows up at their doors asking for a showing.

'Ah, *Pig in a Poke* again, Galahad? I must admit it's one of my favourites.'

He turns. His employer and the king's right-hand man stands there, not tall, soft spoken, with eyes that are sad and deadly in turn.

'Sir Kay,' he stammers. 'I did not realise—'

'Yes, yes. Relax. I came to see the Pict. I must admit I was curious. Bald?'

'As the moon, sir.'

'Imagine that. It will be all the rage in Camelot by morning.'

'She is a talented actress, sir.'

'I do so enjoy a good comedy,' Kay says. He watches the stage, where the aforementioned Pict has emerged from the bath house, and is now confronted by the enormous unsheathed swords of the guards. She stares in shock and admiration at their manhoods before reaching decisively.

'Grab the sword by the blade, dear, that's right,' Kay says. 'I swear to you, Galahad, if only there was a way of somehow capturing this sort of entertainment in a more permanent form. Merlin always does mutter about types of material that may capture and store light... I am sure he is getting crazier by the day. Still! Imagine if we could do that, and somehow sell it.'

'It would rather spoil the art of live theatre, sir, don't you think?'

Kay smiles.

'You appreciate art over money, Galahad?'

'Money isn't everything, sir.'

'My, my, you truly *are* pure...'

'I only mean... Sir, it is power that matters.'

'Money *is* power, Galahad! Don't you ever forget it.'

'No, sir.'

'Your time will come.'

'When, sir?'

'When you've earned it, boy. Now go make me some money.'

Kay looks at the stage. Galahad nods. Galahad turns to go.

'Oh, and Galahad?'

'Yes, sir?'

Kay smiles. He raises his glass.

'Salutaria,' he says.

59

'This is it, boyo,' Gaheris says, all excited. 'This is it, you shit!'

Galahad grins. He can't help it. His friend's excitement is contagious.

They stand on the top floor, looking over the city through the wide windows.

Camelot. It is finally his. Like a fruit ready for plucking.

'You worked hard, now it's your turn, Gally! Now it's your fucking turn!'

'Ain't that right!' Galahad says.

'Amen!' Gaheris says, using the Hebrew word the new Christians are so fond of in their services.

Galahad smiles. 'Amen,' he says.

He'd plucked Gaheris from the latrines and the boy followed his lead. Took everything in his stride. Looked up to Galahad like an older brother.

Became his friend.

What a strange word, 'friend', in this town. Yet there it is. Galahad wraps his arm around his friend's shoulders, and together they stand and watch the lights. The city's spread in the past few years. New quarters outside the city walls, and always there's construction, the carts come in with timber, builders everywhere, and scaffolding, and sewers being dug, then clogging, then drained, until the city stinks, it stinks like rotting fruit and shit.

'Yours, now, Gally!'

'Ours.'

His friend smiles.

'Ours, then.'

The castle is alight with torches, the wizard's tower flashes with its strange illumination, down in the street the hawkers and the punters and the whores converge, a never-ending night in a city that never sleeps.

And it is his, at last. He's done everything right, and when he heard two foreign fellows conspiring against the king he did the right thing and informed on them right away. They were tortured into confession and executed, and he had the king's favour.

So what if they were just some merchants out of Deira with no more thought in their heads as to getting drunk and getting laid?

He did what he had to do. No one can blame a fellow for that.

And now the city will be his.

'I can't believe it, Gally, I still can't!'

'I know,' he says. 'I can't believe it either.'

'Look! There!' Gaheris points. They watch the knights approaching. Lancelot, Kay, Elyan and Bors. The old guard. They come to the doors of the Gilded Cage and wait there.

Wait there for him.

His friend gives him a hug. 'I love you, man.'

'I love you, too. You wait. I'll pull you up the way we've always done. You'll be a knight in no time, too, Gaheris!'

'Me, a knight!' Gaheris laughs. 'And I believe you, too. You make the impossible possible.'

'Alright, alright.' They extricate from each other. 'I'll see you after.'

'Go with God, Gally.'

'Later, then.'

He leaves his friend there and descends the stairs. They're outside when he comes out. They slap his back.

'Come on,' they say. 'We'll take you there.'

'Take me where?' he says, delighted. He is delighted with everything. He's going to get made. He's going to be a *knight*, a fucking *knight* of the Round Table!

'To the party, man! Come on!'

They pass him a bottle of something fermented and strong. He takes a pull, almost chokes.

'Jesus!'

'*He* never had this,' Bors says.

'What is it?'

'Mead and Goblin Fruit.'

'Jesus,' he says again. He takes another pull. A numb, happy feeling.

They lead him away, through the narrow streets, singing.

It is hours later and he is drunk and stoned, mellow and wired at once. His legs wobble. He sees impossible things all around him: faces in trees, unfamiliar colours, the stars formed into lips that whisper out words.

'Oh, man,' he says. 'Oh, man.'

They're somewhere outside of town. There's no one else around. The knights have built a fire and it burns inside a ring of stones. The air is cool but Galahad is sweating.

'It's time,' someone says; Lancelot, perhaps. 'It's time.'

'Time for what?' Galahad says. His tongue feels too thick in his mouth, the words crawl out like worms.

'Draw your sword.'

Galahad does, gladly. The blade glints in the light of the fire.

'To join up you must prove you're one of us.'

'I am.'

Lancelot nods.

'Please, don't, let me go, let me g—!'

Galahad hears the screams but at first they don't really register. He's not even sure they're real. But then he sees them.

Balin and Balan, as large as oaks and as mean as dogs, carrying a smaller figure between them, a hood over that person's head. They reach the small campsite and push the victim roughly down and he falls. His hands are tied behind his back with rope.

'You know what to do,' Lancelot says softly.

Galahad is ready, surely he is ready? But at Lancelot's nod Balin pulls the hood off the victim's head, and Galahad sees with fear that the pulped face that was beaten and stomped on by the twins is known, that in fact he had known the voice, had somehow only pretended he hadn't.

Gaheris looks up at him through his one remaining eye.

'Please, don't,' he says.

Galahad sways.

'Gaheris?' he says. Still not comprehending. 'But what are you doing here? You should be waiting for me, at the Gilded Cage—'

'Please, Gally. Don't.'

'There must be some mistake—' Galahad says stupidly.

Lancelot says, 'There isn't.'

Balin sniggers. Balan farts.

'Gally...'

'Shut the fuck up already!' Balin slaps the bound man on the back of the head, hard. Gaheris, pathetically, starts to cry.

Galahad closes his eyes. He can hear them all around him, he can hear the stars. There's no way out. This is what he'd always wanted. It's such a small price to pay.

He opens his eyes. Looks up at the stars. For just a minute he wishes he could go there.

Then he lowers his head and looks at his friend. Gaheris

kneels there, waiting. He cries without sound, now. The tears and the snot and the blood.

They see each other, then. That thing we know, yet can't accept.

Gaheris gives a tiny nod of acquiescence. Or perhaps it's a trick of the light. It doesn't matter, anyway. Galahad's sword is already swinging.

The soft whoosh of metal, the sick plunge into skin and the hiss of blood, the sound of a bone breaking.

The head rolls in the dirt. The headless body falls forward and is still.

'One of us,' Lancelot says.

One by one, the knights begin to chant.

'One of us, one of us!'

Galahad stands there, the sword in his hand.

'Let's get fucked,' someone says.

'Yeah,' Galahad says. He slides the sword back in its scabbard and accepts the offer of a drinking jug. He takes a deep pull on the concoction, until his eyes water, at least that's what he tells himself. He wipes away the tears.

'Yeah,' he says. 'Let's get fucked.'

PART ELEVEN

THE GRAIL

60

B ut that all happened a long time ago and far away.
And in view of what is about to happen to Galahad,
those really *were* the best of times.

Even if poor Galahad doesn't quite know it yet.

For we have come, at last, to the matter of the grail.

Now the bird that is Merlin rises high in the air above the terrestrial plane.

It's hard to make the crash site out clearly. He can trace the path that the dragon took in its flight all those years before. A trough of blackened earth, as though the heat of the object was so powerful that it eradicated everything around it in its descent.

But where it landed...

Merlin sees trees. A forest grows where a forest has always grown. The trees are dense together and the canopy hides whatever there may be within. The only giveaway is the curious display of light which dances overhead: ghostly, wraith-like ebbs and flows that glow unnaturally in the sky.

The bird scowls, if birds can be said to scowl. The bird watches.

Merlin has done his due diligence. To go within the site is a risky proposition. Many have gone in; only a few have come back.

They would need a specialist.

He waits and watches.

Sees a posse of armed men ride out.

They spread out. They wait.

For what?

The bird scowls. The bird watches.

Sees, at last, a small human figure emerge out of that place and into the world.

They finally catch up with Gawain, the outlaw, on the very edge of the Zone.

There are seven of them. Rough bearded men on horseback, with nasty old swords that they barely even know how to use. But there are seven of them, and there's one of him, and they look pissed off.

'There he is!'

'There's the crawler!'

'Halt where you are!'

'Fuck off!' Gawain calls. He calculates escape. He could make a run back to the Zone – but even as he thinks that he sees three more men emerge at his back, blocking the route.

Fuck.

It's a fucking *ambush.*

He doesn't try to work out how they knew which way he'd come out. He thinks he could take three of them easy. Maybe four. Make a dash for it when they least expect it. He spurs his horse.

'Get him, boys!'

Fucking *peasants!* he thinks. He pulls out a sword and as the first man comes riding at him the sword flashes and the man's head flies off his shoulders and bounces on the hard dry ground. For just a moment, the eyes blink. Something small and black and hard tunnels up from the ground and crawls to the head and *burrows.* This close to the Zone, there are often extrusions.

Two others converge on Gawain with screams of rage. He ducks a blow, stabs one through the chest, hacks an arm off the other. Blood spurts and catches him in the face, hot and sticky, and he curses again. He tries to wipe his eyes and spurs his horse, which gallops towards the distant hills – to freedom, Gawain thinks.

Then he sees the rest of the posse, further back. They had anticipated this, he realises. How many men had they sent for him? Why?

In desperation he pulls out one of the artefacts. It is a round grey-green thing, shaped like an onion, cool at first to the touch. The longer you hold it, however, the hotter it gets, until you have no choice but to throw it.

Gawain waits, bites his lips through the pain until the heat is too strong to bear, and then he tosses it. It arcs through the air and the men fall back when they see it, for they have lived on the edge of the Zone for many years now, and they know its dangers.

For a moment nothing happens. Then the artefact *unfurls*. The grey-green slates of its mysterious composition peel away like the layers of a scarf, almost languidly, and a burst of terrible fire blows out.

Gawain hears their screams and he curses them for making it happen this way. His hand is burned and blood dries on his face. He turns the horse and tries to flee east. The horse is fast and Gawain is desperate, but now there are men pursuing him from all sides, until the air fills with the thunder of hooves and the screams of the burning men, and the dust churns into the air and makes everything vanish.

For one glorious moment he thinks he's made it.

Then a small shape on a horse darts in through the haze of dust and something hard smashes against the side of his head and the pain is like the peal of a clear enormous bell.

Gawain sways on his horse and then feels himself falling.

And then, mercifully, there is nothing for a time.

*

When he wakes up there's a rope around his neck.

Everything hurts. They must have worked him over real bad while he was out. He's pretty sure there's a rib broken, and he can't see out of one eye.

What he *can* see kind of makes him wish he was still out cold.

Or dead.

Which he will be, soon, anyway.

He's standing on a log with a rope around his neck and the rope's looped over the thick branch of an oak. The men stand around him in a semi-circle. It's getting dark and they're holding torches. A horse whinnies softly and paws the ground. In the distance, eldritch lights chase each other across the fading skies over the Zone.

'What's this all about, then, anyway?' Gawain says. He feels so tired, and he needs a piss.

One of the men spits. 'You killed Edward,' he says. 'He didn't deserve it.'

'Which one was Edward?'

'You took his head clean off!'

'Oh, him,' Gawain says.

'And you stabbed Brian real bad. He died not an hour ago, in great pain. And the others all burned! I will hear their screams in my dreams for months to come.'

'Life is pain,' Gawain says philosophically.

'Fuck you, crawler!'

'What's this about, Gaius? I didn't see you complain when I brought out the witch mud that cured your girl Delphine, did I? And you, Crispin, when I caught that starfish in the Zone for you, the one that glows in the night with the light of a thousand stars for your poor old eyes, was I just a crawler then? The Zone's been forbidden for twenty years, but *now* you suddenly feel the need to uphold the law?'

The men, he notices, look at each other a little sheepishly.

'Maybe we should let him go,' someone says, but quietly.

'Shut your mouth, Edwin.'

'We was supposed to take him to the man from Ca—'

'Shut your mouth, Edwin!'

Gaius clears his throat. He unrolls a piece of parchment.

'Gawain of Gwyar, you stand condemned for the crimes of robbery and murder; trespassing into the forbidden Zone; dealing in retrieved artefacts; trading in leprechaun gold; engaging in unnatural activities and being in communication with such things as live beyond the demarcation line. You are accused of being a thief, a killer, and a crawler of some twenty years standing, and you are herefore condemned to hang by the neck until dead, and may the gods have mercy on your soul. Proceed!'

Gawain spits out blood and stares at the men with hatred. The shifting flames of the makeshift torches bathe their faces in an unhealthy pallor, and the shadows crawl on their skin. He laughs at them.

'You're already dead,' he says. 'You just don't know it.'

The men shift, and some curse, but they pull on the rope and he feels the air being choked out of him and he kicks and flails with his hands tied behind his back. The darkness he had just visited creeps back upon his mind as thought flees, but still he fights, and through his one good eye he sees something that, surely, must be a vision of approaching death – only Gawain's been a crawler too long, and he had seen too many impossible things to mistake the real for illusion.

He sees a young, slim figure on a horse. A pale man with the stench of Elfland on him, and cold pale eyes, who smiles at him and raises a hand in greeting.

What the *fuck*? Gawain thinks, as the world turns dark. Gawain chokes, he chokes, he cannot breathe.

Then the young man extends his hand and whispers something, and a flame shoots out and flies over the hanging mob's heads.

It hits the rope, which hisses.

Gawain twists and turns.

The rope breaks.

Gawain falls in a heap onto the dry, hard ground.

'Motherfuckers,' the man says, 'we had a deal.'

'He killed my men!'

'I'm sure I don't care.'

'He deserves to die!'

'And he will. Eventually. Now shut your fucking gob and drive the cart.'

When Gawain wakes up he's trussed up again, and lying in the back of a cart that still smells of overripe cabbage. His throat is raw. His rib's still broken. He thinks, it doesn't feel so good to be alive.

It feels *great*.

The young pale man's sitting on a crate and watches him. He's got some sort of bulbous clay thing in his mouth and, for some reason Gawain cannot, right now, quite fathom, he seems to be exhaling smoke.

It's all very peculiar.

'This?' the man says. 'Habit I picked up off a visiting Scythian. I'm Merlin. You must be Gawain.'

Gawain tries to speak but just ends up coughing. The Merlin smiles at him kindly and without any warmth.

'Spare your breath,' he says.

'Who the fuck *are* you?'

'I told you, I'm Merlin.' He smiles and blows smoke.

Into Gawain's perplexed expression: 'I'm the man from Camelot.'

Ahhh...

Gawain hawks phlegm and blood. His head's pounding, but at least he's still, improbably, alive. The life of a crawler is one of improbable survival. Men have little to offer him in fear compared to the things he's encountered in the Zone.

'What has... Camelot... got to do with *me*?'

Merlin blows smoke. Doesn't answer. 'So, you're a crawler?' he says instead.

Ahhh...

'You can't... prove it.'

'Come, come, Sir Gawain.'

Merlin reaches in his pocket. He takes out a pair of thin, odd gloves. They are transparent, and Gawain thinks they must be made out of some animal's intestines. Merlin puts them on very carefully before reaching for Gawain's bag and opening it.

Gawain stares as all the loot he's brought back from the Zone tumbles out. Gold goblets and strange glass shapes and curious coins and receptacles for samples.

'F... *found* it,' Gawain says. The Merlin only smiles. And Gawain suddenly has the realisation there is no talking his way out of this one.

'They say you're the best.'

Gawain gives this statement all the reply it deserves – which is none. Merlin rummages through the finds.

'What's this?' he says, holding up a cloth bag.

'Witch... Witch mud,' Gawain says. Giving up. What difference does it make, anyway?

'Witch mud?'

'It's mud found in... in certain parts of the Zone, near certain... streams. It has... healing properties.'

'Good for the skin? That sort of thing?'

'They say it can mend... bones. Cure fever. *That* sort of... thing.'

He notices his voice is growing stronger. The night is very quiet. All he can hear is the clip-clop-clop of the horse's hooves, the squeaking of the cart wheels, his own harsh breathing.

'Bet you could use some right now,' the Merlin says, and dumps the bag. He picks an object that resembles a half-wheel, with strange hollow spokes emerging from the rim. It looks like a child's toy, it is made, if it is made at all, for small hands.

'And this?'

'We call it a ghost wheel,' Gawain says unwillingly.

'What does it do?'

'Don't turn it... widdershins twice when the stars are out and there is no moon!' Gawain says, alarmed. The Merlin quickly lays the ghost wheel down.

'Why?'

'It does... No one's sure what it does, exactly. It... changes depending on certain conditions in the firmaments of the heavens.'

'You believe the sky is a solid dome, and the stars are lights fastened to it?'

'You have a... better idea?'

'I do not know,' the Merlin says. 'These mysteries are hidden even from me. But if the sky is a dome, then what is beyond it, crawler? And if it be breached, then what may fall through?'

Gawain stares at the man from Camelot; and some suspicions, at least, have just been confirmed.

'You want to go into the Zone,' he says.

The Merlin just stares. 'We can discuss that later,' he says.

'Why does Camelot suddenly take an interest?' Gawain says. 'You've had twenty years.'

'I meant to,' Merlin says. 'But it turns out consolidating a kingdom takes some doing. It is my fault, perhaps, that this has been allowed to go on for so long. By the time I could drag my attention back to events beyond the Pict's Wall, things had changed more than I'd realised.'

He sighs, unwraps the gloves and disposes of them over the side of the cart. He picks up his smoking apparatus once more.

'I should grow a beard,' he says. 'People respect you more when you have a beard.'

'I'm sorry?' Gawain says, taken aback.

'Don't be,' Merlin says. 'You'll have plenty of opportunity yet.'

61

They rock into Wormwood as tendrils of sunlight begin to crawl their way across the skies. Gawain wakes from an uneasy sleep. Merlin's sat where he was, stares expressionless at the passing terrain. Gawain sees the crude wooden sign stuck into the earth outside the gates of the town.

Wormwood. Pop. 971 853.

All these years and he's still only in Wormwood.

They pass through the gates unhindered, the watchmen jumping to attention at their approach. The cart moves slowly on the pebbled main road. The last of the drunks stumbles out of a brothel, stares at them in the early dawn light, yawns, takes his dick out and pisses.

'Quite a town,' Merlin says.

'It's a shithole.'

Merlin nods.

'You got family?' he says. 'Children?'

Shit, Gawain thinks, but doesn't say.

'You?' he says instead.

'Mostly aunts,' Merlin says. 'No kids that I know of.'

'Well, same here.'

'Hmmm.'

Gawain keeps his face impassive. Could he warn Helena? He'd told the girl to leave town for a while before he went, but she never listened to him. She rarely indicated she could even understand him when he talked. She was always playing with the artefacts and, once, he'd caught her spinning a ghost wheel and every item in the room began to shudder and *sing*, for just a moment it was as though a hole had been punched in the world as he knew it and the music of God came through.

'Ah, here we are,' Merlin says.

The cart stops outside the Toadstool. It is one of the last houses before you abruptly hit the end of Wormwood, a combination inn and brothel often frequented by crawlers. Merlin hops off the cart, nimbly, and two of the posse men who followed them on horseback grab Gawain and dump him on the ground. Merlin kneels by him, a small sharp knife in his hand.

'You won't try to run, will you?' he says.

'Fuck,' Gawain said, 'if that's what you were worried about you could have untied me hours ago.'

'I know. I just didn't want to.'

Merlin slices the rope. Blood rushes back, painfully, to Gawain's wrists.

'Come on in,' Merlin says.

He dismisses the other men; though Gawain notices they linger outside, and that their swords are drawn. There's no getting out for him, not yet at any rate.

But a realisation materialises: whatever it is they're planning, and whoever these people really *are*... They *need* him.

It's dim inside. The windows are shuttered and fat candles flicker and shudder on the low tables. A long lanky man sits in one corner with his feet up on the table, chewing on a toothpick. He raises his head when Gawain comes in but says nothing, and his eyes are keen.

A second man sits by the abandoned musicians' station, holding a lyre. He plucks the strings, looks up at Gawain, goes back to strumming.

Merlin perches on a stool and pours himself a drink.

Something pale and colourless. He downs it in one and his tongue darts out and licks his lips.

'Sit down,' he says.

Gawain pulls up a chair.

'Get you anything? Food, something to drink?'

The man with the lyre stirs. 'There's half a cooked chicken somewhere,' he says. 'And some bread and apples and that.'

The man by the window chews on his toothpick.

'Yes,' Gawain says.

'Yes?'

'Yes. Food. Drink.'

Merlin looks at the man with the lyre. 'Well, Galahad?'

'Oh, alright.' He puts aside the instrument and goes to the back and returns with a tray. He dumps it on the table.

Gawain doesn't wait. He tears a chunk of bread and stuffs it in his mouth. He shoves his hands in the chicken carcass and tears out meat and skin with greasy fingers.

The man by the window raises his head and stares.

'This is the crawler?' he says.

'That it is, Lancelot.'

'He doesn't look like much.'

Gawain ignores him. He's learned to eat when he can. There's no pride here. Inside the Zone food is scarce and it is *always* dangerous to take it. On shorter excursions he makes sure to bring his own supplies, and over the years he had left several dead drops on the more charted routes to hold emergency provisions. But the geography inside shifts abruptly, and anything left there long enough corrupts in strange ways.

On longer excursions he's had no choice but to forage within. He supposes he, too, is a part of the Zone now, in some small way. This might explain the growths on his skin, and as for Helena...

'Tell me about the Zone,' Lancelot says abruptly.

Gawain stares. He chews and swallows.

'Excuse me?'

'What is it like, inside?'

'It… It changes.'

Lancelot frowns. 'Changes?'

Merlin, with a roll of parchment and a pen before him, stares intently.

'Our reports do indicate the terrain is subject to spatial metamorphosis,' he says encouragingly.

Back with the lyre, Galahad plays a note. 'That's a big word,' he complains.

'Shut up.'

Gawain stares at them, wonders what it is they are doing here, what it is they really want. He says, 'It is unpredictable. It's like…' He tries to think. Figures he may as well give them the same spiel crawlers always give civilians when they ask.

'It's like we're the ants,' he says.

'Ants?'

'Yes. It's like we're ants, crawling on the hide of some massive beast. We cannot really *fathom* the beast itself, we can only glance at the small features as we pass and try to make sense of them, and thus convince ourselves we know the whole. The first lesson of a crawler is to understand that we cannot. All we can do is try to survive the passage.'

Lancelot looks at him in a new light, then, it seems to Gawain.

'A beast?'

Unwillingly: 'That's what I said.'

'You are saying the Zone is *alive*?'

'It's a metaphora,' Merlin says. He scribbles something in his parchment. Dips the pen in a small pot of very dark ink. And Gawain thinks of Phoenix Blood, which can be sometimes found inside the Zone. The crawlers bottle it and carry it back, and when you write with it the ink's alive, and crawls across the page.

The hermit told him once that the blood really *was* alive.

That some powerful creatures, too tiny to see, lived within in, and that released upon the page they still attempted to crawl back elsewhere. If so, he feels a kinship with the things. And he wonders where they try to go.

The Blood is prized by augurs and their like. The shapes the ink makes when it settles suggests the future, or so some say. But like most things from the inside, its true purpose, if it has one, is unknown.

'How large is the Zone?' Galahad says.

Gawain shakes his head. 'Nobody knows for certain.'

'Tell me of the people who live within,' Merlin says.

Gawain tears a chunk of bread and swallows. He drinks the wine. The wine is good.

'It depends,' he says carefully, 'on what you mean by *live*. Or *people*.'

He thinks of some of the beings he'd seen in the Zone. There are villages of the mutatio still inside, deformed men and women touched by the star-stone which is said to lie at the heart of the place. They have a semblance of a life still, isolated little villages, thatched mud huts perched on tiny bubbling brooks of tainted water. They hunt the birds and badgers that live inside and catch the fish in the streams for their food. If they have language still then it is not one Gawain can recognise.

And once, in pale moonlight, he saw a procession go past through a clearing, who had no earthly form. But he does not tell the men from Camelot that.

'Tell me about the sightings,' Merlin says. Makes a note, of what, Gawain has no idea.

'The sightings,' he says.

'Above the Zone.'

'Ah,' Gawain says. 'That.'

Flying lights, hovering silver shapes, darting almost like fish in the sky. The men from Camelot have done their groundwork, he thinks. But they do not know the Zone. It is one thing to compile reports and quite another to enter into that strange landscape where nothing is what it seems and all the ordinary human values are reversed.

He humours them. He tells them anecdotes. They are familiar with the more common retrievables: witch mud and ghost wheels and leprechaun gold. He doesn't mention the wishing well or the hermit. The men ask about the centre. The Merlin asks a series of questions about a star stone. Where did it land? Is there an impact crater? What lies at the very heart?

Gawain shakes his head at them. 'The paths twist and at last vanish. When you think you're close you find yourself back near the perimeter. They say there's a heart to the Zone, yes, but even I don't know how to get there. You've got the wrong man.'

They exchange glances then.

They know, he thinks, that he's not telling them the whole truth.

'How far have you got?'

They make him draw them a map. There is always a map in this sort of thing.

He marks stable points: The Witches' Cauldron, Three Hanging Men, The Spider Bite, The Place Where The Gristles Wash.

They ask him about the distribution of leprechaun gold. Someone's minting the coins, they keep saying. Someone holds power within the Zone. Someone human.

Perhaps, he tells them. He doesn't know. He doesn't mention the dark castle and the wounded king and the Pool of Despair.

He knows they have him. Where is he to run?

Only in the Zone is he ever free.

At last they relent. They let him go and wash. He applies witch mud to his wounds. The healing hurts. He curls up on a cot in an upstairs room and, finally, he sleeps.

In the morning, they set off for the Zone.

62

The landscape resolves slowly. At first it's all dusty plains and low brown hills, cracked earth, barely a shrub in sight. A trail of black ants crawls along a precipice. One of the horses farts.

Then you start noticing the wide horizon. The clear blue skies. The sun that is a yolky yellow of a most perfect kind – and what *is* the sun, exactly? The Greek, Aristarchus of Samos, had proposed that the sun is a great ball of fire which lies at the centre of all things, and that the Earth and the planets revolve around it. And furthermore did not Aristarchus propose that the very stars, those fixed in place, were suns themselves, and merely very far away from Earth to seem so small?

Well, under the sun they traverse the distance out from Wormwood. Soon there is no human habitation. There is little water or shade. They see few animals as they pass. Yet it is all – so Gawain, the crawler, tells them – illusory to an extent. Part of the blight or curse placed on this land by the event.

A dragon's breath, some say. A star stone, say others.

Merlin keeps his own counsel.

He'd love to go into the Zone. He has some thoughts as to its nature. Oh, how he longs to go exploring! To catalogue its fauna and flora, make learned notes, draw vibrant illustrations of new species, make charts of their anatomy. He has a thought that what's inside is unlike anything else found on this Earth.

Though who's to say? And he knows that the Greeks and Romans recorded the finding of many curious skeletons of a giant size. The Athenian general Kimon, for instance, excavated just one such on the island of Skyros.

And Merlin thinks that perhaps, long before humans ever trod the Earth, before their imagination could conjure up his kind, there lived upon the land strange giant beings. And if that is so, and humans' time had only just begun, then who's to say what could or couldn't live on other worlds, and what strange manner of creatures could still be found upon the Earth itself?

And yet he knows he cannot go. Predominantly among the reasons is the simple fact that the Zone is poisoned.

For people, yes, but for Merlins, more. If Merlin is right and the star stone he saw fall across the sky in the reign of Uther lies at the heart of that place, then it is deadly to his kind. In his tower in Camelot he spent many nights poring over artefacts retrieved from the Zone. Even then, using care and protective equipment, the experience proved hazardous. The fae are too susceptible to whatever invisible radiance emerges from the matter of the Zone. It kills them with its reason.

So he must stay behind. It is best. While this affair continues there are other pressing matters to consider, namely the problem of the Anglo-Saxon tribes. They are expanding, more and more. With their guttural Anglisc and their keen sense of place and foreign battle strategies, streaming across the channel into Britain, taking up land, making native-born babies, slowly but surely pushing at the borders of Arthur's united kingdom. This cannot go on. The Anglo-Saxons shun the old Roman towns and build their own encampments outside the places that they conquer. They speak not the native tongues. They maintain their own strange customs.

He worries that they cannot be defeated by conventional weapons. He needs something else, something *definitive*.

A weapon to end all wars.

And he thinks: the grail.

But he cannot dally. Arthur's away at war. The years have aged him. Power is like poison, it feeds into the blood. And Merlins hunger for the power of men. So where?

And he has heard disturbing rumours, which draw him west of here. For Morgause has been too quiet of late, and yet he knows she lays her plans. And word has come to him of a new power arising, some dark warrior, youthful and savage, who made bargains with the Irish and reunited the warring gangs of the coast, cut-throat smugglers and brigands the lot of them.

One single name, coming out of the wilds of the west:

Mordred.

And Merlin longs for peace. To study his star charts and the anatomy of frogs. To dream of distant Qin and Aksum, of Greek philosophers and of the infinity of the ratio of a circle's circumference to its diameter.

And this he cannot have.

On the second night they make camp on a low mound in the shape of a femur bone. Lancelot builds a small fire and Galahad, reluctantly, goes foraging. He comes back with a bloodied hare and a sour expression.

'No more hunting,' Gawain says.

'Excuse me?'

Gawain gestures at the darkening horizon. Ahead of them they can now clearly see the skies above the Zone. Fantastical lights chase one another in ethereal greens streaked with crimson and violet.

'Sometimes the smaller creatures cross over the threshold,' Gawain says. 'No more hunting after tonight.'

'Then what do we eat?'

'Not much.'

Galahad scowls and sets to skin the hare. Lancelot stretches his legs by the fire and stares towards the Zone. He has his own agenda being here, Merlin knows. These men of the Round

Table all have that in common: they are unholy sneaks and thieves and liars to a man, and will connive and scheme and murder to pursue their goals. No wonder they all flock to Camelot. It is that great cesspool into which all the loungers and idlers of the kingdom are irresistibly drained.

Merlin slices a piece of dried apple and chews without much appetite. He stares at the Zone. It is hard to avoid it. The eye is drawn to that display of light. The place taunts them with its mysteries.

He observes the men who are about to go within. He cannot trust them, but he can trust in that at least. As for Gawain, the crawler, he no doubt plans to sabotage their journey just as soon as they're inside.

Merlin stirs.

He says, 'Your daughter.'

The crawler is startled, but tries not to show it.

'Excuse me?'

'Helena,' Merlin says, without mercy.

He sees the knowledge suffuse the crawler's face.

'You wouldn't—'

Merlin nods.

'You *knew*.'

'Her mother was from there, was she not?'

Gawain stares into the fire.

'She was so beautiful,' he says. 'And so free...'

The other men stir and pay attention.

Gawain says, 'I was lost. Deeper into the Zone than I'd ever been before. Starving, half-delirious. You were right, wizard. There is a place deep at the heart. A dark castle high on a hill above a pool of black water... You do not want to go there. There is nothing there but despair.'

'What happened?'

'I met her after I made my escape. In a grove of weeping trees. She came out of the night, a pale lady, and her eyes were bright. She took my hand in hers and led me to her abode. There were others like her. Their forms shimmered and changed when you glanced at them sideways. In the moonlight they were translucent. I dwelled with them there for a season. She gave birth to my daughter. Then something happened, I know not what. When I awoke from it I found myself back outside the perimeter, holding a small, rag-wrapped bundle in my arms.' He blinks a few times, turns his eyes from the fire. 'I named her Helena. My daughter... She is not like the other children.'

He stares helplessly at the wizard. 'She is very precious to me.'

Merlin says delicately, 'I wish her no harm.'

'You have her?'

Merlin lets his silence be an implication.

'I will serve you true,' Gawain says. 'But your quest is folly. The Zone does not abide intrusion. I fear you will find nothing but death and despair within.'

Galahad turns the hare on the fire. He stares. Merlin knows Galahad has no stomach for this work. He would cut and run if he could.

Lancelot stretches. 'I'm willing to take that chance,' he says.

'Why?'

'I have my reasons.'

'Reason,' Gawain says, 'does not exist in the Zone.'

Galahad scowls. But Merlin knows the little rat too well. Merlin had made sure to spell it out for him. His fate depends on a successful mission.

He'll stay the course.

They share the hare, some bread baked back in Wormwood. For their supplies Gawain had told them to pack travelling food: hard cheese, dried meat, pickles and dried bread. Lancelot packs a small bag of precious salt. Galahad has an amphora of wine secreted on his person.

They sleep by the embers. The night is almost too quiet. Over the Zone the lights move soundlessly, like green-dressed ghosts dancing in the starlight. Merlin listens to the other men sleep. Lancelot snores, Galahad grunts and mutters as though he's fighting off a leg of lamb. Gawain, the outlaw, sleeps very quietly, he notices. His breathing is so slow and even, almost as though—

'My daughter,' the crawler says. And somehow he's no longer by the fire but standing behind Merlin in the dark. Something cold and sharp touches Merlin's neck.

He licks his lips.

'I saved your life,' he says evenly.

'You set them on me.'

'True. So what do you want?'

'My daughter.'

'She is different *how?*' Merlin says.

'She speaks to the artefacts from the Zone. She can... understand function.'

'And we do not?'

'No.'

'Why do you think that is? Where do these things come from? Ghost wheels and scar-bugs and elf-fingers?'

'You know of these things?'

'I have made study of the objects found within, yes. What do scar-bugs do?'

'They bore. Outside the Zone they go half-dormant, unless the phases of the sun are such as to activate them fully. They are small black things the size of half a thumb. You've seen one?'

And Merlin thinks of the specimens in his tower in Camelot. They had survived for a time and he had occasion to experiment with several at first. They bore through anything: wood, metal, stone. What powers them he doesn't know. But far enough from the Zone they slowly disintegrate, he discovered. He had not been able to *preserve* any Zone specimen for long.

It has frustrated him.

'Why do they do what they do?'

'I don't know.'

'Who made them?'

'I don't know.'

'I *need* to know!' Merlin says.

The pressure of the knife against his neck.

'My *daughter*,' the crawler says.

'She will be safe.'

'I have to know this.'

'Bring these men out of the Zone alive. Bring me that which I seek for my king. And you have my word.'

The crawler hesitates, his hand steady on the knife. Merlin had studied this Gawain, his past, his methods. Twenty years of going in and out of the territory. He could have retired several times over on the loot he'd brought back from inside.

'Crawlers don't usually live very long,' Merlin observes.

'No.'

'Yet you survive.'

'Listen, wizard. In all this time all I have learned is that I know nothing useful. Each trip into the Zone is a blank slate. Each trip can be your last.'

'You must be lucky.'

Gawain gives a hollow laugh. 'Yes, lucky,' he agrees.

'You have my word.'

The knife withdraws. When Merlin turns the crawler's gone. He's back by the fire and gently snoring.

This is no witchery that Merlin knows, but something's in the man's blood that should not, by any rights, be there.

And Merlin doesn't even *have* the stupid girl!

Oh, he had tried. He'd been so careful. They came at night, embedded watchers let them through the gate. The girl was sleeping in the house that her father built her. She hadn't left. How softly they crept in.

And yet she wasn't there. The window open and a dry breeze blowing in and she was gone. The bed still warm. And in the room the ghost wheels spun in unison, and on the wall he saw a star chart drawn in ink, a child's hand, and it showed no constellations that he knew.

She must have sensed their coming. A different magic, he thinks. But then the world is filled with the mysterious and strange, and only Greek philosophers and Merlins ever try to understand its inner workings.

For everything there is an explanation, Merlin thinks. A rationale.

A wizard born of fae and mortal, this Merlin's cursed – for he alone does not believe in magic.

63

A butterfly as large as a fist flitters past Galahad's face and he bats it away savagely. The creature's wings are veined with outlandish whorls of violet and sick-yellow.

'What the fuck,' he says.

'Don't touch anything,' the crawler tells him. 'I warned you before.'

'Fucking thing flew at me!' Galahad says. 'Fuck.'

Gawain, the crawler, is ahead. Lancelot brings up the rear, his lanky frame moving with surprising grace. It's Galahad who's stuck between them.

The branches of the trees here are a vivid green. Their leaves sting if they touch your naked skin. Gawain had instructed them to cover up before they left. It's hot under the rags they wear. The tree trunks are like the exposed bodies of a worm or grub. Belly-white, and strangely alive, they move too much, almost as though breathing.

It's silent in the wood, and the canopy of the trees hides the sun. It's humid and the air is full of flying insects. Twice now Galahad's been stung, each time he'd killed the creature, found a smear of violet blood on his hand.

It's silent but somehow he can hear the trees whispering. They know he's there. They watch him pass. They say his name. Every time he takes a breath he hears Gaheris crying. Gaheris, saying, *Please, Gally, don't.*

The sound of a sword swishing through the air. The sound of a head rolling in the dirt. *Please, Gally.*

Galahad breathes violently. The trees sway and hem him in. He reaches for his sword. He'll fight them, he'll kill them all!

'Hush,' the crawler says. They pause.

'There should be a clearing ahead, if it hasn't moved,' Gawain says. 'It's usually a stable point, but the Zone seems unusually active for this time of year, this close to the perimeter.'

'Oh, shut *up*,' Galahad says. The branch of a tree brushes his shoulder and he jumps.

'Follow on my signal,' the crawler says. Then he vanishes in the trees ahead.

Galahad stands there. They'd parted from Merlin on the outside. There was a way station or an observation post, something the wizard must have dreamed up years ago. Really it was just a shack of wood and crumbling stone. Two ancient knights manned it, two men with long grey beards and weak watery eyes and *sandals.* They barely spoke.

'What have you seen in all this time?' Merlin demanded.

Their faces were as slack as idiot children's.

'Nothing,' they said.

Gawain, Lancelot and Galahad went ahead. In the daytime the sky above the Zone looked blue and peaceful, with nary a white cloud in sight. There was nothing to distinguish the crossing. They had been walking for some time over cracked earth when Gawain said, 'We're in.'

Galahad turned and looked back but everything looked the same, and he felt vaguely disappointed. There were some trees ahead, but that was it.

He'd half figured it was all a con even back in Camelot. Some scheme of Merlin's that he cooked up. Some such nonsense.

Then a thing like a blue giant crab crawled out of the ground beside him and tried to take his fucking leg off.

Galahad swore and stomped and *stomped* again and the creature's shell burst and some sort of *light* burst out of the

LAVIE TIDHAR

creature and then Gawain was there, pushing him *away* as the light turned into liquid and just missed the place where Galahad had been. It hissed when it touched the ground.

'Don't *touch* anything!' Gawain said.

Then they went into the trees.

Now he hears Gawain's low whistle. He follows the man and really does emerge into a clearing. There are signs that people have been here before, and recently. A dead fire in a ring of stones, and when he squats to feel them the stones are still warm. There's an old oak tree with a hollow, and Gawain reaches inside and brings out a leather satchel. The leather had been treated with beeswax. When Gawain opens it they find cheese, cured meats, cucumbers pickled in the Roman way, even a small jar of fermented fish sauce. The sight of these familiar food items makes Galahad ache suddenly for Camelot. He'd give anything to be back there, anything.

But Gawain meanwhile is muttering to himself. He stares at the foods sitting there on the leather.

'…Too fresh.'

'What? Come on, man. Let's dig in,' Galahad says.

'Hello, what's this?' Gawain's attention is turned on some spot on the leather.

'What is it, man!' Galahad says. He ambles over, kneels – 'Why, it's just a pretty ladybug.'

'Ladybugs aren't a bright blue,' Gawain says. 'And the food I left here last was sealed, and there was no—'

The bug bursts into the air with a shudder of wings. It hits Galahad in the eye and he screams. The creature *crawls* on his cornea – he can *feel* those tiny feet on his eye – and then it crawls *under* his freaking *eyelid* – he can feel it *burrowing inside* – he can feel it *moving*! – and then there's nothing, and he blinks.

He can see now the illusion of the food parcel. The cucumbers crawl out of their clay jar and wriggle on the short grass. Galahad can see them raise small antennae, open tiny black eyes. The cheese explodes into a nest of maggots that wriggle and spread rapidly outwards. The meat rots and larvae emerges.

'The spot's contaminated,' Gawain says. 'I worried this might happen.' He turns to the others. 'Quick. We'll go north. The next stable point should be just past the Big Water. If we get separated, look for three burned trees in a row. Something happened there, a long time ago. Something bad. But it's stopped the Zone, in that place.'

Galahad savagely stomps on the maggots. They screech in horrid high-pitched voices as they die.

'Someone came past here, and recently,' Lancelot said.

'Don't be fooled by the fire,' Gawain says. 'For all I know none of this was even here an hour ago. Now hurry. They're growing.'

Galahad stares: the tiny blind grubs are expanding, the green cucumber worms swell up, exposing round, teeth-filled mouths. Gawain vanishes ahead and Lancelot moves in step behind him. Galahad hurries after them but his vision's worse now, everything seems double, and he can see faces trapped inside the trees, pale human forms with lips that move ceaselessly in speech that is at times a curse and others a prayer. They call to him. The branches reach out to him. The leaves stroke his face and arms. He can feel the bug wriggling deeper into his brain.

Galahad screams.

'Where is that useless fool!' Lancelot says.

Then they hear the scream.

'Oh, for fuck's sake—' Lancelot starts. Gawain silences him.

'If you don't mind me saying, you seem far too comfortable here so far,' he says.

Lancelot shrugs. 'It's not exactly what I expected, but...'

'You will tell me later. Follow me.'

'Whatever you saw, crawler.'

He follows Gawain through the trees. They can hear Galahad throwing a tantrum somewhere in the distance. So predictable. Those knights of the Round Table, Lancelot thinks, are provincial thugs with no imagination. Useless cunts the lot of them.

He looks a little uneasily around him. The swaying branches like the slender arms of dancing maidens. The brightly coloured insects like gaudy jewels. The master had never mentioned anything like this in all his talk of the grail. It was as though the grail, by its very being, somehow manipulated reality around itself. Lancelot can feel the hidden energies that go into maintaining this illusion. A word comes into his mind: *camouflage*.

But what is it all in purpose *of*? What is the Zone *hiding*?

'Motherfucking cocksucking Jesus of Judea and all his *shitting* disciples!' Galahad screams. He's close. They burst through the trees and see him just ahead, beside a curiously sloping bit of ground and a violet shrub with agitated, limb-like fronds. Galahad's face is red and Lancelot could swear there's something, some bulge *moving* under the man's skin.

'God damned cunt fucking shit jizzing wank b—'

Galahad stumbles and the ground suddenly *vanishes* and Galahad *falls*—

'...ast...'

Lancelot waits.

'...ards...'

Lancelot waits.

'...Fuck!'

But Gawain is already moving. He unspools a thick rope off his belt and throws it into the hole that had opened in the ground. He tosses the other end to Lancelot, who catches it easily. 'Loop it securely.'

'Sir, yes, sir,' Lancelot says, but the crawler pays him no attention and Lancelot, with a sigh, ties the rope to the nearest tree. He stares at the tree with a little suspicion. So much around him is not what it seems. But the tree seems solid enough – for the moment, at least.

'Is it secure?'

'I guess so,' Lancelot says.

'Is it secure!'

'How the fuck should I know!'

They stare at each other. Gawain's eyes are a disconcerting dark blue, like the sky before the stars appear. How has he not noticed them before?

'Listen, knight,' Gawain says. 'All I am trying to do is keep you two fools alive long enough for you to get through whatever idiotic mission you are on. You understand? The Zone's *awake*, now. The Zone's *active*. And it *likes* newcomers. It's like a new flavour that suddenly enters the mouth and rests on the tongue. You understand? Me, it knows. But you... you make it *curious*.'

'You talk as though the Zone's alive,' Lancelot says.

The crawler shrugs. 'I don't know what it is or why it does what it does. Do you?'

'I have some ideas.'

'Is that so, knight of the Round Table?'

'My name is Lancelot!'

'It's a stupid name.'

'Fuck you!'

They stare at each other.

'Help! Hel—'

'Oh, right.'

'Galahad.'

Gawain reaches for the rope. Tests that it holds. Turns back, says, 'Well? Are you coming?'

'Fuck you,' Lancelot says again, but without malice. The crawler grins, and then he's gone in a flash, feet-first down the hole. Lancelot whistles, some tune half-remembered from childhood, and he grabs hold of the rope and follows suit.

Down and down and down into the belly of the Earth.

They fall a surprisingly long way. Lancelot holds on to the rope and kicks against the sides of the borehole. Clumps of dirt come loose and fall down on Gawain. At last they land. Lancelot falls gracefully and assumes the forward stance; the flying sword, Secace, is drawn and in his hand.

'Put that away,' Gawain says. Lancelot straightens. They are in a small cavity in the Earth and there's no sign of Galahad. Just ahead he can see a strangely octagonal opening.

'What is this place?'

Gawain shrugs. They walk ahead and through the opening. Dim lights materialise all around them. Lancelot touches the walls. They're warm.

'Metal,' he says.

'Yes.'

It is a small room, hot and stuffy, with the smell of faded incense for some reason. The signs of violent struggle are evident. Lancelot sees unfamiliar instruments pinned to the wall, rows and rows of them. They put him in mind of astrolabes and Ptolemaic quadrants. He sees a star chart caught in glass, recognises the Pleiades, Ursa Minor and the star Rastaban, in the Draco constellation. And he thinks Ptolemy would have loved the mystery of this room.

In the centre of the room is a chair. The chair is long and wide and it reclines curiously. Sitting in the chair is a skeleton. It is far taller than an ordinary man, and the skull is elongated, and it has but four long fingers on each hand. The skull grins up at Lancelot as though to say, I've lived and died, and you will never know the things I've seen, and one day you will be as I am now, and who's to say who will disturb *your* bones in their own hidden grave?

'What is this thing? What is this place?' Lancelot says.

The crawler shrugs. 'It's of the Zone.'

But Lancelot's senses are tuned to something deeper. It feels real to him, and sad, somehow.

He says, 'Where's Galahad?'

'I do not know, in truth.'

Lancelot steps out of that octagonal doorway. The walls of earth are sealed around that little cavity and yet he has the sense that *something* came and snatched the man and vanished through. But if that is so then the walls have sealed themselves back around the puncture, and wherever Galahad is now…

'Leave him,' Lancelot says. 'It doesn't matter. A casualty was not unexpected.'

The crawler emerges out of that metal room and stares at him levelly.

'You do not seem surprised. Or upset.'

Lancelot traces fingers on the walls. 'I wonder…' he says.

'Yes?'

'Nothing.'

'What is it, man of Camelot?'

Lancelot has the sense of something beyond the walls, watching, listening…

'It's only,' he says, 'that little shit has a habit of surviving.'

His hand drops.

'It doesn't matter,' he says again. 'We press on.'

'On where?' Gawain says. 'What is it you really seek? How much do you know?'

Lancelot smiles unpleasantly. 'I know you have a way of making it into the inner sections,' he says.

Gawain does not reply, but he returns to the rope and pulls it. It holds, still, and he begins to climb. Lancelot follows, and they traverse that shaft back up to sky and sunlight.

When Lancelot emerges at last out of the hole he sees the trees are gone, and they are standing in a clearing. The rope he had been climbing is loosely held in Gawain's hands, unfastened.

He looks at the crawler, a question in his eyes.

'Then how?'

The crawler shakes his head. 'The Zone's the Zone,' he says. 'Come on.'

Lancelot follows mutely.

They wend their way deeper inside.

64

'You're not *from* around here?' the crawler says, with genuine curiosity.

Lancelot shakes his head. He stirs the embers of the fire with a stick.

'Judea,' he says.

They're sitting under the stars. Overhead the green wraiths of lights chase each other in a mute display. Somewhere, an owl hoots. Something small skitters under leaves. It's strangely peaceful.

'What's it like?' Gawain says. 'I've never been much farther than Wormwood. Ain't never even seen Camelot or Londinium.'

'It's different,' Lancelot says. 'Warmer...' He barks a short, surprised laugh. 'I don't often think about it anymore.'

'Do you ever miss it?'

'I try not to miss things in the past. It's a place you can't get back to.'

The crawler stares at him with that same curiosity. 'So what brought you here?'

Lancelot shrugs. 'I forget,' he says.

'This?' Gawain gestures at the world around them. He catches Lancelot by surprise.

'You guessed?'

'You have a look about you,' Gawain says. 'You're not the first to come here and ask for passage. I'm a crawler, what I do is go into the Zone. Bring stuff out. Take people in. People like you. Drawn here, for whatever reason. You have the same look.'

'What look is that?'

'Fatal curiosity,' the crawler says. 'It's the mystery that gets them, every time. Well, the mystery and, eventually, one of the traps.'

'Yet you survive.'

'I just have the knack for it, I guess.'

Lancelot laughs. 'You've got it all wrong, crawler. I *know* what the Zone is. I've been searching for it all my adult life. Not by choice, you see. My master was convinced it, or something like it, must exist. He spent his life searching for it, across places you cannot even imagine – Smyrna, Arabia, Punt. But he never found it. And I never cared to, before.'

'Then why now?'

'Unfinished business, I guess. And the king wants whatever's here for his war against the Angles and the Saxons.'

Gawain shakes his head. 'It will serve him not.'

'Well, my job is to find out for sure. Besides, you must think me an even greater fool if you think I believe you when you chalk up your survival to dumb luck.'

'Then what, man of Judea?'

Lancelot stirs the embers and sparks fly into the air.

'You're of it,' he says softly. 'You do not trespass. You belong.'

Gawain stiffens. But he does not reply. Crickets chirp in the undergrowth. It all sounds so normal, Lancelot thinks. As though this really was a peaceful field in Britain. As though this was all as it should be.

'What *do* you think it is, then?' Gawain says at last.

'Do you know, I trained under Joseph of Arimathea,' Lancelot says. 'In his young days he was quite the soldier. Trained with the legions, he once told me, what was left of them anyway. Followed the land road to India, went even further than that.

Knew the five point palm exploding heart technique, or so he claimed, at any rate. Never taught it to me. But regardless. When he came back his obsession for the thing we call the grail meant he was often in need of financing. His particular skills lent themselves to a particular kind of job. When Iblis and I came on board—'

'Iblis?'

Lancelot stirs. 'An old friend,' he says. 'Forget about her.'

'Sorry. Go on.'

It's so still. As though the Zone itself is listening.

'When we came on board he trained us to be assassins.'

'I see.'

'It is not a glamorous or respectable job,' Lancelot said. 'And it pays less than you'd think. Regardless. We were very good at it.'

'As fascinating as this is, I fail to see how it answers my question—'

'We could spend days tracking our target,' Lancelot said, ignoring him. 'In an urban area like Rome we could be disguised as beggars or a member of the fire watch, an apple seller or a passing senator. Each environment requires adaptation. In the countryside we learned to track by always staying hidden. We liked the bow and arrow for long-range work. I'd lie on a hill disguised in earth and leaves, and you could pass right by me and never guess that I was there.'

'I...'

'You know, when my master spoke of the grail, I am not honestly sure what it is he had in his mind. When I first became aware of the dragon or star stone and heard the stories – there's, um, there's a lady in court who has seen it for herself—'

'A lady in the court? Pray tell!'

'No, I mean... Forget it. I just meant, I heard the stories. But Merlin said what they had witnessed there was only a minor crash site, where a piece of the star stone came loose. I listened to their stories and charted their path and I thought the mutatio and so on were but a natural phenomenon of the poisonous metals the fallen stone must have carried.'

'I am not sure I follow.'

'Aristotle, on observing the octopus, said that it "seeks its prey by so changing its colour as to render it like the colour of the stones adjacent to it. It does so also when alarmed." The master quoted him often. He was very fond of Aristotle's *Historia animalium*.'

The crawler looks levelly at Lancelot.

'What are you saying?'

Lancelot stares at the dying fire. He listens to the night. An owl hoots. Above the Zone the green wraiths chase the starlight.

'I am saying that *this*, here... This is the octopus.'

In the morning the sun shines and they pass through the trees and reach gentle grasslands. There's an apple tree and Lancelot reaches for a low branch to pluck one before the crawler knocks the red apple out of his hand.

'Don't. *Eat*. Anything!'

After that they walk in silence, and no birds sing. The field they pass through is dotted with white milkmaid flowers and daisies, bright yellow kingcups, bluebells and pink foxgloves. It's all so ordinary, innocent, sublime. The air is sweet with nectar. He listens to the sound of bees but there are none.

It's so peaceful. The sun plays in the leaves of the distant trees. The breeze ruffles the blades of grass. The sun's so warm. The air's so clear. The sky's so blue. White feet whisper through the grass towards him. Long shapely legs, a white sheer dress, her black hair's down, her eyes twinkle in the sunlight, she comes towards him, she reaches her hands, her lips curl in a smile, he's suddenly as hard as anything—

'Guinevere,' he says, enchanted. He'd dreamed of this moment, how often have they been together, just the two of them, and not a word between them, nothing but glances, all in the eyes, but he knows, and she knows, and that knowledge of each other is forever between them. 'Guinevere, I—'

She reaches for him, he can see the swell of breasts, her taut stomach, her lips so red and full, ready for kissing, she reaches for him, her lips move without sound, whispering his name – he goes to her.

'Don't you fucking *move!*' the crawler shouts. Somehow he had loaded his crossbow and now an arrow flies sure and true. It hits Guinevere in the chest and she bursts apart, becomes a cloud of white butterflies with dark spots on the wings.

The cloud hovers there as though uncertain, for a moment it attempts to reform and Lancelot can see the curves and lines of his secret love redrawn, the secret sorrow in her eyes. He tries to go back to her, then, but the illusion breaks, the lines become jagged, and the cloud of butterflies disperses to the skies and is gone.

'Motherfucker, what did I *tell* you?' the crawler, Gawain, says. 'Don't eat anything, don't touch anything, and for the love of your countryman Christ, don't try to *fuck* anything in the Zone!'

Lancelot whirls and catches him with his fist. The crawler staggers back, regains his balance, stands there.

'*You* did!' Lancelot screams.

The crawler's fist smashes into Lancelot's face.

Lancelot lets it.

He falls back, assumes the first position of the Praying Mantis school.

'Are you sure you want to do this?' he says.

Gawain says, 'You look ridiculous.'

They trade stares like two men over a crooked game of dice.

Gawain starts to laugh. Lancelot lowers his hands and straightens.

'That's years of practice,' he says defensively. 'I once killed three men with just a reed pen.'

'Sounds like a waste of a pen.'

'It wasn't a very good pen.'

He laughs. He does feel a little ridiculous.

'I just wasn't expecting that, you know?' he says.

'Who was she?'

'A... a friend of mine.'

'The lady from the court?'

Lancelot nods.

'Seemed nice.'

'She is.'

'You two...?'

Lancelot shakes his head. 'She's married.'

'Ah.'

Gawain looks at him with some curiosity. 'And that bothers you? That she is?'

'It's complicated.'

'Come on,' Gawain says. 'The Zone's too reactive at the moment. We should be safer when we cross the water. If you see any other manifestations ignore them. Can you do that?'

'I... Yes.'

'Good.'

Gawain hefts his bag and then they're back on the path, and soon the field is gone and they are back in the trees. It gets murky and humid again and the sweat irritates Lancelot's skin. But soon he can hear the sound of rushing water.

When they come on the river they do so abruptly. The ground ends and falls down to a raging torrent of black water. White jagged rocks like teeth peek from just under the surface.

'The Big Water,' Gawain says, and slaps Lancelot on the back. 'Come on.'

They follow the river for a while, until they come to a place where some vast oak had fallen down in time past. Now it overhangs the two sides of the river, the branches black and twisted, and Lancelot suppresses a shudder at the sight.

'You have got to be joking.'

'I've used it in the past. It's a real tree. Solid. It's been on this land for far longer than there's been a Zone.'

'It could be riddled with worms, and hollow.'

'Only one way to find out.'

With that, Gawain simply climbs the fallen tree. He makes his way cautiously but swiftly above the black river, bare-footed, holding on to the thinner branches that poke out from the trunk. Only moments later he's across.

'Well?'

Lancelot breathes, exhales, and runs across the bridge. And he remembers one winter, high in the Sirion, that grandfather mountain that looms over the Lebanon: the master had taken him there in pursuit of some ancient relic. There had been a monastery there, on the highest peak, held by the priests of Ba'al. The only access was a narrow plank across a chasm. The master trained him in the art of cloud walking but the very sight of the abyss made Lancelot falter, and he almost fell, there, at the end.

Then there had been the whole question of the relic, its authenticity or otherwise; and the master got into an argument with the priests of Ba'al, and he and Lancelot had to fight their way out, flaming arrows chasing their escape, the blood of priests hot on the blades of their swords.

'There you go,' Gawain says. 'See? Not so bad.'

Lancelot turns, and he regards him with suspicion. Where is this man really taking him? Lancelot had learned from the master that those who wish to lead us astray nevertheless may lead us where we want to go. And so he follows in the footsteps of this crawler, and knowing all the while that there is a plan in place for him – a trap. The secret to getting out of traps, the master taught him, is to know they're there.

'Sure,' he says. 'No problem.'

'Come on. There's a place nearby where we can camp for the night.'

They walk until they reach the place. It is night by then. Three blackened tree stumps in a row mark it. A ruined stone house stands on the site. It hovers precariously over the precipice, above the Big Water. The bricks are blackened on the inside, as though some enormous fire had erupted there at some point in the past. As they approach, Lancelot can see a small campfire burning in the ruins.

A dark cowled figure sits hunched near the flames.

But Gawain strides confidently. In moments more they arrive in the circle of light and the figure raises its head and looks at them mournfully. Lancelot beholds an ancient face, heavily lined, with a thick beard streaked now in white.

'Oh, crawler, it's you again.'

'Hermit.'

'Who's your friend?'

'Man from Camelot.'

The hermit's eyes are still bright and clear; and they turn on Lancelot with newfound interest.

'From the king's court?'

'Yes,' Lancelot says. He sits beside the fire as Gawain stows their equipment in the ruins.

'How is the dear boy?' the hermit says. 'It's been so long... What are the latest fashions? Do men still style their moustaches with beeswax?'

'Beeswax?' Lancelot says.

'Is that not a thing?'

Lancelot shrugs. 'The king is fine. I do not know about moustaches. And the fashion is as it always was, or so I presume – drinking, fucking and picking fights. Are you...?'

'I was.' The man smiles. It doesn't make him look any younger. 'The name's Pellinore. I served the old king, Uther.'

'But that... You must be...'

'I'm pretty old. I'm not *that* old,' Pellinore says. 'Which reminds me, is Merlin still around?'

'He is.'

'He's a bit of a shit, really, isn't he.'

Lancelot laughs.

'He is,' he says. 'I'm Lancelot, by the way.'

'A pleasure to meet you.'

'And you.'

'Care for a drink? I boil water infused with a lily that grows only in the Zone. It's most calming. And you can taste colour.'

'No... Thank you.'

'No problem. So what brings you here, Lancelot? You're not the usual type Gawain brings into the Zone.'

'How so?'

'For one... You're still alive.'

The old man chortles.

'I'm here on behalf of the king.'

'Is he still fighting his wars?' Pellinore says. He sighs. 'Sometimes I miss it,' he says. 'Old Uther was always fighting. Would have died fighting, too, only his guts gave out.'

'Oh?'

'Poison.'

'Oh.'

'There is nothing here your king could use, you know,' Pellinore says. 'This isn't how the story's written. There's no happy ending for kings. They become by beating or killing the competition, then they rule, then...' He makes a chopping motion. 'Another upstart comes along. And he's young, and he's hungry, and he's just a little bit more vicious and *he's* not scared to die. The king is dead. Long live the king.'

'You know something I don't, old man?'

Pellinore chuckles. 'Word filters in, even here. Heard a name, recently. You know it, perhaps?'

'Mordred.'

'So you have.'

'He's a nobody.'

'Wasn't Arthur a nobody?'

'He was the son of a king!'

'Word is this Mordred is also the son of a king.'

Silence falls between them. The fire crackles in its ring of stones. There are no stars, the clouds have amassed in the skies above.

'Besides, what is a king but the last guy to take power?'

'Why do you say there's nothing here?'

'You're searching for a weapon?' Pellinore's shrewd eyes examine Lancelot. 'Even if there was one, you can't kill everyone. People will come here. They will continue to come. If it isn't the Angles or the Saxons it will be other people, at other times. Europa's just there, beyond the water. What are you going to do, kill them all?'

'Maybe, yes.'

The old knight shakes his head. 'There's no profit in it. And very little humanity. But listen to me blather on. I've grown old and the world beyond seems often like a dream to me. Somehow, the Zone is more real.'

'What *is* the Zone? And how is it that you've survived in it so long?'

'Accommodations have been made.'

'I... I see.'

The old knight laughs. 'Relax! You worry too much. I know why you're really here. It's the mystery that captivates you. You want to *know*. I think, like me, you had a harsh master.'

'I... Yes.'

'And love? Do you have that?'

'I... Yes.'

The old man relaxes. 'Then that is sometimes all you have,' he says. 'Ah, Gawain, there you are.'

The crawler reappears out of the shadows. 'Went scouting ahead,' he says. 'But all is clear.'

'That is good, that is good,' Pellinore says. He yawns. 'I will sleep now. See you in the morning...'

He turns and lies down on his side. In moments he's asleep, his chest rising and falling, loud snores escaping from his lips.

'Go to sleep,' Gawain says shortly. 'We'll start early tomorrow.' He moves into the shadow of the ruins.

Lancelot ponders. He stares at the flames. But the fire's dying and the night's long and dark. He settles on the hard earth. He slows the beat of his heart. He summons sleep. For just a moment he allows himself *her* face in his mind. She turns and the sunlight sparkles in her eyes.

It's all he needs.

In the night he wakes abruptly. He cannot breathe.

Opens his eyes to see Gawain's face above his; Gawain's hands round his throat, choking the life out of him.

65

Lancelot flails wildly. His training's lost. Thumbs press into his windpipe. Gawain seems to be using the classic Green Frog Crouches on Ground hold. Lancelot struggles to emerge out of sleep and fear. Gawain's face swims before his eyes. For one moment it changes, and he sees Guinevere.

Lancelot knife-hands Gawain in the neck. Gawain grunts but keeps the pressure on. Lancelot twists on the hard ground. Raises a kick and spins up in the air. He lands on his feet.

'Mother*fucker*!'

It comes out as a croak.

Gawain comes at him with the same unchanged face. The hermit snores softly on the ground. The fire's dead in the ring of stones. Gawain's fists flash, once, twice, Lancelot counters with the Arimathean Sand Spider. He sweeps Gawain's feet and the flying sword, Secace, comes to his hand. He raises it and strikes.

Gawain comes apart at the blow.

A thousand tiny black spiders scatter away from the blade.

Lancelot sees the real Gawain appear through the trees then, a bewildered, angry expression on his face.

'What are you—'

The false Gawain reforms around the blade. It pulls it out. Its face remains expressionless. It launches a vicious attack then, driving Lancelot back, he whirls and falls to avoid the apparition's fists. His sword flashes and it cuts the false Gawain in half but does no damage. He launches the Monkey's Paw and the King in Yellow and the Turn of the Screw but the thing that is wearing Gawain's face pays them no heed and it pushes, pushes—

Too late, Lancelot realises what's happening. He loses his footing and hears the rumbling of pebbles—

The real Gawain appears behind the apparition and knocks it over the head with a rock. The thing falls on Lancelot, who reaches helplessly up—

For a moment Gawain catches his hand, but then the weight of the apparition pushes him down, down, and he falls, and the false Gawain breaks apart into tiny spiders again and Lancelot hits the cold dark water.

The impact's like hitting stone. He cries out and then the spiders reform and the apparition drags him down, down under the surface. Lancelot flails wildly. He cannot breathe. He kicks with the Boiling Frog and slams his fist into the apparition's cheek with simple brute force but it just won't do, the creature has no real physical form, it cannot be harmed, the air departs Lancelot's lungs, the blackness crawls like spiders into his eyes.

Then, from above, an arrow falls. It pierces the water. When it hits the surface it bursts into a white, intense flame. The arrow flies through the water and pierces the apparition's chest.

The thing screams.

It lets go of Lancelot. The fire burns underwater. The arrow's coated in some material unknown to Lancelot. He kicks desperately upwards. Bursts out of the water, gulps in air. The thing that wore Gawain's face burns in the river. It screams and the sound travels in bubbles up to the surface. For just a moment the thing changes. For one moment more it wears again Guinevere's face. Her eyes are filled with agony.

Then the flow of the river pulls and shoves Lancelot away.

Caught in the current, he can't get out. The river carries him fast and far. It's all he can do to stay afloat. His power wanes. The water tries to suck him back down, to bash him against the rocks. It is an enemy he cannot fight for long.

No stars overhead. It is so dark. But bright yellow eyes watch him from the banks. He is aware of notice being taken. He hears a rumble right ahead.

A waterfall.

Then he does hit rocks; but he goes over them, and down, down again.

Stunned, weakened, he floats in calmer waters. A rock pool, and reeds. He drifts to the bank. Crawls onto hard ground.

Throws up.

For a long time after there is nothing but darkness. When he opens his eyes again it's to rough hands turning him over. Blurry faces look down on him. Then they drag him away and, when he weakly protests, someone hits him matter-of-factly over the head with the hilt of a sword and then there's nothing but darkness again.

'Lancelot... Laaaancelooooot...'

The voice is like a mother speaking to her babes. He can't remember much of his mother or father. Vague images, without sound. Soldiers screaming. His father with a spear in his chest, blood blooming. His mother is just a presence in the memories, he can no longer recall her face. She holds him close, her arms are soft and warm. Then the soldiers pull her away and take Lancelot and he never sees her again.

They sold him in the great slave market of Yathrib. The traders who bought him had little use for him at first. They crossed the desert in a long caravan, the camel men cursing and the hot dry wind blowing all the while.

In the night he woke up and there was a knife in his hand and it was dripping with blood that wasn't his.

'Laaancelohhhtt... Wakey-wakey...'

He tosses and turns. *Go away*, he wants to say. He doesn't *want* to get up. He's had enough of it all. It's all so pointless.

That was when the master found him. Dazed and wandering in the desert, alone, nothing but his footprints in the sand behind him, the pale and merciless moon overhead. Bruised, covered in blood... Alive, somehow.

The master was a shadowy figure. Strangely, he'd left no footprints of his own. It was as though he trod so softly on the sand that he was never there at all.

'I am Joseph,' he stated. 'Of Arimathea. And you look like you could use some help.'

The boy who was not yet Lancelot just stared at him mutely. The master examined him closely, then sighed.

'What tribe?'

The boy just stared.

'Banu Harith? Banu Shutayba?'

The boy just stared.

'Al-Kahinan?'

The boy startled.

'A Jew,' the master said, marvelling. 'How would you like to go back to your ancestral home? I myself am heading to Judea. The order to which I belong is assembling there, in the city of Tiberias. I seek a most precious thing. We call it a grail, but that is just code, to confuse those who would do us harm. Really it is something else entire, something marvell– do you understand anything I am saying right now?'

The boy stared, stubborn, unyielding, and the master laughed.

'You will do, boy,' he said. 'You will do.'

'Lancelot... Lancelot! Get up, you fuck!'

He opens his eyes. A woman's face framed in the light, staring at him furiously. He smiles.

'Hello, Iblis.'

'You *fuck*!'

'So you made it, huh?' he says weakly. He sits up and rubs his head. It thumps with pain.

And something else. He realises he's felt this thumping for a while now. It comes from underground. It comes from the walls. It's like the beat of a great big heart. He stares around him. Old stone walls, a cold floor, torches burning in their alcoves. A dark ceiling.

Doef doef!

Doef doef.

'I always knew you would,' he says.

'Is that why you came here?' Iblis says.

He stares at the walls. They seem to move in time with the beat. Contract and expand, as though they are the lining of some giant lung.

Doef doef. Doef doef.

'No,' he says, distracted. What had he been dreaming, moments back? Something about the desert...

'You shouldn't have come.'

He looks at her properly then. It's still the same Iblis, the one he'd trained with, the one he worked with, the one he hated, the one who knows him better than he knows himself.

Twenty years have changed her. There are new lines round her eyes. A new scar on her cheek. Her hair is short, and streaked with grey. But her eyes are the same, and they are ferocious. The eyes of a bird of prey.

'Why?' he says. 'But it wasn't my choice. I was sent here.'

'We had a deal!'

There is a strange panic in her eyes. He rubs his head. He has no energy for yet another argument. Once upon a time the two of them would argue for days.

'But I honoured it,' he says. 'You had the map and all the time in the world. You must have—'

Doef doef. Doef doef. Doefdoefdoefdoefdoefdoef!

'He's coming!' she says. 'Quick, we don't have long.'

She leans over him. Her features change, are seized somehow. Her lips open and she leans in for a kiss.

'What the—!' he says, and tries to push her away. Her mouth opens fully and something black and wet comes flopping out on his chest, and then another and another – he sees in revulsion they're black slugs.

He jumps up and wipes them off him savagely and stomps and stomps on them until there's nothing left of the creatures but a wet sort of sludge on the floor.

He looks at Iblis and she looks back at him in real horror. Then that strange convolution overtakes her again and her face goes blank and beatific, and she smiles.

'He's here,' she says.

Lancelot can hear the heartbeat fully then and the walls contract and expand and how could he have *ever* thought this was a castle? They are inside the stomach of some giant living thing, they must be, and then he hears the footsteps, slow, and one foot stronger than the other, and a man appears.

He is not a tall man and he is walking with a limp, for he is wounded. There is a pussing open wound, infected in his groin area. A sword slash long ago, perhaps, which never healed. The man is short and old and fat but weirdly he is beaming happily.

'Hello, hello! You must be Lancelot. I've heard so much! We get so few visitors round here. I bid you welcome!'

'Um... Thank you?' He stares at the man, who wears a golden crown on his head, perched at an angle. 'I do not know—'

'Oh, but of course! I am King Pelles. Lord of all that I can see!'

He laughs, and stumbles slightly, and only then does Lancelot realise that the man is blind.

'Won't you join us for a feast? I fear we've grown accustomed to the local food, but Sir Gawain assures me he has some provisions from the outside.'

'Gawain? He's here?'

'He worried that you might be lost and came to seek me. Luckily, I was able to assuage his fears.'

'We are ever so happy here,' Iblis says.

'Ever so happy,' King Pelles agrees. He beams at her and she weaves her arm in his.

'Shall we?'

Lancelot follows them, for all that every instinct screams at him to run.

Through endless corridors like arteries, the torches flickering and the ground shivering and shaking with that endless beat, until they arrive at last at a cavernous throne room, where a small table, rough and inexpertly made of wood, is laid with simple clay plates and spoons for a meal.

Lancelot does not comment, not on the rough uneven chairs, not even on the guest already seated.

Gawain raises his head to him.

'They have soup,' he says.

'Soup,' Lancelot says.

'Mushroom soup,' King Pelles says. 'They grow in profusion in the lower chambers.'

'The lower chambers?' Lancelot says.

'Of the, err…' He waves his hand vaguely. 'The castle.'

'The castle,' Lancelot says.

'They have soup,' Gawain says.

'And drink!' King Pelles says. 'Boiled mushrooms. Very good for the digestion.'

'Digestion,' Lancelot says. Then he gives up.

They sit down. Lancelot does not eat, nor does he drink. From somewhere, Gawain materialises a sealed wine amphora. He opens it and pours.

'How about you?' Lancelot says to Pelles.

'Oh, no,' the king says earnestly. 'I never drink… wine.'

He beams at Lancelot.

'This is so very pleasant.'

'This is so fucked up!' Lancelot screams. He kicks the table over and pulls out his sword.

'Lancelot, no!' Iblis screams.

King Pelles beams. His blind eyes dilate, become black holes. *Something* shoots out of the ground and penetrates him. It animates him like a puppet in a child's play. It makes his mouth move, pumps air into his lungs. When he speaks again it's with a different voice.

'You are... intruder...'

'You bet your fucking ass I am!' Lancelot screams.

'Intruder... alert...'

The torches, for some reason, begin to burn red. The light seems demonic on the contracting and expanding walls. Iblis reaches for Lancelot, he sees the desperation in her eyes. Then she is taken over by whatever *it* is, but she tries to fight it. She opens her mouth and vomits slugs.

'Lancelot... Get... *out!*'

'Iblis!'

The ground shakes. The walls burst at the seams and tear. The heartbeat swallows up all sound. Pressure builds behind Lancelot's eyes, his nose begins to bleed, he staggers back.

'Iblis!'

'Lancelot!' She reaches him. For just a moment her eyes are her own again. She clutches him and holds him tight. A hole opens in the floor. It grows. Something vast and metallic begins to rise out of the ground then all around them. The floor they're on rises. Iblis pushes Lancelot, he rolls, hangs from the side of the fast-rising edifice. He stares down, at the ground far below.

Then Gawain is there, above him. He reaches for Lancelot and Lancelot grabs his offered hand.

Gawain strains to pull him up. Then the world shakes and Gawain loses his balance; and he and Lancelot are thrown from the ledge.

They fall.

Down and down to the ground.

66

Not far from there, at the epicentre of the grail crater, the 63rd reiteration of Galahad the Pure wakes up and screams.

Every small unkindness and minor cruelty he's ever dealt is played through in his brain. Every murder (and really there haven't been *that* many). Every theft and every lie and every terrible action he had perpetrated, at some point or another, in pursuit of his goals.

He really *was* somebody. He was a *knight*, a knight of the Round Table! His word was law, he ran the Gilded Cage, a staff of two hundred hurried to fulfil his every whim! Even the noblest of the lands had to respect him. He had Sir Kay's *ear*!

'You don't *get* it!' he screams.

He is suspended inside a glass vase filled with a green, viscous liquid. The liquid is in his mouth and lungs. Metal filaments run through his body and out again. He squints against the awful murky light. He can just make *them* out outside his prison, studying him.

The real masters of the Zone; the real keepers of the grail.

Then tell us, they whisper, into his mind. He thrusts and struggles against his cage.

'Let me *go*!'

He can see two shadows behind the glass, whirring and

clicking. A terrible light shines through the green murk of the liquid they keep him in and he screams again.

They reach into his mind. They draw the words out of him. They want all of him, all he knows, all he is. The sum of his parts.

He sobs.

'You don't *get* it,' he says. 'It wasn't like that. Those were the *good* times.'

He tries to tell them then. He goes over the story one more time. Starting with Uther. His glorious ascension—

So he murdered the other man? This Vortigern? For power?

'It's not *like* that, don't you ever *listen*—'

He explains about Igraine, Uther's love for her, how it overcame him, how he transformed his features just to be with her, while her husband was away—

He raped her? the voices say, angry, confused.

'No, it wasn't like that, it wasn't—'

They just don't *understand*. He wants to convey to them the *warmth* and *nos*-fucking-*talgia* of the tales. The *glory* of it all! The... The fucking *chivalry*!

But they don't fucking *listen*, do they. They make him question everything. As though it's all so awful, this story of Arthur, just a sad, simple tale of violence and greed.

He sobs again. He sounds like a wounded dog.

His eyes are closed, but there is so much light.

'Alright,' he says. 'Alright.'

We tried so hard, they say, almost in apology, *to keep you all away. It is almost done, now. That thing you call a grail is not a weapon. It will be no use to you. We will go, now, and take it with us. Will you come?*

'No!' he screams. 'I fucking won't!'

We could show you worlds...

He screams and bangs his fists against the glass. But they don't listen. They never do.

In time the light fades. Consciousness flees.

Galahad dies.

His body decomposes. The waste material is reassembled. They are almost done, and yet they cannot leave. They do not understand. They do not understand this story.

Just one more time...

The 64th reiteration of Galahad the Pure wakes up and screams.

Gawain and Lancelot stand at the foot of the hill and watch the ascension of the grail. It really does look a little like a drinking cup, if you squint hard. It's huge and metal and it rises out of the ground and it keeps on rising, until it casts its shadow over the entire Zone.

They're still alive, remarkably. Some unseen force had cushioned their fall, let them escape.

They wait and watch. There is nothing much to say.

A hatch opens in the side of the object. Light shines out. Figures appear.

Lancelot can only see them as shadows. Tall, willowy. The real keepers of the grail.

How his master would have wished to see them. Give them a message, perhaps. But what it would have been, Lancelot has no idea.

He wonders whatever happened to Galahad. But he doesn't really care.

A small figure emerges out of that frame of light. Gawain runs to her and hugs her, crying. When they turn back, the girl's mute but Gawain's smiling through his tears.

'My daughter,' he says.

'Yes,' Lancelot says.

The girl touches her father's face with one finger. Her expression's serene.

'No,' Gawain says. 'No, you can't, please.'

She hugs him again. He hugs her back as though he would never let go. 'Helena, stay—'

She strokes his short-cropped hair and then parts from him. For just a moment, she smiles. It transforms her face, makes her radiant. She lifts her hand and it's goodbye. Then she vanishes into the light, and the door closes.

A terrible screeching and keening sound erupts behind them then. Lancelot turns – nothing surprises him, not anymore – and sees some hideous beast run in a shambling gait towards the vessel.

Behind her comes a figure he now knows – Sir Pellinore.

'Don't go!'

The beast halts. She turns back. She looks at the elderly knight and screams in rage and pain and affection. Then she darts past the vessel and vanishes into the woods.

Sir Pellinore passes them by on his way after her. He smiles as he passes, and waves.

Lancelot waves back. The ground shakes and, with no sound, the great silver vessel rises into the air.

In moments it becomes a mere dot in the sky.

Then it's gone.

'When I file the report back in Camelot,' Lancelot says, 'it might be best to leave out the otherworldly apparitions.'

'It might,' Gawain agrees.

They ride through the old forest. Gawain looks around him in marvel. The trees are just old trees, and the grass is grass. Earlier, he'd picked up a ghost wheel but it crumbled in his hand. When he checked for his stash of leprechaun gold he found that it, too, had vanished.

He reaches for an apple tree, plucks fruit and bites it. It tastes like apple.

The Zone is gone.

'What will you do now?' Lancelot asks him.

Gawain shrugs. 'Rustle cattle, perhaps,' he says.

'You could come with me, back to Camelot. We always have need of good men.'

Gawain says flatly, 'There are no good men in Camelot,' and Lancelot laughs.

'True,' he says affably. 'But the king's coin's solid, all the same.'

Gawain thinks of his daughter. He's all alone. Already the past twenty years seem like a dream. Did the Zone really exist at all? Or was it not so much a place as a state of mind? Had he been trapped there all along?

He grieves for what he'd lost. They ride over the Big Water – now just a gentle river, and with an old but solid bridge still spanning it – and by dusk the next day they reach the edge of the old forest and come back out.

They find the way station much as they had left it, though the building's old, decayed, and the two ancient watchmen who had occupied the place are gone as if they never were. Lancelot opens a wine amphora and they drink it, watching what had been the Zone.

'Look,' Lancelot says. He points to the sky.

Gawain squints. A bright star, floating in the heavens. It grows bigger in the sky. The radiance turns night to day, erases stars.

'Uther's dragon,' Lancelot whispers.

Something plunges down from the skies above the Zone. It falls to Earth. The brightness grows. It almost blinds.

And then it hits.

The burst of light is followed by a towering cloud. The sound only rolls over them later, an earth-shaking, monstrous wave.

'Well,' Lancelot says. 'I guess that's that.'

Somewhere high up in the firmament of heaven, the 65th reiteration of Galahad the Pure wakes up and screams.

PART TWELVE

MORDRED

67

The blade of a sword is subjected, throughout its lifetime, to extraordinary stresses. It is forged in fire, then tempered and quenched. To last, a sword must be pure, without the tiny imperfections that could break an inferior make.

A sword is wielded, and it has one use.

And war is but the use of violence in service of the state.

Outside the window the nights grow long. Camelot's festive, same as it ever was. The merry drunks are crammed into the many hostelries, and on the avenues the prostitutes wear fur. The torches burn over the city. The year is turning, and the winter's cold.

The wizard broods. The air in the castle is draughty, but that is not what bothers him. It feels emptier, somehow. The tapestries are drabber. The servants walk more quietly. As though someone is ill.

It is the *taste* of things that is different. He remembers it with Uther. The taste of power is so strong in youth. So... intoxicating.

But a blade when subjected repeatedly to force must suffer stress. Eventually, all swords shatter. No weapon's made to last.

The taste of it is on Merlin's tongue now. Sour, like an old man's sweat. Bitter, like ground mint leaves after they've been soaked too long. Still with hints of greatness, though: the warmth of blood and the salt of tears and the false sweetness of a poison when administered to an unsuspecting dinner guest.

And Merlin wants it all. It hurts him when it weakens. He craves it like a blind man craves the light, like a knight craves murder, like a junkyard dog needs rats on which to feed.

Merlin is *hungry*!

The very thought makes him ill-tempered and rude.

In the queen's chambers, he can hear Lancelot and Guinevere rutting like pigs.

They had given up all decorum or pretence. Since the knight's return they had been at it all but openly. Earlier, the king himself walked in on them as they fucked. They didn't even stop. Guinevere's pale legs wrapped around Sir Lancelot's brown buttocks. The king said nothing, walked out quietly and shut the door.

They'd always had an arrangement, the queen and he. He isn't sore. But now propriety's abandoned, and in the stories they will write of him, in centuries hence, is this how they will tell it? That he's a cuckold, old and weak? And why? Because a woman dared to choose her own affections?

He knows she doesn't love him. And as for him, he has no love for anyone but the sword.

He's waiting, Merlin knows. He's counting down the days to battle.

'Fuck this,' Merlin mutters. He jumps on the windowsill and turns into a bird once more. He seems to be spending a lot more time in avian form these days.

He flaps his wings. They're stiffer than they used to be. He takes to the air, plunges down, catches a thermal and rises again. Used to be easier, he thinks sourly.

But then, even Merlins get old.

Camelot's a shining pattern of fire below him. In moments the clear cold air takes him away and it vanishes behind, and then there's mostly darkness below. Here and there an isolated village with a fire or two still burning. He flies over a darkening island, with only the stars to guide his way.

And what will they say about *him*? he wonders. Will they portray him as the wild man of the woods? Some have called him that. Will they make him a councillor, a wise man, a guide to kings? Or will they see him as he truly was, just a guy like all of us, just a stranger on a crumbling truss, trying to make his way home?

Will they make him *fat*? Will they give him a *beard*?

The bird that is Merlin shudders. He dives and swoops on the currents.

Merlin follows the stars.

He comes, first, to a place he'd hoped never to visit again.

A ring of standing stones, casting shadows in moonlight.

Like a watching eye.

He thinks of a night long ago, a night much like this one, and a naked figure tied with ropes, and the flash of a blade, and the dark colour of blood as it seeped into the earth.

From above, it just looks like a few big boulders standing there.

But he knows what it really is. What's hidden below. The extensive network of burial chambers.

The *graves*.

This is the Giants' Dance.

Stone-fucking-henge.

This is where the bodies are buried.

He lands a little crookedly in the circle. Stumbles as he turns back into a man.

There are only so many ways into Fairyland but this here's a door painted in blood and grounded in death.

Every scream, every cry, every time someone begged in vain for forgiveness had written and rewritten the world here in runes.

Merlin lifts his staff and *knocks*.

'What do you want now, you cunt?'

A Jenny Greenteeth crawls out of a hole in space and peers at him irritably. 'Shoo! Shoo!'

'Mistress Greenteeth.'

'Oh, Merlin, it's you. *Again*. What do you want?'

'I wish to speak to those who live by water.'

'The mistresses are busy. Come back later.'

'No.'

She sighs. 'Then come through.'

'Not this time.'

'Listen, you little fucker—'

But then someone does come from the other side.

She materialises between the stones and smiles at him. The air shimmers around her and the stars, above, fade and reform, for here they truly are but the lights of the firmament. Merlin can see now the constellations above Fairyland, the Swift and the Gibbet, the Tax Collector and the Door Into Air.

'Hello, little man.'

'Morgause,' he says with loathing.

Her teeth are so white and so sharp. The Jenny mumbles something and slithers back into the other place. Morgause and Merlin circle, the stars keep shimmering, the constellations form and change. Not quite the one world, not quite the other.

'A merry dance,' Morgause comments. 'A merry dance we've led.'

'You won't get away with it.'

'Oh, Merlin.' She laughs at him. 'I already have.'

'I won't let you.'

'Come, come, little man. You've had your fun. You've hogged the sandbox. Now it's time for someone else to play. You can't say we've not played you fair. You've had your golden age, your mythic time of peace and calm, prosperity, the bards will sing of this age of marvels—'

She doubles over herself laughing.

'Screw you!' he screams.

'You wish, you little turd!'

The venom's always there, just below the surface.

They circle and circle each other.

'So what now?' he says.

She shrugs. 'The game's the game, same as it ever was.'

'He's just a delinquentis,' Merlin says. 'A, a *punk*.'

'You hush your mouth. He's mine. And he's got a legitimate claim to the throne.'

Merlin snorts. 'As if *that* ever mattered.'

Morgause's eyes glint in the starlight. 'Don't overreach yourself, little Merlin. What's done is done. Your boy is weak. He's had his time. Now scram.'

'Alright.' He's breathing hard. 'Alright. I'll go.'

She flashes those teeth at him again. Twirls in a dance. 'Such good times we had here, in the old days. Do you remember?'

'Yes,' he whispers. 'Yes.'

The screams, and the earth so very dark with blood...

'I'll see you soon,' she says. She blows him a kiss.

Then she's gone like the mists. The stars assume their ordinary shapes, as recorded by Ptolemy: Andromeda, Cassiopeia, Hydra and Sagittarius.

'Fuck you,' Merlin mutters. Then he transforms into a bird again and gets out of there fast.

The starlight guides him.

In bird shape, Merlin flies towards the sea.

From high above the Earth, everything looks simpler.

The bird can see the torches on the sand – lit, then hastily extinguished.

Can see the long boats glide silently along the waves, coming in from Ireland.

Eire-land. Merlin shudders. There is a reason Arthur never ventured beyond the waters to that godsforsaken place. Not only are its inhabitants half-giants and man-eaters, so it's said, who'd suck the tender flesh right off your bones and smack their lips for more. But worse, they have their own wizard, some Christianist magic man, Pádraig they call him; and even Merlin fears the wily old codger. They say he has the staff of one of those Egyptian magic men of old; that he can speak to ghosts and make trees come to life, and that he'd driven all the snakes from Ireland.

Now Merlin's not saying this is true. Far as he knows they never had no snakes in Ireland to begin with. But he's not saying they're *not* true. You mustn't underestimate the power of this new church out of Rome. They have their own fanatics, worse than druids, and they're as fond of a sword as any greedy knight. No. Best leave the Irish to their pirate ways. You don't know what they're capable of, not with the Judeans' god on their side.

He watches the smugglers meet the pirates on the shore. The offloading is brisk, efficient. The bird swoops, circles.

Notes grain, leather goods, freshly slaughtered beef.

The bird crows.

Then notices the other two ships coming in.

Heavier loads.

Sees the boy, Mordred, open one crate and take out the goods.

A sword, newly forged.

Bundles of arrows, neatly tied.

The smugglers offload. Crates and crates of the things.

Weapons, changing hands. An arms shipment – a hefty one. Interesting.

Money's exchanged. The pirates count their gold and leave.

The smugglers take their shipment and skedaddle.

They run dark and fast. Unmarked paths with no light to guide them. But they know the way. The bird follows at a distance. They depart the beach and climb a narrow cliff. Rough stairs hewn into the stone. Tunnels that weave and part.

One can vanish there without a trace. Even the bird finds it hard to follow.

They come at last to what must be their nest. Shouts of triumph, and greetings to those who were left.

The bird huddles in an alcove and waits.

Torches are lit. In their light the boy, Mordred, freezes.

He drops his sword.

His men on their knees on the ground. A stone table laden with goods, and around the table sit men with the tans and hard lines of life spent on the sea.

'We *told* you, boy, not to cross us.'

'Master Brastius, I—'

'Save your breath.'

The older man stands. Spreads his arms. His soldiers surround Mordred's men. No one moves.

'We are the Legionem Maris!' the man roars. 'The Council of the Sea! Who rules the coast?'

'We do!'

'Who runs the goods?'

'We do!'

'Who pays the tax?'

'We don't!'

The man roars with laughter. And Merlin thinks of all these riches smuggled in from Ireland past the king's taxmen. A fortune lost to Camelot. Grain and leather and beef.

But it is the swords that bother him; and what's more, he had not seen the ones carrying the swords arrive yet in this hall.

'Not a finger of leather goes through these ports without me getting my share!' this man, this Brastius, says. 'Not a single drum of wine leaves from here to Ireland without my say so! Who has the best steaks?'

'We do!'

'Who has the finest Irish wenches?'

'We do!'

'Who rules the coast?'

'We do! We do! We do!'

The man lowers his arms. He stares sourly at Mordred.

'And yet you thought you could do as you wish? You thought you could circumvent *us*? What gives you the *right*, boy!'

Mordred stands straight. Merlin can admire that about him. He looks this Brastius straight in the eyes. He shrugs. Almost apologetically.

'This,' he says.

Then the air is full of whispers. An arrow hits Brastius and goes through his left eye. He opens and closes his mouth like a fish. Then flops down lifeless on the table.

The archers step forward from the shadows. The men of the Legionem Maris are all dead, and so are their soldiers.

Mordred smiles.

He turns to his men.

'Gentlemen,' he says, 'Please take a moment to pay your respects.' Then he laughs, turns, and hawks a gob of phlegm on Brastius' corpse.

'Brastius! You useless old shit! This is a new day, a new dawn, for the coast – and for all of Britannia! Who rules the sea?'

'We do!'

'Who'll rule this land?'

'You will!'

'You bet your fucking asses I will! Somebody grab this bird.'

Too late, Merlin tries to flee. Someone has crept up on him all this while. A black sack comes down on him and the string tied up. He struggles wildly but he's blind. He's lifted, pulled, and before he can do anything he's taken violently out of the sack and shoved into a wooden cage.

He's trapped.

A young, smiling face peers at him through the bars of his tiny prison. A hand holding seeds. Mordred feeds them into his cage.

'Hello, uncle,' Mordred says.

★

Merlin pecks at the seeds. Merlin watches the boy. This Mordred.

He's handsome, he'll give him that. Dresses in black, and there's a jaunty sword at his hip. A cruel smile, cold eyes, sensuous lips. So young. He's like a newly forged blade.

But what arrests Merlin is the taste in the air.

The boy *reeks* of power.

The bird's so hungry for it. Mortals live so quickly but intensely. Merlin watches the men unload. Swords and knives and bows and arrows. How long has this been going on? he thinks. In Camelot, he did not think to look this way until too late.

And yet, and still – it's nothing! Arthur has an *army*, he has a *kingdom*, he could crush a hundred Mordreds without working up a sweat.

There's something Merlin's not *getting*, here.

Something he's missed.

He watches them move about. There's an air of quiet efficiency. And it dawns on him that they are preparing to depart from that place. That all this – whatever *this* is – has been planned and put in motion long ago.

'Enjoying the hospitality, uncle?'

Merlin crows and takes a shit in the cage. The bird droppings fall on the table and Mordred laughs.

'It won't be long,' he says. 'I promise.'

He mimes twisting a bird's head off and laughs again. It's all he seems to do. Merlin's wings beat in panic against the bars of the cage.

'Oh, don't worry,' Mordred says. 'You're family. Although I wonder what you'd taste like, roasted on the coals and basted in olive oil and wild garlic. Oh, *relax*!' He knocks on the cage and moves away.

Merlin dozes through the long hours. The men come and

go, and they take their crates of arms with them. Somewhere, Mordred will be assembling an army, but what army could he possibly raise against the king?

Delusions of grandeur, Merlin thinks. The boy's a provincial, he has no true idea of what it is he thinks to do.

And still, that niggling worry that he's missed something.

The bird dozes until weak sunlight, stealing in through holes high in the stone ceiling, wakes it.

The warehouse, Merlin sees, is all but abandoned now. The crates are gone, and the men with them. He sees Mordred at the far end, in the shadows, pacing.

Like he's waiting for someone important, and the someone important is late.

The bird feigns sleep. Watches the boy. Pacing and pacing. Glances sharply, just the once, at Merlin, but the bird's asleep.

Pace, pace, pace, p—

Hello. What's this, then.

Someone does appear. Who is it? Merlin strains but he can't make him out. An indistinct shape, not tall of stature. Military bearing, though.

Speaks very quietly.

Mordred listens. Nods. Aha. Aha.

Like the boy's not the king in waiting he makes himself out to be.

Almost like he's being given *instructions*.

Interesting. Yes. Yes. For just a moment the bird's wings erupt. They bang against the side of the cage. The other man, the one Mordred's talking to, turns and looks. For just a moment the light from above catches his face and his *attire*, and Merlin *sees*, and he thinks, Oh, shit!

It all makes sense now!

He tries to flee his cage. He needs his *magic*, damn it! But the bars are soaked in some magic-dampening potion, or he'd have fled hours ago.

He has to get *out*!

'Shoot that fucking bird!' Mordred screams.

Merlin panics. He slams against the bars of the cage, over and over. The cage shakes, tumbles, and takes him with it. It crashes to the floor.

Mercifully, the door springs open upon impact.

Merlin bursts out. An arrow whistles but he's not *fucking around* anymore and he snaps it mid-air as he transforms, and kills the archer with a contemptuous click of his fingers; though it costs him, this transference of energeia, or what*ever* it is: don't ask Merlin to explain fucking *magic*.

He limps a little. He's *really* not as young as he used to be. He throws a bolt of unholy fire at Mordred, which the boy repels – too easily. Then the boy charges at him with a sword, and Merlin turns and stumbles.

He curses.

They fire arrows at him but he dodges them, using the last of his strength. He transforms once more into a bird, takes to the air, heads for those distant holes in the stone ceiling. He almost reaches...

Then he looks down, and sees no one's firing anymore.

And the boy, Mordred, is *smiling*.

Then Merlin reaches the exit and he beats his wings against the cold air and shoots up, and out.

Dawn kisses the horizon over the grey sea. Ireland in the distance, and white-sailed ships out on the waves. Fish leap in the shallows. Dolphins rise to the surface out beyond the breakers, call out a greeting to this new day.

How he loves this fucking land, he thinks then.

He crows into the rising sun and the waves answer his call. He swoops on the wind, loosens his bowels and shits down the rock hole, where he hopes it will hit Mordred in the eye.

Then he races the sun back to Camelot, to warn the king that Mordred's working in cahoots with the Anglo-Saxons.

PART THIRTEEN

THE LAST BATTLE

68

t is an overcast day when they go to war. The dogs bark in the alleyways of Camelot and all the sundials are out of commission. It is as though time itself has momentarily stopped. In the brothels and beer houses the workers peer out of windows at the marching knights. The drums that beat the march are muffled. Ravens huddle on the rooftops like fat drops of rain.

'Eli, Eli, Lama Sabachthani?'

A priest in a Christian burial ground on the outskirts of the city prays as he looks up at the sky. Will it rain?

Washing hangs on the lines. The flower sellers do no trade. Street kids dart to look at the army. So many men, so many swords. Had there been sun, its light would shine off metal helmets, shields. The men move softly. If it rains there will be mud.

Horses with carts pull their supplies. The horses whinny softly, perhaps impressed by the gravity of events. They shit big steaming piles as they go. A lone black cat sits curled on the stone steps of a mithraeum. She has placed her bet long ago. Now she watches to see who will come on top in this game of soldiers.

It's still morning.

Remember Camelot. This city built of mud and magic, where the Round Table sits, where Merlin's tower shines across the plains like a beacon. Where knights who are legends in their own lifetime walk the streets like ordinary people, stop for a piss against the wall of a leatherworker shop, where a vicious knife fight might erupt at any moment outside the Gilded Cage, and draw the betting men and women as spectators.

Here is the forum and here is the zoo, and it is said the queen keeps peacocks and adders. Here are the sellers of Goblin Fruit and candied apples, here are the temples and brothels to satisfy every need and urge. Here come some Christian missionaries, long used to the turmoil of empire, pulling a cart laden with manuscripts. Here the *Novum Testamentum* and Augustine's *Confessions*. Here is Chrysostom's *Against the Jews*. Here is James's *Second Apocalypse*, here *The City of God*, here a book of simple hymns.

The missionaries are making a run for it, it seems. They pick no sides beyond that of the winner. Their gospel, born in hot Judea, tempered in the blood of Rome, is ready like a blade to pierce the hearts of infidels on this remote, cold island.

Black clouds amass on the horizon.

It will rain.

It always rains, in this God-forsaken land.

'Will he come?'

'Will he come?'

In the rooms the women come and go. Edith holds a scented handkerchief to her face. She stands by the window, looking at the men passing on the street below. Already some of the women speak of following the troops. The men will need company, and what need do tomorrow's dead have for today's coin? There is money to be made on the battlefield. Already in the courtyard the mules and wagons are assembled and the women pack all that is needed: tents and pillows, curtains and Greek ticklers, Roman candles and nightcaps and sheaths, oils and perfumes.

'Will he come?'

But Edith has made other plans, and now this king's war for the soul of the nation has ruined them. Will he come, already? She breathes in the scent of crushed roses. The knights in their passing raise a vast cloud of dust. The sun's hidden behind the clouds, and it's cold. She shivers in her gown.

Then he's there – 'Edith!'

'Bedivere!'

He grins and lifts her in a crushing hug. Oh, he *does* love her, he does, he does! She covers his face with kisses.

'I cannot tarry long. We ship today, to Camlann.'

'Camlann,' she says, 'Camlann, where the fuck is Camlann!'

He cups her breast. His breathing comes faster then.

'I do not know, nor care,' he says.

'Oh, Bedivere! Let's run away together! Forget this war! I see nothing but death foretold.'

He pulls her closer. He's so hard, so desperate. She responds to the heat of his body. He pulls off her shift and she pulls him out. He's so stiff. He cries out when she touches him.

'I can't,' he says. 'But you will see, we'll come back covered in glory.'

He enters her. She runs her fingers in his short-cropped hair. He's fast, relentless.

Scared, she thinks.

Yet it excites her, too.

'...Don't go.'

'I must.'

He's already buckling on his sword again. The army marches outside.

'I'll never see you again,' she says.

He gives her a kiss on the cheek, strangely chaste.

'I'll come back and buy you from the house and we shall live like man and wife and make a family.'

'I want a little boy,' she says. 'I'll name him Arthur, after the king.'

'You will have all you want and more,' he tells her. 'Servants so you'd never have to lift a finger. Cooks and gardeners and nannies for the children. We'll live upriver in a mansion outside Londinium, and piss downstream.'

She cries in his arms. He is so hard and so young and so untampered. A blade is not a blade if it's not used to kill. A sword's no good for chopping up cucumbers.

'...Goodbye.'

He leaves her. She looks out the window, trying to pick him among the throng. But all the soldiers look the same, and the dust of the road swallows them until they're gone.

But always there are those for whom the great event simply doesn't matter, who are playing Roman ball and ghost in the graveyard on the edge of town, in a muddy field.

'Look at them all,' Little Bevan says, and he spits on the ground. 'All going to war, like. They say this Mordred's a demon with black ichor in his veins.'

'Never!' Crazy-Eye Arty says. He kicks the ball and it bounces off the ash tree and hits Chicken-Feet Calum in the face.

Everyone laughs.

'*I* heard he eats the hearts of little babies!'

'Shut up, that ain't true!'

'*I* don't think anything's gonna happen,' Gildas says. He's a little bigger than the other boys. '*I* think there is no enemy. *My* daddy says—'

'Your daddy's a deserter!'

They all laugh and Gildas's face turns red. He chases Little Bevan round the field but Little Bevan can move fast when he wants to.

'*Your* mummy smells!'

'Take that back!'

'You take it back!'

Finally cornered, Little Bevan squares up to Gildas. They start punching each other in the dust as the other children cheer them on.

Along the road, oblivious, the soldiers march on and on.

'Tell them...' the boy says, and then he looks uncertain. The old letter-writer working on the steps of the forum as he has for years looks up at him with eyes that have seen everything already. 'Tell them... You take dictation, right?'

'I do.'

'You just write whatever I say?'

'That's how it works.'

'But I don't know *what* to say to them.'

'Your ma and da?'

'And young Elsbeth, what thinks I'm lord and master of Camelot.' The boy smiles fondly.

'Girlfriend?'

'My sister.'

'Ah.'

'Tell them...' The boy stares. 'Tell them we're shipping out today, to war. Tell them we're going to a place called Camlann. I don't know what it's like, there. The king says it will all be over as soon as it's begun. A new day for Britain. A new dawn. Tell them... We are resolute of spirit and ready for battle. No. I don't know.'

'It's alright,' the old letter-writer says gently.

'Just tell them I love them.'

The old man writes. The young man pays him his coin.

Then he, too, is gone, to join his comrades on the long march to their war.

But for many, life must carry on as normal:

'But this is not what I ordered.'

'This is the suit.'

'But I asked for the forest green. This is spring green.'

'Sir, the pigment we use is exactly as the sample you picked.'

'This is not what I ordered. And also it does not fit neatly round the stomach.'

'Sir, the measurements were quite precise at the time of their taking—'

'Are you saying I gained weight?'

'Sir, I am not saying—'

'I demand to speak to the manager.'

'I am the manager, sir.'

'This is unacceptable. I have a function tonight at the Merchants' Guild. I must look my best!'

'Sir, we can offer a discretionary ten per centum discount, seeing as—'

'Very well. And you can make the adjustments?'

'Right away, sir.'

'Get to it, then, man!'

'Very good, sir.'

'Here comes Papa,' Deirdre says to the baby in her arms. She rocks it and croons. 'Here comes Papa now, to say how much he loves you.'

The tread of footsteps in the yard. Sir Morien, in battle dress. He kneels down, kisses Deirdre on her brow.

'Shh, he's sleeping.'

Sir Morien strokes the baby's head. Can feel the pulsing soft spot on the baby's skull. How much he loves this little creature. He kisses him, inhales that smell of baby and sweet milk.

'Papa is off to war,' Deirdre says, and smiles at her baby.

'I wish I didn't have to go,' Sir Morien says.

'You'll make us proud. You serve your king and country. Defend us from the traitor, Mordred, and his rebel kin. It will all be over well before the winter solstice.'

'I hope so,' Morien says. 'Can I...?' he says.

She gives him the baby, gently. He holds him in his arms.

'Morien,' he says, marvelling. His son, how is it that he has a son?

'He'll be a knight like you,' Deirdre tells him.

He looks at her – so vibrant with the birth, her skin aglow, her huge brown eyes are so alive. He knows she's tired, the child has been keeping her up, always hungry the little creature, hungry and strong. They'd lost the previous one, a little girl. They never talk about it. When this one was born healthy they had hugged without words.

He wishes for his son to grow. To live. He doesn't wish a soldier's life upon him. But Deirdre does, she's always full of stories from the washing yard, of what the queen said today and what the king wore for the parade, and everyone says this Mordred's but a bastard child with a ragtag group of men – it will all be over well before the solstice. So she says and he loves her too much to disagree. He hugs the baby to his chest and wishes time would stop but it does not. He hands him back. He kisses Deirdre. And then he leaves them, and there is only the tread of his boots on the muddy ground, the tread of his boots on the muddy ground until the sound fades away and is gone.

The giant, Maelor Gawr, catches up with her by the stables.

'My lady queen,' he says.

She's busy saddling the horse. He notes she's back to her old outfit. Her hair's cropped short and she's wearing dagger and sword. She whistles 'Let All Mortal Flesh Keep Silence', but stops when she sees him.

'My Lady Guinevere, I cannot let you—'

'Fuck off, Gawr,' she says shortly.

'My Queen, you cannot ride to join him in the battle!'

She stops, startled, and actually laughs.

'You think I am going to *him*?'

The giant looks confusedly at her. 'But where else—'

'You fucking giant fool. I've had it with this crap. Shitting Arthur, boys and their wars. This was only ever a temporary arrangement.'

'My Queen! You *married* him!'

'Are you really this naïve, or merely stupid?'

The giant rumbles. Guinevere ignores him and mounts her horse.

'I'll go to Europe, maybe,' she says. 'They have plenty of riches to plunder. All a story needs is a woman and a sword.'

'My Lady Guinevere?'

'Fuck off,' she says; not unkindly. Then she spurs the horse and, before the giant knows it, she's gone for good.

In a copse of trees outside the city, three of the Ladies of Water stand beside the bubbling cauldron.

'When shall we three meet again, in thunder, lightning or in – oh, fuck, it's raining.'

'It always rains, dear Cailleach,' says Thitis sweetly.

The Queen of Winter turns an icy gaze on her. 'Oh, fuck off,' she says.

'Fuck you!'

'Ladies, ladies!' Morgan says. She stirs the water in the cauldron. The reflection of the dull skies and grey clouds shifts and changes when the raindrops hit the surface. An image forms: black hills, a distant shore, a wide plain shorn of grass. It might have been one of those places that the Romans mined for silver, back when there was still a Rome to matter to anyone here. An industrial landscape, blasted and gouged and bleak.

It will do, she thinks. It is as fine a place for men to die as anywhere.

'When the hurly-burly's done,' she says softly. 'When the battle's lost and won.'

'But lost and won by who?' says Thitis.

Cailleach stirs from her pondering. 'I am sure you have your favourites, dear Thitis.'

'As do you.'

'I care not for either. My Picts will hold the Romans' wall against whoever wins. My white-skinned devils care not for British Celts nor the Germanic Saxons.'

'Your Picts are hooligans who think meat pudding's a gastronomic miracle.'

'Fuck you.'

'Fuck you!'

'Ladies, *please*,' says Morgan. She stirs the cauldron. The water shimmers. The sea is not far from the plains. The mermaids sing beneath the waves. She sees white sails and dark clouds, a storm on the horizon. Sea spray and crying birds, and a single boat, sailing on the sea towards a distant shore.

An islet illuminated in searing white light like a beacon.

A premonition. She stirs the pot and the water turn to dull reflection. The rain falls down. She knows the ground will soon turn into mud. The knights will spend a miserable first night on the road.

'I'll see you later,' she says.

'Not if we see you first, Morgan.'

'Whatever.'

She turns into a raven and flies away. Thitis slinks into the distance, a cat: Graymalkin. The Queen of Winter summons fog. She drifts away, a cloud.

The cat will feed tonight on soldiers' scraps. The fog will cling to their clothes and dampen their spirits, and hide the world from their sight. And as for Morgan...

Morgan has business elsewhere.

69

The torches burn over Dinas Emrys. They burn over Londinium. They burn over Tintagel.

And in their light the soldiers march.

They march away from hearth and home. They do not know what's waiting there, at Camlann. But they go all the same, for king and country, to give their blood for this land.

Merlin watches them all. And he wonders what it is about mortals, who are so ready to die. For what is land? he thinks. It isn't for a people. It can't be *owned*. Land knows no *fealty*. It was there before people ever trod upon it, and it will be there long after they're gone. In time even the memories of these marching ghosts will fade. The Earth will turn and turn. The sun will grow dim, burn red – in time even the sun will fade.

All people are is the dust of old stars.

Yet here they are nevertheless, these conscious beings of reconstituted matter. Marching blithely along, ready to die for an idea that makes no sense if you stare at it head on. This island's just a piece of Europe with the land bridge submerged, just another clump of dirt in the middle of an ocean, on a world that spins through space, in a universe older and weirder than anything even a Merlin can imagine.

Why would you die for this? he wonders. Would it not be better to simply *live*?

But he has learned such questions have no answers a Merlin, with his mere logic, can answer. And so he watches the soldiers march to Camlann.

It doesn't really matter, he thinks, this matter of Britain.

Just another way to pass the time.

'Da? Da, it's me.'

Bors the Younger stoops by the bed. The window's open. He can smell roses in bloom, and the rain.

'Da, you should see them go. Perfect formation. Roman legion standard. Drilled and trained, full kitted. Swords polished and sharp. Shields clean and oiled. Oh, Da, they look glorious! If only you could see them now, just how you trained them all these years.'

But Bors the Elder doesn't speak. Bors the Elder doesn't stir from his bed. How small he seems. How thin. His eyes are milky-white and blind. And Bors the Younger takes his father's hand in his and feels how fragile the bones have become. How cold the old man feels. And he tucks the furs tight around his father's body.

'Oh, Da!'

The nightjars call outside. The rain patters gently on the rose bushes. Bors the Younger shakes his head, perhaps to clear it. When do our parents become our children, he thinks. And he stokes the fire to drive away the chill in the room, and he sits by his father's bedside, and he talks late into the night, telling him fairy-tales: of fabulous battles and glory and blood, of chivalry and wild romance.

'I got a bad feeling about this one, Lucan. If our guts don't spill in that bullshit valley, first thing when we get back to Londinium I'm paying my two denarii so that Brastius here can dip his wick in the inkwell of an Aldgate tart.'

The men laugh.

'Brastius here's gonna die a virgin, boss. Chances are he'll have his guts splayed in the dirt before some fisherman's feet 'fore he ever gets to bite the fruit on that tree of knowledge.'

They huddle round the small fire. All about them, extending to the horizon, are encampments, men and tents, equipment, livestock, carts and campfires. Brastius takes the ribbing with a smile. These men are his best friends. He'll die for them just as they would die for him.

'You ever finger a holy grail, Brastius?'

The men laugh. Brastius wraps the greased leather coat over himself. He stares into the flames.

'When do we get there?' he says quietly.

'A few more days of marching, I reckon.'

'A few more days...'

'Play us a song, Lucan. You're good with the harp. Something cheery and bawdy.'

'You know "There Once Was A Girl From Dubris"?'

He strums the strings of the harp. His voice is lovely there, under the stars. The soldiers quieten down as Lucan sings. They laugh when he mentions the girl's golden fleece, and roar when he gets to her altarpiece. Other soldiers, round other fires, join in, and the tune spreads, across the length of the camp, until it seems to envelope the entire world.

'What are they doing *now*?' Kay complains. He turns to Agravain. 'I do wish Galahad was here. He was always good with the logistics.'

'Galahad was a shit.'

'Galahad was a *useful* shit. Which is more than I can say for you.'

Kay rubs his temples. This is a nightmare, he thinks. He is against this march, this battle Arthur's so bloody keen on. The administration of this march alone is making his ulcer worse. Supply lines and road maintenance and setting up camp and feeding the troops, and *trying* to maintain *some* sort of latrines in a field situation... This is the problem with kings, he thinks, equal parts fond of Arthur and exasperated. They don't think of the *implications*! To go to war, someone has to hire *cooks*! Maintain discipline, make sure the roads are clear after the rains, ensure provisions, medical supplies, lines of communication—

Arthur thinks it's just like in the old days, when they were boys, when all you needed for a fight was a knife and a yard, and somewhere to stash the bodies after.

Fuck this, he thinks. He's too *old* for war. All he wants to do is be back home at the Gilded Cage, where you can never tell if it is night or day, and there is always music...

'What do you want me to do?' Agravain says.

'Do? Everything!' Kay says. 'Look, go and talk to the company commanders at least. Get these idiots to shut up and go to sleep. We march at first light tomorrow.'

'Come on, they're just letting off steam. They're kids,' Agravain says.

'Just... do it, will you? Go!'

Agravain gives him a sullen look but complies.

Kay stares at the paperwork on the desk. Bills of lading and promissory notes, endless lists of inventory and accounts... He lifts up the pen, takes a fresh sheet of parchment, and starts to do sums.

'Daddy? Daddy!'

The green children run to the giant figure that comes striding towards them through the forest. Bercilak lifts them up in a bear hug, tosses them to the sky as they shriek with laughter.

'Neve! Mercury! Shana! Acanthus! Jack-in-the-Green! Penny! Oh, hello, which one are you?'

'He's only a *baby*,' one little girl says. The Green Knight picks up the baby and strokes his green hair. Tiny foliage already grows behind the baby's ears.

'I'll call him Bolton.'

'That's a stupid name! And it's a girl.'

'I'll call *her* Bolton, then!'

'Daddy, you're *silly*!'

The Green Knight roars and the children scamper as he chases after them.

'You'll never catch *us*!'

'Quick, in the canopy!'

'I'm a root!'

In moments they vanish in the forest. Only their eyes gleam bright, staring at him as they try so hard not to giggle.

'I'm sure I can't see you,' Bercilak says. 'Anyway, where's your mummies and things?'

'All about.'

'All about, eh?'

'Daddy' – a small boy rematerialises from the bark of an oak – 'are you going to the war?'

'Sure am, kiddo.'

'But isn't it… dangerous?'

Bercilak laughs. He pulls out his long sword and shows it to them. 'I am a knight!' he says. 'A knight of the Round Table! I am the bestest fighter in the land! I eat the hearts of men and sheath my manhood with the lining of their intestines! Also, I am a primeval manifestation of the forest given human form. So, you know. Not that easy to kill.'

'Daddy, you're the bravest!'

'I know, kiddo. I know.'

'Can we play catch again?'

'Let's play hide and seek!'

'Grr!' the Green Knight roars. The children scamper, shrieking.

He gives them a count of ten before he gives chase.

*

Day turns to night and night to day and back again. The moon streaks across the sky. Stars blink and fade, the Earth – as propounded by Aristarchus of Samos, at least – revolves around the sun. Time, which Parmenides has argued is nought but an illusion, nevertheless passes.

The soldiers march.

They come from Camelot. From Londinium. From Tintagel and from the Glastonbury Tor and from the line held against the Picts along the Wall.

And they converge, at last, on that bleak and barren plain men call Camlann.

Where the enemy's army is waiting.

70

The clash of steel on steel. The screams of dying men. A horse breathing his last in the mud. It rains. The whisper of arrows flying overhead. The hiss of a flame. The dull thud of a lance as it pierces bone. The hiss of warm blood from an artery. The distant crackle of thunder and the muffled beat of the enemy's drums.

All that and more.

Lightning illuminates the battleground. It's like a war painting by Aristides of Thebes. The bright vermilion of mercury sulphide. The black of charcoal. The startled white of lead. Perhaps a hint of ochre yellow to complete the classical four-colour composition of the picture. The sun, perhaps, the promise of a dawn hidden just behind the curvature of the Earth.

'White Company, to me!' screams the Black Knight of the White Hill Gang. They charge across the battlefield. The swords that flash, the spears that bite! Beware the White Hill Gang, and run, before the fearsome knight!

'South Londinium company, to me!' shouts Sir Daniel von dem blühenden Tal of the Frankish mob. His men give cheer, and follow him to meet the foe. And on, and on:

'Bors Company!'

'The Bastards!'

'Men of the Hard Hand, to me!'

'Attack!'
'Attack!'
And snicker-snack, there's only forward, there's no way back. The glorious battle, the wounded and dead, the mud and the screams and the blood and the blood and the bl—

'Nasty business,' Sir Pellinore says. He's perched on a rock, on a crag, overlooking the field of battle. He munches on an apple.

The Questing Beast warbles in an awful, mournful cry. Sir Pellinore passes her a slice of apple and she chews it.

'Perhaps it's time for you and I to retire,' the old knight tells her. 'Things are going to be different, after this, I think. The world is changing. There will be less room in it for fanciful things. And my bones ache in the cold weather.'

The Questing Beast warbles in affection; but whether she's convinced or not, the old knight cannot tell.

They watch the fight unfold. It's hard to tell who'll win. The old knight learned, a long time ago, that there aren't really any winners in a war, just lots of losers. Life's such a fleeting thing. It's gone in moments. Sometimes he wonders if his true achievement isn't simply that he's lived so long.

What is it all *for*? he wonders. The apple's sweet, with just a hint of sour. More and more now he's glad of that long-ago viper's bite, and the birth of his daughter, which took him away from court and set him on this different path. Forever questing, in pursuit of that which eludes you – and isn't that, in microcosm, life?

Those men on the battlefield, they're barely stories. Just build-up with a sudden end. At least Sir Pellinore, say what you will of him, will have beginning, middle and an end.

A bird comes to rest beside him. It turns, not unexpectedly, into a man.

'Well, this is a giant fuck-up,' Merlin says.

'It's nice to see you too,' the old knight says.

'I *tried* to warn him. But he wouldn't listen.'

'His father never was a man for listening when calls the blood.'

'This Mordred,' Merlin says, 'he's joined up with the Anglo-*fucking*-Saxons.'

'I say, that's bad!'

'That little *cunt*!'

'Indeed, indeed. Well, some would say they have a right to live here too,' the old knight says, then instantly regrets it. Merlin's fury's like the sudden storm that tosses fishing boats into the depths.

'I will see them wiped off the face of the Earth!'

Sir Pellinore somehow doubts that; but he wisely keeps that to himself. They're not so bad, these Johnny Anglisc, these Johnny Come-Latelys. Strange, for sure, with their guttural tongue and their continental manners. And they're fond of bloodshed as much as the next man. But they love their children, and they make beautiful jewellery, there really are some talented artists in their midst. And who's to say whose land this is, really? Land's just land. You may as well say it's owned by the ants or the birds or the stags who live upon it. Do *they* not have a claim?

But Sir Pellinore is just a foolish old man, surely. And so he keeps these thoughts to himself.

'Apple?'

'Thank you.'

They chew this fruit of the Earth in companionable silence, and watch the battle commence.

An arrow through the eye takes down Daniel von dem blühenden Tal.

A dagger through the ribs for Escanor the Large.

The Black Knight of the White Hill Gang: trampled to death under the hooves of panicked horses.

★

'Regroup! *Charge!*'

The main forces of Hengist and Horsa and their clans are not even *there*. They wait beyond, as Mordred and his men do battle. Only a select engagement of Angle and Saxon mercenaries swell up Mordred's ranks – but it just might be enough.

Lancelot sweeps through the battlefield like a dancer. He slashes and kicks, flies overhead with his sword arm extended, separating heads from their owners, hearts from their beats. He is a one-man war engine, like some Trojan War hero summoned from the feverish imagination of Homer's whacked-out brain.

Beside him Bercilak, the Green Knight, roars as he swings a giant tree he's using as a club. It sweeps up men and horses, it impacts with a thud that breaks whole skeletons inside their meat coats, that bursts eyes as though they were jellied sweets.

'Vivi tu, vivi, o Santa Natura!' screams the Green Knight.

'Im ein ani li, mi li!' screams Lancelot, quoting Hillel. *If I am not for myself, then who will be for me?*

'Die!' screams Geraint, before he gets a lance in his guts and speaks no more.

Tor, set on fire by a flaming arrow.

Gareth and Cynric, hacked to pieces with long fishermen hooks.

Elyan the White: heart attack in the midst of battle.

So it goes.

'*Fuuucking* Anglo-*Saxons*,' Merlin says, with feeling.

Sir Pellinore shrugs. 'Don't take it to heart,' he says kindly.

'For all you know in a few centuries some other lot will come with swords and an attitude. The Franks from Gaul, maybe.'

Merlin shudders. 'Can you imagine?' he says.

They stare at the battlefield.

'Shouldn't you be down there?' Pellinore says.

'Yeah, I guess. Not really into swords, though.'

'No, never had you pegged for the scut work.'

'It's just all the... the *blood* and shit. It's filthy.'

'Got to get your hands dirty sometimes.'

Merlin stares at the battlefield. 'My hands have been dirty for a very long time, Pellinore,' he says softly; and the old knight cannot but concede the wizard's point.

From their vantage location they watch the soldiers make war: it doesn't look too bad, from up there; from a distance.

'Kay? Kay!'

Bors the Younger is cold; so cold. He looks up but all he can see are the clouded skies. Then, miraculously, Kay's face appears above him.

'Bors! Oh, Bors!'

'I'm so cold, Kay.'

'You'll be fine,' Kay says, 'We'll get you back to camp, the medics will make you as good as new.'

'I can't feel my legs, Kay.'

'Stay with me, Bors! Stay with m—'

'Kay, I... I love you.'

Bors tries to smile. Kay is so close. He blocks out the skies. His lips are warm.

'I love you, too.'

Then the world fades for Bors. He can hear something, he thinks. Some distant cries. He puzzles over them. Then even that last vestige of thought flees.

'Bors! Bors!'

⋆

'Oh, Bors,' Kay says. He lets go of the corpse. He's too old and too fat to be fighting this war. And he can hear the distant cries.

'Victory! Victory's ours!'

But he has no idea who's shouting.

He turns and turns. His men surround him, dispatching any enemy who dares approach. Where's Arthur? Where is the king?

He cannot see him.

That stupid boy!

Surely they've had enough, he thinks. More than their fair share of things. But it was never enough. There's always more, and more, until you hit something even bigger than yourself, and it swallows you whole. Alexander of Macedon reputedly wept when he beheld that there were no more worlds to conquer. But the idiot died of gut rot at the age of thirty-two all the same, in distant Babylon.

There is *always* something bigger, ready to eat you up.

'Arthur? Arthur!' Kay screams. He shoves the loss of Bors and all his love and fear deep under. He hefts his sword. He's still a knight. He's still alive. And this is war.

'To me, knights of the Round Table! To me, Britons! *Charge!*'

Oh, how they roar. Oh, how they cheer! Swords flash, the knives come out, and they surge, one last great desperate heave against the enemy, to turn the tide of war.

Bercilak, the Green Knight, takes a sword in the side. He looks down, surprised. Green sticky sap seeps out of the wound. Bercilak laughs and slaps the head of his opponent clean off. The head bounces on the dark ground.

'Long live the king!' Bercilak screams. A veritable rain of arrows flies down from the enemy's archers then and hit him full in the chest. Bercilak stares in surprise at the arrows sticking out of his chest like the branches of a tree.

'You think *wood* could stop me?' he screams. He plucks out an arrow but the wound stays open, and more sap bleeds out. Bercilak roars and wields his sword, but there is no one to strike. The enemy's pulled away, the Green Knight's isolated in their midst.

They throw lances then; and it is possible the lance heads are fashioned of the metal that was found on the site of the grail, for it tingles unpleasantly when it cuts through his flesh, and the wounds stay open, and more and more of his blood comes pouring out. He roars and tries to charge them but they simply move away, and fire from a distance. He cries in pain, and it's such an unfamiliar sensation that he laughs in delight.

'You can't kill me!' he screams. 'I have *natural* immunity!'

They come closer then. With swords and shears. With gardening implements. They hack at him. They cut and chop and *trim* him. And Bercilak, too late, realises even a mighty oak's no match for a man's axe.

'Fuck you!'

But more and more they come. And his blood sprays the black ground, and where it falls new, green shoots emerge, and tiny plants take root and grow. Nature finds a way.

Bercilak sinks to his knees.

'I am undone,' he says. The spirit that animates him must return to the primordial forest from whence it came. And yet he resists.

To live, he thinks, has been so *glorious*! He wishes to remain in this realm but a moment longer. To savour one more time sweet life, its contradictions, its strange allure.

Then the final axe falls for the final instance, and *this* time it's Bercilak's head that rolls. He blinks, surprised, sees feet and skies, and then the spirit's gone.

A mound of twigs and leaves and moss, dry branches.

In moments a fire arrow hits the pile and it bursts into flame.

But the shoots of green around that place of death remain.
The ash will fertilise the ground. In time new plants will grow
and flowers bloom. In time the deaths on that wide expanse of
plain will vanish, and only the blooms shall remain.

In time...

'*There* you are,' King Arthur says.

Mordred, the traitor, turns with a grin to face him.

PART FOURTEEN

THE DEATH OF ARTHUR

71

Excalibur strikes.

But Mordred with a litheness born of youth jumps out of way's harm. He parries the attack and slashes savagely at Arthur, who falls back. Mordred uses the momentum to push him harder. Arthur parries the next strike, then lunges with a nasty little knife. It grazes Mordred's rib. Mordred kicks and catches Arthur in the chest. They fall back from each other, stare.

Neither of them is smiling anymore.

They are so much alike: Mordred as thin as a young branch, and Arthur as the older tree that birthed him, still straight-backed and standing tall. Mordred's all in black, and Arthur's battle wear is dusty, green and brown, but the look in their eyes is identical: it is furious and focused, and signals someone's death.

But whose?

Arthur stabs and Mordred slashes, hacks and kicks. Arthur roars and comes at him with Excalibur and Mordred, almost contemptuously, parries the attack and shifts his stance and grins.

You little prick.

There's only the two of them now doing battle. Around them the great sea of the wounded and the dead lies over the plain of Camlann. It moves in the tide: waves of freshly dying soldiers peaking in final screams, but mostly traced in shallow eddies of whimpers and cries.

Then great big silences.

Here and there sporadic fighting still takes place. Somewhere high up a few archers still track moving targets, from the safety of the hills they take down human prey.

But mostly now the battle's done. It's hard to say who won, who lost, there's no one left to take a proper tally of the living and the dead and do a count.

The men who *are* left surround the two fighters in a circle now. They give them a wide berth. Kay is there, for always there must be someone to keep an account. Owain, the Bastard, and Agravain of the Hard Hand. They're too hard to kill. They remain.

Arthur and Mordred fight like shadows. They leap and their swords clash in mid-air. Mordred turns and runs and Arthur gives chase. Mordred feigns and lashes at him and Arthur laughs and Excalibur flashes and the sound of steel on steel echoes through that valley of death.

And so it goes.

Hack hack slash stab feign thrust parry stab stab knife.

They don't really fight like soldiers. They fight like the gutter rats they are. Arthur kicks dust into Mordred's eyes and slashes at his legs but Mordred recovers, jumps, screams, 'Somebody shoot him in the fucking back!'

But the last of the hidden archers has been taken down. Lancelot has been busy, sneaking up on them, slashing throat after throat, silently. No archers come to Mordred's aid, and none to Arthur's. The two men are alone there on the battlefield.

One by one, the Ladies of Water materialise ringside. They form wherever there is moisture. They emerge like shadows out of puddles of blood. They are drawn to the power on display here like flies looking to lay their eggs in rotten meat. They watch so avidly. Their eyes shine and their lips are wet.

'The boy is strong,' Sir Pellinore says.

'Arthur is stronger.'

They've come down to watch. Pellinore gives Merlin a reproachful sideway glance.

'After this, me and the old girl were thinking of retiring. All this questing, it's hard on the knees.'

The Questing Beast croons affectionately. The sound, terrible as it is, does not even distract the watchers from the final fight.

'Oh? Where to? Somewhere nice?'

'Ever hear of a place called Avalon? They say the air is good there and the hot springs are most conducive to one's health.'

Merlin shakes his head. 'Sounds good,' he says distractedly.

He watches the two men fight. He and the other fae can taste the power arcing through the air here. It's like a cocktail, an intoxicating scent and taste and tingle all rolled into one. They're getting high on it. Arthur's weakening, though he doesn't outwardly show it. It's only really there in the slight tightening round his shoulders.

But Mordred, too, is slowing down. He's ill-accustomed to this type and length of battle. He has been trained, but this is the sort of street fighting as they do in Londinium, and the only rule is that two men go in and only one can come out.

He's tiring.

And slash and hack and stab and *hurt*.

Mordred stares in horror at the blood dripping onto his hands. Excalibur has slashed him savagely across the left side of the face, cutting through skin to expose the bones beneath. What is a man? How does this thing, a skeleton clothed in blood and skin, move and live and think? It's so improbable.

They fight back and forth; back and forth.

When it finally ends, it happens quickly. At first the onlookers don't even register. There's a surprised look in Mordred's young eyes. He sits down, heavily, on his ass, and his booted legs stretch out in front of him.

The sword, Excalibur, sticks out of his ruptured stomach.

It's gone right through, and to the other side.

'*Fuck* you, Dad—'

Then the light of reason in his eyes fades. Whatever mystery takes place in that moment, that *cessation* – it happens. The heart stops beating and the pain is gone and the brain no longer thinks or feels or knows. There's nothing so very miraculous about it all. And as for souls? Try catching *those* like butterflies in your net. Merlins can taste power; but when something dies it's just... no more.

Arthur pulls out the sword, bloodied with the other's guts. He stares around him, bewildered. It's so very quiet on the plain of Camlann then. The wind has picked up and it ruffles his short-cropped hair. Somewhere in the distance, a gull cries. On the edge of the battlefield, far away, someone sobs.

Arthur turns and turns. He looks at them all: Merlin and Lancelot and Kay, Agravain of the Hard Hand, the Questing Beast. He stares at the Ladies of Water and the ladies stare back at him.

He looks around him at the battlefield, and what remains: dead men, dead horses, fallen swords. Already some scavengers have snuck into Camlann to loot the corpses. Impish figures, clad in rags, going through the pockets of the dead. Kay, eventually, will have to hire some work gangs to pile up all the corpses and cart them away. The profits and the loss.

Arthur turns and turns.

He's bleeding from the side. They can all see it now. And the dirty knife that went in, and the blade that broke inside the wound.

It doesn't *look* like much.

It's so quiet there. From somewhere in the distance, the sound of the waves against the shore. A hint of moisture in the air. A chance of rain.

Then the king falls.

They stare at him. Nobody moves. He falls to his knees and the great sword drops at last from his fingers. He stares at them all in disbelief. Falls down on his side, and shudders. That open wound in his side, it gushes blood.

He tries to crawl. He pulls himself, like a sick dog, across the ground. Leaves a smear of blood in his wake. Still nobody moves. No one comes to his aid. The Ladies of Water watch and some lick their lips. Arthur's body shakes with pain. He turns on his side, slowly and painfully brings himself into the foetal position.

He cries.

Then they run to him. Lancelot and Merlin and Kay. The Questing Beast howls fear and rage and despair into the air, her mouths open in a terrible scream, her tongues clicking. Then she departs from there, goes haring away into the distance, and the old knight, Sir Pellinore, rides after her, tears in his eyes. He would not watch another king of his shit himself to death.

Kay sits by Arthur's head. He strokes his hair. He murmurs soothing words. Merlin examines the wound, but he already knows what he'll find.

It's bad.

'Lancelot, help me carry him.'

'Carry him where?'

The Ladies of the Water stand watching. Nimue quietly melts away. She'll wait with her mermaids at sea. A deal's a deal, and she would not be cheated of her bargain.

'You and Agravain. Fashion a litter. Just do it!'

Merlin stands up. He stalks to the Ladies of the Water. They look at him in amused contempt.

'Took your best shot, you shouldn't feel bad,' Morgause says insincerely.

'*You* should fucking talk! *Your* horse barely made it out of the gate.'

'Poor Mordred,' Morgause says, and wipes a tear. 'He *almost* made it. It was worth a go.'

'So what's it now? What will it be?'

'You know what's what.'

'So why are you grinning, Morgan?'

Morgan is more glamorous than ever. She's dressed anew, he sees. New, unfamiliar gold bracelets on her arms. A pendant round her neck.

Continental designs: savage, sophisticated.

'You *didn't*.'

'The Angles and the Saxons are here to stay, dear Merlin. And so are we. In time they will forget they ever came here as invaders. They'll tell this story and think it is about themselves it's told. This Golden Age of yours could never last. You can't preserve the past. Embrace the new! Accept the change. There will be plenty of new kings to come – among the Angles.'

'You made a deal?'

She laughs delightedly. 'Thitis thought she had them, but I undercut that stupid bitch!'

Merlin feels so tired then.

'What will you do with him?' Morgan asks.

'Give him an ending fit for a king.'

'Alright, little man. Alright.'

She melts away and, one by one, they all go.

Perhaps, he thinks, they were never there at all.

He directs the knights. The king is in his litter. He is delirious in pain. They carry him across the plain of Camlann and past the countless dead he'd fashioned.

It is a benefit of the dead that they feel nothing.

Or what would they say?

He was a good man? He was a righteous man?

What would they say, that it was all worth it?

Would they quote Horace, and exclaim that dulce et decorum est, pro patria mori? That it is sweet and glorious to die for one's country? That old lie?

What would they say? Would they cry bullshit?

Who knows. Who cares. They're dead.

The knights carry the king in his litter through that sea of death until they come to the ocean shore.

A boat with white sails, sedately approaching. Clouds on the horizon. The wind picks up, has a tang of salt.

Merlin sees the ferryman, Haros. Somewhere a flute is playing the old Greek melody, the Seikilos epitaph, and Merlin whispers the words along with the music, 'Life exists only for a short while and time takes its toll...'

'What will happen to him?' Lancelot says.

Kay's eyes are wet with tears.

Agravain, Owain, they stare at Merlin mutely, like lost children.

He has to tell them *something*.

'There's, like, a magical island I can take him to,' he tells them. 'Where he'll be healed of all his wounds. He'll rest, there. Time flows differently there. He will be gone, perhaps a long while. But when the land needs him, he'll return.'

Oh, he can see the look Lancelot's giving him! Lancelot's heard worse bullshit than this in Judea, where they specialise in this sort of crap. But Owain, Agravain, even Kay – they *want* to believe in the story. They want their happy ending, the warmth and comfort of a lie well told.

'Just put him in the boat,' he tells them tiredly.

They watch from the shore. They see the king ferried away. White sails and dark clouds, a storm on the horizon. Sea spray and crying birds, and a single boat, sailing on the sea towards a distant shore.

'Merlin?'

'Yes, my lord.'

He grips his hand. Below them, the mermaids sing, and bare their teeth in shark smiles as they wait their turn.

'I don't feel so good.'

'Yes, my lord.'

Then it is done. The grip slackens and the eyes go blank. The king is dead.

They're far into the open sea by then. Merlin stares down at the depths, sees Nimue and her mermaids. He drops the useless sword down to the depths.

Then he rolls Arthur's corpse over the side until it hits the water with a splash and sinks.

Afterword

Some time in the twelfth century, a man called Geoffrey of Monmouth sat down with the purpose of writing an imagined history of Britain. The resultant manuscript – the *Historia Regum Britanniae* – is a wildly inventive fantasy text.

It is only in the second part of the book that Geoffrey introduces his greatest creation. Uther Pendragon makes his entrance much as is described here. Arthur is born, rises, and eventually dies at the hands of Mordred at Camlann. The first outline of a new story is given life – though in an overall shape often unfamiliar to the modern reader.

The manuscript proved popular. It was widely copied and translated, and led to the creation of a new genre of Arthurian romances on the continent. Each subsequent writer sought to expand on the tale. Each added new elements, characters and plots. It is thanks to the otherwise-obscure Norman poet, Wace, for instance, that we get Excalibur and the Round Table. An unknown English poet in the fourteenth century gives us Gawain and the Green Knight.

But it is three European writers – two of them French and one a German – who give us much of the Matter of Britain as we know it today. Indeed, it is one of the greatest ironies of the material that the stories of Britain were mostly made up by those on the continent.

Chrétien de Troyes, a poet working in the court of Marie of France, first gives us Lancelot. Even more importantly, he then introduces the grail, though it is not yet the Holy Grail of later versions.

The German writer Wolfram von Eschenbach took de Troyes' work and elaborated it. His grail is a *Lapis Exilis*, or fallen stone, and it is thanks to him that we first have the structure of the *quest* for the grail.

Finally, Robert de Boron creates the backstory of the grail as – explicitly – the Holy Grail we know now. He then invents the story of Joseph of Arimathea as the keeper of the grail and, along the way, also gives us the Lady of the Lake.

And so it goes on. By the mid-thirteenth century the various stories add up to several cycles (The Lancelot-Grail, the Post-Vulgate, and so on), incorporating a whole range of new additions (including the story of Tristan and Isolde, only briefly hinted at here) – but then they fall out of fashion again.

These texts, of course, make no attempt at historical accuracy. They transpose twelfth- and thirteenth-century notions of knighthood and chivalry to the Dark Ages, much as Geoffrey's original text bears no relation to actual history.

Geoffrey's intention was most likely political. He wanted to provide a unifying story for the new Norman masters of Britain. And de Boron's, certainly, was religious – the grail becomes a Christian symbol in his hands. But mostly, I suspect, people enjoyed the tales for simply being rousing stories of magic, adventure and bloodshed (just as they were fond of a good public hanging).

In 1485, a man by the name of Thomas Mallory brought the story back to life. His *Le Morte d'Arthur* was one of the first books printed by William Caxton on his new press, during a time when Britain was once more unified – the Wars of the Roses would end a year later. This Mallory was, by all accounts, as reprehensible as any character depicted in this book: a murderer, robber and rapist, he was eventually buried near Newgate Prison.

Mallory first brought together, and gave final shape to, the various and often conflicting stories of the Arthurian romances. He incorporated Geoffrey's Arthur with the later grail sections; added Lancelot and his romance with Guinevere – and so on and so forth.

The book was popular. Once more, it provided mass entertainment while serving an essentially political purpose: giving the people of Britain a shared (if entirely made up) past, made of glory.

But the tales sooner or later fell into obscurity once more. It was not until the nineteenth century and the Victorian era that Arthur was called again from Avalon: as the new British Empire spread across the globe, the stories of King Arthur and his knights found a new, enthusiastic audience. The tale's nationalistic sentiments had never been more appropriate.

Since then, of course, Arthuriana only flourished. The twentieth century saw an explosion of new material, from books to films, and the story's underlying structure and motifs inform much of twentieth-century fantasy from Tolkien onwards. Its Merlin, originally a waif-like youth who changes his appearance to a bearded old man just to be taken seriously by Arthur, has since become the stock character of the wise wizard – proving that Merlins, truly, are everywhere.

And the debate, improbably, still rages on in the newspapers of this day: was Arthur *real*? Well, to accept that we must go back to Geoffrey's *History*, in which the isle of Britannia was first inhabited by savage giants before Brutus of Troy came, slaughtered them, and built New Troy, which we now call London...

The true history of Britain looks much different. The island

– a part of Europe until the Doggerland sank under the rising seas some 8,000 years ago – was inhabited for nearly a million years by various humans. The Romans arrived in 54 BC. By the second century, and after the failure of Boudicca's revolt, the Romans had conquered much of the island. They built cities and roads, mined for silver, exported slaves, and generally kept Britain as what it was – a distant, dismal part of the great empire that had its seat in Rome. The Romans built London, Bath, York and Newcastle. The roads they constructed are still being used today.

Then they left.

With the fall of the Roman Empire, Britain became susceptible to a wave of new arrivals from the continent. Those tribes – Angles, Saxons, Jutes – had no doubt different motivations. Some were driven from their homes by rising sea levels and floods. Others might have come in search of fortune. The new arrivals established their own kingdoms and principalities, and slowly pushed at the borders of the Britons.

Little is known for certain of that time. Christianity had come to Britain with the new missionaries from Rome, but it was not widely accepted by the new arrivals until well into the seventh century. By the tenth century the Kingdom of England was formed by King Athelstan, and in the eleventh century the Norman conquest of Britain arrived in full force.

It is in those Dark Ages that the tales of Arthur and his court flourish. Though there really *was* an extreme weather event in 535 AD, which led to global famine, and which I've used as the marker for the appearance of Uther's dragon in this book.

As much as possible, I drew on original sources. The Nine Sisters appear in Geoffrey's *History*, and I opted, similarly, to keep Merlin in something of his original form. The monstrous cat, Cath Palug, has long plagued the Arthurian romances in various disguises. For the grail I could not resist but incorporate more than one of the early versions.

In no source to my knowledge, however, does Lancelot know kung-fu.

The attentive reader will no doubt find a great many and various references scattered throughout this novel. To them, my congratulations.

About the author

LAVIE TIDHAR is the World Fantasy Award-winning author of *Osama* (2011), *The Violent Century* (2013), the Jerwood Fiction Uncovered Prize-winning *A Man Lies Dreaming* (2014), and the Campbell Award-winning *Central Station* (2016), in addition to many other works and several other awards. He works across genres, combining detective and thriller modes with poetry, science fiction and historical and autobiographical material. His work has been compared to that of Philip K. Dick by the *Guardian* and the *Financial Times*, and to Kurt Vonnegut by *Locus*.